Praise for Nora (

"Bravo!"
— ALICE MUNRO, winner of t

Advance Praise for *Fields of Exile*:

"Nora Gold's *Fields of Exile* is a gripping tale. It is also a novel of ideas in the tradition of George Eliot, Doris Lessing, and Marge Piercy, but one that is filled with real characters, a literary sensibility, and a powerful example of the near-fatal consequences of anti-Israel aggression. The heroine Judith's vulnerability, dreaminess, erotic imagination, and knowledge of Jewish traditions in both kitchen and yeshiva drew me close and kept me there, and I could not put this book down. I wanted to scream to her, though: 'Danger Ahead! Proceed with Caution,' but she could not hear me. I hope and pray that this novel's readers do."
— PHYLLIS CHESLER, author of
The New Antisemitism and *An American Bride in Kabul*

"Nora Gold's *Fields of Exile* is a fine novel: poignant, passionate, compelling, and funny, an adventure of the heart and mind. I don't think anybody has nailed the way anti-Israel feeling gives the license for antisemitism as well as Gold has here, and you won't find a more unflinching examination of the terrible ironies inherent in the Israeli-Palestinian conflict, or a more compelling portrait of the personal toll exacted from those who face these ironies with courage. This is an emotionally fraught, distinguished novel, often as humorous as it is harrowing."
— STEVE STERN, author of
The Frozen Rabbi and *The Book of Mischief*

"In *Fields of Exile*, Nora Gold succeeds fully in making her characters debate social and political themes as an expression of their personal complex contradictions. They are luminously alive. This novel is about men and women who are trying to understand and define their relations to each other, as well as their place in society. Wonderful reading."

— NAÏM KATTAN, author of
Farewell Babylon and *Reality and Theatre*

"Nora Gold's *Fields of Exile* restores one's faith in the possibilities of the novel. It is truly a novel of ideas, a brave book that ventures into territory from which non-fiction has shied away and even obscured the truth. With a lyrical flair Nora Gold has delivered a novel that casts a light onto the ivory tower in ways that should unsettle the faculty lounge."

— THANE ROSENBAUM, author of
The Golems of Gotham and *Second Hand Smoke*

"'My heart is in the East and I am in the far, far West.' Seldom has anyone expressed so well as Nora Gold the yearning for Zion that remains within every fibre of one who has been torn away from a life of fulfillment in Israel and condemned unwillingly to return to the anti-Zionism/antisemitism of exile. A brave book that courageously takes on the ambivalences of Jewish life in the Diaspora — ambivalences that mirror those of the protagonist, torn between two very different lovers.

— ALICE SHALVI, Israel Prize laureate

"The yearning for true peace and human compassion blooms in these fields of exile. Judith, the protagonist, much like Nora Gold, the author, searches relentlessly for ways to fix the flaws of our world. This is a novel written with an open heart and a loving hand, and with the hope that literature can somehow make amends. After crossing many fields of exile we, like Judith, shall finally find our way home."

— NAVA SEMEL, author of
And the Rat Laughed and *Paper Bride*

"A novel about a difficult subject — antisemitism in the university — written with passion and fervor."

— ANN BIRSTEIN, author of
Summer Situations and *The Rabbi on Forty-Seventh Street*

FIELDS OF EXILE

a novel

Nora Gold

DUNDURN
TORONTO

Project Editor: Shannon Whibbs
Editor: Cy Strom
Design: Jennifer Scott
Printer: Webcom

Library and Archives Canada Cataloguing in Publication

Gold, Nora, author
    Fields of exile / by Nora Gold.

Issued in print and electronic formats.
ISBN 978-1-4597-2146-3 (pbk.).--ISBN 978-1-4597-2147-0 (pdf).--ISBN 978-1-4597-2148-7 (epub)

    I. Title.

PS8563.O524F54 2013   C813'.54   C2013-905473-1   C2013-905474-X

1 2 3 4 5   18 17 16 15 14

Conseil des Arts du Canada   Canada Council for the Arts   Canada   ONTARIO ARTS COUNCIL CONSEIL DES ARTS DE L'ONTARIO

We acknowledge the support of the Canada Council for the Arts and the Ontario Arts Council for our publishing program. We also acknowledge the financial support of the Government of Canada through the Canada Book Fund and Livres Canada Books, and the Government of Ontario through the Ontario Book Publishing Tax Credit and the Ontario Media Development Corporation.

Care has been taken to trace the ownership of copyright material used in this book. The author and the publisher welcome any information enabling them to rectify any references or credits in subsequent editions.

J. Kirk Howard, President

"Exile," a childhood poem by Leah Goldberg, was first published by Tuvya Ruebner in *Leah Goldberg: A Monograph* (in Hebrew) (Tel Aviv: Sifriyat Po'alim, 1980), p. 10. "Exile" was translated into English from this monograph by Michael Gluzman, and cited by him in his chapter "Modernism and Exile: A View from the Margins" (pp. 244–245) in David Biale, Michael Golchinsky, and Susannah Heschel, *Insider/Outsider: American Jews and Multiculturalism* (Berkeley: University of California Press, 1998). "Exile" appears here with the written permission of Professor Gluzman.

The publisher is not responsible for websites or their content unless they are owned by the publisher.

The archway and flowers on the cover of this book were adapted by Joseph Weissgold from a painting, "Tranquillity," by Mikki Senkarik (www.senkarik.com), with the artist's permission.

Printed and bound in Canada.

Visit us at
Dundurn.com | @dundurnpress | Facebook.com/dundurnpress | Pinterest.com/Dundurnpress

Dundurn	Gazelle Book Services Limited	Dundurn
3 Church Street, Suite 500	White Cross Mills	2250 Military Road
Toronto, Ontario, Canada	High Town, Lancaster, England	Tonawanda, NY
M5E 1M2	LA1 4XS	U.S.A. 14150

For David, my best friend and true love

Exile

How difficult the word how many memories
of hatred and slavery
and because of it we have shed so many tears
exile

and yet, I'll rejoice in the fields of exile ...

— Leah Goldberg

CONTENTS

1   In Exile, but Just for a While   11

2   Friends and Enemies   113

3   Winter Chills   199

4   Taking a Stand   251

5   Love and Hate   349

6   Next Year   399

    Glossary   419

IN EXILE,
BUT JUST FOR A WHILE

She is sitting on the edge of her father's bed, holding his hand. She thinks he's dead, but she isn't sure. He seems strangely still and lifeless; he can't be dead, though, because he's her father.

His hand is still warm and dry, as it always was. Like when he took her hand at the age of three, to lead her for the first time safely across the street. And when he touched her on the cheek, in a kind of wordless blessing, the day she left home for Israel.

Her father was not happy about her going to live there. Neither he nor her mother could understand why she would give up a safe and comfortable home to go "halfway across the world, and to a war zone, yet." But they didn't stand in her way. Now, though, ten years later, her father brought this up again. Just yesterday he said, "I know you want to return to Israel, Judith. And that's fine, if that's where you've chosen to make your life. But first you have to go back to school. You need a Master's degree so you can stand on your own two feet."

"Never mind, Daddy," she said. "I'm fine." Which is what she always said whenever he raised this topic.

But this time he didn't accept her answer with his usual resigned silence. She was older now, he said: thirty-two, not twenty-two like when she first went to Israel, and here she was, still alone — *gantz aleyn*, he added in his native Yiddish. By which he meant she was unmarried, and with no prospect of marrying any time soon. She did have a boyfriend, and even one her father liked, but this wasn't somebody she could imagine ever having as a husband. Firstly, because she planned to return to Israel, and as soon as possible, and he would never follow her there. And secondly, because he was conservative and right-wing, a tax lawyer who had little in common with her socialist ideals or her passionate temperament. But they had known each other since high school — they went out in grade eleven, and then again during her final year in university, for those last few months before she left for Israel. When nine months ago she came back to Toronto, Bobby seemed to always be around. They started going to movies together, and dinners, and in no time at all they fell back in step with each other and became a couple again. She was lost, disoriented, and depressed being back here, and he was comforting and dependable with his weekly Saturday night dates and daily phone calls and invitations. He also felt familiar, and maybe even familial, because he saw her much as her father did. As a wonderful, talented person who had wasted herself and her Bachelor of Social Work by moving to Israel for ten years, living hand-to-mouth in Jerusalem for the last nine of these, and before that working on a kibbutz where she did various odd jobs. Some of them very odd, like simultaneously sucking turkey sperm up one side of a two-pronged straw and turkey ovum up the other, to try and artificially unite them for fertilization. An unpleasant job because sometimes she sucked too hard and the foamy foul mixture came up into her mouth. They were right, Bobby and her father, that since her two social work jobs in Jerusalem were both only short-term contract positions, she hadn't developed her career very far while in Israel. But still she doesn't consider those years to be wasted time. She'd really lived while she was there. She'd had friends, lovers, and a community, and she felt truly alive. On kibbutz she rose every day before dawn and worked in the dark, cold fields picking artichokes while the sun rose slowly before her. In Jerusalem she cooked meals with her friends and ate with them and celebrated and demonstrated and laughed and mourned and belonged.

But now she's here in Toronto, supposedly back "home" — though home for her is still *there* — because her father, aged seventy-two, got sick. Her mother had been dead for nine years and there was no one else to take care of him. So, loving him, Judith has been doing this as well as she can for the past nine months. (Nine months — long enough to have a baby.) Nine months of watching her father gradually weaken, and get thinner, yellower, and bonier, the life leaking out of him till there was nothing left. Fortunately, he has had relatively little pain, and this is easily brought under control by morphine. His could be called *A Very Easy Death*, she thinks now, recalling the bitterly titled book by Simone de Beauvoir about the months leading up to the death of her mother. At least Judith's father has remained lucid all the way through, and this has been a great blessing. Even as recently as yesterday he spoke to her and made perfect sense. Half-sitting up in bed, propped against pillows, he took her hand in his, and said, "Judith, dear, you must go back to school. You said last month that in Israel it takes forever to do a Master's, but that here it's just a one-year program. So stay here, Judith, for a year, and do it. I'm not a rich man — I can't leave you provided for the way I would have liked to. You're going to have to stand on your own two feet." He didn't say "when I'm gone," but it hung in the air between them. And now he looked at her expectantly. She realized he was asking her a direct question — he wasn't, as she'd thought, just making a suggestion. She looked back into his eyes. Dying eyes, she thought. But no, those eyes couldn't be dying. His body maybe, but those eyes of his, so full of intelligence and warmth, would never die.

"Okay, Daddy," she said. "I'll do my Master's."

There was an obstruction halfway down her throat when she said that. She'd held out a long time against this. She didn't want to leave Israel, even for twelve months, and she didn't want to do the same thing as everyone else, following the usual well-worn path. She wanted to be different. But yesterday, though that lump in her throat was still there when she spoke — a physical hurdle in her voice box that she had to leap over, like a horse over a fence in an obstacle course — it wasn't as hard as she'd thought it would be. Maybe because of the relief, joy, and hopefulness that immediately suffused her father's face. It filled her with astonishment — it had been so easy to make him happy. Then he turned his face away and instantly fell asleep. This conversation had cost him a great effort.

Now, just one day later, she is again sitting on this bed and holding his hand. This hand is warm. Though she knows it won't be for long. In a couple of hours — or maybe even less than that — her father's hand will turn cold and rigid. But this is not important. All that matters, all that's real to her, is that for now it's warm. It is still Daddy's hand, the same as always. Tears stream down her face, but she doesn't feel sad. Why should she? Daddy's not dead. He can't be dead; he's her father. It is late afternoon, and she sits for a long time staring out the window at the slowly falling night, holding — as if this moment will last forever — her father's unmoving, gradually stiffening hand.

Four days later she tells one of the women at the *shiva*, an old friend of her father's, that she's planning, at her father's request, to go back to school here in Toronto. She asks this woman what she should study now — should she stay with social work, or try something new?

Flora laughs her big horsey laugh.

"You should study, of course, what you already know, my dear. It makes things so much easier."

Two days later, on a hot June day, Flora returns to the *shiva* house, carrying a tub of pistachio ice cream and an application package for the only Master of Social Work program within driving distance that has not yet closed its admissions.

Judith frowns at the name on the envelope. "Wasn't Dunhill in the papers a few months ago because of a student riot?"

"Yes," says Flora. "A rally there got out of hand. But never mind about that. You don't have to have anything to do with the Students' Union. You just go to your classes and do your homework, and everything will be fine. Anyway, at this point you don't have any choice. This is the only school still accepting applications — it's the only game in town."

The only game in town. Her father always said that. She thanks Flora and puts the big brown envelope on the kitchen shelf. A few days after the end of *shiva*, Flora phones and comes by again. From the shelf where she saw Judith place it, she takes down the unopened application package, and with Judith sitting dully next to her, dazed and paralyzed with grief, she painstakingly fills it out. Three weeks afterwards, Judith receives a letter saying she has been accepted into the M.S.W. program at Dunhill University.

— 2 —

A glorious sunny day in September, and after a one-hour drive, Judith arrives at the gates to the university in Dunhill, Ontario. She doesn't want to be here, in exile; she wants to be home in Israel where she belongs. She resents being stuck here for the year because of the stupid promise she made to her father. She stomps around the campus for a half-hour looking for the School of Social Work. She's here for Orientation, but she feels totally disoriented. The social work school is housed in a silo-like building, the Franklin Ardmore Rutherford Tower, which, for obvious reasons, the campus map does not refer to by its acronym, FART, but simply as FRANK. She climbs the front steps. Once inside, she waits for the elevator with two chatting women. One is a very plain redhead, the other pretty, dark-haired, and flamboyant. The three of them ride up to the eleventh floor. Room 1104 is a big square corner room with large picture windows on two sides, and through these windows Judith sees a big grey-stoned quadrangle eleven floors below her with students crossing it back and forth. The room itself is bright and cheerful, thanks to the large windows flooding it with sunlight, some of this refracted through orange woven curtains, giving everything a warm, fiery glow. It is full of talking, laughing people, mostly women, and Judith, not knowing anyone, mills around, nodding and smiling at whoever she passes, trying to look unobtrusive, un-lonely, and un-lost. She keeps walking as if she's preoccupied with looking for a friend or has a destination — perhaps someone she knows on the other side of the room. After ten minutes of walking in circles and picking at the handouts and cookies on the long table at the back, she hears a loud thumping. A burly grey-haired man in a green cardigan is pounding on a table at the front of the room.

"Okay, everybody," he calls out. "Take your seats so we can start."

Almost all the gold or orange easy chairs are already taken. Within seconds nearly everyone is seated except Judith. She alone will be left standing, with everybody staring at her, like the loser in a game of musical chairs. Desperately she glances around.

"Here," says a cheerful voice. A young blonde woman in a lime-green blazer is smiling at her and patting the chair on her left.

"Thanks," Judith says, gratefully sitting.

"No problem," says the woman, extending her hand. "I'm Cindy."

The hand is dry and cool to the touch. "Judith," says Judith, and is about to say more, but the burly man is rapping the table again and starting to speak.

"Good morning," he says. "I'm Lawrence Weick, Director of the Dunhill School of Social Work, and it's my pleasure to welcome you here today. You've made an excellent choice in selecting this school for your graduate studies. As you'll soon see for yourselves, we have an outstanding faculty, as well as a very select group of students. It may interest you to know that this year, for your one-year M.S.W. program, there were eighty-four applicants and only twenty-eight spots. In other words, for every one of you sitting here now, we turned away two others."

A buzz, surprised and pleased, runs through the room. Judith and Cindy grin at each other. Cindy shrugs.

"So you should all feel very proud of yourselves," Weick continues, "and we're delighted to welcome you to the 2002–2003 academic year. As most of you already know, we at Dunhill take a Structural approach to social work. Our mission, as you can see on the orange handout, is the advancement of knowledge in the service of social change. This means, firstly, educating ourselves about the oppressions, injustices, and structural inequalities in Canadian society today, as well as around the globe. Secondly, it means preparing our students to engage in the struggle against inequity and oppression, whether you're working with individuals, groups, or communities."

Judith is starting to feel at home here. This mission statement sounds almost verbatim like the one at the university where she completed her B.S.W. ten years ago. The same language, the same concepts. Apparently nothing has changed.

Now Weick introduces Phoebe Browne, the school's Administrative Coordinator and student advisor. Phoebe is a dumpy-looking woman of about forty, wearing an apricot-coloured polyester pantsuit, and she speaks for about ten minutes, describing in mind-deadening detail all the course requirements for Dunhill's one-year M.S.W. Judith, being in the Practice, rather than the Policy, stream, will need to take eight half-courses — six required and two electives — over the course of the year; alternatively, she can take only six courses and write a one-hundred-page thesis. *Thesis*, she writes. She's forgotten to bring paper with her today, so she is writing in the margins of a fuchsia handout that invites all the first-year students to the Lion's Den, the student pub on campus, for the first meeting of the school's GLBT committee. *GLBT* looks strange to her — she's used to seeing the term *LGBT* instead. So for a moment GLBT strikes her as some variation on a BLT — maybe a Greek Lettuce-Bacon-and-Tomato, something for the Greek students? Then she understands. Phoebe, finished now, sits, and Weick pops up again like a jack-in-the-box.

"Thank you, Phoebe," he says. "Now let's have a go-round of the faculty, who will each tell you what they're teaching this year, and also speak a bit about their research." Judith notices now for the first time the long lineup of professors at the front of the room, sitting in a row on plastic orange chairs to the left of Phoebe. *Oh God – a dozen speeches!*

"Don't forget," says Weick, "some of you will need to find someone next term to act as your thesis advisor. So, as your profs are speaking, listen carefully for common interests you might have."

A short, friendly-looking woman with close-cropped black hair stands. Judith's pen is poised, waiting, above the pink page. "My name is Terry Montana, and this term I'll be teaching the course on women and social work, which focuses on the relationship between the social policies affecting women in this society and the everyday problems faced by our women clients." This interests Judith. "I'm also co-chairing the GLBT committee this year, and for those of you who don't know, this stands for gay, lesbian, bi, and trans."

Judith, smiling, lowers her eyes to the page.

Terry continues, "My research is a study I'm doing with five women colleagues from universities across the province, documenting the kinds of barriers lesbian graduate students face, and the ways heterosexism and homophobia are manifested in the academic environment. If you're interested in this topic, or anything to do with GLBT, feel free to come chat. My office hours are Thursdays from two to four."

Terry Montana, writes Judith on the pink invitation to the Lion's Den. Feminist. Lesbian. GLBT. She means to write down what Terry said, but she's tired, and with the next guy already starting his spiel, she writes without realizing it, *Gay Lesbian Bacon and Tomato*. The next guy is named Greg Smolan, then it's Corinne Marajian, and by the time the following guy stands up, Judith is spacing out. A short round bald man resembling Humpty Dumpty introduces himself as Tom Reggel. *Reggel eggel*, thinks Judith. In the prophet Ezekiel's "vision of the chariot," the *reggel eggel* was an ambiguous part of the four-headed creature's body, which has traditionally been translated as a foot, a third and extra foot. But she knows from a night course in Jewish mysticism she took one winter at the Beit Ha'am Institute in Jerusalem, that *reggel eggel* actually means a penis. Automatically she glances at Tom Reggel's crotch — no bulge there at all (maybe he doesn't have one?). Then she catches herself and, blushing, looks away. Professor Reggel is speaking now, but she isn't listening to him at all. She's thinking about the penis of Moshe, the married man she was with seven years ago in Israel for about six months. Until her father's death, she hardly ever thought about Moshe. But he's been on her mind a lot since the funeral. As she sat there that day in the front row, surrounded by people but feeling all alone, Moshe's image appeared before her like an apparition, like Hamlet's father, and ever since then he has come to visit her once, twice, three times a day, even more if she's bored or lonely. She isn't so much thinking now about Moshe as feeling him. Feeling his taut, strong body, his thighs, chest, and penis pressing hard against her. Every Monday and Thursday morning he'd wait for her at the train station, at Hartuv Junction near the town where she worked. She'd get off the train from Jerusalem drained by the ecstasy of the ride: forty minutes of meandering through magnificent sun-slashed forests, up and down the back-roads of the Jerusalem hills. Unsteadily she'd step off the train onto the almost-deserted outdoor platform, and at the bottom of the hill, Moshe's white van was always waiting quietly under a tree, with the back door open, like an invitation. She would go running toward it: half-running, half-tripping down the hill, stumbling over the protruding tangled roots from the olive trees and their Y-shaped broken-off branches, nature-made slingshots.

At the bottom she'd hurl herself against Moshe's body, and he would catch and embrace her, one hand on her buttocks, and pull her tight against him. His body was hard and muscular, the body of a man who worked his own fields. No softness. No slack. But there was softness in his mouth, in his lips and tongue, when he kissed her, and in his eyes when he smiled at her tenderly. Then his kiss would turn hard, and he'd pull her down, and right there on the floor of the forest — on top of pine needles, and pine cones, and dead and living grass — they'd make love. Quickly, and urgently, always quickly and urgently, because there was never much time.

"Never enough time," Moshe often said, feeling old at forty-two, and having, as she thought then, "intimations of mortality." But also, objectively speaking, there wasn't much time. The train from Jerusalem arrived at seven-thirty in the morning, and they both had to be at work for eight. So as soon as they'd finished, they stood and brushed themselves off, with him sometimes picking debris out of her hair (reminding her of Rabbi Akiva, who did the same thing with his bride almost two thousand years earlier). Then he'd drive her up the hill to the lone office building in the town centre, where she was working for eight months on a community development project to help the poor and infirm.

While in the middle of this thing with Moshe, she didn't think much about it, because she couldn't understand it. And she couldn't understand it because she couldn't find a word for it. *I still can't*, she thinks, sitting here at Dunhill, while at the front of the room a cheerful but tough-looking blonde woman named Harloffery does her spiel. Moshe wasn't a "boyfriend." Boyfriends were the Jerusalem boys around her own age, innocent and eager, who took her out on Saturday night dates to movies. Moshe never took her anywhere; he just waited for her by the train. He wasn't a boy either; he was a man, and an older man at that: forty-two to her twenty-four. Forty-two, twenty-four: opposite numbers, but matching opposites.

The other word that didn't fit her relationship with Moshe was *love*. They never used this word between them, not once. Though this thing between them was deep, maybe even as deep as love. Because Moshe was a man of the land. He had five *dunams* of land on a *moshav* that he farmed himself with his own tractor, growing artichokes, melons, and orange and lemon trees. To her, he smelled of the earth, the fields, the orchards, and the sun. Sometimes, after they'd made love, she would lie face down on top of him — the same way she liked on nature trips to lie face down flat on the Israeli earth and inhale its deep scent — and she would smell him. As if Moshe were the Land, Israel itself. Once, lying on top of him like this, she wished she could just for a while be male, so she could scatter her seed on Israel's earth, and in this way help to — as Ben-Gurion put it — "make the desert bloom."

Now at the front of the room a tall, skinny man is making his presentation. The blonde woman is gone: Judith didn't even notice when they switched. In fact, she's not even sure there hasn't been someone else, or even two other people, in between Blondie and this guy. Now she feels anxious: maybe she's missed something important. So she tries to focus and listen to this man. He is talking about the elusiveness of language, and how, from a postmodern perspective, the meaning of a word is not static, but something that constantly shifts, depending on its context. What he's saying sounds very interesting and seems to resonate with depth. Yet she keeps feeling that she *almost* understands what he's talking about, but never 100 percent. As if he were an ad for his own product: Elusive Language. After ten minutes of increasing frustration, she asks herself what Moshe, if he were here, would say.

"Bullshit," comes his immediate answer. Judith suppresses her laughter and looks down at the arm of her chair. Of course he'd say that: to Moshe, language was a simple matter. He spoke without thinking about the words he used. But she found them fascinating because they were Hebrew. Moshe was a man of Hebrew words. A "real Israeli," a *sabra*. This was *his* language, his and Bialik's and the Bible's — this language she had just borrowed, acquired through painful study, "breaking her teeth" on it, as the Hebrew expression goes. And which even now she knew — though unusually well for an immigrant — in only a fractured way. It was still for her a second, "other," language, like being the "other" woman, someone's second love. Yet this language, this holy tongue, belonged in Moshe's mouth. Sometimes when he kissed her, she imagined thousands of Hebrew words, tiny as sperm, being transferred from him to her, along with his saliva and desire. Planting themselves within her, taking root, and then blossoming inside her into a tree, with hundreds of Hebrew words hanging off the branches, instead of pink flowers. Making her a "real Israeli," too.

She looks at the postmodern guy. No — words for Moshe didn't shape-shift. They each had a meaning that was constant and clear. She used to ask him for words, and his answer was always unhesitating.

"How do you say this in Hebrew?" she'd ask him, scooping a palmful of soil from the ground.

"*Karka.*"

She held up a pine cone.

"*Itztrueball.*"

She pointed to a pink wildflower.

"*Hotmeet.*" A hot meeting, she thought. Hot meat.

She was like Helen Keller asking Anne Sullivan to tell her the names of things. Moshe always told her. But he couldn't understand her hunger for words. He'd say to her, tenderly joking, "What do you need all these words for, Judith? What will you do with them once you have them? When are you ever going to have a conversation about pine cones?"

But she kept asking. Earlobe. Spider web. Cum. (*T'nuch. Kurei akavish. Shpeech.*) Which, written, looked to her almost like *Speech.* Slurred speech — shpeech — like when you come. When Moshe asked her halfway into their relationship what she wanted for her birthday, she told him "a word."

"A word! What word?"

"Any word. As long as it's one I don't already know."

"But how am I supposed to know what words you don't know?"

She just shrugged.

"Crazy girl," said Moshe.

25

But the following week, when she turned twenty-five, he gave her two presents. First a plastic, imitation-alligator-skin purse — the kind of thing she'd never be caught dead with. Then he gave her the word *ta'ava*. Craving, or longing. Because, he said, she seemed so much to want, and to want so much. "Greedy girl," he chided her gently. "You must learn to be satisfied with less. *L'histapek b'm'at.*" Which she realizes now was probably his way of reminding her he was married, and she shouldn't hope for too much from him. He concluded his little birthday speech by quoting from Ethics of the Fathers, disconcerting her since he was so staunchly secular: "Who is rich? He who is content with his portion."

He ... his, she thought. That male language doesn't include me, so *I* don't have to be content. She said this out loud to Moshe, half-knowing he wouldn't understand. And he didn't. *But that's okay*, she thought. *L'histapek b'm'at.*

Now at the front of the room, there has been another changing of the guard: a skinny woman with wild hair like a cavewoman is talking. *From postmodern to premodern, or even prehistoric*, thinks Judith, and listens for a few moments. Blah blah blah. She returns to Moshe. Yes, he was married. He had two young daughters who adored him, and a wife who didn't like sex. And who he in turn didn't seem to much like, his lip curling involuntarily whenever he mentioned her. What Zahava did like, though, was lampshades. Apparently she had over a hundred of them, and bought a new one at least once a month. Judith pictured a small house crammed full of lampshades, all tawdry and vulgar, and Zahava as tawdry and vulgar too. But actually it was thanks to Zahava that she met Moshe. It was only because he had to keep up with the cost of Zahava's wild shopping sprees that he started moonlighting and took the six-month part-time contract in the town where Judith worked. He was hired as a contractor to renovate this small, run-down development town. In the thirty-ninth year after the town's founding, and in anticipation of the fortieth-year festivities, a group of leading citizens had convinced the municipal council the place needed some sprucing up. So, twice a week, Moshe wandered in and out of decrepit abandoned shacks, houses missing half their roofs, and never-used "community centres" with all their windows broken — donated by well-meaning but naive Jewish communities abroad — as he chewed thoughtfully on a piece of straw, considering what to do. She watched him and thought, *This is a man who fixes things. Takes that which is broken, and makes it whole again. Perhaps he could do this for people, too.*

She soon discovered, though, that he didn't work alone. He had a Moroccan guy helping him, a skinny younger man named Koby, who measured everything in sight, listened to Moshe weigh the pros and cons of various repair plans, acted as his sounding-board, and helped him come up with price estimates that were neither too high nor too low. Once Judith came with Moshe to visit one of his sites. Koby looked with surprise at her, then questioningly at Moshe; Moshe just smiled and shrugged. For the next fifteen minutes, she watched the two men work together and saw how heavily Moshe depended on Koby: he couldn't have managed this project without him. But that didn't stop Moshe from saying when they were alone again back in the van: "Never trust a Moroccan, Judith. You're not from here, you don't know what they're like. They're lazy, and primitive, and they'll rob you blind the second you turn your back."

She looked sharply at him to see if he was joking, but he wasn't. She felt nauseated, and couldn't think of anything to say. Other than, "But Koby —"

"Koby's okay — he's a good worker," Moshe said. "But he's the exception. Most Moroccans aren't like him. And even he sometimes says very primitive things."

Not like you, she thought, but didn't say it. She stared straight ahead at the road as they drove through the town, and her nausea steadily increased. She couldn't believe she'd been intimate with this man — she'd let him inside her body — and he was a racist. She was disgusted by his comment, and by him and his body, calmly arrogant in the driver's seat next to her. Yet she also half-admired, or anyway envied, him. She wished she had his male self-confidence, his unquestioned assumption that it's his God-given right to say whatever he feels like. She was always worrying about sounding nice or not-nice, saying the right or the wrong thing. But Moshe just talked. He didn't know about political correctness, and even if he had he wouldn't have cared. He'd have felt it was his right to express, to expel, whatever words had collected in his mouth. Not just the "nice" ones, but all of them. She can see his mouth now: his sensual mouth, full of words. Full of words like the mouths in the Shabbat morning prayer:

> Even if our mouths were as full of poetry as the
> sea is full of water, and our tongues sang your
> praises like the roaring waves ... we could never
> thank you, God, for even one thousandth of
> your countless gifts and miracles.

Moshe's mouth was like a sea. And his red lips like the banks of the Red Sea. She remembers the first time he kissed her. His kiss was careful, exploratory, tentative, like dipping a toe into the sea. She'd just gotten off the train from Jerusalem, he was at the station picking up a small shipment of building materials that had been delivered there, and even though they didn't know each other, he offered her a lift up the hill to the centre of town. It was a long, hot, dusty walk, and that day there was a *hamsin*, a burning, dry desert wind. She looked up the hill doubtfully, and nodded yes. In the car, they drove in silence. But at the top of the hill, Moshe leaned over and his mouth softly covered hers. Then his lips parted like the parting of the sea, and his tongue, just the tip of it, reached down hopefully into her mouth. She waited a moment, wondering what would happen next, but it just stayed there — hanging there like a bat hanging upside down on its perch — waiting. Slowly she reached up the tip of her tongue to meet his. Carefully, though. She'd been told by previous men she was too intense, too passionate. She didn't want to frighten Moshe. But then she couldn't help it: she trembled — a huge tremor ran through her body, and made Moshe tremble, too. His face flushed and filled with desire.

"On Thursday I'll pick you up again," he said hoarsely, somewhere between a statement and a question. She hesitated, then nodded before getting out of the van. She was sitting high up and she had to be careful stepping down. As she did so, she felt swollen in between her legs, and reaching the pavement, it was hard for her to walk.

Remembering this now, she keeps her eyes lowered to the arm of her chair. She's not sure how much of her feelings show on her face, and she doesn't want everyone here at the Dunhill School of Social Work to see written across it all her naked longing and desire. Once on a Jerusalem bus, she was daydreaming and forgot to watch herself — and not only did she miss her stop, she actually moaned out loud at one point, recalling the night before with her lover, and a man sitting two seats away shot her a sharp glance. Now too, she senses someone watching her. She looks up: it's Weick. Peering at her intently. She blushes and looks down. *Oh God. He knows. He can tell.* She keeps looking at the orange armrest. When she glances up again, he's still gazing at her, frowning slightly, as if trying to puzzle her out. Then he looks away and stands. Now alone at the front of the room, he instructs everyone to look at the rose-coloured page, which lists all the teachers and their areas of specialization. Judith studies the list. It looks like they have one of everything here, like a smorgasbord. One lesbian, one gay guy (the interest in HIV/AIDS is always a dead giveaway), one black prof, one Native one, etc. Given these identity politics, she can't help speculating whether the prof who will be teaching poverty grew up poor, if the guy teaching about housing was ever homeless, and whether Tom Reggel, specializing in child abuse and neglect, was, as a child, neglected and abused.

Someone's handing out canary-coloured sheets. It's the schedule for first term: every Monday she will have Weick in the morning, Greg Smolan over the lunch hour, and then in the afternoon someone named Malone for "Social Work Practice with Individuals, Families, and Groups." Weick loudly clears his throat, looks around the room to get silence, and explains there are four profs on the list who couldn't be here today: Hetty Caplar, Marie Green, Bruce McIvor, and Suzy Malone. Suzy Malone — that name, spoken aloud, sounds familiar to Judith. But she can't place it. "Malone, Malone," she whispers under her breath, as if speaking the name aloud will help. It doesn't. But hearing it repeated like that makes the name seem different, like an abbreviation for "I'm alone": 'mAlone. And she does feel alone. Terribly alone. There's no one here — in this school, town, or even country — who really understands her. Who she could talk to about Israel, who shares her feelings about that place. Bobby loves her, but he doesn't understand her. She achingly misses her friends in Jerusalem. *I'm alone here*, she thinks. 'mAlone. *Gantz aleyn*. In *galut*. In exile.

"We, the faculty," Weick is saying — rather grandly, like an American saying "We, the People" — "have just told you something about ourselves. So now we would like to hear from you:

who you are, what you've been doing, and what you're interested in." He stops abruptly and turns sideways to listen to Phoebe, who is hissing something at him. He turns back to the group with a short laugh. "Unfortunately, however, Phoebe reminds me that in only twenty minutes Labour Studies gets this room. So please tell us something about yourself, but try to keep your comments brief. Just a few sentences, starting with your name, of course."

Judith's stomach starts convulsing. This type of public speaking always makes her very nervous. But at least, she sees, she won't have to go first or even anywhere near the beginning: she's sitting smack in the middle of the room, and Weick has started the go-around on his immediate left, with a startled older woman. As this woman speaks, and is followed by other students, Judith listens for clues about what to say when her turn comes. Anxiously she plans a presentation of herself that will make her look interesting and will also fit in with the "mission" of this school and what others are saying. Among the first seven to speak, there are those who proudly declare themselves gay, poor, "of colour," physically challenged, learning disabled, and "culturally diverse" (Native, Caribbean, Pakistani, Portuguese). Some are just one of these things; others are two or even three, like Macario, the gay, dyslexic, Portuguese guy. Judith struggles over what to say about herself. There's nothing particularly oppressed about her — nothing she can think of, anyway. She's white, middle-class, heterosexual, not disabled intellectually or physically, and neither old nor young. She knows that being female and Jewish, she has been in various ways oppressed by both sexism and antisemitism. But the truth is, she doesn't feel particularly oppressed, and doesn't see any reason to put herself across that way. The go-around continues, and as it moves closer and closer to her, she gradually figures out what to say.

The person talking is three seats away from her. Then two. Now it's Cindy's turn.

"I'm Cindy Hanson. Since getting my B.S.W. five years ago, I've been working at Mindy's Place, a group home for teenage girls with physical and developmental disabilities. Quite a few of them have been sexually abused. So I guess what interests me is why that is, and if it happens to these kinds of girls more often than others because of being disabled. I'd also like to know how they think about these abusive experiences, and also about their bodies in general." There are nods and murmurs of support. "So this is what I'd like to do my thesis on. Maybe approaching it from a feminist perspective, even though I don't know very much about that. But I hope to learn." Cindy looks at Terry Montana, and Terry nods back.

Now everyone looks expectantly at Judith.

"I'm Judith Gallanter," she begins.

"Louder," shouts someone from the other side of the room. "We can't hear you."

Judith raises her voice. "I'm Judith Gallanter. Is that better?" But somehow the volume has increased with each word, so that by the end she's shouting. Heads turn sharply toward her and a few people laugh, as if she's made a joke. Blushing, she continues, somewhere between her normal voice and a shout.

"My area of interest, like Cindy's, is teens. But what I've been involved with were discussion groups between Jewish and Arab adolescents in Israel. I was part of a group called Friends-of-Peace. They have a branch in Toronto. We ran meetings twice a month — with discussions and activities — to foster mutual understanding and tolerance between the two groups. To try to build bridges for the future between these two communities, instead of just conflict and hatred." She pauses. Everybody's looking at her and listening attentively.

"So while I'm here, I'd like to focus on cross-cultural dialogue, especially with adolescents, and examine what makes it work when it works — or not work when it doesn't. In more general terms, I'm interested in how people talk to each other. I'm interested in hate speech, and also" — she smiles, scanning the room — "in love speech. In coexistence speech. In the language we use to communicate with each other." She pauses for a moment. Then she shrugs. "I guess that's it."

Lots of people are smiling back at her or nodding approvingly. With relief and happiness she realizes she's done well. She's managed to translate herself, and her life in Israel, into Canadian terms: into something these people can relate to. Several of the professors are regarding her with interest. Cindy touches her arm and whispers, "That sounds very interesting." "Thanks," says Judith. Soon the go-around is complete, and Weick stands. But before he can say a word, there is loud, raucous noise coming from the hallway — yelling, laughing, and banging on the door, like an approaching mob.

"That must be the Labour Studies people," says Weick. "An unru-u-uly bunch." Someone laughs. "It's their turn for the room now, so we're going to have to adjourn. Please make sure you've got all the handouts, and we'll see you in class. Welcome."

Judith is glad this orientation is over. It felt considerably longer than one-and-a-half hours, and she's tired. But she feels much better now — less alone — than when she walked in here this morning. She gathers her papers.

"Thanks again," she says to Cindy.

"No problem. You know, we should talk sometime about working with teens. That's not an age group many people like."

Judith laughs. "I know." She watches Cindy, who is trying to straighten out all her different-coloured handouts, and then, giving up, just stuffs them impatiently into her brown leather satchel. There is something endearing about this, and while Cindy bends over, buckling the straps, Judith says to her back, "How about now? I'm not doing anything."

Cindy looks sideways at her with china blue eyes, reminding Judith of Loretta, her favourite doll when she was growing up: the one with the real open-and-shut eyes. "Sounds good," Cindy says, standing and slinging the satchel over her shoulder. "But I have a few errands to do first: I have to drop by the administration office to pay my fees, and I need a library card."

"I have the same list. So we could do them together."

"Great!" says Cindy. They move toward the door. "That'll be more fun than doing it alone."

"Yes. I hate doing stuff like this. It's so boring."

"I know. Plus even though I did my B.S.W. here, they've changed the campus since then, and I can't find my way anywhere."

"Really?!" Judith is surprised. "You seem so ... at home here."

"Me?" Cindy laughs. "Not at all. I haven't been in a classroom in five years, and I find all this quite overwhelming. I'm not sure I'm ready for this grad school thing. Plus the faculty for the B.S.W. and M.S.W. are completely different. I don't know a single person here."

"Yes, you do," says Judith. "You know me."

Now it's Cindy's turn to look surprised. They look at each other for a moment, then smile. "You're right," says Cindy. Together they leave the room. And on the way out, Judith, feeling triumphant, snatches one last cookie.

Five hours later, driving back to Toronto, she hits bumper-to-bumper rush-hour traffic. She probably should've left Dunhill earlier, right after finishing lunch with Cindy at the Lion's Den. But she was too excited and happy. She had a great time talking with Cindy about social work and life in general. Cindy knew nothing about Israel except what she read in the papers, but seemed genuinely interested in Judith's life there. Then she showed Judith some pictures of her baby and husband. And the weather was glorious: it felt like the perfect day to walk around the campus under those magnificent oaks, and find out where the gym, library, administration office, and cafeterias were. To physically orient themselves, it being Orientation Day. A strange word though, *orient*, it seems to Judith now in her unmoving car, since at this point she is not in the Orient. Dunhill shouldn't have had an Orientation Day; it should have had an Occidentation Day, since, being in Canada, it is located in the Occident. Which sounds like Accident. *Yes,* she thinks, *it's an accident I'm here in the Occident. I wouldn't be here if it weren't for Daddy getting sick. I didn't choose to leave Israel — I'm not one of those chickenshits who fled because of the intifada, betraying Israel in her time of need.*

She glances at the clock. It says 6:12, like the insect repellent she grew up with, and she frowns at the clock like at some horrible bug, as if it is personally to blame for the time. It's late. And Bobby hates to be kept waiting. So there's no time to stop off and change her sweaty, smelly T-shirt before going to his place for supper. The stalled traffic irritates her. She looks around: off the highway there are barns, crops, and some grazing cows, everything in a mix of sun and shade. She breathes deeply, inhaling the pungent smells of animal dung and the sweet hay and clover from the fields. Her father loved the country — he loved barns, of all crazy things — but she pushes this away, she doesn't want to start thinking about him now. Or about his house, where she is now living all alone — so empty and desolate without him there, the house grimy and filthy, and her dirty dishes piling up precariously high in the sink.

Instead she reflects on the coming year. Tomorrow night is Rosh Hashana, and she hopes it will be the beginning of a good, sweet, and happy year. It can't be worse than the last one: the year she watched her father die. She'd like the year ahead to be easy, light, and pleasant — even slightly boring, so she can recover from what she's been through. Bruria, her friend in Jerusalem, thinks a year in Toronto may be the perfect thing. Last week Judith wailed on the phone, "What am I doing here, Bruria? Why am I stuck here for a year? I want to come home!"

Bruria answered calmly, "Try and enjoy it, Judith. It's not like things here are so great right now. Some people would kill to be in your position — to have a year away from Israel forced on them by circumstances, no guilt attached. So enjoy yourself. Make the most of it. Think of the coming year as an anthropological experiment: a chance to study life in Canada. It could be interesting."

"Okay," Judith said, "I'll try." Grateful to be "given permission" — as Bruria, a therapist, would say — to enjoy herself. Now she reaches into the glove compartment and pulls out a tape labelled *Israel at Forty*, and in seconds her car is filled with bright, tinny music, unsophisticated and hopeful. No such hopeful music, though, emerged from Israel's fiftieth birthday. By 1998 the country was traumatized by Rabin's assassination, the first intifada, and a series of crises one after another, political, economic, and social. The songs on that tape are sombre and anguished. So she prefers to listen to *Israel at Forty* instead. She listens to a line or two of "The Honey and the Bee Sting," and then starts singing along, loudly, whole-heartedly, in Hebrew, in the privacy of her car. She knows every word of this song and of every song on this tape — she has sung them year after year with her friends at Yechiel and Miri's annual Independence Day sing-song — and when it comes to the chorus of this one,

> Please, good Lord,
> Preserve all these.
> The honey and the bee sting,
> The bitter and the sweet,

she feels like she's singing it together with them, no longer alone in her car in Canada, in *galut*.

But then the song ends, the car is silent while she flips the tape, and maybe because she *is* alone, and in *galut*, the words of this song now strike her as odd. She wonders who would want to preserve the bitter parts of life along with the sweet? Who would pray to God asking for that? And why, if you want a bit of honey in your tea, should you first have to suffer the pain of a bee sting? Is this what we in Israel have come to believe now? That we only deserve to be happy, or to live, if first we count out *x* number of pain tokens per year, like poker chips, to pay to God? That's sick. It's like domestic violence — like letting someone beat you so you can have his "love."

She does understand, though, all those battered women who stay with their men. Because her love for Israel is something like that. Unconditional. The way many people love their family members. You know all their faults, but still you love them. There are things about Israel she can't stand. At the top of the list, the occupation, and this government's treatment of Palestinians.

(Another definition of domestic violence: domestic policies that are violent.) But it doesn't matter: Israel is her love. *I am my beloved's, and my beloved is mine.*

One of her boyfriends in Israel, Micah, once joked that Israel was the only real love in her life. Recalling this now, she knows it is basically true. She has loved various men, just as she currently loves Bobby. But nothing has ever come close to her passion for Israel. Israel was her first love, and it's the love of her life. Only there has she ever felt fully alive or at home. She never felt at home in her parents' house. It wasn't a "bad" home, or anything like that. There was nothing particularly wrong with her family. Her parents loved her. But they were both busy running their little dry goods store, and for as long as she could remember she'd let herself into a silent, empty house after school. When her parents finally did come home at seven-thirty, they were tired after being on their feet for twelve hours, serving customers. There was a quick supper, and she did homework while her mother did housework and her father paid bills. Her parents always had more to do than there was time for. And her mother was short-tempered and given to moods.

But then Judith found Israel. The summer she was twelve she went to a Zionist summer camp, and after that she never felt that loneliness again. She was part of something larger than herself. Her life had meaning and purpose. But not in just a dutiful way. Rather in the way that life has meaning and purpose when you're in love. She fell in love with Israel. With its soul, but also — a few years later, on her first visit — with its body. She loved this country's red earth, its mountain-deserts, streams, forests, birds, fish, and flowers. She loved the star-studded night sky, with its sliver of moon lying horizontally on the bottom like a cradle, instead of standing vertically, like in Canada. She even loved the air in Israel and the water — including the salt-heavy water of the Dead Sea, the lowest point on earth. In Canada she'd always found geography and history boring, scoring low on her high-school leaving exams in both these subjects. But in Israel she was fascinated by every mountain range, by every excavated *tell* or Biblical battlefield. Because it was hers. It was about her people, and it told the story of what had happened to them, and therefore to her.

One morning, on one of the many nature-and-archaeology trips she took with the Israeli Nature Protection Society, she awakened in her sleeping bag on the cold desert sand near Timna, the location of King Solomon's mines, and also a modern reconstruction of the Israelites' tabernacle during their forty-year desert journey. Everyone else in the group was still asleep, their sleeping bags dotting the desert floor like multicoloured rocks, and she watched the mountains gradually turn visible in the early morning light, until the whole valley was bathed in a strange grey-yellow haze. Nothing else seemed awake, or even alive, except her and an ibex, its horn arced backwards, staring at her. She followed it. After ten minutes, she abruptly stopped walking. The sun, a brilliant orange, illuminated the mountain before her, making it radiate in the sun, and the whole world was perfectly silent and still. Suspended, as if waiting for something. Feeling rather foolish, she said, "I promise." She didn't know exactly what she was promising, she couldn't have articulated it if you'd asked her. But she had promised herself to this land.

Of course, she's never told anyone about this. It would have sounded too corny — ridiculous even. Who wouldn't laugh at a too-earnest pretty young woman swearing herself to a desert at dawn? *No one*, she thinks now as she drives. But from that point on, her life — as if with a will of its own — bent in a new direction. That glowing throbbing orange of a vow sat in the centre of her like a hot coal she had swallowed, burning and transforming her all the way down. Nothing mattered to her anymore except taking her place in Jewish history and on Jewish geography. Coincidentally, her cousin wrote her around then that history and geography were now being taught together in Canadian high schools under the heading *Social Sciences*, which felt exactly right to Judith. All she wanted to do at this point was to help realize the Zionist dream. To come home again after two thousand years of exile — of *galut,* which she noticed laughingly back then, rhymed with *dissolute* and *pollute*. To rebuild the land, and on it to reunite all the Jews scattered and in exile from every corner of the globe. As soon as she knew this was what she wanted, she found herself in a circle of young people like herself — Zionist dreamers, new immigrants from everywhere: the United States, England, Australia, Argentina, Chile, Russia, France, Switzerland, Italy, Finland, Holland, Algeria, Morocco, India, Ethiopia, even China. She learned scraps of a dozen new languages, heard music and tasted foods she'd never encountered in Canada. *It's ironic*, she wrote then to her father, newly a widower. *I was afraid living in a Jewish state would seem culturally narrow and parochial after Canada. But here I'm for the first time living a truly multicultural life.*

She swerves — something dark and furry darted onto the highway — a cat? a groundhog? — and she's missed running over it by mere inches. Lucky there were no cars near her on the road. She looks around and gets her bearings: she's only about fifteen minutes away from Bobby's house. The traffic is thickening again now, but so far so good. That's Bruria's expression, "so far so good," and Judith smiles thinking of her. But quickly the smile fades. Yesterday she got a long email from Bruria, and things in Israel are terrible now. Economically, politically, every way. At least, though, all their mutual friends are okay — "okay" meaning none of them were hurt in the latest suicide bombing three days ago at a café where some of them hang out. Five people were blown to bits and eight more lost arms, legs, parts of their faces. But her friends, who that day chose to meet elsewhere, were mercifully untouched.

Bruria's email also gave Judith an update on their friends. Yechiel and Miri, she wrote, are doing all right, still demonstrating against the occupation every Friday afternoon in front of the prime minister's residence, as Judith sometimes used to do with them. Usually they'd get a turnout of about forty people, but last week there were just fifteen because of the nearby bombing that morning. Still, that's not too bad, wrote Bruria, for a moribund peace movement gasping its final breaths. Rina and Michel were there, too, and so was Yaacov, who's starting his Ph.D. in archaeology next month, and is excited but nervous. Sammy didn't come — he had pneumonia but is feeling better now. Then on Saturday Tamar and Benny went with some friends in their broken-down van to visit a Palestinian family whose house had been demolished by the army, to help them rebuild it. Yonina usually goes with them, but this time she declined. She's fed up with politics, and says she doesn't believe anymore that these little gestures make any difference. Besides, she's working very hard — her art show opens in two weeks at the Artists' House. Miki, Bruria's brother, has started going out with Miri's neighbour's sister-in-law, Hedva. They came for cake and coffee on Saturday — she's nice, and the two of them seem to get along well. "So far so good."

Last but not least, Bruria writes, Noah has just finished his first six weeks of army service. Judith remembers the first time she met Noah. He was home from school with a fever, and Bruria, whom she'd met only a few months before, was spoon-feeding him warm milk with honey. He was an angelic-looking seven-year-old with silky blond curls, blue eyes, round flushed cheeks, and a heart-shaped mouth. More recently, for the two years before he went into the army, Noah was head of Youth for Peace Now, Jerusalem branch. About six months ago he had his four seconds of fame on CNN: they filmed him at a peace rally, holding a huge placard saying in English, Hebrew, and Arabic: END THE OCCUPATION — NOW! *Now*, though, he's in the Tank Corps in the occupied territories — terrified of being shot at, and only slightly less terrified of shooting at others. Bruria wrote that a few weeks ago, on his first day on patrol, Noah was confronted by a group of what the Canadian media calls Palestinian "children," but in fact were teenage boys his own age, some just a year or two younger than him — sixteen or seventeen. They were throwing rocks and rusty metal pipes at him and his friend Doron, and they were both terrified, but Doron actually shat his pants. When Noah came home a few days later for Shabbat, he just locked himself in his room and wouldn't come out. The next day he joined them for lunch, but hardly said a word. Now, after a few weeks, he seems to be getting used to it.

But what does that mean,"getting used to it"? wrote Bruria. *Getting used to being shot at, and to shooting other people? This is insane. Aside from all the obvious things, which I won't — can't — even name, I worry about what this is doing to him inside. To his heart and soul.*

Anyway, she concluded her email, *we hope for the best. Shana tova, Judith — a good, sweet year. I hope it's much better than the last one for you, and for all of Israel. Love, Bruria*

Music is blaring in the car. Judith forgot the tape was even on — it just drifted into background music. But now she hears "Hallelujah," the song that made Israel the winner of the Eurovision song competition in 1979. *Back then, when the Europeans still liked us.* ·

Again the traffic has stopped moving. *This sure is Canada,* she thinks: *everyone just sitting in their stalled cars in polite silence.* If this were Israel, there'd be dozens of horns honking, louder than a hundred Canada geese. She gives a tiny honk, just something symbolic, which doesn't make any difference to the traffic, but makes her feel better. The traffic begins moving, and soon she arrives at Bobby's house. He's standing on the porch, suntanned and handsome in a golf shirt, neatly pressed shorts with two perfect creases, and deck shoes. A bit preppy for her taste, but she can't help noticing how good-looking he is: she always forgets this when they're apart.

"Sorry I'm late," she says, getting out of the car. "The traffic was horrendous."

"I was getting worried, you took so long."

"It was rush hour — next time I'll know to leave earlier. What are you doing out here?"

"I live here."

"No, seriously."

"Waiting for you." Judith, nearing the porch steps now, gives him a skeptical look. "It's true. I was putting out the garbage and saw your car coming down the street. So I figured I'd just wait and surprise you."

"That's nice," she says, and gives him a quick kiss. Bobby puts his arm around her as they go into the house.

"So how was it?" he asks.

"Great!" She takes the sunglasses off the top of her head and shakes out her hair. She's flushed and radiant, and Bobby gapes at her.

"Wow!" he says. "I haven't seen you this happy in ages." Then, slightly resentfully, as if Dunhill were his rival: "What was so great about it?"

"I don't know," she says, her back to him as she lays her

sunglasses and purse on the room divider. Turning around to face him, she's aware of a feeling of reluctance, like she is not quite ready for him yet. He's so demanding. Always challenging her. "Mostly it's just good to be part of something again," she says. "The people seem very nice, too. And some of them are doing interesting things."

"Like what?"

Bobby is leading the way into the living room, and she glances warily at his back as she follows close behind. They don't see eye to eye politically, and Bobby views social workers as a bunch of bleeding hearts. She hopes tonight they're not going to have another one of their arguments. Sitting with him on the black leather couch, she tells him about the profs and students she met today, the unexpectedly splendid tree-lined campus, and the smoky, noisy Lion's Den, smelling sourly of beer. Bobby sniggers appreciatively at her description of the identity politics at Dunhill, and laughs at "Gay Lesbian Bacon and Tomato." But when she mentions the school's "mission," and its focus on anti-oppression, he looks testy.

Ignoring this, she continues: "They genuinely care about social justice at Dunhill. They may not all be, as you'd say, rocket scientists" — he stares back at her stonily, refusing to smile — "but they strike me as people with ideals."

"Ideals?" he cries. "Is this what you call that left-wing crap? I can't believe you're buying into that anti-oppression bullshit. All it is, is, 'I'm a victim, you're a victim,' and you're way too smart to fall for that."

She feels her anger rising. "I'm not falling for anything," she says. "And stop being simplistic. You know as well as I do, that isn't all it's about."

"Yes, it is." His handsome hazel eyes flash. "That's exactly what it's about: the Moral Superiority of the Victim. Anyone who's not a victim — who's at all successful — is an 'oppressor.' According to these people I'm supposed to feel guilty and apologetic because I'm a lawyer earning a half-decent salary, but I don't. I've worked for it — nobody handed it to me on a silver platter."

"Oh, c'mon," she says impatiently. "No one's saying poor people are morally better than rich ones. Just that they've been socially disadvantaged, 'oppressed' if you will, and deserve a fairer share of the pie."

"Ah, but that's the question: Do they, Judith? Do they? Why do you lefties assume whenever people are poor, or have miserable fucked-up lives, that it's always society's fault? Maybe sometimes it is. But mostly these people have fucked up their own lives, and shouldn't blame this on anyone else. Let me finish." He holds up his hand to stop her from interrupting. "People aren't always at the bottom of the social heap just because of your 'structural oppressions.' Some people don't work hard. Some are dumber at birth. People aren't all equal at the starting line."

"That's exactly the point. But never mind — forget it." Judith crosses her arms across her chest. She's getting angry, but is trying to control her temper. "I'm not having this conversation with you again. We've been through this a hundred times, and you never understand."

"I never understand because it doesn't make sense."

"It doesn't make sense because you're not trying to understand."

They glare at each other from opposite sides of the couch. Then Bobby sighs.

"Okay, Judith," he says quietly. "Try once more. Explain what you see in this that I can't. Because if this is where your head will be for this whole next year, we have to be able to talk about it."

Doubtfully she looks at him. His voice has lost its combative, prosecuting lawyer's edge, and he seems to have retracted his claws, but she isn't sure. *The voice is the voice of Jacob, but the hands are the hands of Esau.* "All right," she finally says. "I'll try one last time, but that's it. Yes, you're right this anti-oppression stuff can have a silly side. But that's true of everything. There's nothing in life that can't be ridiculed — even your precious tax law. As for your argument that some people 'at the bottom of the heap' have fucked up their own lives, yes, some have. But most of them haven't. A single mother, black and on welfare, has a million barriers working against her. So social workers — we 'lefties,' as you'd say — try to eliminate these barriers and redress structural inequities, like racism, sexism, and heterosexism, so people can live lives of dignity. C'mon, Bobby, don't look at me like that. You know perfectly well what I'm talking about."

"*Avanti popolo.*"

Bobby spent one childhood summer in a socialist Zionist camp singing "Hatikvah," the Israeli national anthem, every morning, and "The Internationale," the socialist worldwide anthem, every night, and this was the worst summer of his life.

Judith, sitting cross-legged, facing his sullen profile, touches him on the knee. "You must admit at least it's a good dream."

"It's a stupid dream because it's just a dream, and built on false premises. You and your 'idealistic' profs, and your lefty friends in Israel, you all believe deep down no one can be rich and also have a social conscience. Well, you're wrong. Some of my clients are extremely wealthy, and donate millions of dollars to charity."

"So what?" she asks, feeling tired. It's been a long day, and this isn't what she was hoping for when she came here tonight. "It's just a tax break. One of the legal loopholes you find for them so they can pay as few taxes as possible."

"Fuck, Judith. You spend one day at Dunhill, and you come home a left-wing Moonie."

"That's ridiculous. I've had the same politics, as you know, ever since high school, when I started thinking for myself. Anyway, if I *were* a Moonie, I'd rather be a left-wing Moonie than a right-wing Moonie like you."

"I'm not right-wing. I'm normal."

"Oh, I see. And I'm abnormal?"

"Well, you're sure different from everyone else I know."

"Maybe you know the wrong people."

"Maybe *you* do."

She doesn't answer. Just stares down at the carpet, thinking fiercely that there's nothing wrong with her or with the people she met today. She likes them. They make sense to her. A lot more sense than Bobby, who in under a half-hour has managed to ruin all the happiness of her day — the first day she's felt truly happy or hopeful about anything since coming back to this country almost a year ago.

"Judith," he says.

"What?" she answers without looking up.

"Judith."

"*What?*" She whips her head upwards, glaring.

"I hate fighting with you. Why do we keep fighting?"

"Because we don't see life the same way. We have different values, politics, *weltanschauung*. Trivial things like that."

He sighs. "But that's what's so aggravating about you. I don't believe you actually see life so differently than me. You know as well as I do exactly how things are, and underneath all that lefty shit you're as hard-headed as they come. But you pretend not to know. You blather on with that mealy-mouthed crap when, underneath it all, you understand exactly how the world really works."

She turns and looks straight into his eyes. "Yes, Bobby. I do know, as you put it, exactly how the world really works. But maybe I want there to be more to life than just being born,

47

accruing as much wealth as possible, and then dying. What's so awful about that? At least I'm not just giving up on the world."

He looks at her more gently now. "Fair enough. I agree, as you know, that there's more to life than making money. But Judith, don't waste yourself on lost causes. Don't throw away all that talent and passion fighting windmills. It's one thing to try and change things where you have some reasonable chance of success. But banging your head against a brick wall isn't going to help you or anybody else."

"I'm not banging my head against a brick wall. Anyway, what would you know? You always play the game — you never challenge, or try to change, anything. You weren't like this when we were in high school. What happened, Bobby? How did you become so conservative? How did you turn into such a right-wing shmuck?"

"A right-wing shmuck?!" says Bobby. "Well, how did you turn into a left-wing shmuckette?"

"*Shmuckette?*"

"Well, if there's a shmuck, there must be a shmuckette."

She tries not to smile, but can't help it. "You learned that word in French class, I suppose," she says.

"From Madame Benoît." Now they're both smiling, picturing their wizened prude of a grade nine French teacher teaching them the word *shmuckette*. "She also taught me this," he says, leaning forward, bringing his face close to hers: "*Ma chérie. Je t'aime.*"

"Yeah, sure. Madame Benoît taught you to say, 'Je t'aime.' Madame Benoît was your '*chérie.*'"

"*You* are my *chérie*. My one and only *chérie.*"

"Oy," she says, but smiles. Then she grins.

"*Ma chér-r-rie,*" says Bobby in what she recognizes as his best attempt at a Parisian accent, and he swoops and plants a kiss on her laughing mouth. His lips feel smooth and firm. Younger than Moshe's. Then he kisses her neck. Her ear. Her eyes. And again her mouth. His lips on hers are somehow both cool and warm at the same time, like sun-drenched marble. His lips move down and kiss her throat, and now they are sucking gently on her left nipple. Then harder. She forgets all about politics. She forgets about everything.

An hour later she wakes up, *déshabillée* on the living-room carpet, to the sound of pots and pans clanging in the kitchen and the smell of burning meat.

— 4 —

On Monday Judith makes the hour-long drive to Dunhill, again listening to *Israel at Forty*. When she arrives, there's an atmosphere of excitement: that special crackle in the air of the first day of school. Her first class today is with Weick, and he starts off with another class go-around. When her turn comes, Judith speaks briefly, offering an abridged version of what she said four days ago. But she adds, since this course is "Knowledge and Values in Social Work," that knowledge interests her more than values because it seems to her that most social workers' values are anyway quite similar, and she's eager to increase her knowledge about the latest social work theories, having been out of school for the past ten years. When she finishes, she sees Cindy off to the right, waving two fingers at her, and she waves back. Then she recognizes, a little past Cindy, some of the other students from Orientation, including the two women she rode in the elevator with that day. They're sitting together in the row in front of Cindy, and the pretty dark-haired one is wearing a magenta Chinese-style jacket. Judith didn't pay much attention to their spiels during Orientation, but now when they introduce themselves, she listens closely. The one with the magenta jacket, Aliza, used to be a jazz dancer, and the plain redhead, Pam, was in honours economics and poli sci. They both speak ironically and are obviously bright, and Judith decides she wants to know them better.

After the go-around, Weick begins to teach. He's a stunningly terrible teacher. Among the worst Judith has ever had — lecturing in a monotone from ragged yellowish notes, and hardly ever raising his eyes to look at the students, even though there are only twenty of them in the class. Furthermore, the material he's droning on about is stuff she already knows backwards and forwards from her B.S.W. Weick is teaching Systems Theory, a theory that was revolutionary in the late 1960s and 1970s, but now is old and tired. It was already stale even thirteen years ago when she first learned it. *This theory is past its expiration date*, she thinks. *If they put expiration dates on orange juice, why can't they put them on theories?*

Weick keeps droning on, and after twenty-five minutes — when it looks like even he is about to fall asleep from boredom — he, for the first time, asks the class a question: "Can anyone give me an example of a system?"

Nobody answers. The question is too stupid. Every student in the room, having done a B.S.W., has already written three, four, maybe five term papers related in one way or another to Systems Theory. He can't possibly be asking them what he seems to be. It would be like asking, "Can someone give me an example of a fruit?"

At the front of the room he waits. The silence becomes awkward. Finally he answers his own question. Proudly, like a five-year-old triumphant at knowing the answer. "The solar system!" he cries, drawing on the board a big circle and some smaller surrounding ones. "The sun with the planets revolving around it —"

Judith nearly groans out loud. *I can't stand this*, she thinks. *I really can't. I know I promised Daddy I'd do this M.S.W., but there's no way I can take a year of this. I can't stand even another half-hour. It's unbearable.* She doesn't dare glance at Cindy, or even Pam or Aliza, for fear that if they make eye contact, she'll roll her eyes, giving herself away. So she keeps her eyes lowered to the page, like an ox with its eyes glued to the ground as it circles endlessly with its yoke. But after a minute she picks up her pen, and on the blank page before her, writes: *I can't stand this. I can't stand this.* She continues writing this over and over, like a pupil being punished — which is exactly how she feels — and forced to copy the same phrase a hundred times. She isn't counting, but she writes this many times, punctuating it now and again with *Stupid stupid stupid* or *Fuck fuck fuck.* Once she writes *Weick is weak. Weick's a freak.* Then there's the sound of chairs scraping the floor, and it's over. Weick has dismissed them early because it's the first day. She approaches Cindy, who introduces her to Pam and Aliza. They all chat together politely, waiting in line to get out of the classroom. But once in the hallway and safely out of hearing distance, the four of them, huddled together, explode.

"Do you fuckin' believe it …?"

"Systems Theory?! Fuckin' Systems Theory!"

"Not one new idea — not one — I didn't already know."

"God! So boring! I thought I'd die!"

They go on like this in joyful outrage as they leave the building and then cross the quadrangle toward the cafeteria.

"What if all the other classes are like this?" Aliza asks.

"They'd better not be, or I'll quit this program," says Pam. "Can you believe they're still teaching Systems Theory? It's shocking. Hasn't anything new happened in social work in all these years?"

"Apparently not," says Aliza.

"Anyway," asks Cindy, "what is Systems Theory doing in a course on knowledge and values?"

"Well, theories are a part of knowledge," says Aliza. "But it's probably the only theory he knows — that's why he's teaching it."

"Or maybe he doesn't have any," says Judith.

"Any what?"

"Knowledge. Or values."

"Ooooh ..."

They arrive at the cafeteria. Entering the door, they all agree this is a class to be merely survived, nothing more, and the one good thing about it is they'll probably all get *A*'s. Soon they're carrying their coffee and donuts to a small, square table.

For several minutes there's silence: they just slurp, munch, and swallow. But soon they're sharing how anxious they were about coming back to school after years spent out in the field, and how relieved they are to have at least one easy course, though they hope their other classes aren't quite as vacuous as Weick's. It turns out Pam and Aliza, like Judith, are feminists, and while Cindy listens, they talk about the deadly style of the traditional male lecturer — Weick being the perfect example — and then about men in general. Including their own men, past and present — except for Pam, who gets completely silent for once, making Judith wonder if she's a lesbian. Then Aliza starts telling funny anecdotes. She's almost like a comedienne, and for a while they just sit around and laugh as she entertains them. Judith flashbacks to how her father loved to just sit around and "chew the fat," as he'd call it, listening to people tell funny or fascinating stories and throwing in some of his own. Without warning it's back: that grief that's always waiting, crouching and ready to pounce, like a cat hidden in the pit of her stomach. She sits, stunned and staring, for several minutes. Then it passes, and she's back again. Aliza is now in the middle of telling a dirty joke — Judith missed the beginning, so doesn't fully get it when Aliza delivers the punchline — but it has something to do with a leaning tower of penis. Pam has a high-pitched screech of a laugh, like a monkey's, and this, with all the glee and giddiness from the others, makes Judith start laughing, too. Then Cindy says, "Look at the time! It's five to eleven," and they hurry back for their second class.

From eleven o'clock to one, it's "Introduction to Social Justice" with Greg Smolan. Greg is short for Gregory — he's named after the saint, he tells them with a grin — not that he believes in any of that stuff anymore. If he believes in any religion now, it's the religion of social justice. This class is fun: a cross between a gossip column about the Canadian elite — the rich-and-famous (or the rich-and-infamous) — and a detective thriller built around a conspiracy. Greg, although he doesn't use this exact word, sees everything as a conspiracy. For two hours he describes how the white, Christian, male elite of Canada uses its power, influence, and wealth to shape virtually all of Canada's social and economic policies, which in turn help to maintain, and even extend, this same power, influence, and wealth. "Of course," he explains, "these policies also maintain and extend the marginalization and oppression of those who are poor, old, female, ethnically diverse, GLBT, and/or disabled, physically, intellectually, or psychiatrically. This is just how things work."

Sitting in Greg's class on a wooden chair as hard as a pew, Judith listens to his succession of stories about the connections between government, business, inherited wealth, social celebrity, and the media. He describes as vividly as a scene from the movie *Howard's End* how, even in Canada now in 2002 — no different, in fact, from the British upper classes in Victorian times — the rich and powerful intermingle familially, socially, professionally, and financially. At their golf games and formal dinners, fundraising galas, garden parties, and weddings, they interact and intermarry, thus keeping within their little circle all that wealth and power. It's been ten years now since Judith left Canada and became active on the Israeli left, and in all this time she hasn't had direct contact with any Canadian leftists. So it's fascinating for her to now hear what their issues are. The left in Canada and Israel have certain obvious similarities, but here the concerns of the left have nothing to do with war and peace, national survival, security, or land. Their issues all seem relatively theoretical to her, and removed from everyday life. She glances at Cindy to see how she's reacting to this class, but Cindy's face is bent low over the page she's scribbling notes on, and Judith can't make out her expression.

Greg is getting more passionate by the minute, waving his hands around in the air as he speaks, and his voice is rising in volume, and soon he's so carried away he completely loses track of the time and continues straight through until one o'clock with his charming amalgam of Marx, Freire, and Foucault. Judith hasn't studied in depth even one of this trinity of guys (*of course they're all guys*), but they don't seem to fit very well together. She can't picture them being in the same room and having anything in common. But Greg keeps saying he's "eclectic," and in his eclectic electric blender, Marx, Freire, and Foucault mush into a kind of sweet social justice strawberry milkshake that has its own internal logic. Greg's political views seem to Judith not very different from her own, so she doesn't feel he's convincing her of anything new. But listening to him speak in his flowing, per-suasive, almost poetic way, she wishes Bobby could hear him. She's sure Greg could make even Bobby, defender of all things capitalist and corporate, see things differently.

As soon as this class ends, Judith asks Cindy to hold a seat for her in the next one and races to the bathroom. There she pees with immense relief, and then for another minute sits on the toilet, daydreaming. Bobby may see her as a left-wing freak-o, but to the people here she makes sense, and they make sense to her, too. This might turn out to be a good year, after all. It could be interesting, even fun, to spend some time here in Canada. In exile, but just for a while. It sounds like the title of a song, "Exile but Just for a While," and she starts humming a tune to go along with it. For the first time since promising her father she'd return to school, she doesn't feel trapped or resentful about it. Maybe her father knew something she didn't. Maybe he was smarter than she thought.

From 1:30 to 3:30 she has the last of her three courses: "Social Work with Individuals, Families, and Groups," with Suzy Malone. (Or "'mAlone," as she now thinks of that name.) Arriving from the bathroom, Judith gets stuck behind a dozen students filing slowly into the classroom, most holding sandwiches and drinks. When there's no longer anyone ahead of her blocking her view, and for the first time she can see the teacher standing at the front of the room, she does a double-take. She knows her. They've met before. But where? It takes several seconds to remember, and then it all comes back. It was at a country club in May, at a boring retirement party for a founder of the law firm where Bobby had just begun. Suzy's husband worked there, too, but as a senior partner. She and Suzy met in the bathroom — a gorgeous, spacious bathroom full of elegant peach-coloured gladioli — and after they somehow discovered they were both social workers, they chatted for about ten minutes. There was something very intimate about standing together in that bathroom while other women came and went, and the toilets kept flushing over and over. Suzy was very interested in the work Judith had done in Israel at a kindergarten for developmentally challenged children, and she told her about the problems of her eleven-year-old daughter, Natalie, who had autism, and how this was affecting her other two kids. Judith, coincidentally, had just heard from a friend of her father's about a new summer camp for "special needs" kids, and she passed this information along to Suzy. They had a long, lovely conversation — the kind you have when you never expect to see that person again — and she hasn't thought about Suzy since.

Now Suzy is smiling brightly at her. As Judith approaches, she is struck by how pretty and petite Suzy is. A short, pretty woman in a fuchsia silk shirt.

"I didn't know you were coming here to study!" Suzy says.

"Neither did I," says Judith. "It was sort of last-minute."

"Well, welcome to Dunhill. How are you finding it so far?"

"Okay."

"You'll be fine," says Suzy. "There's a lot to absorb at first. But you're so smart —" Judith looks at her in surprise. "You are. You'll be great. You'll see."

"Thanks." Then Judith feels self-conscious. Glancing around, she sees some of the other students are listening to their conversation. Awkwardly, she says, "I should probably sit down."

"Sure," says Suzy. "We'll be starting soon anyway."

Judith sees Cindy waving at her from the middle of the room and goes to the chair Cindy has saved for her.

"How do you know her?" Cindy asks as Judith sits. "I thought you didn't know anyone here."

Judith starts to explain, but stops abruptly as Suzy says, "Good afternoon," and begins teaching. In front of a class Suzy is the same person she was in the bathroom: unpretentious, friendly, and open. She's a good listener, too, obviously sincerely interested in students' points of view, allowing lots of time for class discussion, and apparently not minding at all — even liking it — when students interrupt, make jokes, or briefly take over. In response to something funny that one student, Tyler, says, Suzy laughs — a natural, tinkly laugh, and now Judith feels happy and at home. Part of this, she knows, has to do with the content of this course: her B.S.W. and all her field placements were in the area of "individuals, families, and groups," so here in Suzy's class she feels on solid ground. But more than this there is something about Suzy that makes Judith feel comfortable and safe. Like who she is and what she knows is good enough. Suzy now says she believes in empowerment and androgogy. Judith wonders if they're back to GBLT.

"Not androgyny," says Suzy, startling Judith as if she's read her mind. "Androgogy, the theory of adult education. Androgogy as opposed to pedagogy. I don't believe in teaching adults as if they were children." She goes on to explain that in this course she wants to help them retrieve, organize, and utilize the rich stores of knowledge they've all acquired from their years of experience in the field, and from life in general.

What a relief, thinks Judith, *and what a contrast to Weick. Suzy's going to treat me like an adult. An equal. Instead of like I'm in grade four.*

Suzy tells them about her own professional background. "You have a right to know where I'm coming from," she says sweetly. She's worked in a number of different jobs, but currently has a private practice, specializing in therapy with single women in their late twenties and thirties. *That's me!* thinks Judith, feeling embarrassed, and more than that, a bit naked, as if Suzy, like Supergirl, has X-ray vision and can see right through her. The rest of the class passes quickly, with Suzy doing a cursory run-through of all the most important theories and models used in working with individuals, families, and groups. Then she asks the class what other theories they know about and like. Judith puts up her hand: "Cognitive Theory," she says.

"Sure," says Suzy approvingly. "This is another very useful approach. Coincidentally, a new book just came out called *Cognitive Therapy for Social Work,* and yesterday I received a complimentary copy. So if anyone's interested in borrowing it" — she looks straight at Judith — "I'd be happy to lend it." Judith vigorously nods. "Just come by my office after class."

Then Suzy says, "Before we finish today ..." and Judith, glancing down at her watch, notes with astonishment there are only five minutes left of this class. Suzy reviews the assignments for her course. There's a term paper worth 75 percent due the last day of the term, and for the other 25 percent they're supposed to keep a weekly log. "A running dialogue with yourself," Suzy explains, "about everything you're learning. A place to begin integrating theory and practice, including your reactions to the readings and class discussions, your thoughts and feelings, and anything else you want to write about. Your logs will be kept strictly confidential," she assures them, "so feel free to express yourselves there. I'll return them each Monday to your box."

After class is over, Judith waits for fifteen minutes while Suzy attends to a lineup of students with questions. Eventually she and Judith, alone in the classroom, talk. To Judith it feels not so much like a conversation between a teacher and student, but like they are just picking up where they left off, back in the bathroom of the Toronto Country Club. Suzy thanks her for the name of that summer camp for her daughter — it worked out very well, she says, and gave them all a much-needed break from each other. Judith tells Suzy how much she enjoyed her class. Suzy says it was great for her to have someone there she already knew. Then, walking together to Suzy's office to get the book, they commiserate about the major restructuring at the law firm where Bobby and Dennis both work. It's called "Bonham Bailey Bomberg" (which makes Judith think of the Barnum & Bailey circus). She says BBB should no longer be called a firm, but a shaky, and Suzy laughs. Judith follows her up two flights of stairs and along a gloomy, serpentine corridor with two bends in it right before the end. Inside Suzy's office, there are red flowering plants hanging from the windows, bright and cheerful French Impressionist posters on the walls (all Mediterranean sun and sea, with ships in the harbour), two bookcases filled with books and knick-knacks, and a deep cream-coloured carpet on the floor. The carpet looks so inviting she wants to kick off her sandals and wiggle her toes in it. But instead she stands politely in the doorway while Suzy searches for the book. Judith is starstruck by the many thick, professional, knowledge-filled books, and the two framed diplomas on the far wall. Suzy, she guesses, is only a few years older than her — maybe five, eight at the most. More the age difference of a big sister than another generation. *But look*, she thinks, *how far ahead of me she is. I'm a student and she's a professor.*

"Here it is," says Suzy. "Hot off the press. The publisher just sent me this. But keep it as long as you want — I'm not in any rush for it. Just let me know what you think of it when you're done."

"Sure," says Judith, taking the book. "Thank you."

Suzy stands there silently, apparently waiting for her to go.

"Bye," says Judith.

"Bye. See you next week."

She starts down the long, dark hallway. She feels strangely emotional, almost ecstatic, yet also wanting to cry. Something about the way Suzy stood with her back to her as she searched among the books reminds her of her mother. She had that same lightness, slightness of build. Trim, tidy, and self-contained. She and her mother were never close, but now for some reason she misses her. And this missing her is laced with guilt. She was in Israel when her mother first got sick, and no one at the time realized how serious it was. So she didn't rush back to see her, and the next thing she knew, her mother was dead.

"How could you have known?" her father said. "None of us knew. Don't blame yourself."

But of course she did. She could have known. She should have known. Now she forces herself to keep walking, and to distract herself, she opens Suzy's book and starts reading. She skims the Table of Contents, then starts on Chapter One: "Cognitive Belief Systems and Their Impact on Emotion." It's engagingly written and very interesting, and she gets immersed in it as she walks down the deserted hallway. She's going at quite a good clip, frowning down at the page as she reads, when, turning a corner, she crashes right into someone coming toward her.

"I'm sorry!" she cries, leaping back.

"Well, well," says Weick. "A student already engrossed in her schoolwork. How admirable. What are you reading?"

"A book," says Judith, immediately feeling foolish. But she doesn't want to share Suzy's book with him (even its title), as if it were something secret or private, like an intimate gift.

"Yes, but which one?" asks Weick, and before Judith knows what's happening, he reaches out and snatches away the book. She stands there empty-handed, feeling naked somehow, while he peers at the cover and then leafs through the pages. He's reading the words she was just reading, and she feels almost like he is leafing through her. "It's on cognitive therapy," she says lamely.

"So I see," he says, still reading. Then he thrusts the book back at her, and contemplates her with open curiosity. She feels herself blush and looks down. He says, "You're here rather late for the first day of class. I thought everyone buggered off as soon as they possibly could. You must be a keener."

"I was talking to someone," she says uncomfortably.

"Were you now?" Weick cranes his head theatrically in all directions, looking around the empty hallway. Judith notices for the first time that it's very ill-lit. *Ill-lit*, she thinks, *and illicit. Just one letter different* (*c*). "I don't see anyone here," Weick says, bringing his face quite close to hers, his breath smelling of liquor. She wants to pull away, but can't. She's frozen. But she manages to choke out a sentence: "I was talking to Suzy."

"I see," he says, drawing back. As if Suzy's name were a magic charm that brought instant safety, like a cross held up to the devil. "Is she still in her office?"

"Probably. I just left her a minute ago," says Judith, comforted by the thought of Suzy still relatively nearby. Maybe just a shout away.

"Oh, good, I have something to ask her." Now Weick squints at Judith. "You're in one of my classes, aren't you?"

"Yes. I'm in 'Knowledge and Values.'"

"That's right, I thought you looked familiar. What's your name again?"

"Judith Gallanter."

"Oh, yes. Teenagers in Conflict, wasn't that you?"

Judith smiles in spite of herself. She's surprised he was even listening during the student go-around and flattered he remembered her. But also it's comical the way he said "Teenagers in Conflict." Like a headline from one of those sensationalist tabloids: Man Beats Wife To Death With Boiled Cauliflower.

"Yes," she says, "that's me."

Weick's eyes narrow. "Very interesting. I must hear more about that sometime. Well, nice 'running into' you, Judith. See you in class."

"Sure." She turns and watches his back as he strides toward Suzy's office.

In the parking lot, Judith sees Cindy carrying a wobbling armful of books toward a green van. She hurries over and helps her unload them onto the back seat, already cluttered with a carseat, baby toys, and a huge bag of diapers. Cindy's been in the library since Suzy's class ended, and she shows Judith all the books she's signed out, offering to pass them on to her when she's finished with them. Judith thanks her and shows her Suzy's book, making the same offer. Then Judith tells Cindy about her little run-in with Weick. Cindy snickers, rolling her eyes.

"Typical," she says.

"What do you mean?"

"Well, let's just say ..." Cindy says hesitantly, "he has a reputation for getting a little too friendly with some of his female students."

"Really?! How do you know this?"

Cindy shrugs. "You're from Toronto, but I live here. In a place the size of Dunhill, word gets around. Everyone knows everyone else's business. He had this very nice wife, apparently. A social worker at the school board, but she left him for someone else — five, maybe six years ago. It all started then. But don't tell anyone I told you."

"Of course not. I would never."

Cindy nods. Then she says, "Be careful, Judith. He's not just a teacher; he's also the Director of the school."

"I know," Judith says glumly. Then she brightens up a bit. "Well, at least I have just this one course with him. After that I'll hardly have to see him."

"I hope you're right. Anyway, I gotta go. I have to get Mikey by five."

"Right. Of course. Thanks, Cindy."

"No problem. See you next week."

Cindy climbs into her van and drives off, and as soon as she's out of sight, Judith lifts Suzy's book to her face and smells it. She loves the smell of new books, and this one is fresh from the publishing house, its binding not yet cracked. Deeply she inhales this book, as if, like a dog sniffing a human, she can determine from this alone whether or not it is good. This book, after sitting for a week on Suzy's desk, smells like her: slightly perfumed with a musk-type scent and at the same time academic. A musky-musty smell, she thinks, and gives the book a kiss.

— 5 —

The next morning she goes food shopping and makes tuna salad and canned tomato soup for lunch. Then she does laundry and goes to the University of Toronto Library, just a seven-minute drive from her house. To her delight there's an inter-university agreement allowing her to use it. Still, hunting down the readings she needs for school makes for a long and tedious afternoon. Eventually she finds and photocopies fifteen journal articles and four book chapters, over two hundred pages in all. She gets home gratified to have almost all the readings she needs, but totally exhausted. She has another bowl of soup, lies down for a brief rest, instantly falls asleep, and at eight-thirty gets up to meet Bobby at the restaurant near his office for a bite. Afterwards they stop by a jazz club and catch the second set of a trio from New Orleans.

The next day, Wednesday, she starts reading her stack of photocopied articles. Or anyway, she tries. It's harder now to concentrate on studying than when she did her B.S.W. She keeps catching herself rereading a sentence for the third or fourth time and still not absorbing what it means. On Thursday, though, it goes much better. Her mind is clearer, and by five-thirty she's finished the six most important readings — the two required ones for each course — and treats herself to pizza for supper. Bobby's working late tonight, same as every Thursday, so she spends the evening watching *Seinfeld* and catching up on email. Tonight she has eight messages waiting from friends in Israel, and she answers them all, cutting and pasting certain general paragraphs — like the one about her first day of school — but for the rest of each email, writing back long, personalized, detailed letters.

Then while she gets ready for bed, she pictures each of these friends reading the letter she just sent. The clock says it's five after ten now, so back home in Israel it's about five in the morning, and everyone is still sleeping. But in a couple of hours they'll all be awake, and soon afterwards they'll check their email and find her letter. In Israel it will be Friday morning, and her words will be mixed in with their busy preparations for Shabbat, like the sweet raisins in a *chalah*. She knows the exact take-out place on Bethlehem Road where in a few hours they'll all buy their hummus, carrot salad, and stuffed vine leaves, and also the hot side dishes for Friday night dinner that they don't have time to make: spicy roast potatoes, ratatouille, fragrant rice with currants. Afterwards, they'll go next door to the bald guy's bakery and buy their *chalah, rugelach,* and cream cakes. While doing their shopping, her friends will all bump into each other, and briefly chat and laugh and wish one another "*Shabbat shalom*" before rushing off to the next errand. Later in the day, around one-thirty or two, just before the stores close, husbands, at their wives' bidding, will run out for some final purchases: flowers, more wine, or extra take-out side dishes and desserts to plump up the meal for last-minute unexpected guests. There will be frantic house-cleaning and cooking and pressing of clothes. It's in the midst of all this that they will receive and read her emails, and in that way she will be there together with them as they get ready for Shabbat. She goes to sleep, dreaming of Jerusalem.

The next morning it is Friday in Canada, and while studying at the kitchen table, she keeps one eye on her bubbling chicken soup. All day long she cooks and studies. That night, Bobby comes over. They light Shabbat candles, do the blessings over the wine and *chalah*, and leisurely eat the meal she's prepared: chicken soup, roast chicken, salad with dressing, and sweet potatoes, and for dessert, a home-made apple cake and tea. They sing *zmirot*, the special songs for Friday night. Afterwards, feeling full — full of food, music, and happiness — they make love. On Shabbat morning (as always) they sleep in, eat breakfast at noon, and for the next few hours just lie around the house reading newspapers and books, playing cards or Scrabble, and snuggling in bed. It's lazy and lovely till mid to late afternoon; then, as usual, they both start getting edgy, and quibble over nonsense, like who's going to do the dishes. Their arguments typically are tinged with politics, such as gender roles and household labour, and sometimes this escalates into a big fight. Today, though, they make up by making love. Sex being their favourite peace-pipe.

Afterwards Judith says, "Too bad Arafat and Sharon can't solve their problems, as we do, by just getting into bed together and fucking."

"What a nauseating image," says Bobby. "Though they do, on a regular basis, fuck each other *over*. Or *up*. Or *around*."

On Sunday morning (as always) they get up around nine, shower, eat, and go straight to work — Bobby at his office, Judith at her home — just as if they lived in Israel, where Sunday is a regular workday. On Sunday night they each sleep alone at home. Then on Monday the work week starts all over again, with Judith in her car at 8:00 a.m., driving to Dunhill.

This same week repeats itself over and over: it is the routine of her new life as an M.S.W. student, and she enters more quickly and easily than she anticipated into its rhythm. Or as her father would say, "into the *shvung*." *Shvung* conjuring a little girl on a swing being pushed from behind by her father, back and forth, back and forth. There's something deeply satisfying about this rhythm of her new life — something comforting about having an external schedule, as steady and predictable as a metronome, after the year she's just been through. A year of broken rhythms, syncopations, and skipped beats. Her father's heart was skipping beats, the doctors discovered. In addition to his malignant tumour, there was an irregular beating of his heart, and they diagnosed him with arrhythmia. That whole year was arrhythmic.

So it reassures her now, grounds her, to have to be at school every Monday morning at nine o'clock for Weick's lecture, and to know that, boring as it is, she can count on this happening at the same time, and the same place, week after week after week (Weick after Weick after Weick). It's gratifying, too, knowing she is expected there, and if she doesn't show up, there are people who will notice and miss her and wonder where she is. On each of the past two Monday mornings, whenever she walked into Weick's class, she's been greeted with smiles and waves and "Hi, Judith"s by Cindy, Pam, and Aliza, her new little gang. They've pointed to the chair they saved for her (like all the others at Dunhill, a peculiar chair, with an armrest growing out of it on the right — *like a tumour*, she thinks every time she sits). Or the one time Cindy, Pam, and Aliza all got to class too late to save her a seat, they were sitting on the bench at the back when she arrived and moved their bums over to make room for her. They're all in the Practice stream of the M.S.W., and therefore in all the same courses. They sit in class together, take their breaks together, and go out together for lunch. They have also, at Aliza's initiative — inspired, she said, by her grandfather, a Communist and union leader — formed a collective to save themselves both time and labour. Each of them finds and photocopies just one-quarter of the readings, then makes copies for everyone else.

"Now we're not just a social support system," Pam says on the third Monday of the term. They're sitting in the cafeteria, exchanging for the second time the articles they've photocopied for each other. "We're an economic system, too."

Judith looks at her admiringly. Pam is smart in areas she isn't, like economics and politics. Aliza is smart, too, but in a different way. Judith always thinks of the two of them together, "Pamanaliza," because they're inseparable, and also because they stand out at this school for having done interesting things with their lives so far — not just coming to the M.S.W. straight from a B.S.W. or a social work job, like most of the other students. Until three years ago, when one of Aliza's knees went bad and she had to quit, she danced in a jazz troupe. Aliza looks like a dancer: slender and lithe, delicate yet dramatic, with sleek long black hair and skin as white as paper. Pam, on the other hand, is plain: a bushy-haired redhead with thick lips and eyelids who never wears make-up. She came to social work with a first-class honours degree in political science and economics, and also an impressive-sounding part-time job at the CBC.

Now Judith looks to her left at Cindy, seated in profile at the square table, twisting her hair. There's nothing particularly interesting or impressive about Cindy. She's a blonde, good-hearted, small-town girl who has lived all her life in Dunhill, and is clearly not as bright or sophisticated as the other three of them: all verbal, intense Torontonians, and Jewish at least to some degree. Aliza, like Judith, has two Jewish parents, but Pam is only one-quarter Jewish — through her mother's father — and she also went at one point to a Catholic girls' school, so she isn't truly Jewish. But still she feels Jewish to Judith. Cindy continues to daydream and twist her hair, and Judith thinks: A heart of gold this person has. Definitely a person of the heart rather than the mind — someone wonderfully kind and caring — and the first one Judith calls whenever she has a question about homework.

There is silence around the table now: Aliza is sipping coffee, and Cindy and Judith are just waiting while Pam, scribbling on a napkin, does the math on what they owe each other. *What we owe each other*, thinks Judith, staring out the window at the rain. Until they started divvying up the articles a few minutes ago, they'd been having a discussion, prompted by a comment someone made in Greg's class, about "privilege" and oppression: What constitutes real privilege or oppression, and what are the relative weights of different types of oppression? For example, this person asked, is it "worse" to be black than gay? Is it worse to be poor than disabled? Obviously, as Greg was quick to point out, one can be more than one thing — one can be poor, disabled, and gay — and anyway there shouldn't be a "hierarchy of oppressions." But it seems to Judith there probably is a hierarchy of oppressions, and a hierarchy of privilege, too.

Watching the rain lash against the windows now, she feels peaceful and contented. She can hardly believe it's only been three weeks since school began — three weeks ago she didn't even know any of these people. Yet now they've become, for this year at school at least, this year in *galut*, her home base, almost a substitute family. It is strange in one way, but in another way marvellous. Miraculous, even. All she did was enroll in the Dunhill School of Social Work, and now, presto! she has a life. An instant life: just add water and stir. People to be with. Things to do. A whole world she's a part of. Temporarily, of course. This is not her real life; *that* is in Israel. But still, this is amazing. It's as if she came home one day and found on her doorstep a big gift-wrapped box with a huge gold bow on the top.

Judith speaks, and her voice, raspy with emotion, breaks the silence. "I don't know about being 'privileged,'" she says to her gang. "But I feel very, very lucky."

Ten minutes later, after swapping bills and coins and putting on their coats, they hurry in two pairs across the street, heads down against the rain, dodging the puddles and the racing river of mud near the curb. Aliza stops to prance in it joyfully in her tall red boots while Cindy and Judith reach the other side of the street, and as they run toward FRANK, Cindy mutters, "I wish we could just go home now."

"Well, at least it's Suzy and not Weick," Judith answers.

Cindy doesn't say anything. Judith has the impression now, and not for the first time, that Cindy is not as big a fan of Suzy as she is. Maybe she's even a bit jealous that Judith likes Suzy so much. Together they run up the stairs, duck into the building, and stand there panting, waiting for the others. Aliza and Pam soon follow.

"You're out of your mind," Pam's saying to Aliza, and Aliza is laughing, showing perfect white teeth, her long hair dripping. "You're nuts, I mean it."

The elevator comes and they ride to the fourth floor. *"Nuts,"* says Pam, as they walk into Suzy's class.

Suzy sees them and smiles. Judith feels instantly happy and at the same time an inner ache. A part of her has been waiting all week for this class. But not, in fact, for this class; for Suzy. She has been wanting to see Suzy again.

Everyone takes a seat, Suzy begins to speak, and Judith feels, as she always does in her class, a fine, almost invisible thread, like a spider's, stretching between them. Suzy looks at her often when she lectures, more so than at anyone else, and whenever she asks the class a question, she turns first toward her, as if appealing to her silently in some way. It's as if Judith, on Suzy's compass, is north, and the needle keeps flying there. Sometimes Judith answers Suzy's questions (almost always correctly), but lately she's started looking down or away, not wanting to be seen by her classmates as a suck. Either way, this class feels like a dialogue between her and Suzy, with everyone else mere spectators. She's asked herself if she was just imagining all this, but apparently it's noticeable also to others.

"Teacher's pet," Cindy said to her on the second Monday of school, during the break in Suzy's class. They were walking to the cafeteria, with Pam and Aliza not far behind. Suzy had just been teaching them about paralinguistics, a form of nonverbal behaviour that includes, among other things, people's tone of voice, and can tell you a lot about how a person really feels. So before answering, Judith replayed Cindy's comment in her head, listening for envy or meanness in her paralinguistics, but there didn't seem to be any. It sounded like Cindy was just saying what she saw.

"No, I'm not," said Judith. But she blushed and felt gratified. She wanted Suzy to like her best of all. She got her wish, too: at the end of that class, she lingered behind to ask Suzy a question, and Suzy invited her to once again walk back with her to her office. Then this became something of a tradition between them, every week after class walking together down that dingy serpentine corridor (which each time made Judith think, *"Yea, though I walk through the valley of the shadow of death ..."*), to the sounds of Suzy's heels click-click-clicking, and their voices echoing eerily off the dismal walls, and Suzy's tinkly laugh. That day in Suzy's office, they were standing under the ferns near her desk, and Judith, who had never seen mistletoe, wondered if this was mistletoe, and if so, isn't that what people kiss under? They talked for almost an hour about all sorts of things. Judith discovered to her delight that Suzy, like her, was religious. Christian, of course, not Jewish, but that didn't matter. In many ways, she thought, religious people from two different faiths have more in common than a religious and secular person from the same one. Religious people understand each other: they can talk about faith, holiness, and God — they can use the "G word"! — without apology. Without having to be embarrassed or ashamed of that love. Just as Judith isn't embarrassed or ashamed of her growing affection for Suzy. They also talked that day about Judith's work in Israel with Jewish and Arab kids, and about some of the teachers at Dunhill. Suzy was professional enough not to say anything against anyone. But Judith could tell from her body language — her kinesics, as Suzy had taught them — which people Suzy did or didn't like. All it took was a little shrug of her petite right shoulder, naked that day in a sleeveless yellow blouse, or a roll of her expressive eyes. It was quickly obvious Suzy couldn't stand Marie Green, the former Director of the school whom Judith had never met. Judith felt privileged to be let into what Suzy truly felt. To be a trusted insider.

Now Suzy says to the class, "Many people, maybe even most people, are afraid of their feelings. But there is no reason to be, because there's no such thing as a wrong feeling. I mean it. Some of you are looking at me like you don't believe me. Okay, then — give me an example of a feeling that's 'wrong.'"

A few hands fly up. Suzy points at Martin, whose family lives in Ethiopia. "Anger," he says.

Suzy nods and points again. "Hate," says Genya.

"Fear," says someone else.

"Right," says Suzy. "These are all unpleasant feelings — negative emotions, if you will. But they are also perfectly normal, and they are, after all, just feelings, part of being human. We need to learn how to accept these emotions in ourselves and in our clients. Otherwise, they'll feel we are judging them and they won't be able to open up to us. They'll feel we are not accepting them for who they are. And they'll be right."

It's true, thinks Judith.

Suzy is writing on the blackboard now, in a flowing, feminine script:

UNCONDITIONAL POSITIVE REGARD

"We'll discuss this concept more in a little while," she says, turning back toward the class, still holding the chalk in her right hand as she gestures. "But this is what we have to strive for. To truly accept our clients in spite of the things about them we don't like, whether these are emotions or behaviours. This is probably the hardest thing you'll ever have to learn. But it's also absolutely necessary for working effectively with clients."

Suzy has brought a guest with her today, an acting student from Dunhill's Theatre Arts department. Judith gazes at the square-faced woman sitting sullenly at the front table: she reminds her of a picture she once saw of a *kapo*. *That's one tough broad*, she thinks. Suzy is explaining to the class that soon one of them will get to role-play a social worker working with a "resistant" client — a great opportunity to practise all the interviewing skills they've learned in this class, including Unconditional Positive Regard. She scans the room and selects Margie, a skinny redhead from Halifax, to take the hot seat. Margie sits nervously across the table from her "client." Cordelia is a crack addict on welfare who, according to Suzy, has just had her two kids taken away, a three-year-old girl and a two-year-old boy, because a week ago she left them alone in the house for a whole weekend, without any food, so she could go off on a holiday with her crack-pusher boyfriend. During Cordelia's absence, the two-year-old, Tommy, fell down the basement stairs and is now in hospital with a severe concussion and possibly permanent brain damage. Cordelia hasn't visited him even once and appears completely unconcerned about him. She also, on her return home from that weekend, hit her three-year-old daughter Angela repeatedly, leaving marks and bruises, for "not taking care of her brother," and for getting her in trouble with the authorities.

Margie looks anxious. She approaches Cordelia gingerly, trying in a soft timid voice three friendly and empathic openers, such as, "It must be awfully hard having your kids taken away from you," but each time Cordelia just slaps her down. After her fourth attempt, to which Cordelia responds, "Why don't you just go fuck yourself?," Margie looks helpless and pale, her freckles standing out like so many tiny failures, as she tries to come up with what to say next. A long silence is finally broken by the click-click-clicking of Suzy's heels as she goes and stands beside Margie.

"At this moment," Suzy asks her, "how do you feel about this client?"

Margie looks confused by the question. She glances at Cordelia as if afraid to answer in front of her. Then she looks away and shrugs. "I don't know," she says.

"You don't much like her right now, do you?"

Margie laughs and shakes her head. "No."

"Of course you don't," says Suzy. "She frightens you. She angers and repulses you, and she makes you feel incompetent. Right now you feel totally alienated from her and I'll bet you can't think of one single thing about her you like or respect. Am I right?"

Margie looks sheepish. "Pretty much," she says. "Am I really that transparent?"

Suzy laughs that charming laugh of hers. "No," she says. "That's what most people would feel in this situation."

But Judith can see Margie is a bit spooked.

"Now *I'm* going to give this a try," says Suzy. "Watch what happens when you make use of Unconditional Positive Regard. Thanks, Margie." Margie stands, looking relieved her turn is over, and Suzy replaces her in the hot seat facing Cordelia, who is now staring at Suzy as blankly and impassively as she stared at Margie. But Suzy doesn't seem fazed by it: she's smiling at her kindly, encouragingly.

Judith starts taking notes — "smile encouragingly at client." But soon the pen is forgotten, and she watches enthralled as Suzy once again works her magic. And magic it seems to be. Cordelia's face softens. Then she starts pouring out her heart to Suzy about how hard it was being a young mother, only sixteen when the first baby was born, alone all day and all night with that baby, and then there were two of them, two crying babies, and they just cried and cried all the time, no matter what she did. They demanded and demanded, and there was nothing left for her, not five minutes for herself, to watch TV or just sit and have a smoke. If one of them was finally sleeping, the other one was still awake, crying, wanting her, needing her, and she couldn't stand it anymore, she had to have a break, she had to have something for *her* for a change, even if it was only a week-end, one weekend away in three and a half years. Cordelia is wiping tears from her face with the palms of her hands. This woman sitting across the table from Suzy is now a fully human person. A pained, mixed-up, maybe even messed-up person, but a real person all the same. Suzy has accomplished this — she has gotten to Cordelia's "story" — in under ten minutes.

Suzy turns away from Cordelia and faces the class. "This," she says, "is the power of Unconditional Positive Regard," and dismisses them, earlier than usual, for their break.

Judith files out slowly with the others. Many of the students around her are talking excitedly about what just happened and a few are laughing. But everyone gives Cordelia a wide berth, even though they know intellectually she is just an actor. Only one student, Lola, goes up to her and starts a conversation. On her way past Suzy, Judith says, "That was amazing."

"Thanks," says Suzy. Then she adds, "Judith, can you stay behind after class today? There's something I'd like to talk to you about."

"Sure," says Judith. But walking to the cafeteria, she feels worried. Has she done something wrong? Was there a problem with the logs she handed in last week? Has she perhaps offended Suzy? Throughout the entire fifteen-minute break, while Cindy, Pam, and Aliza talk, Judith sits silently at the square table, nursing a coffee and fretting. Finally she tells them what Suzy said.

"Maybe it's something good," says Cindy.

"Yeah," says Aliza. "You can see how much she likes you. Why do you assume it's something negative?"

"You're right," says Judith, surprised, and brightens. "It's probably not."

But just the same, the second half of the class passes interminably. They are still on the topic of Unconditional Positive

Regard — or as Judith has now acronymed it in her mind, UPR, or "upper." Suzy has embarked on a long lecture about it, telling them among other things that this is "the *sine qua non* of any good counselling relationship," and that with a little effort it is always possible to find the place in oneself that is non-judgmental, that accepts each client as a valid and valuable human being, regardless of what they may have done during their lives.

"It's like, 'Hate the sin, but love the sinner,'" Suzy says cheerfully. *Sinner?* thinks Judith. *We don't have sinners in Judaism. Or even sin. The word translated into English as sin — chet, in Hebrew — just means an error. We have people who get off track, people who make mistakes. But in Judaism there is no original sin — or even any unoriginal kind.* Still, in her stomach now, there's a sick, dread-filled feeling about her upcoming meeting with Suzy, as though Judaism is wrong and there *is* such a thing as sin, and she has committed one. Eventually 3:30 rolls around. She waits impatiently as Suzy deals with a long line of students, and after twenty-five minutes, the two of them are alone at last. Judith compliments Suzy again on her interview with Cordelia.

"Thanks," Suzy says. "You'll be able to do that too, one day, with some practice. It's incredible, the power of Unconditional Positive Regard." Then she asks Judith if she knows what SWAK is.

"I think so," says Judith. SWAK is short for Sealed With A Kiss: what she and her friends in high school wrote on the backs of birthday card envelopes after they'd licked them shut, with the letters SWAK inside a picture of two lips. But as Suzy continues to look at her eagerly, she understands it must also mean something else. Then she remembers SWAK with a "C" is the acronym for a committee at the school. The most important one. The Social Work Anti-oppression Committee, which coordinates all the school's anti-oppression activities, publishes an evaluation every spring of each professor's handling of anti-oppression issues in their classes, and is always co-chaired by a faculty member and a student.

"What I wanted to talk to you about," says Suzy, "is being my co-chair for the coming year. The peace work you've done in Israel is very impressive, and also very relevant to SWAC — encouraging people to work across difference, etcetera. Plus, I think you'd be terrific. If you're interested, that is."

Judith nearly laughs with relief. She feels flattered, too: this is a great honour, especially for a first-year student.

"Of course!" she says. "I'd love to."

"That's great," says Suzy, looking pleased. "It'll be a lot of fun doing this together. Our first meeting is on October 17. Is that okay for you?"

"It's fine."

"Good. What are you doing now? If you're free, we could go over a few things. I have an orientation package for you in my office."

"Sure. No problem." Judith's cheeks are burning hot, and she feels she can't control her face.

"Great. Let me just stop by the main office for a second — I have to pick something up. Then we can get started."

They walk down the hall to the main office. But just outside the door, Suzy gets stopped by a tall, gaunt woman. Suzy excuses herself from Judith, and starts talking with this woman in a low voice. Judith goes partway down the hall and waits near the bulletin board, feeling useless and not sure what to do with herself. There's no one else in the hallway to talk to, and nothing to read on the bulletin board she hasn't already read. So, for lack of anything else to do, she watches Suzy and the tall, gaunt woman. They're too far away for her to hear what they're saying, so she practises "observing their nonverbals," as Suzy called it in class last week. She notices how intensely Suzy is talking, leaning forward with her face very close to the other woman's, and also putting a hand on her arm, on the pale green sleeve of an exquisite silk jacket. Suzy smiles and the woman smiles back. They say things to each other, and both of them laugh. *Clearly a warm and friendly relationship*, thinks Judith. Suzy was right: "It's astonishing how much you can learn without hearing a single word." A moment later they draw slightly apart, and Suzy starts looking around the hallway.

"Judith," she calls when she spots her, and beckons. Judith trots over, self-conscious under the gaze of the two older women. "I'd like you to meet someone. This is Marie Green, the former Director of the School, who has just returned from research leave in China. Judith," Suzy says to Marie, "has just agreed to be my co-chair this year on SWAC."

"Congratulations!" says Marie Green, vigorously shaking Suzy's hand. "Good for you!"

Judith, startled, is already muttering "Thank you" when she realizes with a jolt that this is Marie Green — the same one Suzy dislikes, who Suzy has rolled her eyes about several times during their after-class chats in her office. *But no — I must have misunderstood something. Misread what I saw. Suzy's not a phony.* She and Suzy walk together to Suzy's office. On the way, Suzy explains that the committee meets every second Thursday night at seven o'clock — sometimes, if need be, slightly more often — and is composed of students, faculty, and community people. They organize one major event per year: Anti-oppression Day, the core of which is usually a lecture by a prominent guest speaker — hopefully a star whose name will draw a good turnout — and constellations of other events surrounding that star. Suzy suggests, if it's convenient for Judith, that they get together before each meeting at around five or six, perhaps over an early supper, to review the agenda. The thought of supper alone with Suzy every second Thursday causes Judith's stomach to somersault with excitement, and not trusting herself to speak, she just nods in agreement. They reach Suzy's office and sit at her desk side by side for a half-hour going over some of the background and basic information about SWAC. Then Suzy takes from one of the bookshelves a fat binder containing all of last year's minutes, and hands it to Judith to read at home. When they're standing by the door, Suzy asks brightly, "So we're all set, then?"

"Yes," says Judith.

Suzy beams at her. "Great!" she says. Then she reaches out her hand, and shakes Judith's. Half-mockingly, but also half-seriously — ceremoniously, even. "Welcome to SWAC."

"Thanks," says Judith, their hands still clasped. Last week Suzy taught them about contracting with clients in social work, and it feels now like she and Suzy have just formalized an important and solemn contract. Or even more than that: like hands and lips are in a way interchangeable, and this contract is being Sealed With A Kiss.

Driving off the campus and through downtown Dunhill, Judith is grinning from ear to ear. "Me!" she crows to herself. "She picked *me* out of everyone!"

Turning onto the highway toward Toronto, she can see herself sitting with Suzy in Le Petit Café, the mini-cafeteria at Dunhill — not the main, big cafeteria in FRANK, but the smaller, quieter, less crowded one a few buildings over, where you go if you want to be able to hear the other person and have a real conversation. They'll sit at one of the small, round aqua-and-pink tables, like knightesses at the Round Table, while they work together, tête-à-tête, their dirty dishes from onion soup, salad, or pizza pushed to one side. After their work is done, and the agenda for that night's meeting all worked out, there will still be a half-hour or even more till the meeting begins. So they'll linger over coffee and talk about more personal things. Suzy will confide in her about Natalie, and about the rest of her family, too; maybe Judith will confide in her about her problems with Bobby. It won't take long, she's sure, just a few of these dinners, before they're talking intimately and become real friends.

The traffic moves slowly, but Judith doesn't mind — she's happily daydreaming about her dinners with Suzy. Eventually, on her right, the huge Brick warehouse appears, telling her she's already halfway to Toronto. Suddenly she feels tired and her elation starts to fade. She reflects now more soberly on how much work the SWAC committee will entail. Probably more than the "few hours a week" Suzy mentioned — committees usually do. And what exactly will be expected of her as co-chair? Suzy wasn't very specific. Though she did say that one reason she picked Judith was that she had a strong sense of social justice. *It's true*, she thinks. But it's funny, because she has no idea where she got this from. Bobby's asked her about this: "Why do you burn like this over social and political issues? Why does injustice bother you so much?" She's never had an answer for him. No terrible injustice or "oppression" has ever personally happened to her. But now, driving past farms, silos, white fences, and grazing horses, she remembers her beloved grandparents, Bubba and Zayda, and the stories they told her when she was little about when they first came to Canada from Russia, fleeing the pogroms. And it seems to her that maybe all of that is still in her — in her blood or her heart, in a place so deep she never even knew it was there. The place of stories buried in the blood. She can hear the hoofbeats of the Cossacks as they ride into her grandmother's *shtetl*, and sees them sitting high on their horses as they beat, spear, and murder Jews. Then they pillage, loot, and set fire to everything, and through it all they're laughing their drunken laughs. As they ride off, they're singing boisterous carefree songs, leaving behind them the lingering stench of smoke, blood, sweat, vodka, dying bodies, destruction, and fear. Mingling with this smell, there are sounds: the wailing of women and children, dogs barking, and the moans of the wounded. Her heart is pounding now. *We need a safe place*, she thinks. *That's what people need — especially the vulnerable, persecuted, and powerless.* She glances around her with a hunted look. That's what SWAC is for. To be a safe haven. An island of justice. A place to stand up against oppression in every form.

— 6 —

At home, the house is dark and cold. *Soon it will be winter*, she thinks. She raises the thermostat and walks through the darkness to her computer. This is always her priority and first point of contact when she comes home from school: her emails from Israel. She works on her computer in the dark, liking the shiny square screen surrounded by the night. This evening there are the usual dozen messages from the Israeli listservs she's on. There are two peace groups — at war with each other, of course — as well as a feminist social action forum, a left-wing chat room, and an organization that promotes civil rights and pluralism in Israel. But tonight she also has three personal letters. *It will be a good evening*, she thinks — an evening spent connected to people who love her and whom she loves. She will be "virtually" in Jerusalem.

But she doesn't open her little treasure trove right away. She wants to postpone these moments of love and comfort. Like postponing in sex so you can enjoy not just the act itself, but also the pleasure of anticipating it. She goes into the kitchen and drinks a cup of cocoa. Then she returns to the computer and studies her inbox. Of the three emails from friends, she decides to read Rina's first. Rina's letter opens by saying how delighted she is that Judith is enjoying Dunhill, and she doesn't doubt for a moment that she'll succeed splendidly in grad school. Judith, reading this, is gratified. Rina has always had this iron confidence in her — it's one of the bonds of their friendship. Then Rina writes about her new job teaching Shakespeare at the university, about Michel's job (there are cutbacks at the hospital now, but so far he hasn't been affected), and about their three teenagers: Gidi, Uri, and Yael. The oldest, their son Gidi, is going into the army in two months, and the twins, a boy and a girl, will go a year and a half later. Then Rina writes:

> *Apart from "the situation" — if that isn't an oxymoron, because of course there is nothing that is "apart from the situation" — we are okay. We don't go out much, though. With suicide bombings now almost weekly in Jerusalem, it's safer to just stay home, huddled with those you love. Many restaurants now offer home delivery: that's the only way they keep from going bankrupt. You can order in not just pizza and Chinese food, but everything. The main thing now is not to go out. Downtown is still the worst place, but actually we don't go anywhere we don't absolutely have to. My daily routine, my life, is remarkably reduced now. It's just from home to work, and then back home again, except for essential errands like buying food.*

Judith can picture Rina and Michel and their kids — all three teenagers with red hair and freckles — pacing like caged leopards around their claustrophobically small apartment, with Rina's shrill voice yelling at the kids five times a day for leaving their stuff in a mess all over the house or for playing their music too loud, and Michel withdrawing more and more into his study. Rina writes that last Shabbat, at the end of a tense afternoon, Gidi, Uri, and Yael, in a rare united front, confronted her and Michel.

"You can't keep telling us not to go out," they said. *"We're not babies anymore — two months from now Gidi's going into the army. And all our friends are allowed to go out. There's a concert downtown tonight — Mashina's performing and everyone's going, and we want to go, too. Just because you guys want to stay cooped up at home doesn't mean we also have to. If you want to bury yourselves alive, go ahead. But we're young ..."*

Better buried alive than buried dead, I thought, but I stopped that before it came out of my mouth. Because I wasn't sure if it was even true. What sort of a life, I asked myself, am I advising my children to live? What am I really teaching them — to live lives so full of fear they just hide in their holes all the time like little mice? That would be a victory for the terrorists, if anything would.

So in the end, with all my doubts and hesitations I'm no better than Hamlet. Like him, I'm weak. I caved. I gave in. I let them go to that club downtown with their friends. I told myself: Life, youth, hope must triumph over fear. Don't you agree, Judith? I hope — I think — I'm right.

Judith frowns. She isn't sure. On the one hand, she is full of admiration for Rina. *She's braver than I am*, she thinks. But at the same time she's appalled: *How could you have let them go? How would you ever live with yourself if something happened to them?* Still frowning, she reads the end of Rina's letter:

> *Anyway, letting them go to the concert had a side*
> *benefit: it gave me and Michel the house to our-*
> *selves for the first time in months. And we had*
> *the most wonderful sex — delicious, drawn-out,*
> *and ... noisy! Something amazing ...*

Judith laughs. What a crazy country. What a crazy world.

The next email is from Yonina. The exhibit of her paintings at the Artists' House closed yesterday. It was quite well received, she writes. A few days after the opening there was a good review in the weekend supplement of *Yediot*. And given "the situation," she supposes she should be grateful any people at all left their homes to come see her exhibit. Anyway, she writes, this will likely be her last exhibit for some time. The arts grants have all been cut — *to free up money for more guns, bombs, and missiles, no doubt* — so pretty soon she'll have to find a job, or jobs (probably some combination of waitressing and teaching art to kids like she did a year ago). *So*, Yonina concludes her letter, *so much for painting for a while.*

Reading this, Judith feels a pang. She loves Yonina's pictures. They are fabulous and vivid, with lots of bright blues and greens, and they're full of parrots and other birds in jungle scenes. Her paintings seem simple, but in fact are subtle, nuanced, multi-layered, and complex. *So much for painting for a while* — and Judith pictures a parrot being shot down by a cannon.

With a deep sigh, Judith stands and arches her back. Then she circles the room a few times before returning, like a homing pigeon, to the dining room table and her third email. She's saved Bruria's letter for the end. The best for the last. She is in much more frequent contact with Bruria than with any other friend: they write each other twice or three times a week. So Bruria's letters have a special quality of immediacy and continuity. Judith opens her letters almost like a fan of a soap opera eager for the next installment. What is the latest development in the ever-unfolding saga of Bruria's life, with all its different subplots: marital, familial, social, professional, and political? But none of Bruria's previous emails could have prepared her for the one she opens now. Bruria's son Noah, Noah with the heart-shaped lips and golden curls, is in prison for refusing to continue doing military service in the occupied territories. He's been there for the past three days, since just after Bruria last wrote. *This has all happened very quickly.* Today's letter, astounding for someone as meticulous about language as Bruria, is full of typos, spelling mistakes, and half-finished sentences. It's hysterical and breathless, and if a letter could be one great long sob, this one is. Or perhaps, rather, it's a series of broken screams, like *shvarim*, the broken blasts of the shofar at the end of Yom Kippur. Bruria writes she is proud of Noah — she knows that what he's doing is morally right. But she is also terrified for him. He's been in solitary confinement for three days, and she and Pinchas haven't been allowed to see him. She doesn't know if he's been given food or water. She's mad with worry that he's losing weight, or that he's very weak or sick and not being cared for, maybe even being mistreated by the prison staff. She and Pinchas spoke today with the best lawyer in Israel for these sorts of cases, but he is only willing to take on Noah as a client if they agree to a group lawsuit with two other boys in the same situation. Bruria and Pinchas aren't sure about this, and are trying to figure out what's best for Noah. They have only twenty-four hours to decide. "Judith, I'm so scared. *Solitary confinement!* Please pray for our boy. Pray for my baby."

Judith would like to pray, but right now she can't. All she can do is curl up on the couch, breathing deeply. This is too much pain for her to bear. It is so naked, coming at her from people she loves. This is how it is whenever she reconnects, even for an hour, with Israel: she feels everything people there feel — they are *her* people, and whatever they feel, good or bad, she feels too. There is no boundary between her and them. She's defenceless against this love. So now she lies curled up on the couch, breathing deeply and steadily. Trying to calm down. And after a while, lying on the couch in the darkened living room, she falls asleep.

— 7 —

Four days later, on September 27, it's the last of the eight days of Sukkot, Judith's favourite holiday. She's standing under the leafy roof of a *sukkah*, the makeshift hut — in this case adjoining a *shul* — replicating the booths the Israelites lived in during their forty-year journey in the desert. Shellacked gourds, ears of purple-and-white Indian corn, pomegranates, and carobs hang from the latticed ceiling; children's colourful drawings of men and women from the Bible adorn the rickety wooden walls; and down the middle of the *sukkah*, a long, thin table is spread with a vegetarian/dairy feast for the worshippers. Services aren't quite over yet, but she's come out early to have some time alone in the *sukkah* before the hordes descend for the meal. She loves its bright, cheerful decorations and dangling fall fruits, the constant rustling of the fresh-cut branches on the roof, the smell of the pine needles on the floor, and the sharp sunlight slicing into the *sukkah* through the slats in the walls. But she also loves being in a *sukkah* because it exemplifies what she experiences as the most essential human truth. That life is fleeting and fragile. This makeshift hut, thrown together out of thin planks of wood and a few boughs for a roof, is a structure a wolf could huff and puff and blow right down. *Nothing*, she thinks, *can truly protect you. Other than God, if you believe in Her. Which I probably don't.*

People start wandering in. They're wearing winter coats — not like in Israel, where people in *sukkahs* sometimes sport sandals and shorts. Now there's a flood of people into the *sukkah* in one huge wave, noisy and exuberant, with many little children running underfoot. Soon Rabbi Elaine in her orange-and-pink *tallis* recites the blessing over the bread. Then Judith piles her plate high with lasagna, salad, tabouli, babaganouj, marinated vegetables, and a brownie, carefully balancing an orange drink on the edge. She is just stabbing a fork into the lasagna when someone shouts her name and touches her on the arm, nearly toppling the whole plate. She rights it just in time, but not before a slice of marinated yellow pepper and a square of purple onion slide onto her shoe. It's Flora, her father's old friend, whom she hasn't seen since shortly after the *shiva*. Her kind, horsey face.

"Sorry," says Flora.

"No problem." Judith surreptitiously kicks away the pepper and onion.

Flora asks how it's going at Dunhill. Judith says, "Fine." Flora asks if it's hard being back at school.

Judith smiles. "Everything's relative. It's easier than trying to bring peace to the Middle East."

Flora laughs.

Judith adds, "Thanks again for helping with that application form. Without you, I wouldn't be there now."

"My pleasure. You know how I felt about your father."

Judith nods automatically, but then something in Flora's tone makes her look sharply and more closely at her. *No*, she thinks, *actually I don't — what do you mean exactly?* But Flora is looking down at her food and her face doesn't give anything away. For a while they eat in silence. Judith is relieved to not have to talk and eat at the same time. She's never understood the logic of socializing over food, when good manners prohibit talking with your mouth full. Furthermore, the eating now is difficult: her marinated vegetables are as slippery as wriggling snakes. Two small boys dart between her and Flora, laughing and shouting.

"How's the atmosphere at Dunhill?" Flora asks.

"Good. Friendly."

"No more rallies or riots, I hope? Last year the worst incident there began as an anti-Israel demonstration. Nothing weird going on there now?"

Judith takes a sip of her orange drink. Now she understands the question about the atmosphere. "No," she says. "There's a strong anti-oppression movement at Dunhill, and there's an anti-oppression committee at my school. But I've just been asked to co-chair it, so I don't see any cause for concern. All that must have just been last year."

"I'm delighted to hear it," says Flora. "I've thought about you numerous times, Judith, and I admit I was worried." Judith looks at the kind, lined face. She's touched to discover that, without her even knowing it, someone has been thinking about her, and concerned for her, all this time. "It's only the beginning of the school year," Flora adds. "Let's hope things continue as well as they've begun."

Judith can't keep back a smile. Flora sounds just the way her father used to. What can you do? It's that generation. Always anticipating something bad, always fearing the worst for the

Jews. It used to drive her crazy when her father said things like this, as if he were deliberately acting gloomy and pessimistic just to put a damper on her natural hopefulness. An undertow trying to drag her down. But now she gazes tolerantly at Flora. There's something almost quaint about her comment. Flora, like others of her circle, still lives in the past. Not in the extreme way of a teacher Judith once had, an old man who, whenever a balloon or a car tire exploded, would dive under his desk, still traumatized from the war. But something changed in that whole generation of Jews, she thinks. Even her father and Flora, who both spent the war years here in Canada. Judith feels wistful now, reminiscing about her father. And compassionate, too. She has an impulse to put her arm around Flora (*Did Daddy ever put his arm around Flora?* she wonders because of her strange comment), and to say, "Don't worry, Flora, the world's not like that anymore. Antisemitism is a thing of the past. That's all behind us now."

But she can't. Because even though she first met Flora back in high school, she doesn't actually know her well enough to put her arm around her. It might even seem condescending. Also, Judith isn't sure it's true that antisemitism is a thing of the past. Some people are saying it's back, and even on the rise. But she doesn't believe it. Sure, there's a lot of criticism nowadays of Israel. But some of it is justified. The constant expansion of settlements, the excessive use at times of military force — these things deserve to be criticized. But antisemitism, as she pictures it, is something quite different from criticizing Israel. The mainstream Jewish community always equates the two, she thinks, but that's because they don't know enough, or care enough, to be critical of Israel, and they always rubber stamp whatever the Israeli government does. No, she decides, antisemitism is not a problem anymore. There's nothing to worry about now.

But still ... *When in doubt, kiss* — a rule she came up with when she was four and her cousin Paul, who was three and a half, cried all the time — she'd kiss him and like magic he'd stop. So now, moved by a mixture of emotions, she leans forward and lightly kisses Flora on the cheek. Flora looks surprised, and her face softens. Then she kisses Judith back and gives her a hug. They wish each other a happy holiday, and Flora leaves. Judith takes another minute to finish her lunch. She steps out from under the *sukkah*'s gently whispering roof, feeling well fed and well sheltered. Succoured. And *sukkah*'ed. Now on her nose she feels something tickle. She looks up and laughs: the first snow-flake of winter.

— 8 —

It's two and a half weeks later now, mid-October, and Judith's classes have all continued, like streetcars, along the tracks laid down for them on the first day. Weick's "Knowledge and Values," for instance, travels along in the same agonizingly slow, tedious, creaking way it began, not having improved one iota since the first day. She hasn't skipped any of his six classes, though: she's too afraid of angering or alienating Weick, especially after Cindy's warning. But mentally she is never there. She walks in, sits, and lets her mind travel where it will. She survives this class week after week only by not being there alone: Moshe comes to keep her company. Today as always he shows up a few min-utes into Weick's lecture, just as her mind is starting to go numb. Moshe doesn't come to talk, to offer her conversation more stim-ulating than Weick's; he comes to make love to her. This is what he is doing now. Though this time he's doing it in an unusual way for him: slowly and very passionately, the way he did on her birthday, the one time they weren't in a rush. He refused to hurry that day: "It's your birthday," he said. "Let them wait." He had informed Koby he'd be late that day, and she called her office too, saying she'd missed the early train and would catch the next one. They lay under the tree at the bottom of the hill. Moshe had smoothed the ground for them, clearing away the pine cones, and even brought a blanket. That day she turned twenty-five.

"A special age," she told Moshe. "Five times five: a perfect square."

"Old enough," he said, "to open your eyes and see what's in front of you." He suggested she keep her eyes open today when they made love, so they could look at each other all the way through.

It was an effort because she felt shy, even embarrassed, but she did keep them open after he entered her, and they stayed like that for a long time. They gazed at each other until she was so deep inside his eyes she wasn't aware of anything else — it was like sliding down the hole in *Alice in Wonderland*, but never hitting the bottom. The love in his eyes was bottomless. Infinite. Then, unexpectedly, he thrust into her. She cried out and writhed, trying to get to the deepest place, but just when she was almost there, he pulled away. Still moaning, she opened her eyes, and he was smiling at her faintly, and his eyes were wet brownness, like rained-on desert sand. Or quicksand, the way they sucked her in. She slid down, getting lost in them again, and there was no him or her; they were just one person. There in his eyes she rested awhile, with no sense of time. Time was gone: they were suspended in an eternal time zone. Then, catching her unawares — how could there be a thought in his mind that wasn't in hers? — she felt him thrusting into her again. But this time all the way into the middle of her — into the inside of the inside of her, into her very core, a place no one had ever been. She cried out. Then she screamed and screamed her way to the end. Afterwards sobbing in his arms for a long time. Sobbing like a baby. Finally she opened her eyes. There he was, Moshe who was also Israel, looking at her, his eyes full of tenderness and love. *Home*, she thought. *At last I'm home.*

Judith looks up. Weick is still at the front of the class. She feels like she's been gone for over an hour, but according to her watch, it's only been fifteen minutes. Weick says: "We all play many different roles in our lives." *Right*, she thinks. *All the world's a stage.* "And when two or more roles," he says, "conflict with each other, this is called inter-role conflict."

Like duh. Judith recalls the classic example of this she learned thirteen years ago during her B.S.W.: being both a mother and a student, and having to choose between caring for your child and getting your schoolwork done. Role Theory was interesting when she first learned it back then, but like Systems Theory, it isn't anymore. Certainly not as interesting as making love to Moshe, or even lying next to him, her body curled around his, in post-coitus contentment, on the grass. So she returns to Moshe. He is still lying where she left him under the tree, but now he has one hand behind his head, and is smoking a cigarette and blowing smoke rings. He too has been listening to Weick, and doesn't think much of him — "A weak man, you can tell just by looking at him he can't get it up" — or of Dunhill. She looks up: Weick is watching her. She lowers her eyes — perhaps he just heard what Moshe said about him. That's crazy, she knows. Of course he couldn't have. But maybe he could somehow sense the presence of Moshe, her invisible friend. Her favourite aunt, Hilda, now dead, always saw, and sometimes even talked to, Judith's imaginary friend Max, whom she pulled around on a string when she was four. *From Max to Moshe*, thinks Judith, rolling her eyes. *Oh, well, whatever gets you through —*

Weick, still talking, is staring hard at her now, demanding her full attention. *Did he see me roll my eyes? Maybe he thought I was rolling them at him.* Just in case, and to deflect his anger, shortly afterwards she raises her hand and respectfully asks a question. Citing the conflicting definitions of inter-role conflict in two different articles, she asks Weick which one he'd recommend. Weick, obviously pleased, says he's happy at least one student's doing the readings, and replies at length while Judith arranges a facial expression of polite listening. She even smiles wanly when he makes a stupid joke. Meanwhile she's thinking this class is a total waste of time. Pam agrees. During their break in the cafeteria half an hour later, Pam sputters that all they're learning from Weick is how to feign interest and respect; how to endure without looking like you're enduring; how to survive long, awkward pauses, some of them excruciating; and how to fake-smile encouragingly at an ill-prepared teacher as he flounders for words. "We are learning," she concludes, "about the power of the guy at the front of the class. Nothing more."

"Well, maybe that's the essence of 'Knowledge and Values in Social Work,'" Aliza says darkly. "The power of power."

"Oooooh," says Cindy, and bites into her donut.

Pam laughs, and Cindy chews cheerfully, but Judith doesn't respond. She's just decided that from now on, she's never again going to be the last one out of Weick's class, or alone with him anywhere. On her way out of the classroom just now, while Cindy, Pam, and Aliza waited impatiently for her in the hallway, she asked Weick a quick question about the topic she'd picked for her midterm paper, and he suggested she drop by his office after class to discuss it further. But she won't. Because when he made this suggestion, he brought his face, flushed and eager, close to hers, and there was the smell of liquor on his breath.

* * *

Next they go to "Introduction to Social Justice" with Greg, or Saint Greg as some of the students have nicknamed him, and if Weick's class was a creaky old streetcar, this one is a turbo train. Today, as always, there is a sense of urgency and dynamism here, and a passion that strikes Judith as almost religious. Greg, waving his hands around, is still, after six weeks, on the theme of how the rich and powerful oppress and exploit the weak, and how it is the obligation of each and every one of us to use whatever power we have to fight for a fairer distribution of resources, both in Canada and around the world. Judith listens, her bum aching from the hard chair, and she vacillates between the exciting feeling on one hand that she's part of a revolution, and on the other that Greg is naive and not very bright. Still, as the term progresses, she finds herself using more and more of what she thinks of as "Greg's words": *socially constructed, classist, marginalized, disenfranchised, globalization.* Or, as Bobby put it several days ago, she has begun to speak, and also think, "in black and white." Even though, of course, that's a phrase you can't use anymore — not unless you're completely politically incorrect, like Bobby. Which she didn't hesitate to tell him.

"I'm not 'politically incorrect,'" said Bobby, looking handsome in a green Ralph Lauren polo sweater with the logo of a horse on it. "I'm free."

"No, you're not," she retorted. "You're enslaved to political incorrectness, which is no different than being enslaved to political correctness. You've just swapped PI for PC. And you're hopelessly out of touch with the world around you."

"Blah blah blah," said Bobby, and gave her a hug.

* * *

Greg's favourite mantra is "Take a stand." Over his desk hangs a tattered copy of the famous poem by Pastor Niemöller written during the Holocaust:

> First they came for the Communists, and I didn't speak up because I wasn't a Communist.

> Then they came for the Jews, and I didn't speak up because I wasn't a Jew.

> Then they came for the Catholics, and I didn't speak up because I was a Protestant.

> Then they came for me, and by that time there was no one left to speak up.

"Don't be neutral," Greg tells them at least once every week. "Truth isn't neutral. Justice isn't neutral. Take a stand."

Suzy's mantra is different: "Know thyself." In Suzy's first class, this sounded terribly naive to Judith. Knowing oneself, she thought, is a lifetime's work. And maybe even an impossible goal, one you can never achieve. "You never fully know a person," her father used to say mournfully. "Least of all yourself." So Judith felt a flash of contempt for Suzy — a quick flash, here and gone, like the sun glinting on the edge of a knife. Contempt for her simple, even simplistic, mind, her lack of intellectual sophistication. As Suzy continued talking, though, Judith realized she only meant self-knowledge in a very limited way: a specific application of this concept to becoming a social work professional, something like "Self-Knowledge for Social Work Practice," or "A Dummy's Guide to Self-Knowledge When Working with Clients."

"For instance," said Suzy, looking cute in a buttercup-yellow silk shirt, "what if you're uncomfortable with certain emotions, like anger? And what if you had, for example, a very angry, hostile client, like Cordelia? I'm sure you all remember Cordelia! Would that be hard for you?" *Yes*, thought Judith. "If so, that's natural. Very few people like anger, or fear, or guilt. Then again, there are people who are also uncomfortable with love, or joy, or tenderness, and will try at all costs to avoid these feelings.

"And it's not only emotions," Suzy continued, scanning the class, sweeping everyone into her range of vision. "It's values, as well. For example, what if you don't like a certain sort of person? Simply don't like — never mind racism, homophobia, or anything like that. For instance, what if you don't like tall people because — I don't know why — maybe they make you feel small and insignificant? So you have to know this about yourself, because if a tall client walks in through the door, you'll react to them a certain way. That isn't fair. That isn't ethical. This is your emotional baggage to deal with, and you have to clean it out of yourself."

Interesting, thought Judith, *that Suzy picked tallness as an example, since she is so short. Funny, too, all this clean/dirty imagery. The assumption that all of us are somehow dirty, or polluted — "sinful"? — and part of the task of professionalizing us into social workers is to "clean us up." Cleaning us through a certain kind of brain-washing. Or is it soul-washing? Maybe they should've put showers in the student lounge.*

But in subsequent days, she gave all this some serious thought. Whether reading articles, hunting down library books, doing laundry, or cutting vegetables for chicken soup, always somewhere at the back of her mind was, *What is knowledge? And what is knowing oneself?* That Friday — the day of the week, she recalled, that God created Adam and Eve, who stole from the Tree of Knowledge — she sat in just a striped T-shirt and panties at her kitchen table, soup bubbling on the stove, and wrote her weekly log for Suzy. She began with Socrates — *the first*, she wrote, *to coin the phrase "Know thyself"* — and some other Greek philosophers. Then she pulled in Nietzsche, Kant, Kierkegaard, Hegel, and psychologists ranging from Freud and Fromm to the cognitivists, including some from Suzy's blue-and-yellow book. Next she peppered in some Shakespeare (Polonius), some Bible (Ecclesiastes), and several relevant scraps of Yiddish and Hebrew poetry in translation (Halpern, Heifetz Tussman, Rachel, Ravikovitch, and Amichai). She knew most of these references weren't from social work and hoped this would be okay. *Well, even if it isn't,* she thought, paraphrasing her friend Sammy, *what can Suzy do — shoot me?* This had become Sammy's favourite expression ever since Rabin's assassination. Then she wrote in her log:

> As the above sources illustrate, there is no one simple thing called "knowledge." There are different kinds: knowledge of the mind, heart, soul, and body, and maybe others. Traditionally, since Plato, the mind and body were split, and the only knowledge valued, or even acknowledged(!), by men was knowledge of the mind: rational knowledge. Women, however, have appreciated different forms of knowledge (Belenky et al.'s Women's Ways of Knowing).

Then, since they were told to include some self-disclosure:

*I've always listened mainly to my mind, so this year
I'd like to be more open to other forms of knowledge.
Hopefully this will help me better understand my
clients, and respond to them more fully, empathically, and effectively in my professional role.*

The following Monday she handed in this log. When she got
it back, on the last page there was a big 10/10 in red pen with a
circle around it, and underneath it Suzy's comments in flowing,
feminine handwriting:

*Excellent work, Judith! Fabulous how you draw
on such a wide range of sources, some of them
unusual, to explore this concept. You do a nice job
of integrating your personal feelings and issues
with the ideas in the literature, demonstrating
your knowledge of both the heart and mind. An
exceptional log from an exceptional student! A
pleasure having you in this class!*

Soon afterwards, Judith's logs began to change. They became
more loosely related to the content covered in Suzy's course, and
more personal, until they felt almost like a diary. The last time she
kept a diary she was twelve and never let anyone read it. But this
log-diary is different, she thinks now, sitting in Suzy's class. Not
because it isn't private or deep; it is. But she doesn't mind Suzy
reading it because Suzy is safe. There's nothing she could write to
Suzy, or say to her in person, that would be unacceptable, or make
Suzy not like her anymore. So everything inside of her comes
flooding out toward Suzy. Not only in her logs; any place, any

time, they're alone together. For instance, walking with Suzy back to her office every Monday after class. Or last Monday sitting with her over coffee at a round pink-and-aqua table in Le Petit Café, just as she imagined it would happen, to plan the first meeting of SWAC, which will be taking place three days from now. Judith likes just about everything about Suzy. Including her petiteness, her tinkly laughter, and her way of dressing: always conservative on the bottom in dark skirts or slacks, but wildly colourful on the top with her blazingly bright silk shirts.

Judith likes, too, how Suzy looks at her. How she is mirrored in Suzy's eyes. "You have an extraordinary mind," Suzy said to her last Monday over coffee. "Yet you're also extremely sensitive and emotionally attuned. This is a very rare combination. I don't think I've ever seen a student quite like you in all my years of teaching."

Later on she added, as if musing to herself, "You remind me of myself a few years back." And she touched Judith on the arm. Softly, like a butterfly resting.

— 9 —

Three days later, on Thursday night, Judith attends the first meeting of the Social Work Anti-oppression Committee. There is no supper with Suzy beforehand because Suzy had an emergency faculty meeting, so Judith, disappointed, worked at home all day and drove in just for SWAC. She arrives at ten to seven and is relieved to see someone there she knows: Lola, from Suzy's class. Lola is a broad-shouldered sensuous blonde with oversized lips and huge blue eyes, and everything about her is theatrical and slightly larger than life. A week ago she told Judith she was born and raised in Montreal as Lola Katz, but now she is Lola Ibn Hassan from Riyadh. As a McGill undergrad she was involved in left-wing politics, and on her twenty-first birthday she married and ran off with another student who took her to his native Saudi Arabia, forced her for three years to wear a burqa, and forbade her to leave the house unless accompanied by him or one of his three brothers. Lola escaped, she said, in the middle of the night, returning to Canada, but she still lives in terror he'll find her. Judith listened raptly when Lola told her this, but now, recollecting Lola's melodramatic style when recounting it, isn't sure how much she believes. Still, they stand chatting together amicably as the other people drift into the room, and then sit beside each other at the rectangular table.

Suzy calls the meeting to order. It's a fair-sized committee: in addition to Suzy, Lola, and herself, Judith counts six other people. Chris is a second-year student in the Policy stream, and the school's representative to the Dunhill Students' Union (DSU). He wears an earring in his left ear and a ratty leather jacket covered in studs. Janice McVitty is a blonde woman whose hairstyle and neat white blouse and sweater are straight out of the 1950s. Janice has a private practice and is working with Suzy on some community project. Carl Lantern graduated from this school twelve years ago, and is now the Executive Director of First Nations Community Services in Toronto, and the alumni representative on SWAC. An abnormally tall woman says she is a faculty member here at the school and will be retiring at the end of this academic year. She looks like some strange big bird with her amorphous black cape, wild grey-black hair, and intense, mournful glare. In a soft, guttural voice with some undefinable European accent, she says, "I am Hetty Caplar," but Judith, who finds her startling, even scary, hears instead, "I am Hedda Gabler." Which makes sense: there is something as grotesquely compelling about this woman as Hedda Gabler herself. The last two committee members are Brenda Chow, a Chinese woman who's a hospital administrator, and James Roberts, a dark-skinned man in a suit who works for the Children's Aid Society. Suzy explains that most of this committee is continuing from last year, except for Judith, Lola, and Hetty, and she's looking forward to these new members' fresh ideas and energy. Suzy tells everyone Judith is this year's co-chair; Judith blushes as some people smile and nod at her and others study her appraisingly.

Then it's down to business. Tonight being the first meeting of the 2002–2003 academic year, the agenda focuses on planning the upcoming year's activities. Judith has been worrying intermittently all day about what would be expected of her tonight as co-chair. She realizes now she needn't have worried, because Suzy runs the whole thing by herself. But she doesn't mind — in a way it's a relief. Suzy is a good chair: task-oriented but relaxed and with a sense of humour, and the committee tonight has a free-wheeling, friendly brainstorming session about this year's Anti-oppression Day, with everyone bandying about ideas, except for Hetty, who sits heavily silent, like a black hole. Several names are tossed around for the keynote speaker — or, as Suzy termed it, "the star." One name keeps coming up repeatedly — Michael Brier — and after the fifth or sixth time, Judith writes down his name, a reminder to herself to google him when she gets home. Chris in particular is enthusiastic about Brier, saying he's heard him speak and he's absolutely brilliant. Ten minutes later Chris brings him up again, offering to contact him and see if he'd be their keynote.

"Ask what he charges," James suggests. "We don't have much of a budget."

"Good point," says Chris.

Janice says she has a cousin who knows Brier personally and maybe can get Brier to come at a cheaper rate. She and Chris agree to work together on this and bring some more information to the next meeting.

"Great," says Suzy.

"The main thing is," says James, "whoever we pick should be passionately committed to social justice. Someone who can serve as a role model for our students and for the profession as a whole."

Everyone agrees.

Suzy asks the group what they want to do about food on Anti-oppression Day. There is a general groan and a rolling of eyes. Apparently last year they offered participants two different lunch options, and when people registered, they indicated their preference. There was a three-course meal for ten dollars, and a five-dollar, lighter option — pizza and a donut — for students and the economically disadvantaged. It all became very contentious, with some complaining that even the five dollars for the latter was too expensive. Suzy says she recently attended a family therapy conference where the organizers dealt with the food problem by just writing on the program: *Lunch — On Your Own.* This is the latest thing, she says, and one easy way to get around all this. But James and Lola object. There is a principle involved.

"I believe eating together on Anti-oppression Day is a crucial part of the experience," says Lola. "That is part of what being a community is about. It's symbolic. The other way you're basically reinforcing a two-tiered system, the same one that rules in society. The profs and the more privileged students will eat one kind of meal, chicken or whatever, while everyone else gets something crummy. That's not what social work is about."

"My feeling exactly," says James.

Oy, thinks Judith. It's true, of course, that often these "small" decisions are microcosms of larger issues in life. But seriously. Everyone eating the same pizza is not going to equalize society's inequities. That's like in *H.M.S. Pinafore* when they sing, "Love levels all ranks." Of course it doesn't. Neither love nor pizza levels anything.

To her astonishment, though, Suzy nods at James and Lola. "I see your point," she says. "Maybe we can all go home and give it some more thought, and revisit this issue at our next meeting. We don't have to decide anything conclusive right now."

Clever. Judith inwardly gives Suzy a thumbs-up.

"Okay," says James, and Lola shrugs her assent. Suzy wraps up the meeting. She thanks everyone for coming and reminds them that next time they'll be striking two subcommittees — Teacher Evaluation and Admissions Outreach — so they should each decide which of these they want to serve on. The meeting adjourns exactly on time, at 8:30 on the dot. Suzy beckons to Judith and they set a date to go over this meeting and plan the next one.

"Do you think it went okay?" Suzy asks in a low voice.

"Yes. It was fine."

"Thanks." Suzy touches her on the arm.

Judith collects her things and starts walking alone down the hallway. Then she hears someone call her and she turns around. It's Hetty, the big bird, walking quickly, her cape flapping like wings. Judith feels her stomach twist with anxiety, and she thinks of Mandelstam's bird: "the grey bird, sadness."

"I hear," Hetty says in her European accent, "you wrote an exceptional paper for your first assignment in Weick's course. A feminist critique of Systems Theory, I understand."

"Yes. I mean, yes, that was the topic."

"There's no need for false modesty, Judith. According to Weick, it was first-rate work. Tell me, have you considered entering it into the school's annual essay competition? I'm on the jury this year for the B.P. Dunhill Award, and we're trying to get all the brightest students to submit their work."

All the brightest students, thinks Judith. *She sees me as one of the brightest students.*

"There's a fifty-dollar cash prize," Hetty says eagerly, "and a big ceremony with the Dean of the Faculty of Social Sciences at the end of the year." Her beady eyes shine eagle-like, not without a certain charm.

Judith blushes. "I'd be happy to submit it. If you believe it has a chance."

"It certainly does," says Hetty. "But we'll need it soon. Could you put a copy in my box this Monday? The jury starts its deliberations next week."

"No problem. And ... thank you."

"No. Thank *you*," says Hetty, and walks off.

Outside it's very cold. Judith sits shivering in her car for a while, collecting herself for the long trip home. Then she drives out into the night. It's the first time she's driven home from Dunhill in the dark, and it feels odd, but somehow also exciting and delicious, like getting to know a new, secret side of someone you thought you already knew. Passing through downtown Dunhill, all the shops are locked for the night, black-windowed, and the streetlamps shine like floodlights over the wet, deserted streets. *One of the brightest students.* She's never been viewed this way before — she was always a voracious reader and full of thoughts and ideas, but she didn't get good marks at school. So it's thrilling now — it even feels to her like something of a minor miracle — that at Dunhill she's seen as smart. It's not just Hetty, she reflects as she drives. She has aced all her assignments so far, she's been nominated for an academic excellence scholarship, and when she walks down the hall, all the profs know her and greet her by name. Just seven weeks — forty-nine days, like the number of days between Pesach and Shavuot — since she first drove to Dunhill for Orientation, and already she is part of the life of this school, and even, because she co-chairs SWAC, something of a big shot.

Turning onto the highway, she does what she always does at this point: she inserts the *Israel at Forty* tape, and immediately "Hallelujah" fills the car. It's the perfect song. "Hallelujah!" is exactly how she feels right now. Joyful. Triumphant. So she sings along with the tape, trumpeting out her triumph and joy. Singing this song differently, though, than she did on the first day of school, when in her mind's eye she was still singing with her friends in Israel. Now she is singing by herself. Here in *galut*. But happy. "In exile just for a while." She grins and sings in the car.

The song that follows "Hallelujah" is a dirge she can't stand. Its opening line is "We were from the same village," presumably about someone who died in an Israeli war. But she isn't sure because she's never listened to the whole song: the music is so depressing that, by the end of the first line, she wants to jump off a cliff. Quickly she ejects the tape and the radio comes on. But instead of the usual classical music, she hears a man's voice: it's the CBC nine o'clock news. In the headlines tonight, there are two main items. The Conservatives are opposing the Liberals' new health care plan, and in response to Israel's incursion yesterday into Gaza, the U.N. is proposing another resolution condemning Israel as an apartheid state in violation of international law. *Oh fuck*, she thinks. *The whole world's against us. Even the U.N. hates us now.*

She used to love the U.N. She was taught to respect and admire not only the concept of the U.N., but the organization itself. For her fifth birthday, Auntie Hilda gave her a large cardboard package with the logo of the U.N. on the front, containing ten different-coloured pamphlets, each about a different country, and telling the story of a child living there who was helped by UNICEF. There was Mozambique, Colombia, Pakistan ... She can still remember some of the children and their stories, which Auntie Hilda read to her while she snuggled up close against her, her thumb in her mouth. One story included a picture of a black girl with a tray of coconuts and tropical fruits balanced on her head. She had gotten glaucoma, and her eyesight was saved thanks to an ointment supplied by UNICEF. On the back of that pamphlet there was a copy of the thank-you letter this girl had written to UNICEF. There was also a boy, Judith recalls, who helped his uncle herding goats and sheep, and a South American girl who wove brightly coloured fabrics on a loom with the old women of her village. The title of this collection was "One World, One Family." What year was that? She quickly does the math ... 1975. Just before the first anti-Israel resolution at the U.N., which equated Zionism with racism. That for her was the end of the U.N. The end of "One World, One Family." Driving, she passes a field that's vacant except for a lone cow grazing in the corner. As alone as Israel, she thinks. Over the past three days, in response to Sharon's intensified campaign against terrorism in Gaza and the territories, the Toronto newspapers have been full of anti-Israel rhetoric. She can't stand Sharon and doesn't support his policies or his recent crackdown. But in the papers, she can feel hatred for Israel bouncing off the page, and if she tries to eat her breakfast while reading them, she can barely swallow.

Judith punches off the radio to silence the news, shoves the tape back in, and presses fast forward to get past "We Were from the Same Village." The song that comes on now is bright and chirpy, but again she ejects the tape in disgust. These cheerful, tinny songs are now starting to sound stupid. And not just stupid; they're a lie. This isn't Israel anymore. Israel's not forty, it's fifty-four, and Israel's song isn't "Hallelujah"; it's "Will We

Survive?" Not Gloria Gaynor's "I Will Survive," that defiant, affirmative statement by an individual, but a question being asked collectively, with anguish, by an entire people. A collective cry like the Israelites in Egypt crying out to God. Only this time no one seems to be listening. The economy is in tatters, poverty and hunger are dramatically on the rise, bombs are going off almost every week in Jerusalem, and the so-called peace process is dead. It's a time of desperation and deep dread. *An aching time*, she thinks. *An* Aicha *time — like the title in Hebrew of the Book of Lamentations.*

In Canada, on the other hand, things are comparatively easy. So even if life here sometimes feels rather shallow, and callow, to her, it's still a great relief after Israel. This wonderfully "bearable lightness of being." Even the people here are lighter. She smiles, musing about her Canadian friends Cindy, Pam, and Aliza, and the fun they have together. As for Suzy, who's not exactly a friend — or anyway not yet, but who in a way feels like the grounding force, the gravity, for her new life here at Dunhill — she too is not heavy. Sure, she can be serious. But she's charming. She's fun. Everyone is lighter in Canada. Well, why wouldn't they be? No one here has a child in the army dodging rocks, bullets, and hand grenades day after day; or in prison protesting against the occupation; or having to take their lives in their hands if they want to go hear a concert downtown. *No one in Canada*, thinks Judith, *ever has to lay themselves on the line for anything. They can if they want, they can voluntarily engage with issues if they choose to. But people here can take for granted their existential survival. They just live their individual lives and enjoy them as much as possible.*

As if to support this opinion, Judith now spots ahead neon signs in red, yellow, pink, and green for Wendy's, Taco Bell, and McDonald's, and further on, a neon dancing girl, and flashing all around her the words SEX SEX SEX. Which reminds Judith of Aliza, who just got a part-time job at Lovetoys, and during class breaks and at the cafeteria over lunch surreptitiously pulls out of her schoolbag fluorescent green, blue, or skin-coloured dildos, and passes them around under the table, after pressing the button and starting them vibrating. Sometimes she even shows off her wares in the classroom to all the students before class begins. Judith laughs every time and blushes: it's vulgar and disgusting yet also fun. Cindy's considering buying one to spice things up with Tom.

"If you're interested in anything," says Aliza, "buy it from me — I get a 15 percent commission." Aliza has brought different items to show them on each of the past three Mondays. The vibrators and dildos come in all different shapes and colours, lengths and textures: slimy, smooth, and with little bumps on them for greater friction. This seems to Judith so Diaspora. So not-Israel. She can't even imagine someone there bringing fluorescent lime-coloured battery-operated vibrators to school to show their friends. In downtown Jerusalem if she walks around in a pair of shorts and a sleeveless T-shirt, she is looked at like a whore. *Yes*, she thinks as she drives, *it's good I'm here for a while. In this easier, more innocent place. I can use a half-year of Canadian lightness.*

And also of Canadian safety. Canada's safe. Everyone here is polite and civil. Civil vs. uncivil, but also civil vs. religious. There's relatively little religious fundamentalism here or fanatical nationalism. No *shaheeds* or Yigal Amirs. You can relax. Last week she and Bobby went to the jazz club they like, and halfway through the first set, in walked a skinny, scruffy-looking guy wearing a bulky down jacket. It was way too big for him, reaching halfway down to his knees, and also much heavier than what the weather called for. It bulged out in front, and she immediately understood: that bulge under his jacket was a belt of explosives. *He's a suicide bomber*, she thought, *and he's about to blow himself up, along with me and Bobby and all the people in this club.* But then she caught herself: Don't be stupid — this is Canada, not Israel. Still, she pointed this guy out to Bobby, and asked him what he thought of the suspicious, anxiety-provoking bulge below his waist.

"Judith," he said, laughing, "that's called a hard-on." Then he pulled her hand under the table, and hidden by the tablecloth, pressed it against his crotch. It was warm and she felt his penis starting to stir. "See what you do to me? Now I have one, too …"

Now her hands, on the steering wheel, are cold. *It's already time for mittens and gloves. Winter is upon us.* It's also very dark out now: pitch black all around her — not a single street lamp on this stretch of highway — and she can't see any of the usual landmarks. Yet it's beautiful too, in a calm, black, deep way. Like watching the sea at night, knowing there are whales beneath the water.

I'm so happy, she thinks. And immediately feels guilty and ashamed. Here she is playing with dildos in *galut* while Israel is suffering. She's fiddling about while Jerusalem burns. She should be there, not here. Not that there's anything she could do if she were there that would be of any help. But still, that's where she belongs. And if she has to be here in Canada instead, the least she can do is not enjoy it. Partying and dancing the night away in jazz clubs — she has no right.

But when she says things like that to Bruria, Bruria tells her she's crazy.

Stop driving yourself nuts, she wrote Judith last week. *Enjoy this year abroad, suck the marrow from the bones, milk every moment for all it's worth. (Sorry to mix milk and meat in the same sentence!) But truly, Judith, it's not going to help anyone here one iota if you have a miserable year there. And don't worry — you'll be back here soon enough sharing all our troubles. Meanwhile, enjoy whatever you can in Canada.*

She's right, Judith thinks. But she pictures guiltily the two dozen emails from Israel sitting in her inbox at home, waiting to be answered. They started building up two weeks ago, and now every day there are more of them, like additional shovelfuls of earth being thrown on top of a coffin. It's true she's been busy with her midterm papers, but it's not only that. For some reason she's finding it difficult to answer her friends. What, after all, can she write that won't sound ridiculous? *What do I write,* she asks herself, *to someone with a child in a military prison? That I'm stressed out about a term paper that's due next week? That my father's old car is making strange noises and I'm worried it won't last the winter? That Bobby is pressuring me to stay in Canada and marry him, and it's getting harder and harder to stave him off? And how can I tell them my activism here, my social contribution for the year — the only thing I'm doing in Canada that isn't me me me — is co-chairing a committee whose great moral dilemma is whether or not to offer two menu choices for lunch? All these things are nonsense. They're trivial. And I'm trivial because these are my concerns. So I can't write about them to my friends in Israel. Which means that, for now at least, I can't write to my friends at all.*

She is now on a brighter, better-lit stretch of the highway, almost alone on the deserted road. The clock says 9:35 p.m. — in only fifteen minutes she'll be home. Well, not home, she corrects herself — just her temporary home for this year. Her real home is in Israel. Though her parents could never understand that. Especially her mother.

Judith notices the little doll swinging from the rear-view mirror. It's a troll doll, but with a face that is surprisingly, recognizably human: an intelligent woman's face. Something like her mother's. She remembers when they first got this doll: it was fifteen years ago, and came with the new car her father had just bought, the same one she's driving now. This doll was hanging from the rear-view mirror on a gold string, and ever since then it's been swinging there. With everything on her mind this past year, she's barely noticed it till now. But it does look like her mother. There's something about those blue, glistening eyes. It feels like her mother is with her in the car. Her mother asked her, the night before she left for Israel, why she couldn't be happy in Canada.

"Because," she answered, "it's *galut.*"

"*Galut* shmalut," said her mother. "You have all sorts of opportunities here in Canada you won't have in Israel. You have your pick of social work jobs here in Toronto, whereas in Israel you don't even speak the language. Or, if you prefer, you could do a Master's degree. Here you have friends. You could keep seeing Bobby —"

"I know, I know. I could live a typical middle-class Canadian Jewish life. Marry a lawyer. Live in a nice house in a suburb. Maybe have some kids."

"Well, what's so terrible about that?"

"Nothing. But that's not who I am. That's not what I want."

"I'm not saying you shouldn't have a career," said her mother. "Did I ever say that? But don't tell me you don't want a family, too. I know you better than that. I know how much you love kids."

"I can have kids in Israel, too."

"Yes, but life there is so much more difficult. Why should you struggle there when you have everything you need right here?"

She made a sour face.

"Look, I just want you to be happy, dear. That's all I'm saying. It doesn't matter where you live. A person can be happy anywhere. It's a question of attitude. You make up your mind to look on the positive side, to appreciate what you have —"

"You don't understand," said Judith.

And it's true, she didn't. Her mother never understood her. But now, ten years later, Judith reconsiders her mother's point of view. *Of course Mummy's right*, she thinks, *that I could live reasonably happily in Toronto if I absolutely had to. That's what I'm doing right now. I'm not walking around crying. I'm finding things to enjoy, and making friends, and if I were staying here, I'd even find a man to love — either Bobby or someone else. But that isn't what I want my life to be.* Galut *is okay as far as it goes, but fundamentally it's empty at the core. It's life minus the jewel in the crown, and why live without this jewel when you can have it?*

The street lamps whiz by as she turns off the highway and enters the city limits of Toronto. Her hands are cold: the left one she inserts into her pocket for warmth, and she steers with just the right one. *My right hand*, she thinks — *"If I forget thee, O Jerusalem, may my right hand lose its cunning."* Then for the rest of the trip she drives automatically, unthinkingly, through familiar streets. She barrels through the neighbourhood where she grew up, past trees she walked under on her way to elementary school, past stores where as a child she lined up, coin in sweaty hand, waiting her turn to buy candy. As she swerves onto her own street, the sky ahead of her is sprayed with stars and there is a swirl of glowing galaxy at its centre.

Magnificent. But pulling into the driveway, she misses her parents intensely, with a sharp stab. Whenever they pulled into this driveway after a long trip, her father always said the same thing in his warm, guttural voice, and she, as a child and teenager, said it with him, timed together like a duet. But tonight she just listens to his voice alone in the cold, dark night, as he says to her with happiness, "Home sweet home."

FRIENDS AND ENEMIES

The following Monday there are no classes — it's midterm break — so the Monday after that there's a feeling of joy at school: the jubilation of reuniting after two weeks apart. People wave gleefully to each other in the halls. Aliza throws her arms around Judith, Pam slaps her a high five, and Cindy gives her a piece of cake with creamy icing saved from Mikey's birthday party yesterday, along with one of the library books she promised to pass on. Judith feels happy and warm with belonging. Within her gang, but also within the school as a whole. By now she knows everyone in her class by name. There are only twenty-eight students in year one of the M.S.W. — twenty in the Practice stream, and eight in Policy — and in year two there are only sixteen more. It feels like a small community.

"Don't forget to send me your names for the keynote," says Chris when he passes Judith in the hall.

"Right," she says. "Thanks for reminding me."

She'd completely forgotten. Like everyone on SWAC, she has only until this Thursday to suggest at least one speaker for Anti-oppression Day. Michael Brier seems to be everyone's first choice, but "in the interest of democratic process" other names are also being collected. She continues down the hall, smiling and waving at people, glad Chris invited her to submit a name. She's grateful to be included. Even though she doesn't know anyone here in Canada to suggest. If this were Israel, that would be another matter. There she knows all the activists. She knows the scene. But Canada? A total blank. Which reminds her she forgot to look up Michael Brier over the weekend. She'd better do that before the next meeting.

She wiggles into her seat near Cindy, Pam, and Aliza. Aliza is telling a joke about a Jewish boy from New York in the thirties who works for one of the big unions then, maybe the ILGWU. They send him to Tennessee to organize the workers in the South. So he gets on a train —

Thump, thump, thump. Weick is standing behind the long table at the front of the room, pounding on the desk, calling for silence to begin his class. "Tell you later," whispers Aliza, and Judith straightens up in her seat.

As usual, Weick is wearing his trademark green cardigan, lecturing in a monotone from dog-eared notes, and making corny puns no one laughs at. But today Judith is so happy, surrounded by the affection of her friends, that she doesn't care. He seems now more pathetic than any sort of threat. He is dull, slow-witted, awkward, and out-of-touch, and he still gazes at her sometimes in that odd manner. But other than this, nothing weird has happened between them. Today, he's saying, they are just past the halfway point in the first term, so they're going to do a review of everything covered in class so far.

Oh shit. The first time Weick taught this stuff she learned nothing; now she is going to learn nothing for the second time. Two times zero is zero. She tries briefly to pay attention, but she can't. Not even for one minute. His voice makes her feel dead. So she summons Moshe. Like calling forth a genie by rubbing an ancient lamp. One of those old Aladdin lamps, its front protruding like a penis. *Moshe will occupy me*, she thinks. Occupy me, as in keep me busy — but also occupy me physically: enter my body and fill me up. Fill my emptiness. He is a kind of occupation, but a different kind from the Israeli one — not a military occupation. Also not an occupation as in a career: last week in the doctor's office they gave her a form to complete that asked for her occupation, and she wrote *student*. No, Moshe's occupation of her is not an occupation of force or of status, but of love. "Make Love, Not War." She wants him to occupy not just her

West Bank, her left flank, but all of her: her north, south, east, and west. So now Moshe comes to her, and they begin making love. But then, as soon as they're getting into it, she tells herself, *I'd better stop this. I could lose control of myself, right here in Weick's class, in front of everyone …*

So she pushes Moshe away and tries to refocus on Weick who, in all this time, hasn't moved an inch and is still droning on. Two students in the back row have fallen asleep, one of them lightly snoring. Judith does her best to stay awake.

But then at 10:36 a.m., with only twenty-four minutes left to go, the class suddenly flares to life like a damp match still containing some fire no one could have guessed at. Darra puts up her hand, and in a vibrant, totally unsleepy voice offers abortion as an example of how the values of a social worker who is pro-life can conflict with those of the client, and interfere with effectively helping a young woman with an unwanted pregnancy.

"In this one case I know," she says, "the worker was Catholic and, because of this, she kept pressuring her client not to have an abortion. This young woman, let's call her Linda, was only sixteen and couldn't decide what to do. But in the end, since her worker kept telling her to wait, she put it off for so long she had no choice but to have the baby. Then, to care for it, she dropped out of high school and married the baby's father, who was seventeen, and also, as it turns out, violent, so Linda got beaten up by him for three years straight until one night she finally fled with the baby to the shelter where I'm doing my practicum."

The whole class is now wide awake and listening.

"This should never have happened to this young woman," Darra says passionately, "and I hold that social worker personally responsible. I think it's disgusting and dishonest and unethical what she did, and she should never be allowed to practise social work in this province again."

Immediately several hands shoot up in the air and wave energetically at Weick. After some dithering, he points to the closest one.

"I agree with you 100 percent," Genya says to Darra. "Social workers who are pro-life have a professional responsibility to neutralize their values in the workplace, so as not to limit their clients' life choices."

Tyler agrees. So do Lola, Mike, Tammy, and Samantha. Then Weick points to Mary Martha.

"Well," says Mary Martha in a high-pitched voice, "I don't agree."

Mary Martha has spoken in class only once before, and Judith looks at her curiously. She's a pink-cheeked girl with blond pigtails, from a small town somewhere in rural Ontario. Rumour has it she is part of some sect, Amish or maybe Mennonite. Mary Martha's pale white skin is now flushed a deep pink.

"I don't believe in abortion," she says. "And I'm not going to pretend I do, just to fit in with the rest of you. You're all very liberal and that's fine. I respect your right to believe what you believe. But you don't respect my right to hold my values, and that's not right."

Mary Martha's words are strong but her voice turns shaky toward the end and she looks like she might cry. Several people begin talking at once, but Weick, laughing, says "Hey!" and holds up his hand like a traffic cop. Then he points to the far corner of the room.

"No one's saying you aren't entitled to your values," says Roberta. "It's just that you don't have a right to impose them on others."

"Yeah," pipes up Anna without waiting for Weick's permission. "Especially if your values could hurt them. Clients come to you for help when they're at their most vulnerable. You're not there to tell them they can't do something they need to, just because you're uncomfortable with it."

Mary Martha is shaking her head. But the arguments keep coming, everyone trying to convince her she's wrong. It's the whole class against Mary Martha, and Judith feels sorry for her. But she can't leap to her defence because she thinks her position is from the Dark Ages. Weick stands uselessly at the front of the class. He's visibly happy, though — relieved to have something, anything, happening in his class for a change.

Now Cindy speaks, more gently and slowly than anyone preceding her. "Mary Martha," she says, talking directly to her, rather than the whole class. "Of course you have a right to your own values. But what people are trying to say is that none of us has the right to impose our values on other people. Especially our clients. So here's a possible solution. What about transferring this young girl to another social worker — someone who doesn't share your ... beliefs, and can help this girl get an abortion, if that's what she wants?"

Sweet Cindy, thinks Judith. *Always trying to find a middle ground to bridge the gaps between people, and make things turn out all right.* The room falls silent while Mary Martha considers Cindy's suggestion. She is struggling with herself. Her cheeks are even brighter now, a real apple-red, and they contrast strangely with her pale blond braids.

"No," she answers finally. "I couldn't do that. It's nice of you, Cindy, to try and find a compromise. But some things can't be compromised on. I could never transfer this girl to someone else when I know this person is just going to help her get an abortion. If I pass her on to someone else to do something, it's the same as if I did it myself. It's still my personal responsibility. I believe my most important responsibility is to make sure this girl doesn't burn in hell for all eternity for having had an abortion."

There is a shocked silence. Somebody giggles nervously. Then at least half of the class is frantically waving their hands at Weick. *My God*, thinks Judith. *She really believes this stuff. What a nutcase.*

But as Mary Martha is attacked by one person after another, with Weick doing nothing to stop them, and as she continues to hold her ground, Judith begins to feel a grudging admiration for her. Mary Martha may be a nutcase, but she is a principled and determined nutcase.

Mary Martha now has tears in her eyes, and her voice is wobbling, but she doesn't back down. *Daniella in the lions' den.* Judith recalls Pastor Niemoller's poem and once again considers jumping in to defend Mary Martha, but she can't. To her, pro-lifers are not only misguided people; they're dangerous and destructive. Six weeks ago a group of them went crazy and smashed up Toronto's largest abortion clinic, and nearly killed the doctor, too. These people scare her. But she watches Mary Martha facing down the whole room, and thinks: I wish I had that sort of courage.

The back and forth, push and pull between Mary Martha and the rest of the class goes on and on. Finally the bell rings, releasing them all. Gratefully, they file out of the room, everyone talking, rolling their eyes and laughing, except for Mary Martha, who sits by herself, inserting her notes into her schoolbag. Pam, Aliza, Cindy, and Judith head toward the elevators.

"These kinds of people," spits out Pam, "don't believe in compromise. Never compromising is a point of pride with them. They're no different than the guys who flew into the Twin Towers. They're religious fanatics."

Well, not necessarily, thinks Judith. *You can be religious, like me, without being a religious fanatic.* But she doesn't say this out loud. She doesn't feel like getting into an argument with Pam, who always seems so certain about everything.

But Cindy ventures, "Mary Martha does seem kind of nice, though."

"Well, what's that got to do with it?" says Pam. "Niceness has nothing to do with anything. If you're a religious fanatic, you're a religious fanatic. And that's that."

You're sounding pretty fanatical yourself, Judith thinks, but again doesn't speak. She watches the numbers of the floors as the elevator gradually descends. Just before it reaches their floor and goes *"bing!"* she touches Cindy's arm and says, "I forgot something. You guys go ahead, I'll meet you in Greg's class."

"Should we wait for you?" asks Cindy.

"No. Go ahead."

Cindy enters the elevator. Then, just as the doors are closing, she calls out, "Do you want a donut?"

Judith shouts back to the almost closed doors, into the crack: "No, thanks."

Back in the classroom, Mary Martha is alone, sitting in the same seat, eating a sandwich. She looks at Judith. Her eyes are pink — like a rabbit's, thinks Judith. Mary Martha has obviously been crying.

"I forgot something," Judith says.

Mary Martha nods and returns to her sandwich. Judith goes to where she was sitting and pretends to be looking for something. She crouches down, peering all over the place and groping around on the floor under what was her chair. Then, as if talking to the floor, she asks, "Are you okay?"

"Yes," says Mary Martha. "Thanks." Judith glances up and their eyes meet. Then Judith gets to her feet.

"I must've lost it somewhere else," she says. "Are you coming to Greg's class?"

"In a minute," says Mary Martha.

"Okay. See you there."

Judith walks back to the elevator and looks at her reflection in the metal doors. She looks young to herself, definitely younger than her age. *Maybe,* she thinks, *it's because I don't wear makeup. Or maybe it's the way I dress: T-shirts, sweatshirts, jeans, and sneakers. Anyway, I look more like twenty-six than thirty-two. And I look like someone who has never fought in a war.*

When Judith arrives at Greg's class, he isn't there yet, but all the students are talking excitedly and laughing, and there's an electric charge in the air. Probably because of what just happened in Weick's class, she thinks. The lions have tasted blood. She waves to her gang and sits with them.

Greg sails into the class with a grin. He waves back at Mike who's just waved to him casually, almost as though Greg were just another student. *So different,* thinks Judith, *from when Weick enters a room and silence immediately descends like a pall.* Greg senses her watching him and smiles at her, and she smiles back. Gradually the room quietens. Greg, jubilantly, like Robin Williams crowing "Good morning, Vietnam!," calls out: "Good morning, everybody!"

"Good morning, Greg!" shout back Tyler and several female students sitting around him. Some others answer too, though more quietly, including Judith.

"You seem happy today," Greg says, laughing. "That's great! Here we are halfway through 'Introduction to Social Justice.' Last class, we completed the first module of this course: Intersecting Oppressions and Social Justice (and Injustice) in Canada. So before moving on, let's do a brief recap of what we've covered till now. First, we showed how race, gender, class, sexual orientation, ageism, and ableism all interact to oppress Canada's most vulnerable and marginalized citizens, thus keeping this segment of the population — Canada's underclass, in essence — in its place ..."

Judith has heard all this before — every week, in fact — and doesn't feel like hearing it again. She looks around the class. She catches sight of Mary Martha, sitting at the edge of the room near the door, looking down at her desk. Then she scans the faces of her classmates. Some of them, as they listen raptly to Greg, remind her of the baby animals in the early Disney films, like Bambi or Chip 'n' Dale: wide-eyed, innocent, and adoring. Greg continues talking without saying anything new, and only half-listening, she doodles happily, filling two pages with drawings of humans, animals, and creatures that are part-animal and part-human. She draws a half-human-half-chipmunk. A half-human-half-deer. A half-human-half-chicken. Just as she's completing a half-human-half-bird, she hears Greg winding up his review and dismissing them for a break. After they return, knowing Greg will introduce some new material now, she gives him her full attention.

"Okay," says Greg. "So now I'd like to move beyond the borders of Canada and into the global context. Here the question becomes: How do the same oppressions and social injustices that we've been talking about manifest themselves outside of Canada? How do they play themselves out in the international arena? I have my own ideas, obviously. But first I'd like to hear what you think. Like when you feel concerned about oppression or social injustice around the world, what places come to mind?"

Uh-oh, thinks Judith. *Uh-oh.*

"Also, when you pick a country," Greg continues, "ask yourselves why there is oppression there. What social structures and policies in these countries make it possible for these abuses and injustices to occur? When you reflect on oppression, think, of course, about racism, classism, sexism, all of the 'isms.' But I also want you to include political oppression, where citizens' human or civil rights are violated on a regular basis. This may not involve, or be directed against, a country's whole citizenry; maybe just against certain segments of it. Perhaps groups that are ethnically or religiously different from the majority, or from the government."

Oh, shit. Don't let them start on Israel.

A couple of hands wave in the air. Greg points to one on the right side of the room.

"I'd say China," says Mike.

Judith is so relieved she wants to laugh. Greg asks Mike to elaborate. It turns out that Mike's sister has lived in China for the past five years, so he knows what's happening there. He talks volubly about the Chinese government's stifling of political dissent, its control and censorship of the media, the multiple abuses of human and civil rights ever since Tiananmen Square, and how even today people are often arrested for no reason and held indefinitely without trial.

Greg nods gravely throughout. He thanks Mike, and points to another student.

"Palestine," says Kerry.

Judith has been thinking, *Don't say Israel, Don't say Israel,* so it takes her a second to grasp that Kerry has just said Israel. Meanwhile Kerry — whose squishy face looks like someone simultaneously pressed down on her scalp and up on her chin — has begun explaining her choice without any prompting from Greg.

"Because Israel is the most oppressive country in the world today. Israel is just like South Africa used to be before the indigenous people took it back. The Jews stole the land of Palestine away from the Palestinian people, and under this illegal and immoral occupation, the Palestinians are treated like second-class citizens without any civil or human rights. This situation is perpetuated by the social, economic, and military policies of Zionist imperialism and colonialism, which are supported by the international Jewish lobby, which controls the media and the banks, and also by the American government, which itself is imperialist and colonialist. Together American and Zionist interests effectively oppress and subjugate the Palestinian people. Just like people of colour, who have been oppressed and exploited both in the United States and South Africa. So it's no coincidence that, after the U.S., South Africa is Israel's closest ally and trading partner."

Not true! thinks Judith, her heart pounding. She knows that nothing she just heard is true, but she can't speak and she can't formulate anything clearer than *No! Not true!* because she's in shock. She was aware, of course, that there were people who believed this stuff, but she's never before heard it said out loud in her presence. She feels like someone has kicked her in the stomach. Through a haze, she sees that Kerry has finished speaking and is proud of herself, and a number of other students are giving her a thumbs-up, including Tyler. Judith doesn't know Kerry very well — she just lent her a pen once when Kerry's pen started leaking — but she's never struck Judith as particularly bright. Yet her little speech came out in perfect, pre-fab sentences, like something handed to her to memorize, a sort of catechism. As she stares at Kerry's ugly, squishy face, Judith seems to have stopped breathing. The whole world seems to have stopped breathing. All she's doing now is waiting. Waiting for Greg to speak. To say what needs to be said. The way he did a few weeks ago in class when Miguel admitted he is uncomfortable around gay people, and Greg responded by "putting Miguel's feelings into social perspective." He reminded them all how in this society we are taught to hate people who are gay, lesbian, bi, and trans, or at least to feel uncomfortable with them and experience them as "Other." So Miguel's reaction to GLBTs was not merely a personal, individual one, but a socially constructed response, which we must view critically, and challenge in ourselves and others whenever we encounter it.

Judith waits, sure that Greg will do the same thing again now. He will put Kerry's comments into social perspective. He will challenge her "facts" and assumptions, including the idea of a "Jewish lobby." He'll talk about the limitations of the anti-oppression paradigm, and how black/white analogies from the United States or South Africa are not accurate regarding the Middle East. She is sure Greg won't let this pass. She looks at him expectantly, waiting for him to say what she is unable to, having become frozen and mute.

But Greg doesn't say a word. He just nods at Kerry as he nodded at Mike, and asks the class if there are any other places they'd like to mention. There's silence. *This can't be happening*, she thinks. *He's got to say something.* The silence continues, so Greg calls on two students who previously had their hands up, but they both shake their heads: they, like Kerry, wanted to say Israel. Then, just as Greg looks like he's about to start lecturing again, Genya raises her hand and says that she sees Afghanistan as an oppressive country because of its treatment — or, should she say, mistreatment — of women. "Even women with college degrees are no longer allowed to drive cars and can't leave home unless accompanied by a male relative. Not to mention," says Genya, "being covered from head to toe as if your body were a thing of filth that needed to be hidden."

Unexpectedly Greg smiles, and his eyes gleam. "Now, this is very interesting," he says. "What do you all think about what Genya just said?"

Judith is confused. She doesn't understand why Greg is smiling. And she is still waiting for him to say something in response to Kerry. As if through a fog, she hears someone agreeing with Genya and then Greg saying, "Ah. But let's think a little more about this."

Now Greg explains that the challenge in respectfully relating to other cultures is precisely that they often hold values that conflict with ours, even values we hold very dear, like women's rights. "So we have to work very hard," he says, "not to be ethnocentric. After all, if other cultures' values didn't conflict with ours, then it wouldn't be challenging to work cross-culturally, or 'across difference.' This is exactly the nature of the challenge. So if this is their culture in Afghanistan, who are we to tell them that they are wrong in how they regard and treat their women? Where do we come off saying that they don't meet the standards of our Western culture on this issue? Furthermore, we have to be very careful not to be influenced, or even manipulated, by all the post-9/11 hysteria in the United States, that in many obvious and subtle ways is fostering Islamophobia around the world. Which, of course, is just another form of racism and oppression."

Judith is having trouble breathing now. She can't have understood this correctly. That Afghanistan is deserving of indulgence, tolerance, and cross-cultural respect for its diversity, even though it has virtually enslaved all of its women, but Israel is not. Israel is an evil empire, and Afghanistan is okay. *I must have misunderstood*, she thinks, as the room swims around her. *This is Greg. This is Greg's class, "Introduction to Social Justice."* A safe place to learn together — he told them on the first day of class — where all individuals and collectivities are respected, and no one gets trivialized or marginalized.

Greg is still talking but she can't hear him anymore. She is feeling herself disappear. She feels herself getting smaller and smaller, her insides leaking out of her like the ink from a broken pen, until there is nothing left in her. She is not real now, she's just a shell. But no, there is one thing left inside her: a wind. A wind blowing around and around, forming itself into a tornado. Like the tornado in Munch's painting. A tornado that is a scream. And in the middle of her scream, there is only one word.

Israel.

Eventually Greg's class finishes, and there is a scraping of chairs as everyone gets up from their seats. All around Judith, people are talking. Everything seems to be perfectly normal. But she feels a wall between her and everyone else. She is walking out of class as she always does with Cindy, Pam, and Aliza, but she is not really there — she is buried deep inside, floating forward in a little bubble of her own. From safe in there, like inside a one-seat helicopter, she watches a cluster of admirers form around Kerry: Ranna, Althea, and Tyler, and then around Tyler a sub-cluster of his own: "the dipsticks," Kiki and Lana, and Mike. Passing them in the hall, Judith avoids eye contact. With her own little gang she heads toward the cafeteria for lunch. Outside they walk four abreast, their heads lowered against the wind, like rams with their horns down ready to charge. When the sidewalk narrows and there's insufficient room for all four, Aliza, her arm linked through Judith's, drops back, pulling Judith with her, behind Cindy and Pam. For a while they walk in silence. Judith's throat, all the way to the top of it where the tongue starts, feels clogged with fear.

"That fuckin' bitch," says Aliza. "Comparing Israel to South Africa."

Judith turns and peers at her. *So it wasn't just me. Aliza felt it, too.* She and Aliza have never talked about being Jewish; they just wished each other Happy New Year once on Rosh Hashana, and when Aliza heard Judith had lived in Jerusalem she mentioned having a cousin on kibbutz. But Judith didn't know if she cared about Israel. Now there's a slight lightening of the choking pressure in her chest, and her throat loosens up enough to allow for speech.

"We're the worst country in the world, didn't you know?" she says. "Worse even than Afghanistan."

"Sssh," hisses Aliza. Judith follows her gaze: Kerry's gang is passing them on the left, like a car in the fast lane. Tyler smiles blithely at Judith; she just stares at him. She and Aliza are silent until that gang has passed. But before they can speak again, they are already at the cafeteria entrance. Pam and Cindy are waiting there, Pam holds the door open for them, and they enter and get in line. It's warm and cozy inside, and the sound of the bubbling vegetable soup is comforting. But Kerry and her friends, laughing and talking, are just two spaces ahead of them. Judith feels like she should go over to them and say something. But she can't right now; she's too raw. And also she is afraid of them. They hate Israel. Which means they hate everything she loves, and everything she is.

Cindy, Pam, and Aliza have also spotted Kerry's gang up ahead, and by tacit agreement, the four of them gaze up at the menu and talk only about the day's specials. Cindy and Aliza joke around about the revolting-sounding casserole of the day. "Hallowe'en Hash" it's called, because in three days it will be Hallowe'en. *Right* — Judith had forgotten about that. The pimply boy in the peaked white cap behind the counter enumerates for Cindy and Aliza the contents of Hallowe'en Hash: charred Cajun chicken, black licorice, black-eyed peas, butternut squash, orange sherbet, and cheddar cheese. A repulsive mélange of ingredients, all of them either black or orange. It is all Judith can do to keep from lurching to the bathroom and barfing all over the sink. So when it comes her turn to order, she asks only for a roll.

"Nothing else?" asks the guy.

"Only a roll," she replies, feeling like Bontsha the Silent in the Yiddish story, who can't think of anything better to ask for in the world than a roll. Then she sits silently without even touching it while Cindy, Pam, and Aliza eat their lunch, watching the clock so as not to be late for Suzy's class. Cindy enthusiastically digs into her mess of Hallowe'en Hash.

"It's very good," she says with her mouth full. "Not at all as gross as it sounded."

What Cindy is eating is the exact colour and consistency of vomit. Judith has to look away or she'll puke. She remembers Sartre's black-covered book, *Nausea*, that she read in high school. *This isn't a stomach upset I have*, she thinks. *This is existential nausea. I literally cannot stomach this world.*

Aliza, however, apparently can. Judith glares at her tray, piled so high it's almost overflowing with food: macaroni, a tuna sandwich, french fries, a large diet Coke, coleslaw, a fruit cup, and a double honey cruller. *Why is it pronounced "crueller"?* she wonders. *What is it crueller than? Is it cruel at all? And how can Aliza eat at a time like this?* Then she answers herself: *Because Aliza is a galut Jew. It's true she reacted sort of like I did to what happened just now. But not exactly. Aliza has lived here all her life and at some level she's used to this kind of thing. But I'm not. I am not a galut girl.*

Two tables down, Kerry and her crew are laughing with glee, obviously in high spirits. *The joy of triumph*, Judith thinks glumly. *They're winning and they know it.* She looks again at Aliza, who is shovelling in her food like a pig.

"Are you okay?" Cindy asks quietly.

Judith, surprised, looks at Cindy, who is frowning at her anxiously. Judith shrugs, then shakes her head.

"Because of what Kerry said?" asks Cindy.

She nods.

"Don't you pay her no never mind," says Cindy. "That's what my mother says — she's from Alabama. But really, Judith. Don't pay attention to her."

Judith wants to answer, but still she can't speak. Several minutes later, without having uttered another word, she returns with the others to FRANK for their last class of the day.

As soon as she enters the classroom, Suzy smiles at her, and immediately she feels better. The pain from Greg's class lightens, as if Suzy, just by her presence, without even knowing what occurred, is sucking the poison out of it, like the poison out of a snakebite. Suzy begins lecturing on today's topic: how to integrate Unconditional Positive Regard with other interviewing skills, such as confrontation and giving negative feedback. *In other words*, thinks Judith, *how to integrate love and truth*. Which brings to mind Socrates, who believed that love and truth could not be integrated. He felt one had to choose between them. At least that time when he and his friend disagreed on a philosophical point, and his friend begged him to concede out of friendship, out of love. Socrates said to him, "I love you dearly, but I love truth more." Judith isn't sure she would make the same choice as Socrates.

Now Suzy points to a nondescript man of fifty-five or sixty sitting at the front of the classroom. He is a pedophile, she tells them, who has been convicted of sexually abusing fourteen children between the ages of three and eight.

"Not someone with whom many of us feel very comfortable," she says. "So how are you going to establish a relationship with this man? How are you going to overcome your initial reaction and find that place in yourself that is non-judgmental, so you can view him with Unconditional Positive Regard?"

I can't, thinks Judith. *And I'm not even sure I want to. Why should I try to emotionally accept a pedophile? Or someone like Kerry? Or maybe even Greg? Fuck them all.* Stubbornly she sits through the class, while at Suzy's invitation, one student after another goes to the front and tries to connect with this pedophile. They're all more skilled today than when they had Cordelia five weeks ago, but this guy is an even tougher nut to crack. Darra comes closest to "reaching" him, but none of them succeed. So, as in every previous class, Suzy steps forward and shows them how it's done. Her performance today, as always, is impressive. But now Judith asks herself what the point is of all this. Does Suzy genuinely believe that everything in life — every human problem in the world — can be resolved by a little Unconditional Positive Regard — in other words, love? (*All you need is love, duh duh duh duh duh ...*) Love is good for lots of things, but it's no use at all for others — for instance, solving Israel's problems. There's too much hate there. And there's too much hate here, too. Look what happened an hour ago.

The bell rings. Suzy's class is over. Judith waits in line for her turn with Suzy, to tell her what happened today in Greg's class, and also in Weick's. But most of all she wants to ask Suzy questions. Like what she really believes about human nature. Does she truly think a person like this pedophile can ever fundamentally change? When, in her view, can love overpower hate? And when can it not? Judith waits for fifteen minutes. But there are still five students ahead of her, and she's tired, depressed, and hungry, and wants to go home. So she waves to Suzy, with a helpless shrug Suzy waves back, and Judith leaves.

Outside the sunlight is very bright. Walking to her car, Judith squints and, as her eyes adjust, she laughs in astonishment.

Witches, ghosts, and goblins stroll around the campus, and Ronald McDonald, with a stack of books under his arm, flip-flops across the parking lot in big floppy clown shoes. Judith now recalls something about a Hallowe'en party at the Lion's Den, and free drinks if you come in costume. She stands and watches for a while with pleasure. Interspersed among the normally dressed students, there are Batman and Superman, rounding a corner one after the other, Cinderella's plump little fairy godmother all in pink, and a knight of the Round Table — or is it Don Quixote? — in clinking, clunking, shining armour. On a nearby footpath a punk rocker with nose rings and purple hair walks arm-in-arm with a human-sized frog, the two of them gaily singing together. Judith grins. Then, starting toward her car, she sees someone, or something, heading straight toward her from the far side of the parking lot. As it approaches, she sees it has no face; there's just a dark cavernous hood from the neck up, and from the neck down, a shapeless charcoal-grey frock from which protrudes a skeleton's hand waving a long, curved scythe. It's the Grim Reaper. Startled, she turns and walks in the other direction. But the Grim Reaper — or is it Raper? — follows her, walking calmly, almost casually, but inexorably toward her.

It's just someone in a costume, she tells herself. Don't be ridiculous. But she can't help it — in spite of herself she's scared. She walks more and more quickly, and then runs the final stretch to her car, hastily getting in, locking the door behind her, and with a trembling hand, turning on the ignition. *This is absurd*, she thinks, as she backs out, *what's the matter with you?* Only when she's about to exit the parking lot does she dare to glance anxiously into the rear-view mirror. The Grim Reaper is still there, standing perfectly still in the middle of the parking lot, watching her as she drives away. Her hands tremble. Stupid pagan holiday. What nonsense. A day when the souls of the dead supposedly rise from their graves. Then again, what nice nonsense it would be if her parents rose from their graves right now and came to pay her a visit. Even a short one. This idea captivates her, but then she brushes it away. *Nonsense.*

Now she is passing through Dunhill's downtown, and in some of the shop windows there are glimpses of black-and-orange decorations and Halloween costumes. This is only her second Halloween in the past ten years (they don't celebrate it in Israel), and as a child — even though she loved dressing up in costume, and filling her bag with candy and her UNICEF box with coins — all the black and orange of this holiday used to frighten her. The black-caped witches flying on brooms with their pointy black hats, the deep blackness of the night itself when she went out trick-or-treating. The orange jack-o'-lanterns at the entrance to people's homes grimaced at her as she stood hesitating on the sidewalk. And when she approached their front doors, her candy bag open, there would be orange flames licking at the soft insides of the pumpkins, and if she leaned down for a closer look, they suddenly leapt up at her. Flaring up. Like the bonfires on the holiday Lag B'Omer in Israel. During her first hours in the Holy Land, the night she arrived on *aliya*, the whole country was on fire, and she couldn't understand why. She didn't know it was Lag B'Omer, or that this is a holiday where the custom is to build bonfires, and the bigger the better: some were as high as sixty feet in the air. Terrified, she watched Jerusalem burn as the taxi drove her past one fire after another on the way to her new home: a dismal spartan dormitory belonging to the Ministry of Absorption. That night in Israel was orange and black, all fire and fear. And now, she thinks, also here. *Halloweened be Thy name.*

— 2 —

The following evening at seven o'clock, Judith stands before the full-length mirror in the hallway. She's wearing a low-cut red velvet gown, a long gold necklace, and black high heels. She can see objectively that she looks very attractive. But all day today, still reverberating from yesterday at school, she's been in an introverted, fearful mood. Now she feels not like the elegant, sexy woman in the mirror, but just a little girl dressed up in her mother's clothes. A costume for the-day-after-Hallowe'en. Bobby has just been made junior partner at BBB, and they're going out for dinner to celebrate at the fanciest, most expensive restaurant in Toronto. Bobby arrives, and after driving to the restaurant, they eat a leisurely, sensual, seven-course meal. They drink champagne, get very tipsy and laugh a lot, and back at Bobby's place, they make love twice before falling asleep.

The next morning, she awakens at five. She slips out of bed, slides over her naked body a T-shirt of Bobby's that comes down almost to her knees, and pads barefoot across the carpeted house into the kitchen with its cold tiled floor. She brews a pot of coffee, then sits at the kitchen table, drinking from a turquoise cup and reading old newspapers and magazines. Bobby has been very busy lately and never throws out anything until he's read it, so in the corner of his kitchen there's a four-foot stack of reading material. She riffles through the past six months of the *Sunday New York Times*, the *Forward*, *Commentary*, the *Canadian Jewish News,* and the occasional *National Post* or *Globe and Mail*. While she reads she bites her left thumbnail, occasionally muttering softly, "Fuck," or "Oh my God." An hour and a half later, Bobby staggers in, bleary-eyed, wearing his shabby blue bathrobe. He stares at the kitchen table piled high with newspapers.

"What are you doing?" he asks.

She barely glances up. "This is unbelievable," she says. "I can't believe what I'm reading."

Bobby looks around the kitchen as if searching for something.

"The coffee's on the stove," she says. "I saved you some. I don't know how hot it is, though."

He pours himself a cup, takes a sip, warms it in the microwave, and then sits at the table.

"Do you know what's been going on in the world lately?" she asks. "Have you any idea?"

He just grunts and sips some coffee.

"Listen to this," she says. "This is from the *Canadian Jewish News*. It's a summary of the antisemitic incidents all around the world during the past six months."

"Please," he says, his eyes still almost closed like a day-old puppy's. "I just woke up. I haven't even had my coffee."

"Seriously — listen. In Belgium a group of thugs beat up the chief rabbi, kicking him in the face, and calling him a 'dirty Jew.' Two synagogues in Brussels were firebombed; a third was sprayed with automatic weapons fire. In Britain a yeshiva student was stabbed twenty-seven times on a London bus. 'Antisemitism and its open expression,' wrote Petronella Wyatt, a columnist in the *Spectator*, 'has become respectable at London dinner tables.' She quoted one member of the House of Lords as saying: 'The Jews have been asking for it and now, thank God, we can say what we think at last.' In Germany —"

"Okay, okay," says Bobby. "I get the picture."

"No, let me finish. In Germany, a rabbinical student was beaten up in downtown Berlin. In the Ukraine, they smashed the windows of the main synagogue. In Greece, Jewish graves were desecrated. In Istanbul, two synagogues were bombed in the same day, killing twenty-four people, and injuring three hundred. In

France, the situation is worse than anywhere: in Paris alone, there have been ten to twelve anti-Jewish incidents daily. The statue of Alfred Dreyfus in Paris was painted with the words 'Dirty Jew.' In the Jewish neighbourhoods, walls have been defaced with 'Jews to the gas chambers' and 'Death to the Jews.' And this one totally freaks me out: a young girl in Aix-en-Provence was accosted by three masked men who called her 'dirty Jew' and carved a Jewish star into her arm. I can't believe this, Bobby. It's like in the past four months since my father died, the world has gone completely mad."

Bobby is more awake now. With half-open eyes, he looks almost kindly at her. "It's not just the past four months, Judith; it's the past two years. Ever since the second intifada started. On that legal committee I volunteer for with the Jewish community, we've been tracking these incidents ever since then. Even longer. Including what's happening locally — in Ontario and all across Canada."

"This can't be right," she says. "These things weren't going on when I came back here a year ago."

"Sure they were. It had already started before that." He gets up and refills his cup. "You want some more?" he asks, holding up the pot, but she shakes her head. "You weren't here then — you were still in Israel. So of course you wouldn't know."

"I'd have known. There are newspapers. There's CNN. If all this is true, how come I never heard about any of it?"

"I tried telling you several times, but you never wanted to hear."

She considers this for a moment. It's true: he intermittently brought up this topic, and she always brushed it away. "I thought it was just your usual obsession with the Holocaust. I didn't realize things were truly this bad."

He smiles ruefully, takes another sip of coffee, and says, "You've had a few other things on your mind since coming back here."

"Yes," she says, pushing away a short stack of newspapers. She sees herself fourteen months ago arriving at the Toronto airport, one suitcase in hand, not knowing how long she'd be staying. How long her father would live. On the one hand, of course, hoping he'd live forever. But also wanting to get back soon to Israel. Then, once she was here with him, while he was dying, his body growing yellower and more emaciated by the week, she couldn't have cared less about what was happening in the world. Of course, she still followed the news from Israel. But Canadian, or Canadian Jewish, news? Why bother? It's only *galut*, she thought back then. And anyway, if Canadian Jews choose life in *galut*, antisemitism is intrinsic, so they should stop whining about it. Now she cringes at the memory.

Bobby is standing by the fridge with the door open. "What do you want for breakfast?" he asks.

"Whatever," she says dully.

"Toast? Eggs?"

"Sure. No, wait — I should be making *you* breakfast. Your first day as junior partner —"

"Ehh," he says with a shrug, and reaches into the fridge for the eggs. She gazes at his bent-over back and then speaks to it.

"I didn't tell you last night — I didn't want to ruin your celebration," she says. "But something occurred two days ago at school." She proceeds to tell him about Greg's class. He turns to face her and stands perfectly still, listening, with the fridge door wide open behind him. He's holding a carton of eggs and a block of butter, and his lips are tightly pursed.

"Fuckin' antisemites," he says when she's finished. He kicks the fridge door shut.

"I don't know. Was that really antisemitism? *This* is antisemitism," she says, tapping the article in the *Canadian Jewish News*. "That bit Kerry said about Jews controlling the banks and the media, okay. That's straight out of *The Protocols*. But the rest of what she said — I'm not so sure. It's like she was attacking someone I love — and unfairly, mentioning nothing about them but their faults. But it's not illegal, or even immoral, to attack someone I love. Even if it hurts me."

He puts down the eggs and butter. "Of course not," he says. "Legitimate criticism of Israel is obviously not antisemitic. For instance, you and your friends in Israel are all very critical of Sharon and the occupation, and I know a number of people here in Toronto, Jews and non-Jews, who feel the same way. But that's different from anti-Zionism, or the newer term, anti-Israelism, which both involve hating Israel. Anyone who hates Israel, who wants Israel not to exist, is an antisemite."

"Kerry and those guys, they don't hate Israel. They just —"
She stops abruptly.

"They just what?" Leaning against the counter, he watches her.

She looks at him with a peculiar, stunned expression, like someone's just banged her over the head. She says wonderingly, "They hate Israel. They do. They believe we should give the whole country to the Palestinians. That they have all the rights to the land, and we have none. We deserve nothing. You could feel their hatred for Israel. It was scary."

"Of course it was. Antisemitism is a scary thing. What you've just had a taste of is 'the new antisemitism.'"

She frowns. "I've been seeing that phrase all morning. But I don't completely get what it is."

He sighs and sets down the frying pan and spatula. "We were just talking about this at that committee. Basically the new antisemitism isn't that new. It's actually a recycling of the old kind, just in a new form. Traditional antisemitism involved hating, reviling, and persecuting individual Jews; with the new antisemitism it's the Jewish collectivity, in other words the Jewish

State, that is hated, reviled, and persecuted. Israel is the symbol and essence of all evil. In Christian terms, the anti-Christ; in terms of contemporary culture, Israel is the Darth Vader of the world. It is evil and hated and must be destroyed."

She stares at him. "That's exactly how I felt in Greg's class. That Kerry and those guys see Israel as evil. I've never felt that before. Obviously I knew there's a lot of criticism of Israel internationally. But I thought most of that, say, here in Canada, was because people don't like Sharon. But neither do I. So I never thought about it the way you're putting it now: as antisemitism. I thought they opposed Sharon, so by extension they opposed Israel. But now I think there's more to it than that. There's definitely something to what you're saying. I can't believe Kerry mixed *The Protocols* in with her criticisms of Israel."

"Of course she did," he says, folding his arms. "That's classic. Merging the old antisemitism and the new, all under the guise of caring about the Palestinians. It's not coincidental that Israel is a Jewish state. It's precisely because it is a Jewish state that it constantly gets singled out as the worst country in the whole world, and the only one that doesn't deserve to exist. Antisemitism courtesy of your friends on the left."

She blinks in confusion. "My friends? Kerry's not my friend. Anyway, this has nothing to do with being on the left."

He laughs. "Of course it does. This new antisemitism was invented by the left. It's their own special brand of antisemitism. Complete with the PC stamp of approval."

"Oh, Bobby, don't. I can't have this argument right now. Anyhow, you're mixing apples and oranges."

"Are you defending these people, these antisemites, just because they're lefties?"

"I'm not defending anybody." She now feels very tired and physically weak. She's been up since five o'clock, and they went to sleep at 1:00 a.m. "I'm just saying that not everyone on the left is a 'new antisemite' — or an old one, either. And even the ones who are, don't necessarily think this way just because they're on the left — it has nothing to do with that. As for 'my friends,' as you put it, the people who are my friends at Dunhill are good people. Like Cindy and Suzy. They're nothing like Kerry. There are people like Kerry, but there are a lot of good lefties, too, who genuinely care about people and human rights."

"Sure they care about people and their human rights. As long as the people are Palestinians. Their hearts bleed for the Palestinians. But not for Israelis or Jews. No. Israelis have no human rights. Your friends on the left are a bunch of hypocrites."

She feels her temper flare. "Like the right has always been so good to the Jews."

"Better than the left."

"Come on."

"Anyway, I'm not on the right. I'm in the centre."

"That's what people on the right always say. That's how you know someone is on the right: They always say, 'I'm not on the right; I'm in the centre.'"

"Study history, Judith. That's all I'm saying."

"Don't patronize me." Now she mimics him in a nasal, mocking voice, exactly the way she knows he hates being mocked: "'Study history, Judith — study history.' Who do you think you are — my teacher?" But when she sees his stricken face, and he doesn't answer, she's sorry and adds conciliatorily: "One thing I learned from studying Jewish history is that the Temple was destroyed because of groundless hatred — because we fought among ourselves over nothing. So let's not fight anymore. If we can't get along, a lefty and a righty who love each other, what hope is there for the Jewish people?"

He smiles thinly. Silently he brings a bowl, fork, and the eggs to the table, and sits. He cracks open four eggs. Then he begins beating them furiously with the fork. She watches him, searching for something neutral to say.

"In Israel," she offers, "one of the most popular Hebrew expressions is 'You can't make an omelette without breaking eggs.'"

He just glances at her without speaking and goes back to pounding the eggs. She tries again: "Did you know that in Hebrew the word for eggs, *baitzim*, is the same as the word for a guy's balls?"

This one gets a smile from him. "Really?" He looks down quizzically at the fork in his hand. "Maybe I should be doing this more gently." She laughs. He takes the bowl of yellow foam to the stove, ignites the flame under the greased pan, and pours in the eggs. There's a sizzling sound and then the rising smell of eggs cooking in butter.

"Bobby," she says urgently, "what can I do about what happened in Greg's class?"

"What do you mean?"

"There must be something I can do. I can't just let Kerry and people like her go around saying whatever they want about Israel. Spraying all that hate into the air. Nowadays no one gets away with doing that — with racism or homophobia or anything else. They shouldn't be allowed to with this new antisemitism, either."

Something in his face hardens. Sharp lines of bone appear in his jaw. "I'll tell you what you can do," he says. "You can write your papers, finish your M.S.W., and get the fuck out of that school as fast as your legs can carry you. That's what you can do. And here's what you cannot do — what you absolutely mustn't do: try to be a knight on a white horse, like Bonnie Bertha."

"Like who?"

"Bonnie Bertha. That girl in your class."

"Mary Martha."

"Whatever. Anyway, that's not you, Judith. You're not the martyr type. Right now you've got one thing to do, and that's finish your courses and graduate. After that, you can do whatever you want. We could even get married." She frowns. "Okay, scratch that. I know I promised not to bring that up for a while. But I mean what I'm saying. Just get through this year."

He turns toward the stove, flips the eggs, and carries two laden plates to the table. She gets cutlery, orange juice, and glasses, and they eat. He glances at his watch.

"Fuck — it's only seven. What time did you get up?"

"Five," she says with her mouth full of toast.

"Barbaric."

"When do you have to be at the office today?"

"Not till eight-thirty. I'm fine."

They eat awhile in silence. Then she says, "I should've said something. I should've said something right then and there — struck while the iron was hot."

"What would you have said?"

"I thought about it yesterday. I have a whole script. About Israel being the only democracy in the Middle East. Not being like South Africa because in South Africa they didn't have blacks in their parliament, and in our parliament 10 percent are Arabs. Stuff like that. I can answer Kerry one for one. But what I really want to say is, 'Who the fuck are you? How dare you insult my country? What if I got up and insulted yours?' That's what I wish I'd said."

"It's good you didn't. They'd have drawn and quartered you." He wipes up the last bits of egg with his toast.

"I don't care. I should've said something. But I … froze. What do they call that in sports?"

"Choking."

"I choked."

He takes a gulp of his coffee. "Forget it. That incident is behind you now and you don't have to say anything to anybody. Just keep your mouth shut and play the game. In six months you'll be out of there and you won't ever have to see any of those people again."

"But I'm still going to have to look at myself in the mirror every morning. How can I just stand by and do nothing about this? What did Mordechai say to Queen Esther? 'Don't think if you keep silent at this time ...'"

He laughs. "So now you're Queen Esther?! Enough of your fantasy life, Judith. This is the real world. Nobody likes a martyr — it just makes them feel guilty and bad about themselves. You'll ruin your whole year fighting with people for nothing. You're not going to change anyone's mind about Israel. Let it go."

"In other words, play this like a Jew in *galut*. Cringe and cower. Suck up and keep my mouth shut. At least in Israel, Jews stand up and fight back."

"Here we go again. Three cheers for Israel, the most perfect place in the world. No problems, no imperfections, everyone's happy, brave, and heroic all the time."

"I never said that."

"What did you once tell me Israel was supposed to be? A safe haven for all the Jews? Sure. A lovely, safe place to live. As long as you don't get blown up walking down the street."

"At least we're running our own country. We're in our own home."

"*Maîtres chez nous.*"

"Something like that. We're not just guests in someone else's house."

"I don't feel like a guest here," he says. "Canada is my home." She rolls her eyes.

"It is," he insists.

"I know it is. But that's the problem."

"It's not a problem for me."

"It's a problem for me. And a problem for us."

He doesn't say anything. Just gazes at her intensely.

"What?"

"I can't live there, Judith."

"I know that."

"No, you don't. You think at some level you'll be able to persuade me to go back there with you. But that's not going to happen. I can't do it. My life is here."

She looks down at her empty plate. She's eaten everything on it without even noticing.

"I know that compared to you," he says, "I seem very straight and conservative. A typical lawyer, with no ideals, no commitment —"

"I didn't say that."

"But that's what you think, at least sometimes. You think I don't have the guts to make it in Israel. But it's not that. I just don't want to. This is my home."

"You'd like it in Israel if you tried. I know you would. Why won't you even give it a chance?"

"You don't understand, Judith."

"Yes, I do."

"No, you don't. You're not even trying to see my point of view."

"What do you want me to say, Bobby? I'm not going to stay in Canada and spend the rest of my life in this sterile, middle-class, *galut* existence. It's fine for you, joining a committee at the Toronto Jewish Community Board, going to *shul* occasionally, and otherwise living like any other Canadian. But it's not enough for me. I'm not Moses Mendelssohn, willing to live 'as a Jew at home and a man (or woman) in the street'. I want to live as a Jew all of the time. I want to live a fully Jewish existence, and I can't do that here in *galut*. I can do that only in Israel."

They glare at each other in silence. Then he glances at his watch. "I have to go. It's getting late."

"I hate this," she says. "I wish we could start today all over again." She remembers what her father sometimes did when things in the family went wrong. He'd say, "Let's start over," or "Let's rewind," and they'd all agree to erase what had just happened; then they'd redo, re-enact, the discussion or activity, this time making it better, making it right. Now she asks Bobby pleadingly, "Can we pretend we just woke up and none of this ever happened?"

He snickers.

"I mean it. Not just our argument, but everything from this whole morning so far. All those articles I read before you came down. I want it all to go away."

"I know how to do that," he says. "I can make that go away."

"You can?" Her eyes open wide and childlike.

"Sure." With a flourish, he sweeps all the newspapers and magazines off the table onto the floor, where instantly they're out of sight.

Upstairs, after his shower, Bobby comes naked into the bedroom, and sees Judith, also naked, lying on the bed.

"You love me," she says. A statement, not a question.

"I do."

"You'll always love me."

"I will."

"You're sure."

He hesitates. "I'm sure. You drive me up the fuckin' wall sometimes, but yes, I'll always love you."

She opens her arms wide.

"I don't have time now," he says. "I'll be late for work."

She spreads her arms wider and spreads her legs, too.

Blushing, he says, "I can't. I *can't*. It's my first day as a junior partner."

"Just a hug, then."

He climbs onto the bed and onto her, wriggling into her arms for a hug. Her hand creeps down to his ass, and then she is undulating underneath him.

"Judith, I *can't* ..."

But he can. And he does. She makes love to him out of love, and sadness, and fear. She knows this thing between them will never work out, and she knows she'll have to leave him. But she loves him anyway, and she loves his hardness inside her and she loves his little-boy softness. She makes love to him sadly, crying in the middle. But he doesn't see.

— 3 —

The next eight days pass uneventfully. Judith works hard on her schoolwork on Wednesday, Thursday, and Friday till sundown. Shabbat is the same as usual, spent with Bobby, and on Sunday she studies some more. On Monday morning, she drives into school feeling anxious: What if there's another incident with Kerry or one of her gang? But there isn't. Everything seems exactly the same as before that occurred. Driving home from Dunhill, she concludes that what happened last week was just an aberration. There's no reason to believe it will happen again. Relieved and happy, she's very productive for the next three days.

On Thursday night, there's a SWAC meeting at seven o'clock. But beforehand, at 5:30, she's meeting Suzy for supper, so she leaves home early. The drive starts in the light and ends in the dark. She reaches Dunhill at 5:10 p.m., with twenty spare minutes till she has to meet Suzy. Just enough time to stop by the library and try once more to get a book she urgently needs for Greg's paper, due in four days. Three times she's come looking for *Black Women in Canada: Sisterhood and Struggle,* but someone has always had it out. Now she tries again, and here it is, sitting on the shelf as if waiting for her. She can barely believe her good luck. With relief and joy she signs it out. Now that she has the primary sources, thanks to this book — the first-hand stories, or "narratives," as she is learning to call them, of twelve Canadian black women — she's nearly guaranteed an *A* on her paper. This will almost certainly mean an academic excellence scholarship, which she desperately needs. The little money her father left her is going much faster than she expected. Happily, almost affectionately, she thumbs through the book as she goes to meet Suzy.

Le Petit Café is empty when she arrives except for a bearded guy sitting alone in a corner, wearing a beret as though acting out some fantasy of being in a petit café in Paris. The two student cafeteria workers wear peaked white paper hats, just like the ones her mother used to origami-fold for her, in miniature, out of the silver paper from packs of cigarettes. Silently the two workers clear off the garbage and leftover food from the tables and give each one a perfunctory wipe with a greasy rag. Through the narrow slits of windows so high up they touch the twenty-foot ceiling, she sees the black winter sky. This cafeteria is in a basement, and here, underground, everything is lit by glass pipes of fluorescent lighting all along the ceiling. Under these lights, and surrounded on all four sides by green walls, the twenty pink-and-aqua round tables give the eerie impression of strange, beautiful underwater plants, some species of waist-high marine mushrooms made of coral and turquoise. She feels as if she's inside an underwater observatory, like the one she visited in Eilat. Like she is floating in some exotic Red Sea world.

Suzy arrives. Spotting Judith, she smiles broadly and waves, and as Suzy walks toward her, Judith feels a great physical warmth spread throughout her body. Suzy greets her in a friendly way, bringing her face close as she says hello — almost kissing, but not — and touching her on the arm. They stroll to the food counter, where Suzy orders a salad. Judith would prefer something warm and comforting, like pizza, or that nice bubbling onion soup with the thick golden crown of melted cheese on top. But next to Suzy, so neat and petite, she feels big and broad-shouldered, an Amazon, muscular, even masculine. So she, too, orders a salad. They sit at a table in the almost deserted cafeteria, and while eating their crunchy uncomforting salads, Suzy tells her that until last year they served supper at their SWAC meetings. Just a light meal: sandwiches, fruit, cookies, and soft drinks. Still, it was nice. But those days are gone, Suzy says regretfully: there's no budget anymore for these kinds of perks. They chat about the most recent cutbacks at the university: the reduced hours at the library and the gym. Luckily, says Suzy, the School of Social Work has not yet been affected, but who knows what will happen when the new budget comes down next month? She hopes her contract will be renewed.

Judith is shocked. "What do you mean 'renewed'?" she asks. "You're such a staple of this school. I didn't know you were just on contract."

Suzy laughs. "Everyone assumes I'm tenured. But actually I could be fired at the drop of a hat. I never finished my doctorate because right at the beginning of collecting my data, Natalie was diagnosed with autism. So it's one-year contracts for me," she says. "Not that it's ever been a problem. I'm fine as long as there are no major cuts."

"I hope there won't be any," Judith says fervently.

"Thank you. So do I. But this university is in a financial crisis. I don't imagine our school, out of all the departments and programs, is going to be spared." With a sigh, she pushes aside her empty salad bowl, says, "Let's do some work," and pulls out of her pretty woven book bag the agenda she has typed for tonight's meeting. They review it together. Tonight is a straightforward continuation of the meeting two weeks ago: they'll continue planning Anti-oppression Day — hopefully Chris and Janice will have contacted Michael Brier about being the keynote — and then the committee will strike its two subcommittees: Teacher Evaluation and Admissions Outreach. Judith asks Suzy a quick question about the mandate of the Admissions Outreach committee and Suzy answers it. Judith says nothing seems to be missing from the agenda. Good, says Suzy, and now tells her some of the gossip — what Suzy prefers to call "the politics" — of this committee. Apparently, Brenda and James both competed for the same large research grant, and yesterday it was announced that Brenda got it and James didn't.

"So there may be some tension tonight between them," says Suzy.

Judith, happy to be in the know, flattered even, nods.

Suzy looks at her watch. "It's only 6:10! Great. We can relax for a while. I'm going to have a coffee. Can I get you one?"

"Sure! Thanks!" says Judith, reaching for her wallet, but Suzy waves her away ("My treat") and goes to the food counter. Judith, alone at the table, feels happy. Suzy likes her. They're becoming friends, just as she hoped. Suzy returns with two coffees and an enormous raisin cookie. "For us to share, if you like." Judith thanks her, breaks off a corner, and eats it. Suzy takes a sip of coffee and looks warmly at Judith.

"Remember how nervous you were the first day of school, and how I told you you'd be fine? Well, you're more than fine. This year you're our star pupil."

"Really?"

"Really. Last week all the faculty met to allocate the academic excellence scholarships, and your name was on everyone's list. So you'll definitely get a scholarship if you want one."

"Wow! That's great!"

"Yes. But I told them I was also planning to offer you a research assistantship, if my project gets funded."

"That would be wonderful. A scholarship *and* an RA'ship with you."

"Well, here's the thing, Judith: you can't get both at Dunhill. You'll have to choose."

"Oh. I didn't know."

"A scholarship is worth only half of an RA'ship: $1,500 compared to $3,000. So if money's a factor, you should definitely go for the RA'ship. But the trouble is I won't know until January whether I've got my grant, and the scholarships have to be decided on by December 1. So it's up to you. I'd love to have you as my RA. It would be fun. But possibly my project won't come through."

"I see," says Judith. She tries to think clearly while Suzy steadily gazes at her. She needs money. Just heating her father's old house is rapidly burning a hole through her inheritance. Plus it would look good on her resumé to have either an RA'ship or a scholarship. Especially an RA'ship. But what if Suzy's grant doesn't come through? She weighs this possibility and dismisses it. Suzy will probably get her grant. She has every year for the past three. Anyway, how can she refuse Suzy? It would feel disloyal.

As if she didn't value their special relationship. She says, "My first choice is working with you. So I'll take my chances."

Suzy's eyes light up gratefully. "I'm so glad. I was hoping you'd say that. I'll let you know the second I hear anything."

"It's a deal," says Judith.

Her father always said that: "It's a deal." Even when she was a small child. "I'll teach you how to ride your bike after supper if you finish your vegetables — it's a deal." This phrase was the equivalent of the red wax seal on a legal document. An incontrovertible giving of one's word. Sometimes her father followed "It's a deal" with a solemn handshake. But of course she isn't going to shake Suzy's hand right now. It would be too formal. Instead she breaks off another piece of the cookie and puts it into her mouth. *The mouth*, she thinks. *The place of vows.*

"One more thing I'd like to ask you," Suzy says. "The school is currently involved in a re-accreditation process, and each faculty member is supposed to ask two students for their honest evaluation, so we can include the student perspective in our report. So is there anything about the M.S.W. program we should know about? Anything we could improve upon? I truly want to know your opinion."

Judith hesitates.

"We're not quoting anyone by name," says Suzy. "So feel free to tell me whatever you like."

Judith reflects on what happened ten days ago in Greg's class. She's not sure, though, she should tell Suzy about this. What if she doesn't understand? She looks at her face and sees genuine interest and openness there. But still she isn't sure. If she tells Suzy, obviously she will be identifiable in the report. No one else at Dunhill has any connection with Israel.

"Please tell me," says Suzy. "If something is wrong, I want to know. I want our program to be the best it can be."

Judith looks into Suzy's eyes. Suzy has taught them that when in doubt, check out the person's nonverbal behaviour, especially their eye contact. "It's easy to lie with words," she told them, "but almost impossible to lie with your body." Right now her pretty brown eyes, looking back at Judith, are warm. Listening. Intelligent. I can trust her, Judith thinks. She'll understand.

"A week ago Monday in Greg's class ..." she begins, and tells Suzy the whole story. She also tells her about what she read last week at Bobby's house, and Bobby's analysis of the relationship between anti-Israelism and antisemitism. Suzy frowns throughout, looking grave and troubled as Judith speaks. She doesn't interrupt, though, letting Judith pour everything out until she's finished.

Then Suzy says, "I can see how upsetting this was for you, Judith, and of course why it would be. So first of all, I'm concerned about you. But I'm also concerned about the larger issue here. Obviously people are allowed to hold many different opinions at this school — about Israel or anything else. That is part of democracy. It's freedom of speech, and also academic freedom, and you can't touch those rights. One wouldn't even want to. But if there is antisemitism — and I'm not sure about that yet, though I have to say that's a very interesting, even compelling, analysis you just offered, I've never heard any of that before. But if what just happened in Greg's class was, in fact, antisemitism — if it crossed the line that separates free speech from hate speech — then that is something else entirely. That would be completely unacceptable at this school, and we would have to deal with that."

"Thank you," says Judith gratefully.

"Don't thank me," says Suzy. "It's not a favour to you. It's for all of us." She pauses, and then adds with intensity, "Antisemitism is a terrible thing."

Judith, watching her closely, thinks, Yes, she does understand. Suzy now tells her that for two years in high school she had a Jewish boyfriend whose parents were Holocaust survivors, so she knows something about all this first-hand. "I even picked up a few Yiddish words," she says ruefully. "Like *antisemitten*." Judith laughs, astounded. Coming from a non-Jew, Suzy's understanding seems so unexpectedly complete and warm-hearted that Judith has to restrain herself from reaching across the table and clasping her hand.

"Everyone has the right to feel safe at this school," says Suzy. "No one here should ever feel attacked or marginalized. All of us, all the faculty, feel very strongly about this."

Judith nods. She feels quite emotional now — so much so that she doesn't trust herself to speak. Suzy won't let something like this happen again. She will make this school a safe place for her. She'll protect her.

"I'm a bit surprised, though, at Greg," Suzy says, "for not picking up on this. This isn't like him. But he's not himself lately. His wife is sick, you know."

"I didn't."

"It's breast cancer, quite advanced, and Greg is taking it very hard. I'm not making excuses for him. But maybe that's why he missed the boat. That's unlike him — he's usually terrific."

"I know. That's why I felt so bad. I couldn't understand ..."

"You really should go talk to him," says Suzy. "He's a good and caring person, and I'm sure he has no idea how you experienced all this. I'll bet if you shared with him what you've just shared with me, he would be very concerned. I don't know what he'd do about it exactly, but you would definitely be heard and taken very seriously. I don't have to tell you how well-liked and respected you are at this school."

Judith feels not only flattered by this, but also like someone tall and strong. Not small, frightened, or helpless anymore. She is an adult standing five-foot-six, not a child half that height.

She can fight back, appropriately and with dignity. She can assert herself on behalf of Israel, referring to universal rights and principles. *Of course!* she thinks. *Of course I'll talk to Greg. How silly of me not to have thought of it myself. And how unfair to have doubted him for the past ten days, without giving him a chance to explain himself. To not give him the benefit of the doubt.*

"That's a great idea," she says to Suzy. "Thank you."

"No need to thank me, Judith. But I'm glad you're going to follow up on this." Suzy's eyes are so earnest there can be no doubt about her sincerity. "It's a very important thing," she says. Then she glances at her watch. "Six-thirty. Twenty more minutes till we have to go upstairs. Would you like another coffee before we leave?"

Judith shakes her head. "No, thanks. But you go ahead." While she waits, she thinks that their conversation so far has been all about her. It needs a reverse in direction, it needs some reciprocity. So when Suzy returns — looking very professional in her white silk shirt with little navy blue squares all over it and a matching navy blue blazer with a brooch — Judith asks her about her family. Suzy smiles, but Judith sees sadness flash for an instant into and out of her eyes.

"Oh," Suzy says with what looks like bravery, "the usual chaos."

Judith nods. Suzy taught them last week that if you ask a client a question and don't get a real answer, you should ask a second, follow-up question to show you're sincerely interested. So now she asks Suzy how Natalie is and tries using all the other listening skills she's learned from Suzy. She wants to show her she is genuinely interested, and not just a taker, but a giver, too. Natalie isn't doing that well, Suzy says. She has a new teacher this year who neither likes nor understands her, so Natalie is very frustrated, and when she's frustrated, she tantrums a lot and doesn't sleep at night. Which means that neither does Suzy.

Judith is sympathetic. "What about the rest of the family?" she asks.

Suzy gives a short snort of a laugh. "Systems Theory 101," she says. The other kids are not sleeping well either, especially their youngest, Todd, who recently started acting out at school. And Dennis gets annoyed at being awakened all the time — he needs to be mentally sharp for work, he says. So sometimes Suzy is so desperate to get Natalie back to sleep in the middle of the night, she brings Natalie into their bed. But Natalie kicks in her sleep, and after a while Dennis goes and sleeps on the couch. Suzy sighs. "It's hard trading everyone off. Wait till you have kids." Then she adds hastily, "Of course, hopefully yours won't have special challenges ..."

Now it is Judith's turn for a moment of sadness, like the return of a boomerang that she herself threw. Will she ever have kids? Will she ever even get married? But she pushes this away and tries to focus only on Suzy, as a good interviewer would. "It *is* very hard," she says, looking at Suzy empathically. "I know from working with kids like Natalie in Israel how difficult it is for the parents, always trying to balance everything and everybody. I don't think most people grasp what it's like parenting a child like this."

A flare goes off in Suzy's eyes, a flash of gold. "No, they don't," she says, "and people can be so judgmental."

Judith feels like she's back in Israel, working as the social worker at the Beit Aharon kindergarten for children with developmental challenges. There, a statement like this would have led her supervisor, Shifra, to suggest Judith ask for an example, to clarify what specifically is bothering this person. So now, as if reciting lines from an old but familiar script, she asks, "Which people do you mean exactly? Neighbours? Friends? Family?"

"Everyone. Even Dennis's parents. They're so worried whenever we're there, in case Natalie breaks something or stains their precious couch or carpet. All they care about is their stupid furniture. Sometimes I almost feel like setting Natalie up — like telling her, 'We're going to Gramma and Grandpa's now, honey, and while we're there, why don't you go take some of these nice very ripe strawberries and schmear them all over their new white couch?"

Judith squints at Suzy for a second. Then they're laughing — laughing, laughing, laughing — and when they're done, Suzy wipes her eyes. Then they look at each other and burst out laughing again. Eventually, their laughter spends itself. They gaze affectionately at one another, and Judith feels herself sinking into Suzy's brown eyes, falling into them. To make this stop, she asks, "What about Dennis? Does he feel the same way?"

Suzy shrugs. "Well, no — they're his parents, after all. But it's not only that — even in general it's different for him. You know how it is with men: they have their work. They leave the house early in the morning and come home late at night. Don't get me wrong — Dennis is a great guy. But — what can I say? — he's a guy."

Judith laughs and rolls her eyes. "I know what you mean."

"I know you do. Which is why I can say that to you. Speaking of which, how's Bobby?"

Again Judith feels a stab of sadness. *How's Bobby?* She looks into Suzy's kind but discerning eyes. "He's okay," she says. "But sort of like Dennis. He's a great guy, but he's a guy."

Suzy nods appreciatively. But now Judith feels guilty to have spoken this way about Bobby, and she tries to explain. "He *is* great. But I don't know." She pauses. "Lately we're not getting along."

"In what way, Judith?" Suzy asks gently.

She looks into Suzy's eyes, and again, there's that feeling of falling, of losing control. Then, starting with just four innocuous words, "Like yesterday at breakfast," she tells Suzy everything. In a torrent of words she didn't mean to spill out, she tells her not only about yesterday's argument, but also more generally how Bobby doesn't share her ideals or her politics — meaning he doesn't love Israel or hate oppression — so, even though they love each other, they don't, essentially, have anything in common. So it's clear to her now that they're going to break up. She is going back to Israel, and he won't consider moving there, and anyway she probably needs an altogether different sort of man. Suzy listens with her brown eyes warm and entirely focused on Judith, as if she were the only person in the world. And there is something extraordinary, something almost hypnotic, about being listened to this way, so Judith just wants to go on talking, and talking, and talking, even though another part of her knows she should stop. Because she feels vulnerable opening up like this. And also disloyal: she knows she is betraying Bobby. But somehow she can't stop herself. It's as if her centre of gravity has shifted, and now Suzy feels closer to her and more important than Bobby. With Bobby, everything she thinks or feels gets challenged or argued with: every conversation is a battle to be won. Whereas Suzy accepts all her thoughts and feelings, like in her weekly logs. It's such a relief to be able to talk like this.

Finally the hydrant runs dry and she comes to an abrupt stop. "I'm sorry," she says sheepishly. "I didn't mean to go on like this."

Suzy touches her on the arm. A light, soft touch. "Don't be silly," she says. "I asked because I'm interested. If we can't talk about our problems with the people who care about us, then who *can* we talk to?"

The people who care about us. Suzy cares about her. This is Suzy's most open acknowledgment yet of the special relationship between them.

"Whatever happens between you and Bobby," Suzy adds, "remember, Judith, you still have me and all your friends here at this school. I know you have very close friends in Israel. But you're not alone here in Canada."

"Thank you," says Judith, feeling very moved.

Suzy glances at her watch. "It's five to seven!" she says. "We'd better go."

They quickly clear their table and hurry to the elevator. Waiting for it, Judith recalls the joke about two Israelis in the Zionist Federation building. Yoram is waiting for the elevator. When it arrives, the door opens and the man inside it asks him in Hebrew if he is going down: "*Yordim?*"

"Of course not!" Yoram replies indignantly. "We're only here for the year." This joke is a play on the verb meaning "to go down" or "descend," and its related noun. This verb also means to permanently leave Israel, understood as a form of spiritual descent tinged with the shame of abandoning the Holy Land. *Yordim* are the Israelis who have done this. Israelis living abroad are so guilt-ridden about having left Israel that even an exchange about an elevator can be taken as an attack on their spiritual and ideological adequacy. Judith has always loved this joke, primarily because she knows it will never be about her.

The elevator doors open and they get in. Judith considers telling Suzy the elevator joke, but decides it's too complicated. They ride to the sixth floor and walk down the long hallway, to the click-click-clicking of Suzy's heels. Judith notices she and Suzy are in perfect step with each other. And for a while she's aware of nothing else except the musky, sweet smell of Suzy's perfume.

There are only two people in the meeting room. By way of explanation, Janice points out the window. It started snowing heavily while Judith and Suzy were at supper underground. Brenda says everyone will be late: the traffic is terrible, and at the university gates there's a huge lineup of cars trying to get onto the campus. Judith stands by the window, looking down at the cars in the parking lot. Hers, like all the others, is covered with a light dusting of powdery snow. White like the morphine powder she's seen in pictures (her father took morphine pills for pain near the end). As if this drug is spilled over everything tonight. She feels a bit drugged, too, watching the white floating powder land on all the cars and the ground and the trees, everywhere, sharply white against the darkness. In some places, especially near the lamps, the snow on the cars sparkles like rhinestones. Like tiny explosions of light, she thinks. Or tiny bombs of hope. She stays there watching, until Lola touches her shoulder and says, "We're starting."

Judith sits where she put her purse to mark her place. Though there was no need for that: everyone's sitting in the same place as last time, as though they've come to a theatre with personally reserved seats. It's already 7:25 p.m., but Suzy welcomes everyone with her usual relaxed charm, setting a light, pleasant tone. The first of the two items on the agenda is "Planning for Anti-oppression Day," and "1A" is finalizing the keynote speaker. Chris reports that since the last meeting two weeks ago, he and Janice have been in touch with Michael Brier and he's agreed to be their keynote.

"Great!" says Suzy, and people nod and smile. Judith nods, too, hoping she looks as pleased as everyone else — or anyway neutral, since she still has no idea who Michael Brier is.

"For such a reasonable fee, too," says Chris, "considering his international reputation." Apparently Brier agreed to come for SWAC's usual $300 honorarium, a steal for someone of his celebrity. But he's willing to do it, he told Chris yesterday, because Dunhill's Students' Union has, over the past two years, become renowned for its courageous public stands against oppression.

Chris says this proudly, and Judith recalls he's the school's rep to the union.

Suzy thanks Chris and Janice, and the meeting continues. The agenda contains five additional Anti-oppression Day items, and the committee discusses every aspect of Anti-oppression Day in mind-deadening detail: the publicity strategy, lunch arrangements, composition of the mid-morning panel, parking vouchers, who will do the introductions and thank-yous. *What stupid trivia*, she thinks. *Parking vouchers, lunch menus — is this what an anti-oppression committee should be spending its time on?* But then she sighs resignedly. She knows that dealing with this trivia is necessary: fighting the evil in the world must be done one banal detail at a time. The meeting proceeds tediously, prosaically, and she drifts in and out of the discussions, gazing out the window at the gracefully falling snow, feeling almost like she's a snowflake, twirling down slowly in a spiral dance, curling, swirling its way down from the sky. The snow is hypnotizing. It seems extraordinary to her, and enchanting, after all those snowless years in Israel.

The committee finishes planning Anti-oppression Day, and now there's only one other topic for tonight: the formation of SWAC's two subcommittees. Brenda will chair Teacher Evaluation and Carl, Admissions Outreach. Everyone around the table volunteers for one of them, and Judith, as pre-arranged with Suzy, joins Teacher Evaluation. Suzy suggests that each subcommittee report back to SWAC at every second meeting, and people assent.

"Good," says Suzy. She glances at her watch. Judith admires it: a dazzling gold oval studded with emeralds all around its face. It must have been a gift from Dennis. Maybe for an anniversary. Suzy smiles. "We started late because of the snow, and we've finished eight minutes early! What an efficient group! Now we can go home — or anyway, try to in this crazy weather. It looks like a blizzard's brewing. Unless there's other business?"

People shake their heads, looking anxiously out the window. The snow is swirling faster than before. Judith is worried. It might take two, even three, hours to get home. If she can get there at all. She can picture herself stranded in the middle of the highway.

"I have something," says Chris.

"Yes?"

"The title of Brier's talk," Chris says. "Lola and I need this very soon. We can't start on publicity without a title, and Brier offered us three topics he's willing to speak on."

"We do have some time left," says Suzy. "We can take a minute for this, if it's okay with everyone."

It's not okay with Judith. She badly wants to get home. The others don't look happy either. But Janice and Lola, who both live in Dunhill, agree, and Chris proceeds.

"Here's the three titles: 'The New Anti-globalization Movement: Solidarity, Democracy, and Citizens' Rights in South America.' 'Anti-oppression and Equity Around the Globe.' And 'Zionist Imperialism and Oppression in the Middle East.'"

Judith feels her stomach drop, as if she's in an elevator that has fallen too fast. Instinctively she glances at Suzy, but her face shows nothing. A perfect poker face.

"I like the last one best," says James. Judith feels nauseated. "It's very timely and topical, and I expect it'll bring out the most people. Which is what we're after, isn't it? The other two topics we've heard quite a lot about lately. There was that guy who was here two weeks ago — what was his name?"

"Claude Rossignol." These are the first words Hetty has spoken at this meeting.

"That's right," says James. "But the Middle East — very relevant."

"What about the rest of you?" Suzy asks evenly. Her eyes for just a second slide sideways toward Judith. *She understands,* thinks Judith, and immediately feels a bit safer and less afraid. Suzy will manage this.

"I agree with James," says Chris. "This was the topic that leaped out at me. And Janice, too." He looks at Janice and she nods.

Suzy looks around the table brightly. Like a robin, an eager, ever-hopeful, fragile-boned robin. "Anyone else? Any other comments?" Suzy asks. She looks around the table at each person in turn, ending with Judith.

Judith wants to speak, but can't. It's back again, that same paralysis that filled her in Greg's class, starting in the pit of her stomach and freezing everything inside her, up to and including her mouth. As if cement had been poured inside her, turning her into stone. *I must say something*, she thinks. *Speak now, before the moment passes.* There's silence, and Suzy is looking at her expectantly. She trusts Suzy. She will speak to her. But only to her. To Suzy alone, she says, "I like the second title."

"What?" asks Carl. "Could you speak louder?"

She turns toward Carl, and pushes her voice past the knot in her throat. "I prefer the second title," she says more loudly. Everyone around the table is looking at her, and she sees that she needs to say something more. But what? All she can think of is what she feels but can't say, which is: "Leave us alone. Why is it always Israel, Israel, Israel? Go pick on somebody else for a change." Then she hears herself say, "It's a very interesting topic, anti-oppression and global equity. Much more than the others. It's also really important." She stops. With Chris and Janice glowering at her from the other side of the table, this is the best she can do. She knows she hasn't spoken well, she hasn't presented much of an argument. But at least she's said something.

Hetty says, "I agree with Judith." Judith looks at her, surprised. "The first title is not suitable," Hetty continues, "because it doesn't have enough of a focus on anti-oppression, and I don't want the third one, because — unlike James — I feel we've heard a lot about the Middle East lately. Personally I'd very much like to hear what Brier has to say about the second topic: the anti-globalization movement and its relationship to other social rights movements around the world. This sounds fascinating and is very relevant to social work."

She knows how to play the game, thinks Judith admiringly. *She's smarter than I am. She gave reasons, she used her mind. I don't have a mind right now.*

Hetty, sitting at the foot of the table, is looking straight ahead of her. Judith tries to catch her eye to thank her, but Hetty refuses to be caught, holding on stubbornly to her independence, her neutrality.

Suzy looks pale and strained. "Two against two," she says with a tense little laugh. "And only three minutes left till it's 8:30 and our meeting ends, or else we're all going to get stranded and have to sleep here tonight. I suggest we table this decision till our next meeting when we have more time."

"No," Lola says belligerently. "We should decide this now. Chris and I need to know the title of Brier's talk so we can start working on the email flyer. Also, your numbers are wrong. The vote so far isn't two against two. It's three against two — Chris, Janice, and James against Judith and Hetty — and with my vote it's four against two. I vote also for the third topic: 'Zionist Imperialism and Oppression.'"

Judith turns to her left and stares at Lola, who looks proud of herself. *Lola Katz*, Judith thinks. *A Jew from Montreal. How could you?*

"I see what's happening in Israel," Lola continues, "as a fundamental microcosm of all the other oppressions happening now in the world. It's the crucial nexus bringing all of them together. So, to me, side-stepping this topic because we're afraid of offending a few people" — she glances at Judith, and Judith feels this glance like a slap in the face — "is wrong."

"I'm not 'offended,'" says Judith, feeling herself flush.

Lola shrugs and looks away. There's a heavy silence in the room.

Suzy scans the table, avoiding looking at Judith. "Would anyone else like to comment? Brenda? Carl?"

Brenda shrugs. "I'm easy. All three topics sound fine to me, as long as they're discussed" — she glances at Judith — "in a respectful manner. But Suzy's right, we have to finish very soon, or none of us will be able to get our cars out of the parking lot."

Suzy looks questioningly at Carl.

"I agree about ending now," Carl says. "I have an hour-long drive ahead of me. About the title, I'm with Brenda. I'm okay with whatever the rest of you decide."

"Since everybody seems so worried about the weather," says Suzy, "maybe we should adjourn now. Or should I call a vote? What do you prefer?"

"You should call the vote," says Lola, with her big pouty lips. Judith turns away — she doesn't even want to look at her. "Not that I see why you need to," Lola says. "We already cast our votes, and it's clear what the majority on this committee wants. And as far as I understand democracy, the side with the majority is supposed to win. I don't think, Suzy, you should be trying to fudge this vote."

Suzy, startled, turns very pale. But before she can even answer, James says, speaking directly to Lola, "You're right. The people have spoken."

"Yes," says Chris. "We've obviously chosen number three."

There is a brief pause. Then Suzy says, "Okay. Number three it is."

Judith sits numbly. Suzy thanks everyone for coming to tonight's meeting and reminds them of the date of the next one.

But Judith doesn't hear a single word. She's not here anymore. She's outside with the snow. She's a snowflake. Falling, falling, falling from the sky.

— 4 —

It takes her two and a half hours to get home that night, and the next morning she awakens to a great silence. Looking out the window, she sees that the snow is piled high all around the house and the street has all but disappeared: it's nothing but a slight dip in the expanse of snow between her front yard and the one opposite. It has obviously snowed all night, and everything is white — not just the ground, but the sky and even the air. She returns to bed and snuggles under the warm quilt, feeling cozy. Happy, too, because today, November 8, is her birthday. Today she's thirty-three, a "double-same-digit" birthday, a term invented by her friend Marnie when they were both eleven to describe the specialness of their birthdays that year. Judith's birthday is also special because it falls just three days after the date when Rabin was assassinated, and the first memorial she attended for him took place on her birthday. So on birthdays she often reminisces about him. This morning, though, she's thinking what a silent birthday this one is. No incessant ringing of the phone like in Jerusalem, where all her friends called her first thing in the morning to sing "Happy Birthday" in Hebrew in gleeful, off-key voices. Two years ago, her last birthday in Jerusalem, the phone rang repeatedly, and then the doorbell rang too, and there stood Bruria holding out a posy of pink and purple cyclamens from her garden. Maybe this year there will be some Happy Birthday emails from her friends in Israel, although that won't be quite the same. No one will phone her this morning, not even Bobby — he's in court until two o'clock. But tonight, Friday night, he's making dinner for her at his place, even though it's really her turn.

The house is disturbingly silent. Last year at this time, this house wasn't hers, but her father's. He was still alive, even though sick, and sitting up in bed that day, he warmly wished her a Happy Birthday. She hears now his kind, raspy voice saying to her in Yiddish what he said to her every year on her birthday: "*Biz hundert un tsvantsik,*" meaning May you live to 120.

She, as always, answered back: "Why only till 120? What's wrong with 121?"

Now she feels terribly lonely — and as if one can run away from loneliness, she hurries downstairs to the kitchen. In honour of her birthday, she eschews the usual breakfast cereal and instead eats a huge hunk of chocolate layer cake, then steals some icing from the rest of the cake, sucking it off her finger with guilty pleasure. Then she works on her paper for Greg, due this Monday. She starts by reading the book she got yesterday, *Black Women in Canada: Sisterhood and Struggle,* and soon is outraged at the crap that black women in Canada had to put up with in the past, and still do sometimes even now. Some of it reminds her of things that happened to Jews in Canada when her father was growing up. Like that sign he saw as a young boy: *No dogs or Jews allowed.* She identifies easily with the black women in this book, identifying as a woman because of the sexism they experience, but also as a Jew because of the racism, since it's obvious to her that racism and antisemitism are fundamentally the same thing. Hate. Though not all women of colour understand this, she thinks. Some do, but some don't. The same with other groups, too: gays, Native people, whatever. Just because you recognize their oppression doesn't mean they recognize yours. There is something asymmetrical about this. Something wrong. Just like what happened last night at SWAC was wrong. Now the pain and fear from that comes rushing back at her again.

But, she recalls, as she was leaving the room after the meeting, Suzy said to her quietly, laying a hand on her arm, "We'll talk." Which meant, she thinks now, "Don't worry. We'll figure something out. We'll fight this somehow." Judith doesn't understand the administrative workings of the school well enough to know what Suzy can realistically do to alter the outcome of yesterday's vote. But she is sure she'll come up with a plan. There is no way Suzy will let the keynote lecture on Anti-oppression Day turn into a platform for bashing Israel.

Shit, what a lousy birthday. She doesn't want to be spending her birthday reflecting on different forms of hatred; this should be a day not for hate, but for love. For pleasure, not for politics. She wishes at least one person had called her this morning or given her a birthday present. Then she remembers. Before leaving FRANK last night, she checked her mailbox and there was a parcel waiting for her: a gift bag from Aliza with pictures of red and yellow balloons all over it. She'd forgotten all about it until now. She rushes to her schoolbag and takes out the gift bag. Inside it there's something hard covered in soft green tissue paper. Slowly she unwraps it. It's ... oh, no, it can't be. It's a vibrator. Aliza has bought her a lime-green vibrator for her birthday. *Wow*, she thinks, *this is too weird. It is so ... vulgar. So not-me.*

But at the same time she's laughing. It's so weird it's funny. She runs her fingers over the fake lime-green penis with little bumps on it. Then she touches, halfway up the penis, a clear plastic ring containing little silver balls. "For extra stimulation to the entrance to the vagina," it says on the box. And what's this? Jutting out from the base of the penis at a forty-five degree angle there's an appendage with a little cat on the end of it, its tiny tongue protruding. According to the box, this tongue moves, and it's for licking the clitoris. *Oy*, she thinks, blushing. *How could Aliza...? Doesn't she know me at all?* This present is ridiculous and embarrassing. Also a bit scary. Who puts things like that inside their body? Aren't you supposed to keep electrical objects away from anything wet? She read in the newspaper once about a guy who died when his radio fell into his bathwater. Maybe this vibrator could electrocute her.

She goes into the kitchen and eats lunch. Then she plans her paper for Greg. Within a couple of hours she has her outline done, and she has blocked out, as in sewing, all the main ideas in her thesis. At 2:30 she takes a break. Standing at the kitchen counter, she noisily cracks open peanuts in the shell, and happily crunches and munches. Then, walking back toward the computer, the vibrator on the living room couch catches her eye. She picks it up. Her only birthday present so far this year. Her mother always taught her to treat presents with respect. Even if an exchange slip is enclosed, she told her, you should never return a gift, and you should try to use it as often as you can. True to her principle, her mother often wore a hideous olive green scarf her best friend Joyce gave her for her birthday, so Joyce wouldn't know she didn't like it and be hurt. But then because she wore it almost every time she saw her, Joyce thought her mother loved it and had no other scarves, so for her next birthday she bought her another one just like it! Except even more hideous: this one in dark brown, the exact colour of shit.

Now Judith, following the directions on the box, washes Aliza's gift with soap and lukewarm water, and then dries it. She lies on the couch, gingerly puts it in position, and holding her breath, inserts it into her vagina. Nothing happens. Not only nothing bad; nothing at all. Now she gets ready to turn it on. The penis and the cat have separate controls: two adjacent sliding mechanisms, the bottom of each one — the place closest to her body — being zero, and the top — farthest from her body — being ten. With her left hand she holds the vibrator in place, while with her right she feels for the two slide controls and moves them together very slightly upward. There's a low, dull, humming sound, *mmmmm*, like a vacuum cleaner — nothing threatening about it in the least. *It's nothing*, she thinks, feeling only a slight vibration, *like when you lean against a dryer that's on. What a relief.* So now she pushes up the buttons just a bit more, and instantly, with the louder hum, she feels sensations racing through her body, causing an inner trembling. The cat licking her clitoris makes her cry out. She reaches for the sliding mechanism to lower the intensity, but in her confusion accidentally increases it. The vibrator goes wild, the penis and the cat both go faster and faster, more and more frantically. She cries out from the sensations in her body — she's never felt anything like this before. But she's also lost control, and she's frightened — she's been taken over by this machine, and everything's happening so quickly and crazily in her body, she's confused and can't recall how to turn it off.

Then everything stops. There's no vibrating in her body anymore. But there is a vibrating in her hand — that thing is outside her body now, it's still in her hand, she is holding it, she must have pulled it out of her somehow. Thank God. This was like "The Sorcerer's Apprentice" story in the Disney movie *Fantasia*, where the brooms come to life and take over. She peers at the two dials on the vibrator, turns them both off, and exhausted, rests with her eyes shut. After a minute something warm gushes out of her. She dozes off.

An hour later she awakens. At first she's confused. Then she remembers and blushes. Then laughs. She looks curiously at the vibrator. Like at a new friend, but a slightly dangerous one. She touches the cat's licking tongue very cautiously, as if it were a live cat. She studies the volume controls and turns each of them on again, playing with them separately, then together, going back and forth between zero and ten till she has it figured out. Carefully she sets them now at four, and slides the vibrator deep inside her. A few seconds later she says, "Oh God," and starts to moan.

— 5 —

Several hours later Judith is at Bobby's, eating her birthday meal. It's a traditional Friday night dinner but features some of her favourite foods, all Israeli: carrot-and-raisin salad, falafel, and babaganouj, and for dessert persimmons and pomegranates, alongside a gateau St. Honoré. Everything is attractively presented and delicious, and on her second glass of excellent red wine, Judith tells Bobby about her present from Aliza. How weird it was, but still she tried it. She asks if he would like to sometime.

He laughs. "You're serious?" Then he grimaces. "I don't know. Why? Do you think we need it?"

"No. I just thought it might be fun."

"Hmm. Can I think about it?"

"No problem."

"Which reminds me," says Bobby, "I have a present for you, too. Nothing quite so titillating, however."

"That's fine. I've had enough titillation for one day."

He reaches into his pocket and presents her with an emerald ring. "It's emerald," he says, "to match your eyes."

She holds it uncertainly. "What is it …?"

"A ring."

"I know it's a ring. I mean — what kind of ring?"

"Whatever kind you want it to be," he says. "It can be a regular ring, or it can magically turn — *presto magico!* — into an engagement ring. With just a word from you." She is looking down at the ring. "I know you don't believe in engagement rings or any of that stuff — you think it's bourgeois crap." She looks at him gratefully. "So whatever you're comfortable with." Then he adds, "Of course, I know what *I'd* like it to be."

She is closely examining the ring. "It's beautiful," she whispers. "Emerald. Like Emerald City. But —" she looks up at him almost fearfully — "is it really okay if I wear it just as a ring? I can't —"

"That's fine. But remember, it's magic. It can transform anytime. You just have to wish it."

"Thank you," she says, and kisses him.

"Put it on."

She does. Gingerly. Then holds it up to the light. It glints slightly. Like Bobby's eyes as, smiling, he watches her. But when he starts kissing her face and neck, and then leads her, with one finger hooked into one of hers, to the living room couch, she takes off the ring and places it carefully on the coffee table. "In case it cuts you," she explains. But it's also, she knows as he kisses and mounts her, in case it changes anything. In case he thinks he owns her now.

— 6 —

Two nights later, at 1:30 a.m. on Monday, Judith sits at her desk, finishing her paper for Greg. She's typing the bibliography while her printer spews out the final draft of the essay. She's happy with it. Another *A* coming down the pipe. Because it has just the right balance of scholarship and passion. At Dunhill, she's learned, it's just as important to demonstrate one's social conscience as one's intellectual knowledge. She prints her bibliography and staples the paper together. She's about to shut her computer, but first, almost in an automatic reflex, she clicks onto *Ha'aretz*, the left-wing Israeli newspaper. The *Ha'aretz* screen on her computer is always open along with Word and Outlook, and she clicks on it regularly, to follow what's happening in Israel and reassure herself that things there are all right. Or anyway no worse than they were an hour before. She also checks *Ha'aretz* every night one last time right before going to bed, in what has become a pre-sleep ritual — a kind of modern-day version of the *Kriat Shma*, the traditional Jewish bedtime prayer.

The *Ha'aretz* screen has a large headline in red:

SUICIDE BOMBER TARGETS JERUSALEM CHILDREN —
16 DEAD, 28 INJURED

Staring in shock, she reads. This is the fourth terrorist attack in three weeks, but this one is different from the others. This one involves children, and also it's just six blocks away from her Jerusalem apartment. It's in the heart of her neighbourhood, Baka — right at the main intersection, the corner of Bethlehem Road and Yehuda Street. In Israel it's already Monday morning, and the bomb went off forty minutes ago, at 7:50 a.m., the peak of rush hour, since 8:00 a.m. is when school and work begin. There are three elementary schools within a four-block radius: one religious, one secular, and one for the developmentally disabled — she knows kids at each of them. So this intersection forty minutes ago was packed with young children on their way to school, waiting at the light to be led across by the crossing guard. Of the sixteen dead, thirteen were under the age of nine, and of the twenty-eight injured, twenty were children. "Injured," she knows from previous suicide bombings, means these children will have lost hands, feet, limbs, stomachs, spinal cords, eyes, and ears. She knows, too, that soon the volunteers will come, the ones who after terrorist attacks collect the body parts strewn all over the street: fingers, toes, noses, mouths, calves, torsos, and skulls. In order to — in accordance with Jewish law — bury together, wherever possible, the different parts of a human being.

Judith turns on the TV, finds CBC, and immediately recognizes the intersection, *her* intersection, where thousands of times she bought fruit from the fruit store, newspapers from the newsstand, roses from the boy beside the hummus kiosk, and tampons from the drug store to stop her flow of blood. But now the blood is flowing all over the street. On TV she sees her fruit store is gone, just like it was never there, and so is her newsstand. Anxiously she strains to catch a glimpse of Tamar and Benny's home — they live just seven buildings down from that corner, in a white stucco house with a black wrought-iron gate. But she can't. All she sees are children's colourful lunchboxes lying in the street, notebooks riffling in the wind, and some torn clothing.

Now on the screen appears a guy named Yossi, an eyewitness to the attack and the owner of a falafel restaurant a few blocks down the street. Yossi is about thirty-five, and his shirt is unbuttoned almost halfway down to his bellybutton, showing off a hairy chest and a gold chain around his neck. By his dress he looks like a cocky, macho Israeli male. But now he's standing, dazed, in front of his restaurant. In heavily accented English he says, "I am in my restaurant, and I hear a big noise — BOOM! Very, very big. So I look outside, and I see flying past my window a doll, the head of a doll, with blond hair. But then I see this isn't a doll; it's the head of a little girl."

In the background, behind Yossi, there are ambulances and police cars, and men in charge rushing around frenetically gesticulating and shouting in Hebrew, "Move! Move! Out of the way!" There's the sound of sirens, and people are running in every direction, and there's screaming, wailing, and sobbing. A woman behind Yossi is rocking back and forth and screeching over and over, "My baby! Where's my baby?!"

Yossi the falafel guy disappears, and Judith sees, in his place, a Canadian anchorman, wearing a neatly pressed white shirt and holding a mike that says: CBC News.

"The Martyrs of Vengeance have claimed responsibility for this attack," he says calmly, in a voice that is matter-of-fact, professional, and free of regret or any other emotion. "They have also indicated that more attacks on Israeli children can be expected in the weeks ahead."

There's a brief pause, the length of three heartbeats. Now he is gone, replaced by a blonde woman in a royal blue suit and big white-and-gold paste earrings.

"Next in the news," she says cheerfully, and announces the second disaster, the second great tragedy, of the day: someone high up in the Conservative Party has just defected to the Liberals. "A great betrayal," this woman in blue says dramatically. Judith switches off the TV, but she does not go to bed.

Are you okay? Are you okay? Are you okay? Are you okay? Are you okay? Twenty emails fly out from her to the twenty people she cares about the most over there. She knows these emails of hers, which she sends off every time there is an attack, won't accomplish anything: they won't save, prevent, help, alleviate, or change anything or anyone. Whoever is dead is dead. Whoever has lost the bottom half of their body has already lost the bottom half of their body. But she sends them anyway. It's all she can do. It's her way of saying, *I am in the west, but my heart is in the east.* Then she waits. It takes until 5:00 a.m. to hear back from her friends, because the Internet connections always get overloaded after an attack. Finally she receives an email from Bruria saying that Tamar, Benny, and their kids are fine. Luckily they'd all already left the house ten minutes before the bomb went off. Judith sighs with relief. Then she reads: *Their house, however, has been reduced to rubble.*

Shit. How ironic, too, that of all her friends, it's Tamar and Benny this has happened to. Tamar and Benny, who twice monthly travel to Palestinian villages to help rebuild homes unfairly demolished by the army. The builders' house has now been destroyed, she thinks, and a flash of anger runs through her. Let's see how many Palestinians run now to Jerusalem to help rebuild Tamar and Benny's house. Let's see how many of them are willing to stand up against the injustice and violence on their side. This I want to see.

Bruria writes that all of their other mutual friends are also okay. No one they know has been killed or injured in this attack. A few minutes later Judith receives two more emails, and Yechiel and Rina separately confirm the same thing. Only now does Judith shut her computer and go to bed.

For a long time she lies there tensely, unable to relax. Then at 6:30 she shuts her eyes "just for a minute." The next thing she knows, the sun is shining into them, hurting them, and the clock says it's ten past nine. *Oh my God — Weick's class!* She leaps out of bed.

— 7 —

Driving to Dunhill, her hands tremble on the wheel. She's shaky from sleeplessness and hunger — she forgot to eat supper, and there wasn't time this morning for breakfast. Though in a way this feels appropriate: a day of fasting, to mourn the dead and wounded. Marching in front of her eyes in a kind of parade are some of the children-under-nine she knows in Jerusalem, the kids of her friends and neighbours: Adi proudly showing off the purple backpack he got in honour of starting grade one, Leah squeaking away on her violin, Shimmy bouncing his basketball. "Fuck!" she cries. It's now been more than two years since the second intifada started. She was still in Israel for the first year of it: bombs exploding in shoe stores, pizza parlours, bus stations. At bar mitzvahs and weddings. You never knew when or where it would happen. Now this: going after children. What next?

Though she knows very well what's next — in the short term, anyway. Sharon will go in and pound the shit out of Gaza, or Ramallah, or Jenin. The Palestinians will retaliate with some more suicide bombings. Sharon will respond by pounding Gaza, Ramallah, or Jenin even more heavily, plus maybe reoccupying a town or two, or rerouting the fence to cut off more of their land. God. When is this going to end?

By now she is almost at the turnoff to Dunhill, but she's stuck behind a big red truck going forty kilometres an hour. Impatiently she swerves onto the shoulder and bypasses the truck. *Sharon is such an asshole*, she thinks, taking the turnoff. *But Arafat is no better; in fact he's worse. Damn them both. Two stupid old men having a dick-waving contest, each one trying to prove his cock is bigger than the other guy's. And in the meantime people — real people — are dying on both sides.* Bruria always said, "Now if women ran the world, boy, would things be different!" and Judith usually agrees with that. But now she's not so sure. Today's suicide bomber was a woman. A *shaheeda*, instead of a *shaheed*. Yay. It's good to know the Palestinians have made some progress: now they're giving equal opportunity to women.

She pulls into Dunhill's parking lot. On the news she heard — adding insult to injury — that this particular *shaheeda* was from

Umm el Fahm: a village Judith visited three years ago for one of her dialogue meetings between Jewish and Palestinian women. Now she slams the car door shut and thumps up the stairs into FRANK. The lobby is eerily empty — *well, of course: everyone else is already in class* — and alone she rides the elevator to the fifth floor. Her mouth feels dry, mealy, and sour as she walks down the long hallway. *My breath must be atrocious*, she thinks. *It's from not eating breakfast. It's the taste of the night.*

But no, that's not it at all. It's the taste of horror that has filled my mouth. Lord, do not open my lips, because I will not be able to declare thy praise. If God opened her lips right now, death, despair, and fury would come pouring out, leaping off her tongue like little frog-plagues. Alone she walks down the long corridor. So long and so gloomy that she again recalls the valley of the shadow of death. Horror fills her, leaving little room for anything else. Except silence.

Fortunately, silence is fine in Weick's class. There's rarely any discussion — last week with Mary Martha was an exception — and today, as usual, everyone is just sitting there, bored, while he drones on and on. He gives Judith a scowl as she walks in at 10:25 a.m., almost an hour and a half late; she makes a grimace of apology and slinks into the chair next to Cindy.

She tries listening attentively, obediently, to Weick. For some reason he is lecturing about Systems Theory again. He's telling them that the Dunhill School of Social Work is a living organism like any other, and therefore committed to its own survival. So everything that happens here is evaluated in terms of its relationship — its potential contribution, positive or negative — to that end. He looks right at Judith.

"Every part of a system," he says to her, "affects every other part."

Embarrassed, she looks down. Then he returns to his usual drone and she does what she always does to get through this class: she summons Moshe. This time the sexual fantasy she imagines involves a vibrator. She is rubbing it slowly up and down his penis, and he likes it. His eyes close and his face flushes. Even though initially he resisted trying it.

"What the hell is that?" he asked when she first introduced the lime-green phallus. "We don't need that thing. There's nothing wrong with my *zayin*."

Judith likes the word *zayin*. *Zayin* in Hebrew is penis. But *zayin* is also a letter of the Hebrew alphabet, the one that makes the "z" sound. And *zayin*, in both its meanings, phonetically sounds exactly the same as Zion. *Ah*, she thinks — *so maybe a Zayinist is one particular type of Zionist. If Zionism is the national liberation movement of the Jewish people, and is based on ethical and religious ideals, then Zayinism could be a sick offshoot: the penis-oriented ideology of macho militarism and misogyny. Zayinism, the dark brother of Zionism — the Cain to its Abel.* Judith loves Zionism with all her heart, all her soul, and all her might. But just as much as that, she hates Zayinism, which pretends to be Zionism, but is just a perversion of it. She plays with words and with Moshe for the rest of Weick's class. When it's over, and everyone is getting up from their seats, she notices Aliza is missing.

"Where's Aliza?" she asks Pam.

Pam's eyes dart to the side. "She's not feeling well today. But if she's up to it, she may come in later."

Judith, Pam, and Cindy proceed to Greg's class. As they walk in, Greg stands at the front of the room, laughing and calling out like a newspaper vendor: "Papers! Papers! Give me all your papers!"

Judith hands him hers. But when he smiles at her with his usual radiant smile, she looks down. She wonders if he can

tell how she feels about him now. She must talk to him sometime, she knows that, but she just doesn't have it in her today.
The room falls silent. Chris is at the front, about to make an
announcement. He says he needs some volunteers on Monday,
two weeks from now, to help set up the Students' Union's Social
Justice Information Table. If anyone can come in a bit early that
day, say around eight o'clock, and pitch in, that would be great.
Even one hour, if there are enough pairs of hands, should be
enough to get the job done.

"Come if you can," Greg chimes in his support. "Walk the
talk, as they say."

Chris asks for a show of hands from people who might be
able to help. A few hands shoot up: Kerry's, Tyler's, and some
others. Judith isn't sure what this information table is — this is
the first she's heard of it. But whatever it is, no, she isn't leaving
Toronto two Mondays from now at seven o'clock in the morning,
for the pleasure of volunteering with Chris, Kerry, and Tyler, all
haters of Israel.

Greg starts lecturing, and she half-listens, half-draws, or
one-quarter listens and three-quarters draws, all the way through.
As always, she draws creatures that are part animal and part
human. A half-human-half-dog, a half-human-half-bear, and a
half-human-half-lion. Then she does a series of birds, which end
up looking like the bird-people in medieval Passover Haggadas,
where all the illustrations are of birds, not humans, because of
the injunction against drawing images. Human birds. Bird people. This is what she draws today in Greg's class. As though art is
an amulet, something that can protect her from harm.

Greg's class passes without incident. Afterwards Judith, Cindy,
and Pam walk to the new restaurant on campus, Libertad, that

opened last week beside the cafeteria. They've been looking forward to this, since they're all bored with the cafeteria menu. As they approach Libertad, standing in the doorway with a big grin and a red wool cap is Aliza. Judith runs over and throws her arms around her. "I loved your present!" she whispers into her ear.

Aliza laughs. "I knew you would." Then, with a sly, intimate look, "It's good, eh?"

Judith, blushing, smiles. "Yeah, but at first I was scared of it. Are you sure I can't get electrocuted?"

Aliza, laughing, shakes her head.

"What are you two talking about?" asks Cindy. Judith leans over and whispers in her ear. Cindy chuckles and says to Aliza, "My birthday's March 14."

Aliza laughs. But now Judith notices how pale she is, even more than usual: there's a translucence to her paper-white skin. "What was wrong with you this morning?" she asks.

Aliza looks away. "An upset stomach. But now I'm okay."

"Good. I'd lend you my notes, but I didn't take any. You didn't miss a thing."

"I figured."

Libertad has a set-up similar to the cafeteria's, but the menu here is different: half Canadian, half South American, and on the wall menu, between *huncaina: cold cooked vegetables with cheese sauce* and *gallo pinto: rice and beans*, a plaque reads: *Viva el socialismo y la Libertad.* The word *Libertad* is surrounded by little red dots. Everyone orders something except Aliza.

"My stomach," she explains when Judith asks her why.

"But you need to eat."

"I'll be fine. Anyway, I should lose a few pounds."

"You?! You're so slim! You have the perfect body. A dancer's body."

"No, I don't. I'm fat."

Judith rolls her eyes and they find a table. Judith's tuna sandwich isn't bad, but Pam takes one sip of her coffee and spits it back into her cup. "It tastes like a cesspool," she says.

"Life is a cesspool," says Judith.

Cindy looks at her inquisitively.

"Did any of you hear the news this morning?" Judith asks.

"What exactly?" asks Pam.

"There was another terrorist attack in Israel today. Just six blocks from my house."

"Your house?" Cindy asks.

"My apartment in Jerusalem. I still have my apartment there."

"Was anyone hurt?" asks Aliza.

"Sixteen dead, twenty-eight injured." To her embarrassment, tears spring to her eyes. "Most of them under the age of nine. This time they went after children."

Pam's usually rough voice is softer now. "Anyone you know, Judith?"

She shakes her head. "No. At least not that I've heard. But my friends' house was destroyed." She snaps her fingers. "Just like that."

"Animals," growls Aliza. "Fuckin' animals."

Judith looks at her, taken aback. No matter what she feels about this bombing — no matter how immense her pain or grief — she could never call a person an animal. Even a suicide bomber. She can call them lots of other things, but not animals. Though some Palestinians call Jews animals: pigs, monkeys … Also, there are right-wing Jews who refer to Palestinians as animals. Bobby's brother did that several months ago, saying that an Arab and a dog have about the same level of moral intelligence. Judith got up and walked out of the room. Now she looks at Aliza and thinks: She feels what I feel, but not exactly. We're not in the same place politically.

"Where precisely was the attack?" Aliza asks. "Not that I know Jerusalem well — my relatives are in Tel Aviv and on kibbutz."

Judith names the intersection. Aliza shakes her head, not recognizing it. "They were on their way to school," Judith says. "Little kids. This time the suicide bomber was a woman."

"I heard that on the news," says a voice, and Judith looks up. It's Lola. Passing by with her tray, she's stopped at their table. She's a big woman under any circumstances, but now standing while they're all seated, she towers over them, casting a shadow. "What terrible news," she says.

Judith looks at her, surprised. "Really? I didn't know you cared about Israelis."

"Just because I care about the Palestinians doesn't mean I can't care about Israelis, too," says Lola self-righteously. "I have enough caring inside me for everyone." She sets her tray down on the edge of their table. "But let's face it — terrible as it is, Sharon leaves the Palestinians no choice. They're desperate, they feel they have nothing to lose. They have no way except violence to get their country back."

"In other words," says Judith, "these children deserved to be blown up?"

"I'm not saying that, obviously." Lola looks slightly uncomfortable. "But in a way they're just paying for the war crimes of Sharon. If Israelis don't want any more of their children to get blown up, then they should give back what isn't theirs. All of it. Not just the West Bank and Gaza, but Jaffa, Akko, Jerusalem."

Judith stares at Lola. Jerusalem. She's talking about my home. She's talking about giving someone else my home.

"That's ridiculous," mutters Aliza under her breath.

Cindy, looking worriedly at Judith, says to Lola, "Would you excuse us, please? We're trying to eat our lunch."

"Well, sorreee," Lola says. "I didn't realize an alternative point of view would be off limits at this table."

"Nothing's off limits," says Pam. "We're just in the middle of a conversation."

"Well, don't let me interrupt you," says Lola, picking up her tray.

When she's gone, there is silence at the table.

"Asshole," says Pam after a moment.

Judith is still staring straight in front of her. Cindy says her name. She turns and looks at her. Cindy's eyes are china blue and honest. "You heard her," Judith says wonderingly to Cindy. Then she looks around the table. "You all heard her. Am I hallucinating, or did she say that basically all these children deserved to die?"

"Basically," says Pam. "But Judith, don't pay any attention to her. She's a nutcase. Anyone who thinks that Israel should give the Palestinians not only all the occupied territories, but also the whole rest of the country, is obviously out of their mind."

"She's crazy," says Aliza.

But Judith's eyes have a wild, trapped look. Cindy puts a hand on her arm and says, "Forget it, Judith."

Judith, dazed, turns toward Cindy. "I can't believe it," she says. "I can't believe she said that."

"I know. It's horrible. But don't let her get to you. Like Pam said, she's an idiot."

"I didn't say idiot," says Pam. "I said nutcase."

"Nutcase. Whatever."

"Time for a joke," Aliza loudly announces. To Judith's astonishment and consternation, Aliza launches into a story about a gorgeous, sexy French poodle who goes for a walk one day in Paris's Luxembourg Gardens. This poodle is so alluring that, within one hour, no less than three Parisian dogs have fallen in love with her. Judith, in spite of herself, listens. Each of the three dogs tries to impress the adorable poodle, and soon they are fighting over her. She doesn't like this, and tells them that instead of watching them fight, she has a better way to decide between them. Whoever comes up with the most romantic and creative sentence will get to go on a date with her tonight. But there is one condition: the sentence must include the words *liver* and *cheese.*

Cindy, listening raptly, nibbles on her maple donut. Aliza, looking around the table, pauses for suspense, and continues: "So the first dog, a golden retriever, steps forward. 'You are the most bewitching dog I have ever seen,' he declares, 'and I want you more than the earth and sky.'

"'Zeez eez very nice,' the poodle says. 'It is also romantique. But you deed not use zee words *liver* and *cheese.* So I cannot go out weess you.'

"Then the second dog, a huge St. Bernard, comes, kneels in front of her, and says ardently, 'I love you so much, I love you more than liver or cheese.'

"'Merci, zat eez very nice, too,' the poodle says. 'But eet eez not creatif. So I weel not go out weess you.'

"Now the third dog, a tiny chihuahua, leaps toward his two competitors, wagging his tail and yelping at them both in his high-pitched chihuahua yelp: 'You liver alone! Cheese mine!'"

Their table explodes in laughter, and the surrounding tables turn and gawk. Pam goes off into her shrieking monkey sounds; Cindy, giggling, covers her mouth because it's full of maple donut; Aliza smiles quietly at everyone else's pleasure; and even Judith laughs.

"That was so good!" she says as everyone's laughter begins to subside. "It's so good to laugh. There's this Yiddish writer, Sholem Aleichem, who said, 'Laughter is good for the heart.'"

"It is," says Aliza. "But first you have to have a heart."

And as if this were another joke, the table breaks up all over again.

Eventually they calm down, and just sit awhile in silence, glancing at each other with leftover smiles still in their eyes. Then they chat about the papers they handed in to Greg today. Aliza didn't hand one in. She was throwing up all day yesterday and is hoping to get an extension, if she can catch Greg now during his office hours. So she stands up to go back to FRANK, even though there are still fifteen minutes left in the lunch break. Judith notices again how pale her face is. And thin — almost skeletal. She can see the fine bones under her skin.

"You don't look well," she says.

"Thanks."

"No, I mean it. You should see a doctor."

"I'm fine," Aliza says testily, adjusting the red cap on her head. "I just need some makeup."

"Well, don't put it on now," advises Cindy. "Let Greg see you without it. You'll look sicker and he'll feel sorry for you."

Aliza laughs. "Good point, Sherlock."

Cindy happily takes another bite of her maple donut. All this time she's been nursing it, and it still isn't even half-finished. She's the slowest eater Judith has ever seen. Pam stands, saying she'll walk back with Aliza and save seats for them all in Suzy's class. Once they're gone, Cindy and Judith sit in comfortable silence while Cindy leisurely polishes off the rest of her donut, wiping her mouth with a napkin after each bite. After the very last one, she says, "Don't look now," and they avert their eyes as Lola, Althea, and Roberta pass their table on their way out. When they're gone, Cindy says she has to go to the bathroom. Judith doesn't need to, but considers joining her anyway. Bobby always laughs at this: how if one woman gets up from the table to go to the bathroom, almost for sure the other woman will stand and say, "I'll come, too." "As if," Bobby said, "going to urinate or defecate were a social event. A guy would never do that." So now she just says to Cindy, "I'll wait for you at the front."

Waiting at the cash, she eyes all the varieties of candy and gum, and then looks around this new restaurant. Adjacent to the front door there's a beaverboard with dozens of notices pinned to it. They're different sizes, shapes, and colours, and from a distance look like a collage. She approaches it and browses. There's a typed ad for a part-time babysitter with the bottom of it chopped into tear-off ribbons, each with a phone number. The orange index card in the middle of the bulletin board is someone trying to sell a motorcycle, and next to that a guy named Fred is looking for a free ride to Mexico over the Christmas vacation. Fred writes, *I'll do half of the gas.* She laughs. Does this mean he's offering to do half the farting? Now she sees a little alcove with another notice board. But this one is entirely filled with one big black-and-white poster. There's a picture at its centre, but it's hard from this distance to make out what it is. She steps closer, squinting. It's a group of people standing in a circle around something that's burning. A cloth of some kind. No ... it's an Israeli flag. The Jewish star in the middle is half-eaten by flames. She reads the words above the picture:

RALLY IN SOLIDARITY WITH
THE OPPRESSED PALESTINIAN PEOPLE
END ZIONIST IMPERIALIST AGGRESSION
AND THE APARTHEID JEWISH STATE

Judith feels like she has to shit. Put an end to the "apartheid" Jewish state?! This poster is a call to destroy Israel. The picture was obviously taken outdoors and at night, and the people burning the flag look like university students. Their faces in the firelight are savage and full of an almost erotic passion for the flame and its destructive power. They remind her of *Lord of the Flies* and frighten her primordially. Instinctively she turns away from this picture and toward the words on the poster, as if words are inherently more civilized. The words under the picture read:

SPONSORED JOINTLY BY THE DUNHILL
STUDENTS' UNION (DSU) AND
STUDENTS FOR A LIBERATED PALESTINE (SLAP)
FREE REFRESHMENTS! BRING YOUR FRIENDS!
MONDAY, NOVEMBER 18TH, 5 P.M.
IN THE QUADRANGLE IN FRONT OF FRANK.
SEE YOU THERE!

November 18, she thinks. *That's just a week from today. But it's good it's five o'clock. Suzy's class ends at three-thirty; I'll be far from Dunhill by five o'clock — probably back in Toronto by the time this rally begins. And if I don't see it, it'll almost be like it's not actually happening.*

All this goes racing through her mind. But the rest of her is just standing frozen in front of this poster, aware of nothing but the hate in these faces. They want to destroy Israel. Which means they want to destroy *her*. She stares mesmerized at the burning flag. It's impossible what she's seeing. The Israeli flag cannot burn. It's like the burning bush in the Torah: *It burns but is not consumed.* She reaches her hand toward the flames in the poster. Then she hears a voice behind her. A voice saying brightly, "Ready to go?"

As if awakened by this voice, she sees herself now, standing in front of a poster with her hand almost touching it. Slowly she retracts her hand and presses it against her mouth.

"Ready?" she hears again, this time from much closer — so close she can sense the warmth of Cindy's body. Cindy is standing beside her, but still Judith can't speak. She just turns and looks at her. Whatever is in her face makes Cindy frown and look at the poster.

"Oh, no," she says. "Come on, Judith. Let's get out of here." She leads her away.

— 8 —

In Suzy's class Judith sits dazed. As deeply submerged inside herself as if she were underwater at the bottom of the ocean, in a strange deep place where everything happening above the surface of the water, up there in the sunlit world, seems far away and unreal. When the class is over, she wants to just go home. But when she reaches the front of the room, Suzy asks, "Do you have a moment?" and she says yes. She follows Suzy down the deserted labyrinth to her office. Once inside with the door closed, Suzy says she can't tell anyone else, this is top secret, but she learned on Friday that on January 1 there will be some major budget cuts at the school. Judith, picturing the school without Suzy in it, asks, alarmed, "Will these affect you?"

Suzy grimaces. "Last in, first out, as they say. But Weick said he'd fight for me. He's planning to tell the dean I'm 'indispensable to the smooth functioning of the school.'"

"You are," Judith says ardently.

Suzy laughs. "Whether or not that's true, I do hope to keep my job. But seriously, Judith, not a word of this to anyone. It's strictly confidential."

"Of course not!" She feels flattered at being trusted with this secret and wishes she had a secret to share in return.

"I know you wouldn't. I'm just a little, you know —"

"Of course. Who wouldn't be? I hope it all works out."

"Thanks. So do I."

There's a moment of silence and Judith, glancing down, notices the deep white carpet. "I love this carpet," she says. "Every time I see it I want to rub my toes in it."

Suzy laughs. "Then do. Take off your boots and do it."

"Really?"

"Really."

She unzips her fleece-lined boots and removes them self-consciously. She looks up shyly at Suzy, who smiles back encouragingly, and peels off her white cotton socks, inserting them neatly into her boots. She worries momentarily that maybe her feet stink. But then she wiggles her toes in the carpet, laughing with pleasure.

"It's so soft!" she cries, and laughs again.

"I should try it sometime," says Suzy, smiling. Judith wiggles her toes again in the carpet, and stops. Now she feels silly, embarrassed even, to be sitting here barefoot in front of Suzy. It's like being undressed in front of someone who's dressed. But it would feel awkward to lean down immediately and put her socks and boots back on.

"How'd you find today's class?" Suzy asks. "I was worried there weren't enough examples — that it got too abstract."

Judith has no idea. During Suzy's class today, she was deep underwater. "It was fine," she says. "But I've been wanting to ask you something since last week's class with the pedophile: Do you truly believe people can change? That much, I mean — the way he did in the course of one interview? You did great work with him and everything — I'm not saying ... But I don't know if I believe people can change so fundamentally."

"I do," says Suzy. "I think people are full of surprises."

"For better or for worse," says Judith.

"That's a bit downbeat for you."

"I've had a downbeat day."

"Why?" asks Suzy, looking concerned. "What's up?"

So Judith tells her everything, just as if she were writing it all out for her in a log. About the terrorist attack this morning. About Lola saying that basically those children deserved to die. About the poster with the Jewish flag in flames.

"Good heavens," says Suzy when she's finished. "That's quite a day. I'm impressed you're still standing. There are people who'd be in post-traumatic stress after a day like this. What did you do to cope? How do you hold yourself together?"

"Who says I'm holding myself together?" says Judith, and they laugh. It feels good to be laughing with Suzy. But then the phrase "post-traumatic stress" strikes her as very funny, and her laugh starts veering off and getting slightly hysterical. When she finally stops, Suzy is looking at her closely, so she casts around for an intelligent, sane-sounding response to her question. She tells Suzy she has good friends here at school — Cindy, Pam, and Aliza — and their social support over lunch definitely helped. Suzy nods.

"But also ..." Judith says, and as she continues talking, she's aware she's sharing with Suzy something rather personal. But she wants to, anyway, because Suzy just shared a secret with her and she wants to reciprocate. So she tells Suzy that one way she copes — for instance, in Weick's classes — is by fantasizing. Usually about Moshe, a man she had a relationship with in Israel. Suzy looks taken aback.

"Are you still in touch with this Moshe?" she asks.

"No," says Judith. "I haven't seen him in seven years, and doubt I'll ever see him again. It's just, you know ... fantasy."

Suzy's eyes dart sharply to the side, away from Judith, and she doesn't say anything. Judith feels her disapproval and is suddenly aware of her naked feet. Like Adam and Eve becoming aware of their nakedness. "Anyway," she says, to backtrack, "I don't do this often."

"But you just said you do. You said this is how you get by in Weick's class every week."

Judith feels caught. She blushes. "It's just so boring," she says, searching Suzy's eyes, appealing to her. "It's not only me — nobody can stand his classes." She adds, "It's not like your class at all." Which is true, but still she feels like a suck-up saying it.

Suzy's eyes smile slightly, but now there is a watchfulness in them, too. *Something's wrong*, thinks Judith. *Something's going wrong here.* In her anxiety, she rambles on about Weick, telling Suzy it isn't just that he's boring; he also has no control over his class. Like a few weeks back when Mary Martha was ganged up on and attacked by everyone — for a long time, maybe twenty minutes — and he just stood there and did nothing to stop it. He's so weak that some students call him "Weick the Weak."

Suzy is frowning, pained, as though it has given her a headache hearing all this. "I like Weick," she says. "He's the one who hired me seven years ago, and now he's fighting Administration to help me keep my job."

Judith stares at Suzy and then flushes as her meaning sinks in. Suzy is on his side. She's defending him. Just as a few weeks ago she defended Greg. Judith feels a flash of fear. She has made a tactical error in speaking so openly to Suzy. She also feels acutely self-conscious about her naked feet, and now bends down and starts putting on her socks. She is all thumbs and it's hard getting her socks to fit back on her feet.

"À propos of Israel," she hears Suzy say. "I wanted to tell you I spoke to Chris this morning. I asked him to convey to

Michael Brier that when he prepares his talk, he needs to take into account the sensibilities of our Jewish students and faculty. That's how I put it to him. I believe Chris understood what I was trying to say, and he said he'd pass this on, so hopefully this will help tone down Brier. We can't do anything at this point about the title of his talk, but maybe now the content of it will be somewhat more moderate."

Judith has finally got her socks on. She slides her feet into her boots and looks up at Suzy gratefully — this feels like the old Suzy again. "Thanks," she says. "I hope you're right." She zips up her boots and rises. They say goodbye, and things feel sort of okay between them. Not perfect, but more or less normal — just a tiny bit strained. On the drive home, though, she could kick herself. *What was I thinking,* she asks herself, *telling a prof I have sexual fantasies in class? Sure, this was Suzy — Suzy to whom I write my logs, Suzy with whom I have this special relationship. But still, she's my prof. Plus not only a prof; she's a religious Christian who goes to church every week. Was I out of my mind? Whatever possessed me ...?*

Then she realizes with a groan that, in fact, it's even worse than this. Because Bobby is being mentored by Suzy's husband, and now Suzy knows that she's having sexual fantasies not about Bobby, but about another man. *Oy,* she thinks. *Now I've blown it. What a stupid thing to do.* She calls herself stupid for a while longer. Then, to stop herself from doing this and from perseverating on her conversation with Suzy for the whole drive home, she reaches into the glove compartment, takes out *Israel at Forty,* and for the next forty minutes lets music drown out the world.

The following morning Judith awakens depressed. Four times in the past three weeks she has experienced anti-Israelism, and three times in the past five days: the SWAC meeting, Lola's comment at Libertad, and the poster there. Dunhill is beginning to feel not only uncomfortable, but emotionally unsafe. Every week there seem to be more people at Dunhill who hate Israel. It's like a spreading plague. She won't be able to endure this place for another six months. She goes to the kitchen, to the Jewish calendar hanging on the wall. This calendar arrives free of charge every year just before Rosh Hashana, courtesy of the Jewish National Fund where her father once made a donation. The top half of the calendar is a picture of a JNF forest planted in Israel; on the bottom half, now showing November, she finds yesterday's date, November 11, 2002 — Remembrance Day — and draws a big red X over that square. Then in the bottom triangle of the X she's just made, she writes the number *147*. Only 147 days left until she's back in Israel. Classes end on April 7, and that night she'll be on a plane. Everything here will disappear: SWAC, Lola, Kerry. All this crap isn't her real life. This is just a year in *galut*. Her real life is there.

Calmed by this, she proceeds with her usual Tuesday routine: food shopping followed by a trip to the University of Toronto library. But back home in the late afternoon, she feels depressed again. She curls up on the couch and lies there as the room gets darker and darker. At 7:30 the phone rings. It's Bobby — he's coming over soon.

"Sure," she says. "But in case I doze off, let yourself in with the key in the flowerpot."

A half-hour later there's the sound of the key in the lock and in walks Bobby. He flicks on the vestibule light and sees

Judith lying on the couch in the dark living room. "Are you okay?" he asks.

"I guess. I'm just not sure I'm strong enough for this."

They spoke on the phone last night, so Bobby knows what happened yesterday. "Of course you are," he says.

"I don't know. I'm not sure." She's annoyed he thinks he knows her better than she knows herself.

This time, wisely, he doesn't argue. He carries a big paper bag to the dining room table and extracts from it three hot, oil-spattered, fragrant cardboard boxes. "I brought some Chinese food," he says. "Come eat something."

"I'm not hungry."

"Come on."

Several seconds pass. Now right in front of her face appears a container of pineapple chicken. It smells wonderful and her mouth waters. She reaches for it, but he pulls it away. "Come to the table. Come on."

She gets up.

Bobby unpacks paper plates, plastic cutlery, and napkins. The food is hot and good: in addition to pineapple chicken, there's steamed rice, chow mein, vegetable spring rolls, and two fortune cookies. She's barely eaten all day and is ravenous. And the more she eats, the more she wants. She takes seconds and thirds of the pineapple chicken, then empties the whole remainder of the box onto her plate and attacks it voraciously.

"*Es gezunterheyt,*" he says. "Have more rice, too." He fills in all the blank spaces on her plate with what's left of the rice. Then he watches her eat. She's wearing a shabby, ripped sweatshirt, her hair is unwashed and disheveled, and her face is drawn and white. She peeps at him and sees the beginnings of anger in his face. She knows that to him pity, pain, or sadness are weak, soft, helpless things. Whereas anger is hard, strong, and masculine, something that can be ejaculated onto a target.

"Fuckin' lefties," he spits out. "Bunch of phonies, these social workers …" He's just warming up, he's barely gotten started, but seeing her stricken face, and her broken, "Please, Bobby — don't," he stops. He looks down and is silent. But then, unable to help himself, he bursts out again: "Why do you let these assholes get to you? *They* should be the ones who spent today flattened and lying in the dark, not you. It should be the other way around."

She glances at him and finishes the last grains of rice on her plate. "I thought you said I shouldn't fight back. You said I shouldn't be a martyr like Mary Martha, tilting at windmills. Just keep my mouth shut and get through the year."

"Yes, but you can't let them get to you. I meant, Don't take them on, but also don't care. You have to not care about the bastards."

"That's what Cindy, Pam, and Aliza say."

"Then they must be smart."

"How can they be smart? They're social workers."

"A smile!" he cries, pointing at it. "I saw it."

She makes a face.

"I did!"

"You're crazy."

"Crazy about you."

Ignoring this, she slides a fortune cookie toward him, cracks open her own, and reads from the ribbon of paper inside. "*Fear not: your enemas will fail.*"

"Your what?"

"Your enemas." She grins. "My enemas will fail."

"They must have meant enemies."

"This is weird. I was thinking today about enemies. My enemies at Dunhill."

"ESP."

"I don't know. But I hope my cookie's right. I hope my enemies fail."

"Your enemas, you mean."

"My enemies are like enemas. Full of shit."

"Ha. Did you ever get an enema?" he asks.

"No. Yuck. Did you?"

He shakes his head.

"What did you get?" she asks.

"What? Oh." He reads his fortune: "*Someone's going to loose their job.* L-o-o-s-e."

"Loose shit. Sounds like an enema. Someone's got shitting on the brain."

He laughs shortly. "Weird, eh? Anyway, I hope *my* cookie's wrong. I don't want to 'loose my job.'"

"It didn't say *you*. It said 'someone.' And I know who: it's the fortune cookie writer. She can't spell to save her life and she's about to get fired." He laughs again. "She has intimations of her own demise," she adds.

He squeezes her hand. Then he surveys the empty containers and dirty plates strewn across the table. "We didn't do too badly," he says, "for two people who weren't hungry."

She glances around. Not a morsel of food remains. "Locusts," she says.

He nods. Then he says, "Though it could've been worse. We could've had frogs. Lice. Boils. The smiting of the firstborn. That would have meant both of us, since we're both firstborns."

"I'm an only-born," she says. "I was thinking about this today, too."

"About what?"

"Plagues. The plague of hatred."

"Are we back at Dunhill?"

"Yes. But it's not just Dunhill. When you arrived I was thinking about evil, about the overwhelming dark forces in the world. The locusts, so to speak, that we can't ever truly eliminate or escape from."

Her eyes are smoky and troubled, and he looks tenderly into her tormented face. "What can I do to make you feel better, Judith? To remind you there is also goodness in the world? If Chinese food didn't do it, tell me what will."

She is touched by Bobby's sweetness, caring, and desire to help. These in themselves prove there's some goodness in the world. She feels now a little of the sparkle of life. "Read my mind," she says.

"I can't. But I can read lips. Move your lips, George Bush, and I'll try and read them. Seriously. Don't speak — just lip synch."

"Okay." She draws her chair closer to his, leans toward him, and moves her lips around in random shapes.

He frowns. "I can't. You're going too fast."

"Read my lips, Bobby," she says, and places them against his.

"Oh, I see," he mumbles. "Mmmm ..." He slides his hand inside her jeans. "You're warm," he says. "And ... ooh! You're wet."

"Wet for you, baby," she grins. "You don't mind?"

"Do I look like I mind? Read my lips." She gazes at his lips as he mouths something illegible. Then he ducks his head under her sweatshirt and puts his mouth where she loves it. The way she loves it. She feels his lips moving. Then his tongue.

It feels like he's talking Hebrew to her now.

WINTER CHILLS

The next morning, Wednesday, Judith awakens feeling almost like her usual self. She knows that what's happening at Dunhill is by no means over. But she is away from that now, safe at home until Monday when she has to return there. So until then, there's no point dwelling on all that. As Daddy liked to say, "Sufficient unto the day is the evil thereof." So all day Wednesday and Thursday she studies and does email and errands. On Friday morning she cooks for Shabbat. By noon there is chicken soup bubbling on the stove, filling the house with its unmistakable Shabbat smell while she studies at the kitchen table. She's up to her eyeballs now in schoolwork. Only three and a half weeks till the end of term, and by then she has to deliver final assignments in all three of her courses, not to mention four more logs for Suzy, each one taking nearly a full day to prepare. None of this work is intellectually demanding; it's just onerous because of the volume. She has about two hundred hours of straight slogging ahead of her. The book she's reading now is the one Suzy lent her, *Cognitive Therapy for Social Work,* and she's using it for two of her term papers: the one for Weick, which is a comparison between Cognitive Theory and Coping Theory; and for Suzy, an application of Cognitive Theory to social work practice with individuals and families. For Greg's final assignment she is doing a group project. She, Cindy, Pam, and Aliza are surveying and analyzing all the anti-oppression initiatives in Canadian schools of social work over the past three years. This coming Monday they're having a lunchtime meeting to nail it all down. But already they have a general outline. They've divided Canada into four regions — Western Canada, Ontario, Quebec, and the Maritimes — and each of them is taking one region to research.

Because Judith's high-school French, though not great, is better than anyone else's, she got Quebec. This afternoon she will email the social work schools at McGill, Laval, Université de Montréal, and Université du Québec à Montréal, to start the ball rolling. Perhaps once she's already in contact with them, she'll inquire also about their initiatives regarding antisemitism (their "anti-antisemitism" initiatives, if that's even a word).

Now she is curious. She puts down the book and googles *antisemitism social work Canada*. Nothing comes up. Nothing: *Your search did not match any documents*. She types in *antisemitism Canada*: 57,217 entries. Where should she begin? She scans the first page of the list, and selects an article called "Antisemitism and Anti-Zionism in Canada." It matches Bobby's analysis almost exactly, identifying anti-Zionism (or anti-Israelism) as the central hallmark of the new antisemitism. Reading this article, she's surprised to discover that there is some very good activism going on in Canada, though none of it, she notices, is in social work, or anywhere else in academe. There are three main groups doing this sort of activism: two of them longstanding, well-known organizations in the Jewish community, and one relatively new kid on the block, all three competing with each other. Reading, she feels somewhat disoriented. She has always felt, even in high school, alienated from the mainstream Jewish community. It was too straight for her. Too conservative and conventional, too bourgeois and right-wing. The lay leadership of the Jewish community seemed always dominated by rich businessmen and lawyers, not unlike Bobby: men in suits making sexist jokes about Jewish mothers and Jewish American Princesses, and occasionally, too, racist jokes about "*shvartzes*" and other ethnic groups. She was always repulsed by these people and their views, so the mainstream community was something she could never relate to.

But now, reading this article, she finds that, despite herself, she is very impressed by the work being done by the Jewish community. Not only are they taking on antisemitism and anti-Zionism; they're actively involved in anti-oppression initiatives that fight discrimination and hate crimes against blacks, First Nations, Muslims, and the Roma. She notes admiringly how these Jewish organizations have formed successful alliances with various other communities and anti-oppression groups. They've "made the links," as Greg would say. She forwards this article to Cindy, Pam, and Aliza, suggesting that some of this may be useful for their project, specifically the section on the importance of "building bridges and anti-oppression alliances across different ethnic communities." Then, just as she's leaving Google, she sees a link to another article, this one entitled "Anti-Israelism on the Canadian Campus." It interests her, but she decides to come back to it later. *Too much of this poison at once*, she thinks, *and one could get sick.*

She returns to the kitchen, turns off the soup, and makes an applesauce *kugel* — a quick and easy recipe from Israel. Surrounded by its sharp, sweet fragrance, she sets the table for Shabbat, and with practised fingers polishes the silver candlesticks handed down to her from her great-grandmother, who carried them from the old country in two separate pillowcases so they wouldn't scratch. Polishing, she remembers how she, Miri, Bruria, and Bruria's cousin Batsheva studied Talmud together every second Shabbat afternoon around Bruria's dining room table. They would meet in the late afternoon after they'd all gotten up from their Shabbat naps, and they would study, chat, and laugh as outside the day got darker and darker around them, until Shabbat was over and it was time to go home. Once, Bruria's husband Pinchas, a big bulky man, came downstairs while they were studying, and stood listening in the doorway. Pinchas never wore a *kipa*, but he grew up in a religious home and was much more knowledgeable Jewishly than he liked to let on. That afternoon, she, Bruria, Miri, and Batsheva — proud of their feminist project to study Talmud, something traditionally done only by males — heard Pinchas's loud laugh. They turned toward him, annoyed at the interruption.

"What is it?" Bruria asked him curtly.

"I was trying to figure out," he said with a smirk, "what tractate you ladies were studying. Then I recognized it: Is it by any chance the tractate on gossip?"

"Very funny," said Bruria. "As it happens, we're doing Damages, *N'zikin*, and relating it to real-life things that have happened to us and our friends. But even if we *were* just gossiping, so what? You shouldn't expect anything more from us — according to the Talmud, women are frivolous and intellectually lightweight by nature. Of course," she added, "when men study Talmud, digressions never occur. Men are always 100 percent focused: they never slide onto business, sports, politics, women —"

"Certainly we digress," Pinchas said good-naturedly, still smiling. Everyone knew how crazy he was about Bruria. "Didn't I say I recognized this tractate? Tractate Gossip is one of my favourites. It takes one to know one." With a wink he left them to their studies.

Judith is stabbed with lonesomeness for Israel and her friends there. She carries the now gleaming candlesticks into the dining room and places them on the table, on top of the clean white cloth, next to a small vase of pansies. Then she returns to studying Cognitive Therapy and various techniques for controlling one's emotions by controlling one's thoughts. It astounds her that this can actually be done, and she continues reading about it with fascination.

In one case example, a young woman named Babs was terrified of her boss, Helga, a domineering, hypercritical, narcissistic woman twenty-five years her senior. Helga reminded Babs of her mother, who was also domineering, hypercritical, and narcissistic, so every time Helga behaved this way — at least twice weekly — Babs regressed into a snivelling, wounded, helpless, incompetent child. Consequently she performed poorly at work and was in danger of being fired.

These problems also strained her relationship with her boyfriend. Whenever they met, all she could talk about was Helga's latest atrocity, and nothing else, until he'd agreed Helga was horrible, reassured Babs she was wonderful, and calmed her down, which sometimes took hours. Understandably, Doug was getting fed up, and they were on the verge of breaking up. Helga — or more accurately, fear of Helga — was destroying Babs's life.

Babs became so desperate she went to a social worker. After pouring out her heart, she said she knew that what she probably needed was many years of intensive psychotherapy to deal with her relationship with her mother. The social worker just laughed.

"Try this instead," she said, and suggested Babs imagine Helga, rather than as her mother, as somebody else: just as any old mean, rotten, selfish, spoiled stranger. Someone so obviously self-centred and obnoxious she isn't in any way a threat — just ridiculous, maybe even comical. Did Babs know anyone like this?

Babs laughed. "Miss Piggy. I just saw an old rerun of *The Muppet Show*. Helga's just like Miss Piggy!"

"Good!" smiled the social worker. "So from now on, whenever Helga starts acting like that, just look at her and think, 'There goes Miss Piggy again!'"

Babs followed this advice. Within days she was not only viewing Helga as Miss Piggy, she was using this name when talking about her with Doug or her best friend at work. In no time her fear of Helga receded. Now, when Helga went into a tirade or tantrum, Babs, seeing only a Miss Piggy puppet, merely laughed inwardly. Also, because she wasn't cowed by Helga anymore, she began standing up to her and talking back. In fact, Babs became so empowered and fearless that within one month she'd initiated various improvements and innovations at work, and was finally beginning to perform to her full potential. Within six months she'd been promoted, and two years later she had Miss Piggy's job and was married to Doug.

A real success story, thinks Judith, stirring the soup. *The power of the mind. As Hamlet said, "There is nothing either good or bad but thinking makes it so."* So all she has to do now is find a different way of thinking about Kerry, Chris, Lola, and their gangs, and they won't be able to hurt her anymore. This makes her feel hopeful. All afternoon, cooking and studying, she is more cheerful, believing these cognitive techniques can help protect her if there are any future incidents at school.

· Just before nightfall Bobby arrives. They eat supper and then they argue. Bobby has been working for the last three days on a big, new case with Suzy's husband Dennis, and he's exhausted and stressed out. If the case goes well, he tells Judith, this will secure him a spot on Dennis's team, and — assuming he's successful there — virtually guarantee him a promotion to senior partner a few years down the road. Conversely, if it goes badly, he'll be demoted from Dennis's team and sidelined from the firm's next big deal: a contract with a huge multinational corporation that wants BBB to manage its holdings in the Third World. Judith can see how overworked and anxious he is. One part of her wants to be supportive and empathic, especially since he was so good to her just a few days ago. But when she hears him speaking wistfully about working for a multinational corporation, it takes all her self-control not to point a finger into her open mouth, indicating she wants to barf. She is proud of her self-restraint. But when he starts going on and on about "the Third World," she loses it.

"You don't say 'the Third World' anymore," she snaps. "You say 'the Global South.'"

"Thanks to the language police," says Bobby.

And it's downhill from there. They have a long argument about language and politics, followed by an argument about their Christmas vacation. Bobby's sister in Vancouver has just had her first baby, and Bobby wants Judith to fly there with him to see them. Judith hedges. She doesn't want to go. She doesn't like his sister Marla, and she also feels this trip would create a false impression. That she and Bobby are a real, a permanent, couple. That she is his wife-to-be — and his sister her sister-in-law-to-be, and the baby her niece-to-be — when she isn't and won't ever be. She is never going to marry Bobby. So she doesn't want to be cornered by Marla in the kitchen for "girl talk" and have to pretend they are anything more than two random women in a room together. Now he pressures her: It's already mid-November, Christmas is around the corner. If they wait any longer, they won't be able to get a flight.

She balks: "Why are you always pressuring me?"

He fires back: "Why can't you ever make any sort of commitment?"

And so on. In the end, they make love. But there isn't much love in it. They are both still smouldering with anger and it feels like a power struggle. Who's on top. Whose way they will do it tonight.

Thank God, she thinks, when he has fallen asleep. *Only 144 days to go.*

— 2 —

On Monday morning she wakes up cold. Her quilt has half-slipped off the bed; she pulls it back up and hugs it tightly around her. On Saturday, she lowered the thermostat to 65 degrees to try to save on the heating bills, as her parents used to do. But she's not used to these Toronto winters anymore. It is often ten or fifteen below zero outside, and in this old house, with cracks in the walls and around the doors and windows, 65 on this thermostat feels more like 60 or 55. All this weekend of non-stop snowing, she's been chilled and miserable anytime she's not in bed. Now she cuddles under the quilt. She doesn't want to go to school. She tries not to think about the "We Hate Israel" rally today, sponsored by the DSU and SLAP. They're going to slap Israel today, and there's nothing she can do about it. She pictures the quadrangle in front of FRANK filled with people who hate Israel and want to destroy it. People who consider themselves good human beings, caring about oppression and the underdog. Hundreds of them will be there today and perhaps, like in that poster, these demonstrators will burn an Israeli flag. Or a copy of *The Jewish State*. And after that, who knows? As Heine said, "Where one burns books, one will soon burn people." She shudders. She'd better make sure to leave the campus immediately after Suzy's class. Not follow Suzy back to her office. She'll have to make some excuse ...

Reluctantly she gets out of bed. The floor is freezing against the bare soles of her feet. In the bathroom, shivering, she does her "morning ablutions," as her father used to call them. Fear flutters in her stomach. Butterflies. She's ashamed of being afraid like this. But brushing her teeth, she remembers Bubba once telling her that fear is nothing to be ashamed of, because without fear there is no opportunity for bravery. Plus, she remembers, even Rabin was afraid. He admitted publicly after signing the Oslo Accords that he'd had butterflies in his stomach when he walked out onto the White House lawn. Not that that worked out very well. The Oslo Accords did not bring peace. Still, it was brave of Rabin. Just because it didn't work out doesn't mean the act itself didn't take courage. Courage isn't about the outcome; it's about finding the strength to do the right thing.

Or is it? Judith ponders this as she steps into her jeans. Maybe outcome does matter. Is it brave, after all, to do something that's foolish (foolish meaning pointless, ineffective, Quixote-ish)? Or is that just foolish? Can something be simultaneously both brave and foolish? *Anyway,* she thinks, pulling on a sweatshirt, *just because Rabin didn't succeed doesn't mean that what he did was foolish. It didn't necessarily fail because of him. What he did may have been his best option at the time. At least he tried.*

Downstairs she distractedly eats some cereal, still wondering about courage and foolishness. She agrees with Burke's famous statement that all that's required for evil to triumph in the world is for good people to do nothing. But what is fighting the evil in the world, as every good person must, and what is tilting at windmills or self-aggrandizing? Bobby thinks fighting evil is foolish, and maybe even a form of narcissism or martyrdom, unless you use the same strategies as that legal committee he's on, like high-level lobbying and politics. But she can't do that at Dunhill. She doesn't know how, and she doesn't have the power. Yet someone has to take these people on. You can't just let them take over the whole world: her classes, then the School of Social Work, then Dunhill University, then all the universities in Canada, then the whole country. Because once you own the mind of a nation, its intellectual life, you own the nation itself. Someone has to say to these people: "Stop. Stop right here. Not one inch more."

She feels herself getting worked up, her stomach is churning again, and she knows this is not good. She still has the one-hour drive to Dunhill ahead of her, a whole day of classes to get through, and then the long drive back home. Besides, whoever this brave person is who is going to fight these assholes and be the leader of the hour, standing up for "Truth, Justice, and the American (or Canadian) way," it is not her. She's no Superman — or Superwoman. She knows herself: in the courage department she is nothing special. She's sensitive and timid — definitely not hero material. *I'll be satisfied if I just survive this year*, she thinks. *Not get smashed and mashed into hummus, but remain who I am: a single chickpea, whole.*

Driving to Dunhill, she muses about Babs and Miss Piggy, and tries applying this technique to Kerry, Chris, and Lola. She plays around with funny cartoon characters, and people and animals from books and movies. But it's much harder to do than Suzy's book made it sound. She can't find just the right image for each person — something that will declaw them and render them harmless, maybe even humorous. The closest she comes is picturing Chris as a puppy dog, a tiny chihuahua yelping and running in circles around Michael Brier the famous celebrity, hoping to impress him by snapping at the heels of his detractors. Seen this way, Chris shrinks down, small and comical. But still he has teeth. Sharp little teeth that can bite. So this isn't working.

Exhausted by all this thinking, she pulls into the Dunhill parking lot at twenty to nine. Good. She won't be late for Weick's class again. Striding through the parking lot, the students around her look not just pale and tense, but also strangely absent, vacant-eyed like zombies, some without hats or scarves even though it's twenty below. *It's the mid-November blues plus the end-of-term crunch*, she thinks gloomily. But then one of the zombies waves from the far side of the parking lot. It's Roberta. She waves back to her, feeling reassured and warmed. *See?* she tells herself, walking along the path toward FRANK. *Just because Roberta ate lunch with Lola last week doesn't mean she agrees with her on everything and is my enemy. Maybe Roberta's okay.*

Much to Judith's relief, today's classes are all uneventful, and she leaves Dunhill immediately after the last one so as to miss the anti-Israel rally. Driving home, she is glad it's behind her, and figures this was it for the year: the annual anti-Israel rally at Dunhill that she read about in the papers last spring. *Anyway,* she thinks, *put it out of your mind. Use Cognitive Therapy techniques if necessary. Just focus on your schoolwork.* So for the rest of that week, she studies from the moment she awakens in the morning till collapsing into bed at night, and almost never leaves the house. But in a way she doesn't mind. She likes the simplicity of this life: the clarity of purpose, the purity of focusing on just one thing to the exclusion of all else. Like a hermit focusing only on God. The week passes quickly, and on Sunday night she's still so deeply and pleasantly immersed in her papers that she almost decides to skip her classes the next day. But she concludes it's not worth it. It's easier just to go. So she does.

That Monday, she spends the whole drive to Dunhill worrying about her final assignments. She has a lot left to do and really can't afford to waste this whole day attending classes. She parks impatiently in the lot nearest FRANK and trudges up the stairs.

But once in the building, she stands just inside the doorway, disoriented. The whole atrium has been converted into a kind of fair. There are two long tables reaching out toward her like arms, and a shorter table joining them on the far side, forming a horseshoe shape. On top of the three tables are a dozen brightly-coloured poster boards, each with two little wings, like the winged poster boards that ensure privacy in voting stations. What are they voting on here? she asks herself, looking around, dazed. She's too far away to see the small pictures or read the text on any of these poster boards, but she is dazzled by their colours, as cheerful as those at a fairground or circus: orange, lime-green, purple, shocking pink. A dozen students are milling around, some looking at the exhibits, others chatting and laughing, a few in earnest, animated conversation. Judith advances toward the long right arm of the horseshoe, close enough to see the first booth on the right, and then stops cold. In front of her is a black-and-white picture of a beautiful, serious-looking boy with black hair, big black eyes, and sensual lips. The caption underneath says:

MOHAMMED RAJOUB

AGE 10

SHOT DEAD BY ISRAELI SOLDIERS

APRIL 19, 2002

She freezes. Stares at it, stunned. Then moves on to the next picture. This one is of a Palestinian woman holding a dead baby in her open, upturned hands. It hangs there lifeless, looking like an upside-down banana, its two ends — head and feet — limply dangling. In the background, an Israeli soldier watches this woman with narrowed eyes. This mother reminds Judith of another mother, the Israeli one sobbing after the terrorist attack in Jerusalem one week ago: "My baby, my baby ..." The Arab woman in the picture looks vaguely familiar — maybe they met at that mothers' group Miri's sister took her to: Israeli and Palestinian mothers who have bonded together — who are bound together, Miri said, like the Binding of Isaac, or of Isaac-and-Ishmael — through their dead sons. "No more violence, no more war," they chanted in Hebrew, Arabic, and English, demonstrating with trilingual signs in front of the Knesset, to the contempt of passersby.

"Lefties! Idealists! Haters of Israel!" people shouted at them. But that didn't upset Miri's sister. Judith asked her why and she just shrugged: "People who haven't lost a son — what do they know about anything?"

Now Judith has had enough. She does not want to look at any more pictures at this "fair." This unfair fair. But she has to walk past more of them, between two long rows of them, like running the gauntlet, to get to the elevator. She decides she'll just glance at them cursorily, scan them superficially, as she walks quickly past, so they won't go inside her, inside her mind, body, or soul. But even one glance is enough. She sees them and they enter her — how could they not? — pictures of dead Palestinian children, their blood spattered across the photos like spilled ink. She stops walking and turns aside, afraid she'll throw up. To steady herself she gazes down, breathing heavily, at a patch of green tablecloth. A small, neutral circle. She knows these photographs are true. She has seen others like them — there's nothing here she hasn't seen before, or that she and her friends haven't been outraged over, and demonstrated against, dozens of times. Yet these photographs are not true. They are not true because they tell just half of the story and provide no context. There is nothing here, not one single picture, about what the Palestinians do to Israelis: about the incessant suicide bombings, the rockets fired from Gaza on young families, the Israeli children stabbed to death in their beds at night. Someone ignorant visiting this exhibit would get the impression that the Israeli army, sheerly out of naked aggression, completely unprovoked, goes around killing Palestinians. Which isn't true.

She's still gazing down at the green tablecloth, wracked with anger and pain. Then she looks around her. *What is this exhibit, anyway?* she wonders. Against the far wall, there's a printed banner:

PHOTO ALBUM OF OUR PEOPLE:
PALESTINIAN LIFE AND DEATH UNDER ZIONIST
APARTHEID

"Apartheid" again. And again her stomach drops. *I have to get to class*, she thinks. *I have to reach those elevators up ahead.* So she keeps moving toward this banner. Finally she is close enough to be able to read the small print:

SPONSORED BY THE SOCIAL JUSTICE COMMITTEE
OF THE DUNHILL STUDENTS' UNION (DSU)

Now she understands. This is the Students' Union's Social Justice Information Table. The table Chris was asking for volunteers for in Greg's class two Mondays ago. She looks around the lobby. New students are constantly streaming in, initially looking surprised, but then browsing through the exhibit. *Every single student*, she thinks, *from social work, labour studies, anthropology, or sociology who enters this building today is going to be exposed to these pictures. To this lie. And a certain percentage of them, being ignorant and gullible, will believe it.*

She feels someone looking at her. It's Chris, watching her with a smug little smirk, a look of "Let's see what you have to say about this." A look daring her to say or do something. She lowers her eyes. "Just get through this year," Bobby said. "Keep your mouth shut. In six months you'll never have to see these people again." Avoiding looking at Chris, she squeezes through a crack between the tables and slinks to the elevator. Slinking like a snake. Slinking like a worm. Full of angst and shame, she rides up to class.

Walking in, she sees Cindy smiling and waving at her. She waves back, unable to smile. As usual, Cindy has saved her the seat on her left. But on Cindy's right sits Pam alone. Aliza is away again.

"She came in this morning," Pam explains, "but then her stomach went crazy, so she went back home."

Judith nods. Aliza's stomach virus must be more serious than she realized. Or else Aliza took one look at those pictures downstairs and felt so nauseated she couldn't walk past them to get to class. Now Pam leans closer, her body arching over Cindy's like a bridge, and she asks Judith in a low voice, "What did you think of those pictures?"

Judith searches her eyes — eager, grey, and catlike — meanwhile sensing Cindy watching and listening in. "Unbelievable," Judith answers softly. Then: "Well, actually, they're not. That's the problem — they're quite believable. I'll bet lots of people who saw them believed everything they saw."

"So they aren't true?" Cindy asks earnestly.

"They're true but they're not," Judith begins, but stops because Weick is pounding on the desk at the front of the room. *What a Neanderthal,* she thinks. *Pounding like a caveman to get our attention.* She listens to him for a minute, but she's not in the mood right now to hear about how values-driven, ethical, and morally sensitive her social work colleagues are. She's feeling too hurt and cynical. She summons Moshe. He comes immediately, and like her, he's disgusted by this exhibit.

"Disgusting," he says to her first in English, then in Hebrew: "*go'al nefesh*" — literally "revulsion of the soul." His soul is revulsed, she can see, but so is his body: his face is twisted into a scowl as if he's smelled something bad and is trying not to vomit. This comforts her. Here is someone — someone from her own people — who understands things, who feels things, just the way she does. It doesn't matter that their politics are different. They are part of the same drop of water.

Moshe's eyes, brown, warm, deep, draw her in. Then a brightness that she recognizes enters them: it's that "Wanna do it?" look. But she doesn't feel like sex now. She just wants him to hold her. So he does. He wraps his big arms around her and holds her. And in this position she rests, feeling safe, till Weick's class ends.

— 4 —

In the next class, Greg hands back everyone's papers. There are yelps of joy, groans, and silences as people see their marks. Judith's gotten an *A* and is pleased. But Cindy is silent and looks disappointed. Judith tactfully glances away. Cindy taps her shoulder, though, and asks how she did. She just shrugs.

"Come on," says Cindy. "Tell me."

She shows Cindy the last page. There's a big *A* circled at the top and underneath it a paragraph of glowing comments.

"That's great!" says Cindy. "Another *A!*"

Judith checks out Cindy's nonverbals: not a single cloud in those clear sky-blue eyes. Not the slightest trace of envy or resentment. Judith knows in the reverse situation she'd have felt a twinge, but not Cindy. *She's a better person than me*, thinks Judith. Then she asks, to be polite, "What about you?"

Cindy shrugs. "The usual. C+. Like the fruit drink."

"I'm sorry."

"It doesn't matter," Cindy says gamely. "As long as I pass."

Greg starts his lecture. Since that incident with Kerry, Judith doesn't smile at Greg, and she hardly ever speaks in his class. But she lets herself be distracted by Greg and his antics, and does her best to ignore Kerry and her gang — all huddled today, as usual, off to the left — and Lola and her gang, at the front on the right. The class passes quickly. When it's over, Phoebe, the school's administrative coordinator, comes in. Looking dumpy and depressed as always, she distributes pink forms and says she needs their second-term course selections by the end of the day. As everybody rises to leave, Judith proposes to Cindy and Pam that they go for lunch to Le Petit Café, so they won't have to walk through that exhibit again. They can bypass it by taking the elevator all the way down to the basement. Cindy and Pam agree. Over lunch they work, as planned, on their final project for Greg's course, updating each other on what's happening in each region of Canada regarding anti-oppression initiatives in schools of social work. Then they fill out their pink course forms for Phoebe. Judith is astonished to discover she is the only one signing up for "Advanced Social Work Practice," the continuation of Suzy's course. Cindy says Suzy is okay but she's had enough of her. Judith looks at her sharply. Something in Cindy's tone confirms what she has suspected for a while: Cindy is jealous of her relationship with Suzy.

Pam, too, is giving Suzy's course a miss, but for an entirely different reason. She's lost her interest, she says, in clinical work. Lately she's been eyeing the courses in labour studies, and plans to take at least one elective there, maybe more.

Instead of Suzy's course, Cindy says she'll take Terry Montana's on feminism and social work. "I need to get to know her at least a little if she's going to be my thesis advisor."

"True," says Judith, and scribbles herself a note to ask Suzy to be hers.

Then they each pick two more courses. Judith is glad that Cindy, like her, is signing up for Corinne Marajian's class, "Sexism, Racism, and Women of Colour." Judith likes Corinne's look: almost queenly, yet kind and warm. Plus Judith is parched for feminist content, some watering from the feminist spring, after a first term that's been a desert in this respect. For their required research course, it's either Hetty Caplar or Penny Harloffery, whom Judith remembers from Orientation as shiny, hard, and cold, like a brass bugle. She tells Pam and Cindy that Hetty is awkward socially, even slightly odd, but a good egg. So they all choose Hetty.

Pam has taken an extra pink form for Aliza that she can hand in next week. "Assuming she wants to continue with the program," Pam adds.

"What do you mean?!" cries Judith. It never occurred to her that maybe all four of them wouldn't continue together all the way through. They're a unit. A quartet. They're her gang for this year.

Pam shrugs. "I'm not saying she will or she won't. It's up to her. But she's not happy here. She's also not feeling well, which always affects —"

"What about you?" asks Judith. She can barely picture Pam without Aliza. "Are you thinking of quitting, too?" She asks this heartily, in a half-joking tone, hoping Pam will laugh. But she doesn't.

"No," says Pam. "But I'm also pretty fed up with this program. I'm sick of having to listen to morons like Weick and Greg. I mean Greg's a nice guy, but his analysis is very superficial. He doesn't know Marx except from secondary sources. He wouldn't last five minutes in labour studies. Maybe I'd be better off in the Policy stream."

Judith stares at Pam. If she switches into Policy, she'll never see her. And if Aliza quits… She can't imagine being here without Pamanaliza. Of course, she'd still have Cindy, but it wouldn't be the same. Dazed, she turns toward Cindy. *Et tu, Cindé?* is on her lips, but she knows Cindy wouldn't catch this reference. So instead she asks, "And you, Cindy? Are you considering leaving, too?"

Cindy laughs. "Me?! Where would I go? No, I'm here for the whole ride. For better or worse."

"Probably for worse," Pam says jovially.

But Judith doesn't laugh. She looks troubled.

"I didn't say Aliza or I for sure were quitting," Pam says to her. "You just saw me pick my courses for next term. I only said we're both asking some questions."

"Maybe it's just the winter blues," Cindy says hopefully.

Pam shrugs. "I don't know. Anyway, it's time to head back now."

They ride the elevator to the fourth floor in silence and walk into Suzy's class just as she's about to start her lecture. There are very few seats left and they end up sitting separately, each one alone. The class is quite interesting, as usual, but for much of it Judith is studying Suzy's nonverbals, trolling for weirdness of any kind, in case Suzy is angry at her, or even slightly cooler than usual because of their encounter two weeks ago. Last week Suzy had to rush off to a meeting right after class, so they haven't spoken since then. So Judith has been fretting. *I can't believe I told Suzy about my fantasies with Moshe*, she thinks now. *Sometimes I do the stupidest things.* But Suzy today seems the same as always, so Judith is reassured.

— 5 —

The next two weeks, the last of the term, are very busy. Judith is working so hard on her schoolwork that, to save shopping time, she just eats whatever is in her pantry. Mostly canned food — beans, spaghetti — but she doesn't mind. When she's in this state of intense focus, sometimes she tends to forget about her own body altogether. Other than on Mondays, she doesn't shower or get dressed unless Bobby is coming over or she can't stand her own smell. Occasionally she even forgets to eat.

At school, too, things are different during these final two weeks. Everyone is haggard-looking and tense, and the photocopier line is so long that last week she waited forty-five minutes to copy one book chapter, which she could probably have read in less time. This followed an almost physical struggle with another student to get the book. Some people, it seemed, would practically kill their own mothers for a library book. Everyone looks stressed, but none more than Aliza. These past weeks she's been showing up at class only for an hour here, an hour there, and each week she's been thinner, paler, and more fragile. On the last Monday of the term, Judith can't restrain herself anymore, and asks Aliza if she's been to see a doctor.

"Stop it," snaps Aliza, "you sound like my mother. I know how to take care of myself."

They're walking down the hallway a few paces ahead of Pam and Cindy, and now they all reach the elevators. They've just finished Greg's class, and Judith suggests Le Petit Café for lunch.

Pam makes a face. "I'm sick of their tuna sandwiches. We've been there three weeks in a row. Let's go to Libertad."

"No," says Judith. "I'm not going there."

"Why?" asks Aliza.

Cindy says, "Because of that poster, right?"

Judith looks at her.

"Come on," Pam says to Judith. "You can't let that stuff run your life."

"I'm not eating there," Judith says. "I'm not kidding. You go ahead if you want, but I'm not coming."

"It's not that important," says Cindy. "Let's go to Le Petit Café. Tuna fish here we come."

This tone is unusual for Cindy, and Judith peers at her closely. Cindy has bags under her eyes: She told Judith she's been up for two nights with Mikey, who has stomach flu. And Tom's been laid off again, so she's worried about money, including for Christmas presents.

At Le Petit Café, Judith, Cindy, and Pam order tuna sandwiches, and Cindy also has her hallmark maple donut. But Aliza eats nothing, just taking the occasional dainty sip from her Diet Coke. Lately she's been looking for a cheap second-hand car, and Cindy says she heard of one in Dunhill. Searching in her purse for the seller's number, she says his name's Clifford. Aliza writes *Clifford* on her hand.

"What if your hand sweats?" asks Judith.

Cindy reads out Clifford's phone number. Aliza writes it on her arm.

"On your arm?" asks Pam.

"Arm, hand, what's the difference?" says Aliza. "They're both good for remembering. Every part of the body has memory. Especially feet for a dancer." She shows them her arm. On it is a series of seven numbers. *Holocaust numbers*, thinks Judith: *the ID number of a branded cattle-person.* She wants to say, "That's not funny," but she can't get a word out. She stares at Aliza's arm.

"If I lost just a little more weight," Aliza says dreamily, "if I stopped eating altogether for a while, I'd look just like my Bubba, my mother's mother, when she was in Maidanek."

Judith looks from Aliza's arm to her dreamy face. She didn't know Aliza's grandmother was a survivor. Somehow this explains something about Aliza, although she couldn't articulate exactly what. Now Aliza, laughing her bell-like, ringing laugh, dips her pinky into her Diet Coke, reminding Judith of when you dip your pinky into wine, to count the ten plagues at the Passover

Seder. Then Aliza, with her wet pinky, rubs off all the numbers she just wrote.

"Coke removes everything," she explains. "It's pure acid. My grandfather used it during World War II to clean the buttons on his uniform. Did you know that if you drop a brass button into a glass of Coke, after twenty-four hours there will be nothing left of it? It's true. Not a single trace. It'll be completely eroded. That's how powerful Coke is. It eats things alive." Aliza says all this cheerfully, as chatty as a child. Judith wonders: *If you drank enough Coke, could it actually erode your insides? Could it enter your mind and erode all the bad thoughts and memories there? That would be nice.*

Later, on the long drive home, she thinks about Aliza. She's worried about her. But once at home, there's no more time to worry: she goes straight to her desk and gets in another seven hours' work before bed. Classes are already over, but several assignments are due a week from now, so there's still a lot of work to do. "I'm not good at handling stress," Aliza volunteered one day at the beginning of the year, and now, as Judith takes a five-minute break to eat some cold spaghetti out of a can, she thinks this appears to be true. But who *is* good at handling stress? Sure, *she's* not missing classes and she is getting her papers done. But she is having bad dreams at night. Lately about her mother and father. The horror of their being gone. Of their being eroded, dissolved into nothingness, like two brass buttons in Coke. *Being, and* — then, with no warning — *Nothingness.* She forces her attention back to her schoolwork. She works and works until she can't keep her eyes open for even one minute longer.

Four days after the last class, there's another SWAC meeting, the last one in 2002. It is also the last day of the photo exhibit in the atrium. Judith purses her lips and walks through it the same way she has for the past two and a half weeks — with lowered eyes. Her eyes lowered in protest against the lie at the core of this exhibit: that the Palestinians are nothing but pure, innocent victims in this conflict. But they're lowered, too, in shame at what she knows to be true: the violence of the occupation and the excessive force sometimes used by the Israeli army. She cannot bear either the truth or the lie. Trying to see nothing as she walks, she glances only once to her right. Someone with a huge name tag saying *Abdul* is eagerly — with big, bright eyes — explaining something to several students. She hears him say, "The occupation," and keeps walking. Approaching the end of the exhibit, she hears a cheerful voice: "These pictures are hard to look at, aren't they?"

She looks up, startled. But the guy who said this — blond hair, blue eyes, red kaffiyeh around his neck — isn't talking to her. He is addressing three female students, young and innocent-looking, who, studying the photos, scowl.

"Looking at pictures, though, is nothing compared to living inside them," continues the guy with the kaffiyeh. "You and I can close our eyes if we want, or turn our faces away. But little Mohammed here" — he points to the far end of the table, to the first picture in the exhibit — "doesn't have this option."

True, thinks Judith. But she is annoyed by how he's pronounced *Mohammed*: like Moe-hammock, except with a *d* at the end instead of a *ck*. That's not the correct way. She mutters *Mohammed* to herself the way an Arab would, with the proper vowel sounds — not an English *o* and *a* — and with the right guttural Arabic sound instead of an *h*. *This guy is posing as an expert on the Middle East*, she thinks, *and he can't even pronounce* Mohammed *properly.* Disgusted, she rides the elevator upstairs to check her mailbox before meeting Suzy for dinner.

They meet, as usual, in Le Petit Café. In their first ten minutes they dispense with the business of reviewing the agenda for tonight's meeting, which is simple and straightforward. Then they talk. Things between them seem fine. Over the past three weeks, Judith has been only once in Suzy's office, but that one time felt as close and comfortable as always. She was careful not to mention Moshe again. But aside from this subject, she still feels she can tell Suzy anything, and apparently Suzy still likes telling her things, too. Tonight over soup and salad, Suzy describes the Sunday dinner this past weekend at Dennis's parents' house. Natalie, picking up on the undercurrent of tension between the adults, ran around her grandparents' dining room table fifteen times like a whirling dervish; then she expanded her territory, tearing through the entire house, flushed, grunting, and glowing with an almost erotic excitement, sometimes screeching or laughing hysterically. Suzy describes this in a way that invites laughter, and Judith obligingly laughs. But simultaneously she hears the pain behind these words, and she can tell that Suzy knows she does. Now Suzy says, still laughingly, that the one time *she* as a girl went at all crazy — meaning silly, wild, and out of control — her father slapped her across the face, and the next day he left.

"Left?" asks Judith.

"Left," says Suzy. "As in left home and never came back."

"Wow," says Judith, unable to think of anything to say.

Suzy shrugs. She says that over the years she has "come to terms with it." But she hasn't spoken to her father since, and she never will. He'll probably die soon, says Suzy. But that's that. She's done with him. "After what he did, he's toast."

Judith, listening, feels a flash of fear. This is a side of Suzy she's never seen before. And she doesn't ever want to be "toast" to Suzy. A burnt, blackened slice of bread. But then Suzy smiles at her and Judith feels calmer. Nothing like this could ever happen between her and Suzy. Only abandonment or betrayal could trigger such a wrathful reaction in Suzy, and she will never abandon or betray her. Now she wants to say something comforting, like, "Don't worry, Suzy — *I'll* never leave you." But she can't. That would be too heavy — it would openly acknowledge all that naked pain — and Suzy's smirk forbids this. It insists on lightness, despite the sadness in her eyes, and makes any real reply impossible. So Judith mimics her smirk. And their two smirks lock together, as if they were two wounded, smart, smart-alecky kids from *West Side Story:* two jaunty, jocular Jets, each acting tough for the other.

"Anyway," says Suzy. The way she says this word is like a red light. It stops all further conversation on this topic. Now she asks, "What's up with you?"

Judith, still keeping the tone set by Suzy, tells her with humour about her latest fight with Bobby. But soon her bravado drops away and she is confiding in Suzy her ambivalence about marriage, about Bobby, and about marriage to Bobby. Suzy, whom she imagines as very happily married, is more sympathetic to her critique of marriage than she expected.

"It's a strange institution," says Suzy. "It may be the best we've come up with so far, but it's still very far from perfect, and it's especially challenging, even problematic, for women. A woman has to think very carefully before taking this on."

Judith nods, absorbing this. They talk a bit more. Then Judith brings up Brier's lecture on Anti-oppression Day. She was very upset, she says, when she first learned about the rally against Israel that took place three and a half weeks ago at Dunhill. According to the student newspaper that came out a week later, it drew over 250 people, and she wouldn't want Anti-oppression Day to turn into something like that.

Suzy frowns. "Me, either," she says. "But it's a delicate situation."

"Yes, but there must be something we can do."

Suzy sighs. "We obviously can't take on the whole school. Plus there is democratic process — we have to respect that. And maybe just as important, *look* like we are respecting it. I can't come across as a professor who is throwing her weight around, abusing her power. Especially" — she laughs shortly — "since my job, as you know, is precarious now. I'm up for renewal in just ten weeks, and as it happens, Chris and Lola are the two student reps on the Faculty Hiring Committee."

Judith's stomach fearfully curdles, like milk turning sour. What is Suzy saying to her? Is she planning to cave in on this issue? Is she going to sell her out? She can't believe that. But what if all along she's been overestimating Suzy? Tonight she's certainly seen more vulnerability in her than ever before.

But now Suzy says, "Don't get me wrong, Judith. I'm going to do my best on this. I'm just saying I don't know how effective I can be. But I'll try. Tonight I'll say something at the meeting."

Judith nods, her fears allayed. This is the Suzy she knows and trusts: solid, principled, and having a plan. "Trust not in princes," it says in Psalms, but it doesn't tell you not to trust in your profs. Of course Suzy is to be trusted. They're smiling at each other now, the smile not just of colleagues or friends, but of co-conspirators. Partners in a plot.

With twenty minutes left till the meeting, they get more coffee and a large raisin cookie to share, and discuss the end-of-term party at Suzy's house next week.

"'End-of-term' party, not 'Christmas' party, please note,"
Suzy says. She adds, though, that they'll have their Christmas
tree up that night. But if Judith likes she can bring a Chanukah
symbol. Judith, blushing, says no thanks, though she appreciates
the thought. But maybe she'll bring her specialty, her *pièce de
résistance*, a dense, intense chocolate mousse.

"That would be great!" says Suzy. "So far we don't have anything chocolatey."

"This is so chocolatey it'll stand your hair on end." Suzy
laughs. Then Judith offers to come early to help set up.

"What a terrific idea," says Suzy. "You could meet Natalie,
Dennis, and the rest of my family. They've heard so much about
you."

Judith, flattered by this, can see herself becoming friendly
with Suzy's family. Maybe becoming a friend of the family. She is
filled with a warm glow. "I'd love that," she says.

"That's settled, then," says Suzy, briefly touching Judith's
arm. Judith feels the warmth from Suzy's hand seeping into her
skin. Then they walk to the meeting.

— 7 —

They are meeting in a different room tonight. Their usual
room was vandalized last week. The couch was slashed
open, its fluffy white insides spilt all over the floor, the two long
tables had their legs cut off, and the only chairs that weren't
stolen were smashed to smithereens. No one knows who the
perpetrators were, and no one is even under suspicion — which
means, in a way, that everyone is. Tonight's meeting room contains only a round table with ten chairs squeezed around it.

Judith puts her purse on the table, and is pleased when Suzy drops her purse at the adjacent seat before going to welcome the committee members. Sitting, she watches Suzy hobnob, greeting people in her cheerful, friendly way and chatting briefly with everybody, either one-on-one or in groups of two or three. She is now with Elizabeth, a first-year student in the Policy stream who is here today for her first SWAC meeting. Watching them, Judith recollects Suzy saying a while back that she wanted to invite Elizabeth on in mid-year, and Judith agreed. Elizabeth's perfect, straight, long blond hair swings as she laughs with Suzy, and Judith recalls hearing somewhere that Elizabeth and Suzy attend the same Dunhill church.

Soon the meeting begins. There's a report from Brenda on the Teacher Evaluation Subcommittee; then the rest of the meeting focuses on Anti-oppression Day. Judith can barely look at Chris or Lola when, as co-chairs of Publicity, they give their detailed update. After Publicity, the committee deals with the lunch plan, parking arrangements, and who will introduce and thank Michael Brier. Then Suzy says, "I know how much we're all looking forward to having Michael Brier here, and hearing what he has to say. But as we go forward with this event, I'd like to remind us all that the underlying premise of Anti-oppression Day, indeed of this very committee, is respect for all individuals and groups." She looks around the table, ending with Chris, who barely restrains a smirk. Suzy continues, "Specifically, given the subject of Brier's keynote, it's important that we all keep in mind the sensibilities of our Jewish students and faculty." Several people glance at Judith; she lowers her eyes. "Obviously we're not talking about silencing anybody. Just ensuring that all discussions take place in an atmosphere of mutual respect and professional collegiality."

"Hear, hear," says Hetty.

"Of course," says James. "We're all coming together to learn."

Shortly afterwards the meeting adjourns. Chris, Janice, and Lola quickly cluster, whispering, but Judith tells herself it means nothing. She shrugs on her coat, careful not to say anything to Suzy in front of the others — no thumbs-up, wink, or expression of gratitude. Instead she chats with Brenda, James, and Hetty, and says goodbye to them cheerfully in the parking lot. She's happy. Suzy came through. She said what was necessary. She won't let Anti-oppression Day turn into a hate rally against Israel.

— 8 —

That night Judith dreams that a woman she doesn't know is massaging her shoulders and neck, and rubbing warm oil into her back, and then, surprising her, into her bum, into the crack in her bum. She awakens incredibly horny and all she can think about is warm fingers probing her all over her body, and different scented oils being rubbed into every crevice and hole. She wishes Bobby were here now to do these things to her.

She eats breakfast and tries to concentrate on theories of knowledge for her final paper for Weick. But the only knowledge she can relate to right now is the knowledge of the body. She calls Bobby at work and says in a throaty imitation of Mae West, "Hey, honey — wanna come over sometime?"

He laughs. "I'd love to, but I'm going into a meeting. But we'll see each other tonight for Shabbat, and tomorrow night's the Jewish film festival."

"Oh, yeah. What are we seeing? Something light, I hope."

"Amen."

"I'm glad we're in the same mood. But what's the movie called?"

"Amen."

"You mean the movie's called *Amen*?"

"Yeah. It's Costa-Gavras's film about the Holocaust."

"Goody," she says. "Now there's a fun Saturday night date for two bright, sexy young Jews. Let's go watch a Holocaust film and get so depressed we both want to slit our wrists."

Bobby chuckles over the phone. "We don't have to go if you don't want to. I'm happy to stay in instead."

"Did you already buy the tickets?"

"No, we were going to go early and line up."

"Then fuck it," she says. "Fuck the film. Better yet, fuck me. Come over tonight, stay in bed with me all weekend, and fuck me, fuck me, fuck me."

"Okay," he laughs. "I won't say no to that. But what's gotten into you?"

"Nothing. That's the problem. I need something to get into me. Deep, deep into me."

There is silence now at the other end. Then Bobby, sounding distant, says he has to go: Dennis just signalled him from the doorway; the meeting is starting.

"*À ce soir,*" she whispers. "*Mon chéri.*"

For the rest of the day she works hard on her paper for Weick, squeezing in her Shabbat cooking, making a less elaborate meal than usual. By sundown her paper is done. Two down, since she finished Suzy's paper last week. Now all she has left for this term is her part of the project for Greg. It's been interesting but sobering: not one social work school in Canada includes antisemitism when teaching about oppression. Still, she's relieved that she'll be all done in three days, and sings as she sets the table and tidies the kitchen. While tidying, she discovers a bag of Hershey's kisses that she bought last month from a war vet on Remembrance Day. It was a fundraiser, with the money going toward prostheses for war vets. She eats one kiss after another, thinking each one will be the last, until Bobby walks in.

He throws his jacket onto a chair, embraces her, and kisses her hard. "Mmm, chocolate," he murmurs, tasting her mouth. They rip off their clothes, and still standing, grab each other's bums, move together in rhythm, and to the sound of his panting and her moans, come quickly. Afterwards, laughing, they half-dress and she pours them each a glass of red wine. She wishes she had one of those negligées you see in old movies. She's naked except for a long T-shirt. Bobby likes this just as much as a negligée, though, and slides his hand underneath her T-shirt, but she wriggles away. Then they light the Shabbat candles and recite the blessings, and as they eat, she tells him about last night's SWAC meeting and Suzy's intervention at the end. Bobby sometimes grimaces when she starts talking about Suzy, but tonight he says, "Not bad for a lefty."

Then he updates her about the big case he's working on with Dennis: assisting a multinational corporation interested in Canada's oil fields. So far it's been going very well, and Dennis seems pleased with him. In fact, today he said, "If this keeps up, Bobby, I can see making you a permanent member of our team. You could be a great asset to us."

"That's fantastic," she says.

"Permanent status on Dennis's team would be a huge step forward for me," says Bobby. "With the new bonus structure the firm just implemented, this could mean an extra thirty, maybe forty, thousand a year."

"I hope this works out," she says, doing her best to be enthusiastic and supportive, even though she feels talking about money is vulgar. She says she's looking forward to meeting Dennis at Suzy's party next week.

"I wonder," Bobby says thoughtfully, "what you'll think of him. He can be pretty strange."

"I'm sure I'll like him if he's married to Suzy." But then she falls silent.

"What is it?" asks Bobby.

"Nothing."

"Tell me."

Frowning, she studies his face briefly. "Do you think I'm a lesbian?" she asks.

"What?" he laughs. "You? A lesbian?!"

"No, seriously." She tells him about last night's dream. "It's weird. I've never dreamed about a woman touching me before."

"You're not a lesbian."

"Or bi. Maybe I'm bi."

"Right. You're bi like I'm bi."

"Well, are you?" she asks.

"Shut up." He looks at her affectionately. "Here's the ultimate test," he says. "Stand up." When she does, he reaches under her T-shirt and strokes her nipple. Her eyes close and she moans. "This," he says, "is not the response of a lesbian. If you were a lesbian, you wouldn't be making that little sound of yours."

He pulls her T-shirt over her head, and with her leaning back against the dining room table, they again make love.

— 9 —

Three days later, on Monday December 9, Judith attends her first meeting of Friends-of-Peace since returning to Toronto. She has no interest in Toronto's left-wing Zionist scene, but agreed to come this once at the urging of her old friend Mendl. It feels strange sitting in Mendl's living room again, with almost all the same people as eleven years ago when, before making *aliya*, she was part of this group. They were all fifteen years older than her, so she never belonged socially, but she did ideologically, admiring them as the pioneers, the inspiring Socialist-Zionists a generation ahead of her. Yet now she looks at them — all these "Zionists" living in *galut*. What are they doing here? Why aren't they in Israel where they belong?

Then she answers her own question, looking from one face to another. Micky and Shira returned to Toronto "temporarily" twenty years ago because each believed this was what the other wanted. Only ten years later, when it was already too late — when they had three children, a house, a mortgage, and two good jobs: in short, "a life" here — did they have their first honest conversation about this since leaving Israel, and discover their mistake. *Tragic*, thinks Judith. *Like the mistake in de Maupassant's "The Necklace."*

Next she contemplates Efraim. He postponed his *aliya* because his mother was dying. Yet here it is eleven years later and his mother's alive and kicking and could be for eleven more.

Lily, sitting in the armchair: just as she was about to make *aliya*, she fell in love with Henry and married him. Henry, though, doesn't like Israel, so she's never been back since. Lily stayed here for love. In fact, all three of them in a way gave up Israel for love. And love is a good thing. But still, to live away from The Land. The Land that throbs with your very own heartbeat. What love — what in the whole world — could possibly make up for that?

After the meeting, she and Mendl chat. She tells him what's been happening at Dunhill. and he encourages her to give him a call. "We'll come up with something," he says. "We'll make a plan." She's touched. This is vintage Mendl. As if there's nothing in the world too big to strategize over, or fight back against. When they part he says, "*Chizki v'imtzi*." Be strong and courageous.

— 10 —

The following evening, Judith stands in front of Suzy's house. It is a big old brick structure with a peaked gable, and in the darkness it reminds her of Wuthering Heights. Nervously, she rings the bell. But when the door opens and Suzy greets her warmly, she feels at home. She hands Suzy the heavy cut-glass bowl she's carrying. She follows close behind Suzy as she takes it into the kitchen, sets it down on the counter, and pulls back the tinfoil on top.

"This is beautiful!" Suzy exclaims.

"What is it?" asks a red-haired freckled boy strolling into the kitchen. *This must be Todd*, thinks Judith. The boy stands on his tiptoes, peers into the bowl, and says, "Woooow!"

Judith laughs with pride. She wanted to please and she worked hard this afternoon to make this dessert. But it was worth it. The creamy chocolate mousse with the pretty dark chocolate curls on top never fails to impress.

"This is gorgeous!" says Suzy. "You made this yourself?" She nods. "Well, thank you very much! Should I put it in the fridge till we serve it?"

"Good idea," says Judith. She watches Suzy manoeuvre things around in the crowded fridge until she finds a spot for the mousse. "I'm so relieved it survived the drive from Toronto," adds Judith. "I was afraid it would turn into mush on the way."

"It's perfect."

Judith, watching Suzy, sees a flash of movement behind her in the doorway, and then in walks Phoebe. *Phoebe! What's*

Phoebe doing here? Next in walks Darra. *Darra?* Now Judith realizes, with a sinking feeling in her stomach, that she is not, after all, alone here with Suzy and her family. Suzy must have invited others besides her to come early and help. Next Janice walks into the kitchen carrying a large platter, and behind her is someone else whose face, initially obscured by Janice, gradually emerges into view ... Elizabeth. Judith tries to hide her disappointment and returns everyone's greetings. In the dining room she watches them bustling about, putting drinks on tables, flowers in vases, and the right serving utensil on each dish: a long spoon for the eggplant parmesan, a spatula for the quiche. Others are arranging on platters, as attractively as possible, all the smaller items people have brought: carrot sticks, hummus, alfalfa sprouts, cashews. Mike is here, too, hauling folding chairs, several under each arm, into the living room from somewhere downstairs.

Judith stands in the middle of all this commotion, feeling lost. Everybody but her seems to know exactly what to do. She looks around Suzy's home. It's a solid old house furnished in the old-fashioned way: thick living room curtains and heavy good-quality furniture in dark wood, including a glass-doored cabinet displaying fine china. They are obviously well off.

They are also obviously Christian: in the corner there's a huge Christmas tree with shiny coloured balls and ornaments hanging from every branch, silver tinsel draped all over everything, and on the very top a triumphant angel. *What angel is this?* she wonders. *It's white, so maybe it's the angel Gabriel. Gabriel who guards over us.* Now she wishes she were at a Chanukah party instead of a Christmas, or "end-of-term," party, or whatever this is. Though she did enjoy celebrating Chanukah this year with Bobby, lighting Chanukah candles in front of the living room window, singing Chanukah blessings and songs, and eating potato *latkes* with sour cream and applesauce, or jam-filled donuts with powdered sugar on top. *Oh well*, she thinks. *Let's see if I can also enjoy tonight.*

She asks a couple of the people bustling around her, "How can I help?" and Janice replies by thrusting a bottle of wine at her and asking her to open it. Judith takes the wine into the kitchen and rummages through the drawers, looking for a corkscrew. She feels awkward going through someone else's things, but Suzy, whom she would normally ask, is nowhere to be seen. Darra says she's gone upstairs. Judith hears a loud thumping coming from there, like someone is repeatedly kicking the floor. Maybe Natalie is throwing a tantrum.

"Whoa!" Tyler says to her, and whistles, looking her up and down. Judith flushes. She already noticed she is overdressed. Everyone else is wearing almost the same clothes they wear to school, just one step up. She feels acutely self-conscious in her low-cut red velvet gown, long gold necklace, and black high heels. She hadn't known how to dress for tonight, and now she is completely out of place.

"Lady in red," says Tyler with a leer.

Blushing, she rolls her eyes, and he leaves the kitchen carrying three chairs under each arm. She wishes Bobby were here with her — he had an urgent meeting of his legal committee tonight — or at least someone from her gang. But Aliza is apparently still sick. Judith called her twice to see how she was feeling and ask if she was coming, but Aliza didn't call back. Pam is away on holiday — she got a cheap last-minute flight that left this morning for Mexico — and Cindy had to stay home with Mikey because Tom is working nights now on a two-week contract. The kitchen is crowded and full of activity. People are searching for things, opening cupboards and slamming them shut, grabbing items off shelves, hurling dirty spoons into the sink, and stuffing empty containers and cellophane from flowers into an overflowing garbage bin.

"Only twenty-five minutes till everyone arrives," pants Phoebe, perspiration dripping down her face. Suzy enters the kitchen looking flushed and distraught.

"Is something wrong?" Judith asks her.

"You know kids," Suzy tells Judith and Phoebe. "They never want bedtime when there's a party."

"Was that Natalie I heard upstairs?" Judith asks, and then hopes she hasn't made a faux pas. Maybe other people don't know about Natalie. Maybe this is something Suzy told only to her, and in confidence. But Suzy seems unfazed.

"No, she's sleeping at Dennis's sister's tonight. We thought that would be easiest. What you heard was Matthew. He hates going to sleep when there's excitement downstairs."

Judith nods but thinks, They have sent Natalie away. Hidden her out of sight like Quasimodo. Suddenly she feels woozy. She studies the glass she is holding. A few minutes ago Darra shoved into her hand this glass of sweet red stuff, and being thirsty, she immediately drank more than half of it.

"Is this spiked?" she asks Suzy, holding up her glass.

Phoebe laughs. "Of course! It wouldn't be Christmas without a little extra cheer, now, would it?"

"Go light on that stuff," says Suzy, smiling. "It's Phoebe's killer punch."

"Punch that packs a punch." Phoebe grins. "Try saying that ten times in a row," and she leaves the kitchen carrying a tray of plastic wineglasses. Everyone is busy in the dining room now, leaving Judith and Suzy alone in the kitchen, working on a cheese tray. Judith feels happier now. This is how she pictured it, just her and Suzy, the two of them chatting and joking around, while their hands work expertly in perfectly coordinated rhythm. They are laying out some Camembert, Jarlsberg, and Danish blue, along with salmon mousse, grapes, thin round tea crackers, stuffed pimento olives, and tiny sweet gherkins. The finished platter is an elegant mix of colours, shapes, and textures. *Almost like a painting,* she thinks. Then Suzy says, "For the final touch," and pops a flower into each corner of the silver tray.

"Nasturtiums," she says. "They're edible."

"Really?" asks Judith. When Suzy nods, she picks up the one unused flower. It has delicate petals, yellow with tiny red flames in them, and she tries to imagine putting it into her mouth. Eating a flower feels somehow like a cross-species act. Something that must be forbidden somewhere, like sexual intercourse between human and beast. With Suzy watching, she flicks out her tongue and licks the soft petal. Its taste is subtle, or maybe it's not even actually a taste, just a smell, like the faint sweetness of violets. There is nothing terrible about it, though. Nothing weird or disturbingly pungent or sexual, like the taste of sperm. So she eats a petal of it. It's nice. Like eating a tender, slightly perfumed, prettier form of lettuce. "Not bad," she says, and Suzy smiles.

Now they start slicing the Christmas cake Suzy made. Suzy doesn't call it a Christmas cake; she calls it a fruit cake — perhaps, thinks Judith, out of respect for her, or multiculturalism, or both. But she knows a Christmas cake when she sees one: it's got those little candied fruits in it, and smashed-up green and red maraschino cherries. It's pretty, in a dark, dense sort of way, and multicoloured even if not multicultural.

"How's it going?" asks a voice, and an energetic fresh-faced man in his early forties strides into the kitchen.

"Okay," says Suzy without looking up, continuing her careful slicing. "Just finishing the cake." When the last piece is done she turns, knife in hand, toward the man, pointing at him and then at Judith with the knife. "Judith, my husband, Dennis. Dennis, this is Judith. Remember that student I told you about, who I'm hoping will be my TA next term? Bobby Kornblum in your office is her boyfriend …?"

Dennis is holding a bottle of wine and a corkscrew, and he puts these on the counter so he can stretch out his hand toward Judith. "I've heard a lot about you," he says with warmth. "Suzy thinks you're terrific. Obviously so does Bobby. Very nice to meet you at last."

His handshake is warm and strong. "Same here," she says, then blushes, feeling confused. His eyes are friendly, but unusually penetrating. A shimmering blue.

"I'll put this on the table," says Suzy, taking the tray of Christmas cake.

"Do you need help?" Judith asks.

"I'm fine."

Suzy leaves the room and Dennis says with a laugh, "Someone out there asked me to open this wine, but I'm hopeless with a corkscrew. What about you?"

His tone and look are slyly suggestive, but Judith just shakes her head, saying, "I'm hopeless, too. And I'm supposed to open that one." She points to the bottle she left on the kitchen table ten minutes ago.

Dennis opens his bottle. Slowly and sensuously he draws the cork out of the bottle: it comes out cleanly, perfectly, with a polite, muted pop. *Yeah, sure*, she thinks, *hopeless with a corkscrew*.

"Would you like me to do yours, too?" he asks. Which again sounds like a double-entendre, and again she chooses to ignore this. Maybe she's imagining things because of Phoebe's punch.

"Thanks," she says.

Dennis easily opens her bottle of wine. Then, wiping off the corkscrew, he asks, "So you're working with Suzy on her research next term?"

"If the grant comes through. I hope it does."

"Why?"

"Why?"

"Yes — why?"

She tries to consider this. But she's feeling extremely woozy and quite inarticulate. *That stupid punch* — she is hazily annoyed at Phoebe. She does her best to concentrate and answer Dennis.

"Because it's important," she says. "We need research on how the university and community work together on anti-oppression. Social work schools should be part of that, not just stay within the ivory tower."

"Ya think?" he asks, smiling down at her, somewhat mockingly. In her peripheral vision, she sees Tyler coming into the kitchen, taking more chairs and leaving. She and Dennis are alone again. His mocking tone irritates her but she tries overlooking it. He's Suzy's husband and Bobby's mentor. She wants to get along with him.

"That's what they always say on *The West Wing,*" she says. "'Ya think?'"

"You like *The West Wing*?"

"I'm an addict."

"An addict."

"Yeah. I never miss an episode." Her tongue feels swollen in her mouth and her words sound strange and slurred to her.

"Aha," says Dennis. "And what else are you addicted to?"

She looks away. She senses now that she's on dangerous, shifting ground. So it wasn't all in her imagination. It wasn't just the punch. She answers without looking at Dennis, "I don't know."

"Come on," she hears him say urgently. "Tell me. After all, we're almost family. You knowing Suzy. And me knowing Bobby."

She glances at him briefly.

"I know you like social work," he says softly.

This feels safer. She looks at him. "Yes. I love social work."

240

"Love," he says, and she feels the room starting to swirl around her. "What else do you love?" he asks, bringing his face closer to hers, his blue eyes glittering. She wants to turn away, but can't. She's mesmerized by those eyes. Then there's the sound of an explosion: it's Dennis laughing, a laugh that sounds like a sob, like it's been torn out of his entrails. Now, very near them both, almost in between them, stands Suzy with a blank expression Judith cannot read.

"You're right," Dennis says, turning toward Suzy. "This *is* an exceptional young woman. She's been telling me how she loves social work."

Suzy looks at Judith. Judith looks back at her. Her mind is blank from the punch. Something in Suzy's face makes her want to say, "I didn't do anything," but she can't find the words. Then Suzy says, "Judith, would you excuse us for a moment?"

"Sure." Her knees slightly tremble. Leaving, she hears Suzy say to Dennis in a low, intense tone, in a voice she didn't know Suzy had, "You've had too much to drink."

"No, I haven't. I'm just happy. You should be happy, too, Suzy."

"In my own house, Dennis. With one of my students?!"

This phrase, *in my own house*, sounds vaguely familiar to Judith, but she can't recall where from. In the dining room she stands numbly with people bustling all around her. Then she feels nauseated and, afraid she'll vomit, rushes to the bathroom. But she doesn't vomit. Just sits on the toilet for a while. *What if Suzy thinks I was flirting with Dennis?* she wonders. *She can't believe that because it isn't true. I wasn't doing anything of the kind. But still, what if that's what Suzy thinks?* She frets about this. Then, leaving the bathroom, she realizes why Suzy's phrase *in my own house* sounded familiar. It's from the *megilla*, the story of Purim, when King Ahasuerus finds Haman, who tried to destroy the Jews, literally throwing himself upon Queen Esther, begging for mercy. The king, enraged, says to him, "Will you assault my queen even in my own house?" *Haman the Evil*, thinks Judith. *That's how the* megilla *refers to him.*

Re-entering the party, she feels like she has stepped from one world — solitary and silent — into a completely different one: the bright and noisy social world, with its glare, blare, and shallowness. Suzy's house is packed with people now. The party was called for seven o'clock, at this point it's seven-fifteen, and there are at least thirty people in the living and dining rooms who weren't there when she went to the bathroom. People say hello to her, and she says hello back, but meanwhile she squints, scanning the room, searching for Suzy. Eager to find her and get her reassurance that everything is okay between them. But she doesn't see her anywhere. Judith weaves her way through the crowd, passing from one room into another. She wishes Cindy, Pam, or Aliza were here. She stands before the long dining room table, which is covered with attractive platters of food.

"When in doubt, eat," Yonina always said, so bypassing the ham-filled quiche and roast pork, Judith loads a plate with eggplant parmesan and salad. Putting her fork into her mouth, she recognizes someone off to her left. One of the most popular profs where she did her B.S.W.: Deanne MacLean, married to another prof at the school, Don Whitehead. Don and Deanne. Then Judith notices Don, too, standing next to Deanne. But, unlike back then, his hair is now white. He's white-headed, she thinks. He finally matches his name. She approaches Deanne, reminds her she was her student thirteen years before, and says "Family Systems" was one of her favourite courses.

"Thank you!" Deanne's smile shows small, even teeth, and her blond hair swings forward as she leans toward Judith. "And what are you doing now?"

Deanne and Don both beam at Judith like two car head-lights. Don's shiny pink forehead gleams as he beams.

Shy under all this bright attention, she says, "I'm doing my Master's at Dunhill."

"Great!" says Deanne. "And what've you been doing since finishing your B.S.W.?"

Judith feels more cheerful now. She tells Don and Deanne about working in Israel with developmentally disabled children, and running coexistence groups for Jewish and Arab teens. Don and Deanne nod approvingly.

"You know," says Don in a caring, concerned social worker tone, "tonight before coming here we watched the six o'clock news, and afterwards we were so upset about Israel."

"So was I," says Judith. There was another terrorist attack today, this time on a university campus: ten dead, thirty-four injured.

"What we can't understand," says Deanne, her eyes searching Judith's, "is how the Jews, who have suffered so much themselves, can turn around and inflict such suffering on another people."

Judith doesn't understand. She frowns at Deanne in confusion: *What do you mean? We got bombed today. Not the other way around.*

"Haven't the Jews learned anything from their own history?" Deanne asks. "It's absolutely terrible what the Israelis are doing to the Palestinians. It makes us just sick, as I'm sure it does you."

Now Judith understands. And she does feel sick, but not the way Deanne intended. "It's complicated," she says weakly, her stomach turning over. But she forces herself to continue, pushing the words out with an effort. "Lots of good stuff happens there that you never read about here. Many people in Israel, like my friends, are critical of Sharon's policies, and they're working to try and improve the situation. To find a peaceful solution."

"Really!" says Deanne. "This is very interesting. I didn't know that. So you're saying there are some good Jews — I mean Israelis?"

Judith stares at her. Then, in a flat voice, she says, "Yes, Deanne. There are some good Israelis and Jews."

But Deanne and Don both miss this completely. "That's great to hear," Don says heartily, beaming at Judith like she's a student who has just given the right answer. He goes on talking, but she doesn't hear a word. All she's aware of is the reverberations of shock inside her, like a gong being hit over and over again.

"Excuse me," she says, interrupting Don in mid-sentence. Which she knows is a terrible etiquette crime in Canada, but she doesn't care. In response to Deanne's frown and Don's half-open mouth and astonished, popping eyes, which make him look like a fish, she turns on her heel and walks away. She is a little surprised at herself, but pleased that, with two small words, "Excuse me," she has extricated herself from these two stupid people. Fuck the Canadian left. Fuck these people whose hearts bleed for everyone but Jews.

Fuming, she continues moving through the party. *Oh well.* She shrugs, walking. *That's two more down. Two more people transferred from the good side of the scale to the bad one.* In her mind there is always a scale operating: the old-fashioned type with two metal saucers. The first time she saw a scale like this she was watching *The Fugitive* with her father. When they introduced the main character, Richard Kimble, they showed the Roman goddess of justice, Justitia, blindfolded and holding the scales. Ever since then Judith has had a scale like this in her mind. Some days the evil in the world is winning; other days, goodness.

Now she spots Suzy on the other side of the living room. She weaves through the crowd to get closer. Suzy looks at her but does not smile.

"I was looking for you," Judith says, her eyes searching Suzy's. "I wanted ... I hope you don't think —"

"Not now." Suzy glances around them. They are surrounded by people who can hear every word they're saying.

"I just want —" says Judith.

"I said, '*Not now.*'"

This time there is no mistaking the coldness in her voice. Judith frowns in confusion. *I didn't do anything*, she thinks. *You got the wrong impression.* But Suzy's eyes looking back at her are matte, like the eyes of a snake, appearing not fully alive. They frighten Judith. She feels like there is no way to reach Suzy.

But then Suzy says, "If you feel like being helpful, Weick needs assistance bringing in the beer."

She doesn't understand.

"The beer is outside in his car," Suzy explains. "He's parked a few doors down to the left, and when he brought in the first case, I told him I'd find someone to help him unload the rest. He's waiting now."

Great. Alone with Weick outside in the dark. But she doesn't refuse. Almost anything Suzy could have asked her to do, she would have agreed to. Anything to get the two of them back on track. "Sure," she says, "no problem." She tries again to make eye contact, but Suzy's lids are lowered and she has already turned away. She is chirping something hostessy to Kerry and Chris, and then laughing with them. *Laughing with those haters of Israel*, thinks Judith, heading for the door.

She steps out into the winter night wearing nothing but her red dress. She searched briefly for her coat but couldn't find it and didn't want to delay doing what Suzy had asked. *As swift as a gazelle to do your bidding*, like in Song of Songs. So here she is, outdoors in a Canadian winter in just a low-cut dress. Weick's car is parked in shadow a few doors down. She sees him, wrapped in a Phantom-of-the-Opera/Dracula cape, stacking cases of beer at the curb.

"Suzy said you needed help," she says, hoping her voice sounds normal, casual. Weick turns his head sideways.

"You!" He stands, scanning her from head to toe and back again, pausing at her partly exposed bosom. "I was expecting Tyler or Mike. I asked for someone who can carry cases of beer."

"I can carry cases of beer."

"Of course you can. Spoken like a true feminist. Well, let's see what you can do." He gestures toward his open trunk.

She leans down, lifts a case of twenty-four, and stacks it on top of the others. She does this again. The third time, though, she has to bend down all the way to the pavement to start a new pile, and she is aware of her cleavage showing, and of Weick gazing at it again. She tries to ignore this as she empties the last case from the car. Then she starts making trips back and forth between the car and the house, lugging one case of beer after another. She makes four trips in total, she and Weick passing each other as they come and go, and even before completing the first trip, her teeth are chattering. When she returns to the car the fourth time for her last trip, she's sweating down the inside of her dress but the rest of her is freezing. She is simultaneously freezing and burning.

"That's that," says Weick, slamming shut the hatchback.

There is only one case left on the curb, and she nods, relieved. She is glad she can return now to the warm house. Glad, too, that nothing weird happened out here with Weick.

"I stand corrected," he says with a slight, gallant bow. "I'm learning a lot from you feminists."

"No problem." She is shivering, her arms crossed over her partly naked chest, as she waits for him to lift the last case so they can go inside.

"By the way," he says, apparently not noticing her chattering teeth, "I'm curious why you never dropped by my office to talk about your paper."

Oh, that. She looks at him as innocently as she can. "In the end I solved the problem by myself."

"I can't complain about the result," he says. "It was a very good paper. But I was disappointed you didn't come by. I'd put aside some articles I thought you'd find helpful."

"Oh!" she says, feeling remorseful. "I didn't know. But thank you, that's so nice!"

"I guess since the term is over you won't need them now. But maybe in January come by and I'll give them to you."

"Sure." She is starting to feel trapped. Like a spider is weaving a sticky, inescapable web around her.

"I especially liked the part of your paper," he says, "where you wrote that internalized oppression can affect how Jewish women or black women feel about their bodies. Their hair, their noses, their hips ..."

She lowers her eyes. This can't be happening. First Dennis, now Weick. Suddenly she's acutely aware of being all alone out here with him.

"Those were the findings from the research," she says, trying to be as intellectual and professional as possible, even though she's trembling inside and her teeth are chattering. From cold and fear.

"You're cold," he says solicitously. "Would you like some of my cape?" He holds up the edge of the cape attached to his coat.

"No, thanks. I'm going in now anyway."

"So am I. But come under my cape as we walk. You must be freezing."

She contemplates the big, warm-looking cape. It's attached to his coat, so putting it around her means being pulled close against him. "I'm fine, thanks. I just want to go back now." She points at Suzy's house and takes a step.

"Are you running away?" he asks.

"What?"

"Don't run away from me."

"I'm not."

"Yes, you are. Wait a minute," he says, and grabs her arm.

She wrenches free, begins walking quickly, and then runs toward the house. Reaching the door, she tumbles inside, almost crashing into Suzy who's standing alone in the vestibule. Suzy looks at her in surprise. Judith is panting and obviously upset.

"He grabbed me," says Judith, her teeth still chattering, tears in her eyes.

"Who? Who grabbed you?"

"Weick."

"Weick?!"

"Yeah. Outside, near his car."

Suzy frowns. "What do you mean 'grabbed'?"

"He wanted me to wear his cape," she says, trying not to cry, "and when I didn't want to, he said I shouldn't run away from him and he grabbed my arm —"

"That's enough," says Suzy. In her voice there's a flat, hard edge, and that coldness again. "Be careful what you say, Judith. You're talking about the director of our school."

"I know, but ..." She stops. Suzy isn't on her side anymore. Suzy is on Weick's side, because he's helping her keep her job.

"Whatever happened just now," Suzy says, "I suggest you keep it to yourself. It looks to me like you have had too much to drink. You're having quite an evening in that pretty red dress of yours. You need to get ahold of yourself."

"I have a hold on myself." But then, feeling nauseous, she says, "I need the bathroom," and races toward it, and the second the door is shut, throws up all over the lovely navy blue tiles. She leans back, panting, against the inside of the door, tears leaking from her closed eyes. Then she hears the front door slam, followed by Weick's voice saying, "Here's the last of it."

"Thanks, Larry," Suzy's voice answers. *Larry?!* Judith has never before heard anyone call Lawrence Weick by his first name — Lawrence, much less Larry — and it sounds quite intimate. Suzy continues: "Right here would be great. We already have plenty of beer on the drinks table."

"Right-o." Then he says casually: "By the way, did you see Judith come in? We were finishing with the beer and she ran off."

"She's in the bathroom," Suzy answers drily. "I think she's had one too many glasses of Phoebe's punch."

"Ah, that would explain it," he says. "She was acting rather strange."

Now there is silence. Judith tries to picture what's happening out there. But then she stops. It doesn't matter anymore. Suzy sold her out to Weick and that's the bottom line. So much for the "special relationship" between Suzy and her. That's all over now. She sits on the toilet and rests awhile. Then she begins mopping up her vomit with wads of toilet paper. It takes some time. Vomit is everywhere. In the sink, on the floor, even splattered on the walls. But eventually she's done. She stands in the middle of the bathroom, unsure what to do, reluctant to return to the party. She wishes that under these gleaming, winking, navy blue floor tiles there were a secret tunnel she could escape through, so she wouldn't have to face Suzy or Weick again tonight.

Gingerly she opens the bathroom door. Only a few people are in the hallway between the bathroom and the front vestibule. They're chatting and laughing in twos and threes, and on a chair near the front door there is a big pile of coats that wasn't there before, with hers near the top. Now is her chance. As casually as she can, she saunters to the chair, lifts her coat, and edges toward the door. Then she is outside in the cold silent night, on a street lined with snowbanks. *I'm free*, she thinks, slipping on her coat. *I've escaped.* Stealthily, like a thief in the night — as if she were actually guilty of some crime — she skulks down the block to her car, slides inside, and, hoping she is invisible in the darkness, drives away.

TAKING A STAND

The next morning Judith awakens with a fever. She caught a chill unloading the beer from Weick's car, but still over the Christmas holiday she goes skiing with Bobby in Banff for two weeks in sub-zero temperatures, and afterwards they pop over to Vancouver for four days to see his sister. Marla is what Judith, if she ever used this expression, would call a "Jewish American Princess." She usually avoids this term because it's both misogynistic and antisemitic, but Marla is always dressed perfectly in the latest fashions and has earrings, bracelets, and makeup on, even at the breakfast table with little Melinda vomiting all over her. Marla's nails are long, red, and shiny — as shiny as all the appliances in her shiny new house, which she shows off to Bobby and Judith with pride. She gives them the grand tour, and this house trumpets out all its newness and richness, but also its nouveau riche-ness. Then she shows off, with almost equal pride, her husband Gunther — whose name she pronounces like Grunter — a heavy-set man thirteen years older, stolidly bourgeois and deadly dull. *An accountant*, thinks Judith, *but a man of no account.*

She hasn't seen Marla since college. They first met in high school when Judith and Bobby started going out. "Bobby's little sister," just two years younger than her, was at first admiring, fawning even. Later she became jealous of her, and then angry when she left Bobby to move to Israel. Now Marla is cool to her and condescending about her clothes and lack of makeup. She also seems miffed that Bobby still — despite everything — wants to marry Judith, and that Judith, once again, is not jumping at the chance. Marla takes this as a personal insult to her and the entire Kornblum clan.

So Marla, with her long, sharp nails, scratches away at Judith. One day they go downtown together for facials — "an outing for just us girls," Marla says coyly to Bobby and Gunther over breakfast, and Judith plays along for Bobby's sake. After they've had their facials, the beautician dabs some makeup on their faces. Marla looks at Judith appraisingly and says, "You know, Judith, you could be quite attractive with just a little work."

I'm already attractive, you bitch, Judith thinks, but does not say. In fact, I'm beautiful, but you're too stupid to see it. Just last night, Bobby stopped abruptly in the middle of making love and stared at her.

"Do you know how beautiful you are?" he asked. "You're absolutely ravishing."

Embarrassed, she shrugged. But then she grinned at him. "If I'm ravishing," she said, "ravish me."

Which he did. And remembering this now, she smiles at Marla without saying a word.

By the end of their four days in Vancouver, though, Judith and Bobby are at each other's throats.

"Okay, so she's a bit of a Princess," says Bobby, "but she's still my sister."

"I can't stand your family," she says, "and everything they represent."

Bobby's family at this point consists only of Marla and Bobby's brother Richard, and Richard is a racist, the one who believes Arabs have the moral understanding of dogs. Judith knows there is no real possibility of her marrying Bobby. But when occasionally she tries picturing her life if she did, she thinks of inheriting his whole family and, like a caged stallion, wants to make a break for it.

On the plane ride home, they sit in hostile silence, a silence broken only when one of them snaps at the other. She is visibly shivering and he seems to intentionally ignore this, not even offering her his green Air Canada blanket, even though he's not using it. She hasn't stopped shivering since Suzy's party, and spending the last four days in Marla's badly heated, uncarpeted house with its cold, imitation-marble floors has made her sicker. Now on the plane she feels cold in her bones, in their inner-most marrow. Nothing she's done since Suzy's party to try and warm up has helped: not wearing *gatkes* under two other layers of clothes, swaddling herself in multiple blankets, or drinking quarts of hot lemon tea. Nothing helps in the slightest. She is freezing from within.

Back in Toronto on Sunday morning, she and Bobby go home separately from the airport. Her house, as she enters it, is ice cold. She raises the thermostat, drags herself upstairs, crawls into bed under two quilts, pulls one of them over her head, and doesn't come out for the rest of the day. She knows it is hopeless with her and Bobby. They're just too different. He has much more in common with his brother and sister than with her. Never mind marriage; she doesn't want to stay with him even until she goes back to Israel. She wants him out of her life, and the sooner the better.

At 4:30, just as the sun is setting, she falls asleep, but several hours later she awakens feeling sick. Her head is heavy and full of sharp, shooting pains, her limbs ache and move slowly as if she's been drugged, and even though she is lying under two down quilts, she is cold. Then hot. Then cold again. She lurches out of bed and staggers to the bathroom. In seconds she has filled the toilet with smelly brown water. Then she vomits into it, too. For the rest of that night and all the next day, she runs to and from the toilet. She's feverish and confused and in and out of sleep. In the midst of all this, there is a sense of urgency: *I have to speak to Suzy. We have to work things out.* With school resuming tomorrow, everything that happened at the Christmas party has come flooding back to her with the force of a tidal wave. She can't believe how Suzy treated her that night, turning on her when she hadn't done anything wrong. She feels hurt and angry now, yet also willing to forgive. After all, Suzy was under a lot of stress that night. She was hostessing a party for seventy people, she couldn't get her son to bed, and she was terribly embarrassed by Dennis's behaviour. Also she is worried about getting her contract renewed, so obviously she has to stay on Weick's good side. None of this, of course, justifies how she acted. But still, until that night, Suzy was very good to her. That counts for something. Furthermore, this term Suzy is going to give her an RA'ship. So she has to make up with her. She needs things to be all right between them.

But the next day she is still sick. There is no way she can return to school and resolve things with Suzy. The following Monday she is still vomiting, feverish, dizzy, and drenching her bedclothes with sweat. *It's just a flu*, she tells herself repeatedly. She tells this also to Bobby, who is becoming increasingly impatient with her for not seeing a doctor.

But when she has been like this for eight days, and has missed not only the first class this term in all her new subjects, but the second one, too, she begins to worry about her schoolwork. Cindy has been great, phoning her every few days and keeping all her teachers informed about her illness. Cindy has also been collecting extra copies of the course outlines and handouts for her. But now Judith is starting to panic. She can't afford to miss the third class in all these courses. There are only twelve classes in all, and she is afraid of falling behind and maybe even losing the whole semester.

So on the Tuesday morning before the third Monday of the term, she consults Bernie Braunstein, an old schoolmate of her father's who, despite his age, still sees patients in his modest office. She hasn't seen Bernie since her father's *shiva* and he greets her with a kiss on the cheek. After hearing about her symptoms, examining her, and sending her for some tests across the hall, he reassures her it's probably nothing serious.

"It looks to me," he says, "like one of those nasty new flu viruses that are going around that we don't yet know much about. The tests you just did will come back in a couple of days and maybe they'll show something surprising. But if this is what I think it is, a virus, it'll just have to run its course."

"How long will that take?" she cries. "I've already missed the first two weeks of school and soon it'll be the third. I can't keep missing week after week."

Bernie smiles down at the piece of paper where he's jotting some notes. "How refreshing," he says, "to see someone eager to return to her studies. Usually people are asking me to get them *out* of school or work, not back *into* it." Then he looks at her over his glasses. "If this were something bacterial, I could give you antibiotics which would speed up your recovery. But for a virus there is nothing to give you. It has to just work its way through your system. Whether this will take two more days or two more weeks — or even three or four — I cannot say. But there's no point trying to rush it, Judith. If you return to school even one day earlier than your body is ready to, you're just going to relapse and extend your illness. So what's the point? Go home, Judith, rest, drink plenty of fluids — we don't want you getting dehydrated — and forget about school and everything else until you're 100 percent well."

Dejectedly she rises, and on her way out Bernie pinches her cheek.

When she gets home, she's exhausted. She crawls into bed and stays there woodenly, like a doll passively remaining wherever it's been placed. She is too weak and dizzy to do anything at all, even watch TV, but she is also too nauseated to sleep. So she just lies in bed and the day goes by. The rest of the week passes like this, too. Bobby pops in once each day and tries to get her to eat something, but she usually shakes her head and turns away. On Sunday, though, she sits up in bed and hungrily eats a scrambled egg Bobby has made for her, along with a slice of toast spread with grape jelly. Then she swallows a tall, cold glass of orange juice.

"You're looking better," he says, watching her. "If this keeps up, soon you'll be back on your feet."

"I'm almost recovered now," she says between bites. "Tomorrow I'm going back to school."

"What!" He stares at her, aghast. "Are you crazy?"

"I have to go back. If I miss any more classes, I might as well drop out of the program."

"Judith, look in the mirror," he pleads. "Two hours ago you couldn't even sit up in bed. How will you get through a full day of classes tomorrow? Much less survive that long drive."

"I'll be fine. Anyway, I have to go. I have no choice."

"No choice?" His eyes light up with his argumentative litigation-lawyer gleam. "What do you mean you have no choice? If you're sick, you're sick. Your profs will understand that."

She doesn't answer. She is feeling another wave of nausea and doesn't have the strength for a fight with Bobby. She gazes at him, thinking, *You don't understand. I have to make up with Suzy.* Then, feeling dizzy, she pushes away the bed tray, slides into a prone position, and within seconds is asleep.

— 2 —

The next day she awakens at 2:10 p.m. She has now missed all of her classes for the third week in a row. And maybe it's something about the number three — the rabbis consider the third incidence of anything significant — but she's starting to feel distant and disconnected from Dunhill. The routine, the rhythm, has been broken. It's gone. Whenever she returns, she'll feel lost and out of step. For the rest of this term, she'll be discovering that she's missing small, but important, pieces of the puzzle laid down during these crucial first weeks. She'll be disoriented. So it's a relief, almost a reprieve, to be able to stay in bed, and not face all that yet.

And also not to have to face Kerry, Chris, Lola, and all the other people at school who hate Israel. *Soineh-Yisroel*, her father would have called them in Yiddish. She's happy to not have to cope yet with them. Or with Suzy. She and Suzy still haven't had any contact this term. She thought of emailing her, but what for? Suzy already knows from Cindy that Judith's sick at home, and the discussion they need to have about what happened at the Christmas party (which hurts every time she remembers it) is not for email. That will have to wait until they meet in person. Hopefully next week when she's back in school — then everything will get straightened out. In the words of Isaiah, *All that is crooked shall be made straight.*

Downstairs, she eats a sandwich and checks her email. She's only checked it once since getting sick, so now she has eighty-nine emails waiting for her. She sits at the dining room table wearing *gatkes*, a nightgown, a sweatshirt, sweatpants, socks, and slippers, because the house is still cold. It has an archaic and expensive heating system, and she can't afford to set the thermostat any higher than sixty-eight. She reads an email from Bruria, who apologizes for not having written much over the past six weeks. She's been very busy with Noah, who is out of solitary now and has a good lawyer. Then she responds to the email that Judith wrote her six weeks ago after Suzy's party.

Judith!! You wore your red dress to a school party???!!! What were you thinking?!

Bruria knows this dress. Judith wore it for the first time to the housewarming party for Bruria and Pinchas's new house about eight months before she left for Toronto. Bruria loved it: "Vavavavoom!" she said, and Judith knew then that this dress was powerful. Its deep ruby velvet was almost the same colour as oxblood, a substance drunk by ancient tribes to enhance their virility. But over time she got used to this dress, as if it had gradually faded in the wash, muting its sensual and erotic power, and making it less magical, more ordinary and respectable with each wearing. Now, reading Bruria's email, she flushes almost the colour of her dress. What a stupid mistake it was to wear this to Suzy's party. Not that Bruria is suggesting it was Judith's fault what happened that night with Dennis and Weick — both of whom Bruria calls "assholes" in her email. *Unlike Suzy*, thinks Judith, *Bruria knows my wearing that dress wasn't an act of seduction — just an honest mistake.*

Now Judith checks *Ha'aretz*. No terrorist attacks today, thank God. Nothing more terrible going on there this afternoon than any other time. She quickly skims today's top three stories:

A revolt is brewing against Sharon from within his own party, the Likud.

A West Bank rabbi has ruled it is not only permissible, but one's religious obligation, to murder anyone, Jewish or non-Jewish, who gives or sells to an Arab even one dunam of land.

Child poverty in Israel has just reached its highest rate since the founding of the state: one Israeli child in three goes to bed hungry at night.

Heavy-hearted, Judith leaves *Ha'aretz*, and returns to her email. There's an email from Suzy buried in her junk mail for some reason. She opens it with fear and hope. Maybe Suzy is wishing her a speedy recovery. Maybe she's also apologizing, or saying something reassuring, about what happened at the party. To her disappointment, it's just an official note Suzy sent to everyone on SWAC:

Firstly, thanks to all of you who attended last night's meeting. It was very productive and we got a lot done.

Judith checks the date of this email: it was sent ten days ago. She not only missed all her classes that week, but also a SWAC meeting. How could she have forgotten that? But in the blur of illness, she had.

Our next meeting will be two weeks from last night, at 7:00 p.m. on Thursday, January 23.

That's this Thursday.

Please make every effort to be there, and also RSVP your attendance as soon as possible. We're almost at mid-January, Anti-oppression Day is just one month after that, and there's lots still left to do!

In spite of her mixed feelings toward Suzy now, Judith is touched by the exclamation mark at the end. How like Suzy to conclude what would otherwise have been a mundane bureaucratic email with this "Let's go, team!" sort of spirit. *I should be well enough by this Thursday,* she thinks, *to attend this meeting. And perhaps if Suzy is free beforehand, we can have our talk then.*

She clicks on Reply and begins to RSVP to Suzy, but then stops. She can't be sure she'll be okay three days from now. And it's worse to say yes and then not come, than to just not reply. So she turns off her computer and goes upstairs. There she gets dressed, thinking that she couldn't drive to Dunhill now, but she could drive to the local mall just five minutes away. Dressing, she feels in the shadows of the room Bobby's disapproval, but she ignores him. The day after tomorrow is his birthday and she wants to get him a gift. So she sets out for the mall. By now it's four-thirty, already dark and freezing cold. But once at the mall she strolls with pleasure through the long indoor avenues. There are boxes inlaid with ivory, pens made of Venetian glass, a newly invented kind of corkscrew, fancy bed linens and draperies, musical instruments from all around the world, and soap in the shape of apples and pears. Nothing, though, is quite right for Bobby. So she goes to the Men's Department at The Bay. Nothing special there, either, it turns out: it's all the same sort of merchandise they displayed the last time she was here, shopping for what she knew in her heart of hearts would be her last Father's Day gift. Saddened now, she examines the standard male gifts: ties, pipes, shaving kits, fleece-lined slippers. None of these suit Bobby.

"May I help you?" asks a saleswoman, but Judith shakes her head. Out of nowhere she's feeling dizzy and nauseated, and staggers to a bench at the edge of the store. She plunks herself onto it and shuts her eyes. She hopes she doesn't vomit here in public, all over the woman sitting beside her. Gradually the nausea starts subsiding. But still she is light-headed and weak.

"Judith?" inquires a voice.

It's Suzy. "Hi!" Judith says, standing, again feeling dizzy. Guilty, too — she flushes like a schoolgirl caught playing hookey by the teacher. "What are you doing in Toronto?"

"My sister lives near here," says Suzy, looking pretty, petite, and self-contained, as always. "Today's my nephew's birthday, so I'm picking up the birthday cake on my way there."

Judith squints with concentration, but she is only half-listening to these words. She is anxiously searching Suzy's eyes, trying to gauge how Suzy feels about her. But her eyes are opaque, "professional," not giving anything away.

"What are *you* doing here?" Suzy asks. "I thought you were sick at home."

"I *was* sick," says Judith, "but now I'm better." Then she hears how odd this must sound. She is talking to a teacher whose first three classes of the term she has missed, the last of them ending just an hour and a half ago. Feeling muddled, she adds, "I'm not completely better yet. I was sick in bed till an hour ago. I was planning to come to your class today, but I only woke up at two o'clock. But then an hour ago I felt better, so I decided to come out for a bit. Bobby's birthday is on Wednesday and I need to get him a present." She's starting to feel nauseated again.

"You look terrific," says Suzy. "You've got great colour in your cheeks."

That's just fever, thinks Judith, but doesn't say anything.

"What's wrong with you exactly?" Suzy asks. "Cindy said something about a flu, but the flu doesn't usually last this long."

She doesn't believe I'm sick. Feeling on the defensive, Judith says, "My doctor says it's one of those new viruses. You just have to wait them out. Sometimes they can last for even four weeks."

"Four weeks — wow," says Suzy. "I've never heard of anything like that."

"Neither had I. But that's what he said."

"Does it have a name?"

"I don't know. He didn't tell me one."

"Really," Suzy says vaguely.

It's clear she is unconvinced this virus is real.

"By the way," says Suzy, "will you be coming to the SWAC meeting this Thursday? I don't believe you RSVP'd."

"I don't know," says Judith. "I hope so. I really want to come. But I'll have to see. At this point I'm taking it one day at a time."

Suzy openly studies her now, peering at her closely, as if weighing her words, and even her character. After a long moment, she says, "I hope this Thursday is one of your good days."

"So do I," Judith says earnestly.

Suzy nods. They both smile slightly and say goodbye.

Suzy continues on her way toward the bakery, and Judith watches her receding back until she can't see it anymore. Then she drives home. In bed she falls quickly into a fever-drenched sleep. But one thing she knows as she is going under: she'd better show up at that meeting on Thursday. It's her last chance.

— 3 —

On Tuesday and Wednesday she is no worse but no better, so on Wednesday night she and Bobby celebrate his birthday at her place, ordering in Chinese. Then on Thursday at 5:30 she drives to Dunhill. The drive starts out all right, but by the time she arrives she's exhausted and sweating. She leans her seat back and lies down with her arm over her eyes. She shouldn't have come today. But once she's here, she'll attend at least part of the SWAC meeting. She'll warn Suzy beforehand that she may have to leave early. Suzy will understand.

Inside FRANK, Judith heads toward Suzy's office. There is almost a half-hour now until the meeting starts. She'll have time to explain to Suzy about leaving early because of her illness, but she'll also offer to review the agenda with her like always. She'll show her she's trying to be a responsible co-chair.

But when she reaches Suzy's office, Suzy is not alone. The office door is open and Judith hears laughter within. This possibility never occurred to her: that at 6:40, twenty minutes before a SWAC meeting, someone else could be sitting in Suzy's office with her. This was always Judith's time. She pauses in the hallway. She could leave now. But she wants Suzy to know that, despite how sick she's been, she made this effort to come tonight. Approaching the doorway, she sees Suzy in her usual chair, and in the other one, Judith's chair, sits Elizabeth.

Elizabeth and Suzy are laughing. Suzy, dark, cute and petite, reminding Judith of a charming Parisian brunette, a flirt with a glorious, tinkly laugh, and Elizabeth, taller and willowy with that long, straight blond hair. There is something intimate and united in their laugh, like when Suzy used to laugh with *her*. Now Suzy notices her and her laughter stops.

"Judith!" she says, looking guilty. "I thought you weren't coming tonight. So Elizabeth and I were going over the agenda."

The agenda? Judith thinks. *You and I go over the agenda. I'm your co-chair, not her.*

"We're nearly finished," Suzy says smoothly, quickly regaining her balance. "Did you want something?"

Yes, thinks Judith. *I want things between us to be okay again. And I want this blond bimbo off my chair and out of your office.*

"I'm still not 100 percent well," she says. "So I probably won't last the whole meeting."

Suzy looks surprised. "How are you feeling now?"

Judith feels nauseous and so hot it feels like her skin is about to set fire to her clothes. But she replies, "Not bad." Then she blushes. She's not a good liar and senses Suzy knows she's lying. Though Suzy seems to think she's lying even when she's not. She adds, to bring her answer closer to the truth, "Not great, either. It can turn on a dime."

Suzy gazes at her silently with a sad, disappointed look. Then she says, "Let's hope that doesn't happen."

There's another pause. Judith vividly feels Suzy and Elizabeth waiting for her to leave. "I'll let you finish," she says.

"Right," says Suzy. "See you there."

Judith leaves, her face burning from both fever and humiliation. To have made such an effort to come here, perhaps jeopardizing her health, and then to be greeted so indifferently, to even be unwanted. Fighting back tears, she thumps down the long gloomy corridor. At the last bend in the labyrinth, she pauses in a shadowy corner. A grotesque stone figure on an upper ledge — an amphibian man with a tail — looks down at her with pity and mockery. She rests against the wall. Soon she'll be in a well-lighted area, and visible. She collects herself. *Vesti la giubba*, she thinks. *Put on the mask.* And arranging her face into the best mask she can manage, she heads toward the meeting.

When Judith arrives, everyone is standing around in twos and threes like at a cocktail party. Binders or purses have been placed on the round table to reserve seats. Judith positions her purse next to Suzy's and sits, feeling weepy. Suzy asks people to take their seats, and approaches her own, chatting with Elizabeth and Lola. But instead of sitting where her purse is, Suzy casually slides it one seat over and sits there, while Elizabeth squeezes in between Judith and Suzy. *Never mind,* Judith tells herself. *It's not important.* But she's short of breath, as though she's received a physical blow.

The meeting begins with reports from SWAC's two subcommittees. Brenda's, having done nothing, is brief. Carl's committee proposes establishing a satellite M.S.W. program on a reserve up north, with special admission criteria for Native people, in recognition of the oppression they experience. Instead of requiring the usual 80 percent average, marks won't matter, and just having a B.A. or B.S.W. will suffice. Judith agrees that Native people have been oppressed, but believes that students with lower averages will have trouble meeting graduate school's academic demands. There's no point saying this, though. This proposal, despite its flaws, will pass, because no one can vote against it without looking right-wing, even racist. Indeed, it passes unanimously.

Judith feels very ill now: extremely nauseated and burning with fever. *I'm cooking,* she thinks: *I'm being roasted like a chicken in a pan. In an hour, when this meeting ends, I will be done, and they can serve me on a platter, garnished with parsley.* She decides, though, not to leave yet. She can hold on awhile longer.

The rest of the meeting is devoted to Anti-oppression Day. Chris, reporting on PR, distributes copies of the *Clarion,* Dunhill's student paper, which includes an article about Anti-oppression Day. Everyone seems impressed. But Judith stares numbly at the picture of Michael Brier. His arm is around Khaled Jaber, Head of Operations at the Martyrs of Vengeance, and the mastermind of what has now been nicknamed "The Baka Schoolchildren Attack." In an article she read in *Ha'aretz,* Jaber told a Brussels journalist that the Baka attack expressed not only resistance to the Israeli occupation; it should be understood as "a warning to all Jews everywhere." A week later the *Globe and Mail* quoted from an earlier interview with Jaber on *Al Jazeera,* where he said Jews were "the sons of dogs and monkeys."

Looking now at Jaber's photo, Judith sees other photos super-imposed on it: pictures from the Internet, TV, and newspapers, of blown-apart little bodies, and of the empty blood-stained street, with pages of children's schoolbooks flapping in the wind. Here in the *Clarion,* Michael Brier is gazing admiringly, even fawningly, at Jaber, while Jaber gazes straight ahead with the arrogance of a self-styled hero. Judith now reads the article. Brier says he and Khaled Jaber are not only "close friends," but "soul brothers." *Soul brothers?!* Judith glares at Brier's face. *You're a "soul brother" to a murderer.* Jaber is not merely sympathetic to the plight of the Palestinians and critical of the Israeli government, as she herself is. He believes it is morally okay to blow up Jewish six-year-olds on their way to school — in Israel, or anywhere else. This can't be happening. A self-avowed terrorist giving the B.P. Dunhill Lecture on Human Rights.

Chris finishes his presentation, Suzy thanks him, and people smile at him. Then Janice covers lunch on Anti-oppression Day (*of course — food being women's domain!*). Afterwards, the committee discusses some potential panellists for the afternoon session. Judith scans the table. Everything seems perfectly normal, as if this were any ordinary meeting, just a group of social workers planning a study day. When in fact they've just invited a terrorist into their midst, given him a platform for spreading poisonous hate, and presented him as a role model to their students. She looks from one face to another, feeling like an animal at the end of *Animal Farm,* who studies the faces but can't tell the pigs from the humans. *Someone here is crazy,* she thinks. *And I don't think it's me.*

Suzy says, "This is good. We're almost ready for Anti-oppression Day. Well done, group!" Everyone smiles except Hetty, who is typically morose. "Before moving on, does anyone have any comments or questions?" She looks brightly around the table. There's silence. "Speak now or forever hold your peace."

Speak now or forever hold your peace. It's now or never. "Well," says Judith, "I have something."

Everyone looks at her.

She hesitates. Then says, "We can't do what we've planned."

Their faces are uncomprehending. She continues, addressing herself to Hetty, "This picture in the *Clarion* has Michael Brier with his arm around Khaled Jaber. Jaber, in case you don't know, is from the Martyrs of Vengeance and is personally responsible for the recent suicide bombing in Jerusalem that killed sixteen schoolchildren. In this article, Brier calls Jaber not just his 'close friend,' but his 'soul brother.' We cannot have the 'soul brother' of a terrorist giving the keynote address at Anti-oppression Day. Apart from it being morally egregious, we'll look like idiots."

She immediately realizes her blunder, but it's too late. Chris is already saying primly, "Well, Judith, some of us aren't concerned about appearances. We're interested in doing what's right."

"Right?!" she cries. "Right! This is someone whose 'soul brother' is responsible for sixteen children's deaths. Thirteen under the age of nine."

Chris, his earring glinting in the light, says, "Any death is a tragedy. But don't ask me to feel sorry for the Israelis; they've brought this on themselves. The Palestinians, living under the occupation, have no choice but to resist, and what other means do they have at their disposal? People have a right to fight for their liberation."

"Yes," says Judith, "but there are different ways to fight. There are words, there's diplomacy. What Jaber opted for was blowing up a bunch of six-year-olds. That is terrorism."

Chris regards her impassively. "Some might answer that the State of Israel practises terrorism on the Palestinian people every day of their lives. It terrorizes them economically, socially, and militarily. So, in a sense, terrorism is in the eye of the beholder. One person's terrorist is another person's freedom fighter." He draws himself up taller. "I'm not ashamed to say that I consider Khaled Jaber a freedom fighter and would be proud to have him at Dunhill."

Judith stares at him. She knows there are arguments she can make about not equating terrorism with self-defence, and about

Israel's right to protect itself. But her body's on fire and she's dizzy, and she can't rally the words.

Janice jumps in, in her little-girl voice: "In a way it's all just a difference in point of view. Because from a postmodern perspective, there's no right or wrong. It's all just perceptions."

"I'm not a postmodernist," says Judith. "And I don't believe everything is just perceptions. There's truth and there are lies. It's not true that there is no difference between a terrorist act aimed at civilians, and an action aimed at non-civilians and carried out by a democratic state trying to protect its citizens. The two are not the same. I feel compassion for the Palestinians. They're not always well treated by the Israeli government, and they've been screwed over by their own leaders. But Khaled Jaber believes in murdering schoolchildren. And murdering schoolchildren is wrong. It's as simple as that."

"Actually, Judith," says James, "it's not. Because sometimes the end does justify the means. As you know from social work, you can never look at just the symptom of a problem. You have to ask: Why is this phenomenon occurring? What is its root cause?"

"Exactly," pipes up Lola. "Exactly."

Judith is now getting it from all sides. She's been attacked by Chris and Janice across from her, by James on her right, and now by Lola on her left. She feels surrounded.

"We need to ask," Lola says, "why a young Palestinian would even consider blowing himself up. And the reason is that he's desperate and without hope because of the occupation. You can pretend otherwise, Judith. But that's the truth, even if you can't face it."

Lola's tone is openly contemptuous, her face is hostile, and her teeth are slightly bared, like a German shepherd. This palpable hostility, even hate, paralyzes Judith the way a wild animal's snarling paralyzes its prey with fear. She's paralyzed also by confusion. She is in a meeting in a university, ostensibly a place of Knowledge and Wisdom, engaged in a debate about whether or not her people has the right to defend itself against murderers. The right to not be blown to smithereens. In other words, the right to exist.

Suzy says in a bright, tinny voice, "There are obviously different views here." Judith looks at her hopefully. "But just to give some context, when Judith lived in Israel, she did peace work, bringing together Jewish and Arab teenagers for dialogue. And her friends in Israel are active in the peace movement."

She's trying to help me, thinks Judith. *Despite everything.*

"That's great!" says Carl. The faces around the table look at her now in a friendlier way than before. The pack of wolves has turned into dogs. First she's relieved. Then she's angry. *I get it — now I'm a "good Jew." Not an evil, "oppressor" Jew on the right or, God forbid, a settler — they, of course, all deserve to be killed. But since I'm a peacenik and a lefty, sharing their political views (they think), I'm a good Jew, so I deserve to be allowed to live. Well thanks, but no thanks. Go fuck yourselves.*

James says, "Now I better understand, Judith, where you're coming from. But still, on this topic, obviously the rest of us are more objective than you. Your perspective is biased."

"Everyone's 'biased,'" says Judith. "No one is 'objective.'"

"Yes," says James, "but there's more objectivity and less objectivity. Regarding Israel, you're less objective than us."

Judith shakes her head. *If there is no such thing as objectivity, how can one person have more of it than another?* But she doesn't bother saying this. These people are crazy. She's at a party at the Mad Hatter's.

There's silence. Then Hetty says ponderously, with her heavy European accent, "We must walk very cautiously here. It's a fine line between criticizing Israel and sliding into antisemitism. We owe it not just to our Jewish students and faculty, but to our-selves, to approach this carefully, sensitively. Because," she says, and now her voice gets louder with each word, "antisemitism is a scourge." *Scourge* she says so loudly and emphatically it's almost a shout. "A scourge, I tell you! Never will I forget being a little girl in Transylvania, and seeing what happened to our Jewish neighbours during the Holocaust."

Judith stares at her. She didn't know this about Hetty. She feels like jumping up, running over, and hugging her.

Chris says, "The Jewish holocaust, you mean. Other people besides the Jews have had holocausts."

Fuck off, thinks Judith.

"Anyway," Chris continues, "how come anytime someone criticizes Israel, they're accused of antisemitism? I have no prob-lem with Jews." *Well, thanks a lot,* Judith snickers to herself. "But Zionism is a colonialist, imperialist movement whose occupation is brutally oppressing the indigenous population of Palestine. Anyone who cares about human rights has to oppose the Zionists."

"No," says Judith, "you're wrong. That's not what Zionism is. It has nothing to do with displacing or occupying another peo-ple. Zionism is the national liberation movement of the Jewish people, and is every bit as legitimate as the liberation movement of any other people. The Palestinians deserve a homeland, yes. But so do we. So right now it's a hard time. Our two peoples are struggling to share a small piece of land so we can each have a state. Eventually we'll find a way. But meanwhile, people who just keep trashing Israel aren't helping this process. They're doing no good at all."

There's a pause. Then Chris says, "What you describe, Judith, sounds reasonable. But most Zionists don't think like you. Not Ariel Sharon or most Israelis, who believe the whole land belongs to them."

Judith is exhausted. She's sick, and this argument has utterly drained her. But from somewhere inside her, like hauling water from a deep well, she dredges up the strength to reply. "Zionism, like any other movement, is not monolithic. It has a right and a left, and I'm on the left. But that aside, a recent poll showed 70 percent of Israelis favour trading land for peace."

"Really?" Lola asks doubtfully. "I never heard that."

"Of course not," snaps Judith. "You never hear about the good stuff in the papers here. All they report are the suicide bombings and retaliations. Lots of good things happen that no one here knows about."

Chris looks dubious but doesn't say anything. Again there's silence.

"All right," says Suzy. "We have to move on. Judith, is there something you'd like to propose?"

Propose? Judith looks at her, perplexed.

"You've expressed a concern," Suzy explains patiently. "How would you like us to address it?"

Judith thinks a moment. "I'd like another keynote speaker instead of Michael Brier. Someone who doesn't support violence against Jewish civilians."

"That's ridiculous!" says Chris.

"It's only a month away!" cries Janice. "Brier's already agreed! We've done publicity —"

"Let me," says Suzy, holding up her hand. She says to Judith slowly, as if to someone dull-witted, "You can make a formal motion, if you wish. I, as chair, must obviously abstain. But perhaps you'd like to think about this first."

"No, I don't need to. I move that we replace Brier with someone else."

"Okay," says Suzy. "Will someone second this?" Hetty's hand rises. "All in favour?"

Judith's and Hetty's hands go up.

"Against?"

A flurry of hands.

"Abstentions?"

Just Brenda.

"The motion," Suzy says, "is defeated."

Defeated. Judith herself feels defeated. And now all the sickness in her that she somehow managed to suppress during this awful meeting hits her with full force. She's going to either vomit or faint. The meeting moves on: they're discussing parking. *I can't stay here*, she thinks. *But if I leave before the end, it'll look like I'm being melodramatic. Or immature, like I can't tolerate losing a vote. Then again, who cares what these people think? These Israel-haters.*

She stands, lifting her purse and coat. The conversation stops.

"Are you leaving?" asks Suzy.

"Yes." She turns toward the door.

"Come back," says Carl. "You're taking this too personally. There's nothing personal about this."

Judith stares at him. *Nothing personal?!* she thinks. *You're bringing in someone who publicly advocates violence against my people. How "impersonal" would you find it if, instead of Jews, Brier advocated murdering Native people?*

She starts walking. Behind her she hears voices like a cacophonous Greek chorus:

"Come on, Judith …"

"Sit down."

"Don't leave like this …"

She keeps walking, not looking back. Her legs feel like a tin soldier's — stiff, with no joints at the knees — as she continues down the hallway. No one runs after her. Outside, the Canadian winter air is so cold it hurts to breathe, and all around her is snow. She drives away from Dunhill along dark, unlit roads, and on the highway she drives faster than is safe, flying toward Toronto, toward what once was home.

— 4 —

Entering the house, she hears the phone ringing. With her coat still on, she runs to answer it. It's Bobby. "Why didn't you answer?" he asks, his voice very anxious, almost like he's going to cry. "I was about to drive over."

She tells him she went to Dunhill for the SWAC meeting, and in the silence that follows, she can feel his astonishment. Then his anger: "Goddamn it, Judith, where is your brain? How could you do something so stupid? I can't believe —"

"Stop it. I mean it. I've had a hard night."

But he doesn't stop. "I can't believe it. I can't believe you did that. Okay, Judith, fine. Go ahead and do whatever you want. But don't come crying to me when you get sick again. Don't ask me for sympathy."

"Don't worry, I won't," she says, and slams down the phone. She's surprised at herself. It's not like her to hang up on someone. She waits a few minutes for Bobby to call back, and when he doesn't, she calls him.

"I'm sorry," she says the second he answers. "I've had a terrible night. Can I tell you about it? Can you listen now? Or can you only talk?"

There's a pause. "Okay," he says. "I'll listen."

So she tells him everything that happened. "Wow," he says when she's done. "Do you want me to come over? I can come if you need me to."

"No, thanks. I'm feeling sick and just want to sleep. But you're coming tomorrow night, right?"

"Yes, but don't worry about cooking. We can go one week without a homemade Shabbat meal. Why don't I just pick something up on the way?"

She hesitates, then says, "Sure. That would be great."

"Judith, I'm proud of you, standing up to those shmucks."

"Yeah, well. I didn't have much impact, did I? Brier's still the keynote."

"Never mind. I'm proud of you, anyway. Sleep well, okay?"

"Okay."

But in bed she can't fall asleep. Over and over she replays the meeting. *How could they have done this?* she wonders. *Are they stupid or are they evil? Do they truly not understand the implications of bringing in this man? Or do they understand and just not care?* She hopes they're just stupid. She'd prefer to see tonight's vote as the result of people's low IQs rather than their low integrity. A problem of being intellectually defective rather than morally defective. But she doesn't really believe this. She is furious, wounded, and confused, and only at dawn does she fall into a sweaty, fitful sleep.

The next morning, though, she is proud of herself. She's glad she said what she said and glad she walked out of that meeting. Yet she also is mortified. She has never done anything like that before. How is she going to show her face next week at school? Then again, who cares? Bunch of *antisemitten* ... She laughs. It seems almost like it was someone else, not her, who walked out of that meeting last night. Someone with courage. *Kuh-ridge*, as the cowardly lion pronounced it in *The Wizard of Oz*. Or *coraggio*, as her father, a lover of everything Italian, used to say. *Maybe*, she thinks, *I have a drop of* coraggio *in my blood. Maybe I have one little drop.*

The phone rings. It's Cindy making her Friday phone call — as reliable each week as the arrival later that day of Shabbat. Cindy also calls her every Monday on her way home from school, to update her on the classes she missed. What a loyal friend. Out of everyone at school, only Cindy has kept calling during this illness.

"How are you?" Cindy asks, and then answers the question herself: "Not so hot, I guess, if you're at home instead of out doing your Shabbat shopping." She pronounces *Shabbat* "Shobbit," rhyming with "hobbit," so it sounds like "doing your shop-it shopping." Momentarily Judith is baffled. Then she understands, and appreciates that Cindy has taken the trouble to learn this word.

"You're right," she answers. "I've been better." She tells her about last night's meeting. Cindy, dismayed, says, "Good Lord, Judith. You really did that? You walked out in the middle?"

Judith is disappointed and even a bit hurt. She thought that Cindy, like Bobby, would understand, and say this was a brave act and she was proud of her. "What should I have done?" she asks. "Just sat there listening to that bullshit for another twenty minutes?"

"I don't know," says Cindy. "It's terrible what they did. Terrible. But maybe there is something to what Carl said. What happened last night maybe *isn't* all that personal. You know how people are about Israel these days."

Judith doesn't say anything. It was silly of her to expect Cindy to understand.

Cindy's voice is earnest. "Judith, don't get me wrong. I'm on your side. You're my friend, and I don't care about any of those people. But it worries me how you take these things to heart. Who knows — if I hadn't met you and heard from you all about Israel, maybe I wouldn't understand about it, either.

Anyway, I'm not making excuses for them. I'm just saying you can't let people get to you like this. Especially people like Lola or Chris, who are nothing compared to you. They have brains like peanuts."

"Like penis?"

"Like peanuts. I said peanuts. *Penis*, Judith? Where is your mind?"

She smiles. "A brain the size of a penis wouldn't be so bad."

"Depends on the size of the penis," says Cindy. They laugh and it feels wonderful. Then Judith says, "Speaking of peni."

"Peni?"

"Isn't peni the plural of penis?"

"I don't know," says Cindy.

"It should be if it's from Latin. *Amicus amici. Cactus cacti. Penis peni.*"

"Whatever you say. I'm just glad to hear you sounding more chipper."

"You've cheered me up. You're such a good friend." Judith's voice turns husky at the end.

"We're buds," says Cindy. "What do you think?"

Buds. Not buds on trees, but buds short for *buddies*. Since returning to Canada, Judith has been encountering new words like this, each one reminding her that while in Israel, her English did not keep up with the living, changing language.

"Speaking of peni," she says, "is Aliza, with her vibrators, back at school yet?"

There's a pause. "No." Then another, shorter pause. "She's not coming back."

"Not coming back?! What do you mean 'not coming back'?"

"She says it's too much for her right now."

"What do you mean 'too much for her right now'?"

"Would you stop repeating everything I say?"

"I can't help it. I'm shocked. She registered for this term. Pam said she was coming back."

"I know. I was shocked, too, when I heard. It's upsetting. But she's sick."

"What's she sick with? Is it the same stomach thing she had last term?"

Another pause. Cindy sighs. "Remember when Aliza told us that when she was a dancer she was bulimic?"

"Yes." She remembers, though hazily. She hadn't taken it seriously because Aliza said this in a jocular way. And she said 90 percent of dancers were bulimic, as if it were normal. She also implied that since she'd given up dancing and become a social worker, this bulimia was a thing of the past. "She's lost a great deal of weight," Cindy says. "She's down to less than a hundred pounds."

Oh God. Just like her grandmother, thinks Judith. "If I lost just a little more weight," Aliza said, "I'd look like my Bubba when she was in Maidanek." She feels a gulp of guilt in her throat. She called Aliza once after returning from Christmas vacation, but there was no answer and no answering machine, and she didn't try again. By then she was already sick herself. *But still*, she thinks, *I should have given her another call.* To Cindy she says, "I'll call her."

"Wait a bit," says Cindy. "I'm sure she'll want to hear from you at some point. But Pam says she won't talk to anyone now except for one of her sisters and Pam."

After hanging up, Judith lies in bed, thinking. Strange — she and Aliza, the only Jews in the class, are both off sick. She tries remembering exactly when Aliza started going under — when she first got that pale, hunted, haunted look, and wrote that number on her arm. Yes — it all started a week before that photo exhibit in the atrium opened. By the first day of that exhibit,

Aliza was already sick and vulnerable. But on that particular day, according to Pam, Aliza came to school and then turned around and went home. That, it seems, was a turning point. After Aliza saw that exhibit, she left and never returned.

That fucking exhibit. Judith pictures Aliza the way she was before that change occurred. Aliza with her hyper, restless energy, her jokes, her generosity of spirit — that amazing lime-green vibrator. Aliza prancing joyfully in her tall red boots in mud puddles, laughing with those perfect white teeth and beautiful half-open mouth, and her long black hair bouncing. Ebony hair, ruby-red lips, paper-white skin — all like Snow White, who bit into a poisoned apple and then lay with her eyes closed in a strange, deep sleep. "Aliza," whispers Judith. "Aliza'leh …"

Then she feels frightened, as if what happened to Aliza, like a curse, could happen to her, too. She curls up in bed, wishing she never had to return to Dunhill, never had to see any of those people again. If Aliza could do it, why can't she? But she can't, and she knows very well why. Because of that promise she made to her father. The promise not just to try for, but to get her Master's degree. She can't ignore her father's dying wish.

Now she considers what his wish was actually about. Higher education is what it sounded like at the time: a Master's degree so she could "stand on her own two feet." She interpreted this then at the most obvious level: financial security. But if that was all he meant, then she could accomplish this much more easily by simply marrying Bobby. Overnight she would be standing on her own two feet. Well, no, of course not; then she'd be standing on Bobby's. Now she smirks. That was a game she and Bobby used to play in high school: she'd stand on his feet — each of her feet on top of his — and try to keep her balance without holding onto him. Of course sooner or later she'd fall, and he'd catch her, and they'd kiss. They never went much further than that in grade eleven. Just making out and a little petting. And even that, only on top of their clothes. Then at the beginning of grade twelve he stuck his hand under her T-shirt, and then under her bra, and touched her naked breast. She sucked in her breath, and when he gently stroked her nipple, she moaned. Then they took off their shirts and he kissed her breast, sucking hungrily on it. But they didn't take off their pants. They were a good Jewish girl and a good Jewish boy, groping each other feverishly on the couch in his parents' basement.

A few months later, though, on his seventeenth birthday, as a birthday gift, she touched his penis for the first time. She was startled at its aliveness. Moving, wriggling, like a small furless animal. Then standing at attention, as if it was singing "God Save the Queen," and she herself was the queen. She told him this and he laughed.

She was surprised that his penis was warm to the touch. Bonnie Zimmerman had said, "Think of an erect penis like a popsicle," so Judith had assumed it would be cold. "Just suck on it like a popsicle," Bonnie advised, "but it doesn't taste as good." Bonnie Zimmerman was the fastest girl in the class. Also, incongruously to Judith, the winner, two years in a row, of the Toronto Jewish community's annual Bible contest. She could rattle off the twelve tribes and the five daughters of Zelophehad faster than giving a guy a blow job. The thought of sucking on a guy's cock made Judith want to gag — she'd prefer a cherry popsicle any day — and she was relieved when Bobby, back then anyway, never asked her for that.

He loved her comment, though, about "God Save the Queen," and laughed and laughed. In those days he had a free, open-hearted, slightly high-pitched, crazy kind of laugh. Not like now, with his reserved lawyerly hahaha. *Whatever happened to that carefree, lovable, genuine laugh?* she wonders. But immediately she knows the answer. It died when his parents died — killed soon after grade twelve in that car accident.

Never mind about that, she tells herself. *Don't dwell on death. Return to sex.* Though now it seems odd how she was just day-dreaming about sex. The world's on fire, her little corner of it is collapsing, and here she is, lost in erotic memories. She must be nuts. But no. Bruria told her that she once saw on a TV nature show how chimpanzees, after a brush with death, copulate like crazy. Apparently it's a natural reaction when one's survival has just been threatened. *I've just been threatened*, thinks Judith. *Not physically, but existentially. And existentially, the only response to thanatos is eros. The only weapon against death is love.*

Now desire — passionate, almost violent, desire — rises in her. This desire isn't for Bobby, though; it's for Moshe. She can't help herself. She loves Bobby, but he is just a man. Whereas Moshe is a man plus Israel combined. (Like that stupid commercial: two, two, two mints in one.) It's not right, she knows, or even fair, but that's the way it is. So she shuts her eyes and imagines lying on top of Moshe. His penis is deep inside her and she's spinning around on it, around and around in circles, like the propeller on a toy she had as a girl. The top was like the two-blade propeller on a helicopter, the bottom was shaped like a vibrator, and if you kept pulling the string on the vibrator, eventually the top part — the propeller — would fly off. She spins around and around now on Moshe's penis, faster and faster, around and around, until she's about to fly off. And as she feels herself lifting upwards, ascending toward the heavens, she thinks: *Lead me, Moshe, out of exile. Into the promised land.*

— 5 —

Four hours later Bobby arrives hugging two big paper bags, each emblazoned with a Jewish star with an "F" in the middle, the logo of Fireman's, the kosher deli near his office. An hour ago he called and said he was on his way with supper, and she said, "Great!" But now, sick again, she sits listlessly on a kitchen chair, too weak even to help him unpack the bags. Soon a complete Friday night dinner has been laid out on the dining room table in front of her: gefilte fish, chicken soup, roast chicken, *kugel*, coleslaw, fruit salad, *rugelach*, the works. Even two *chalah* rolls and a small bottle of kosher wine — he has forgotten nothing.

"I could get used to this," she says. "This is fantastic!"

He leans down and kisses her lightly. "*You're* fantastic. I'm so proud of what you did last night."

"I accomplished nothing."

"Even so." He bustles about, setting up their meal. She marvels at his dexterous, efficient gestures as he sets the table and sticks serving utensils into each container. He moves briskly and confidently and she is grateful he's here, taking care of her. *I'm lucky*, she thinks. *He is a good man.*

He strikes a match, it makes a whooshing sound, and there is the smell of sulphur. He melts the bases of two white candles and inserts their wet, sticky bottoms into the holes of her grandmother's candlesticks. She lights the Shabbat candles, covers her eyes, and sings the blessing. Then they bless the wine and *chalah* and eat the meal from Fireman's. Bobby says, "I'm so proud of you. What you did took balls."

"I don't know." Her fork stabs a piece of chicken. "I'm not so sure."

"I am. You showed courage."

She just shrugs and lowers her eyes. She does not feel like an argument now. It is pleasant, too, to be viewed as courageous, even if she doesn't believe it's true. She has changed her mind since this morning. Now she feels that whatever came over her last night, it was not real courage. It was only a result of her blood boiling with fever, and when her anger mixed in with it, the two things together exploded, like when you throw a handful of baking soda into a bottle of vinegar. They rose inside her like a frothing tidal wave, drowning out everything else. Including her usual cautiousness. But this is no proof of character or courage.

"Courage," she says to Bobby. "I don't even know where that word comes from. Do you?"

"No."

"Courage. Cou rage," she muses. "*Cou* in French is neck. Plus rage. That's the rage of the neck. Which could work, because the brain stem is in the neck, and that's where our most primitive emotions are located. Including rage. So maybe courage isn't such a high and noble emotion, after all. Maybe it's just neck rage. There's road rage. Neck rage. And courage."

"Interesting," he says. "Now you've made me curious. Where's the dictionary?"

She points. It's above the microwave with the cookbooks. For years, to clarify the meanings of words during their family supper discussions, her mother ran upstairs almost every night to fetch the dictionary from the study. Finally she got fed up with running up and down stairs, and just left the dictionary in the kitchen. It now sits among the cookbooks as if someone were planning to make a meal out of words. Bobby brings it to the table, sets it down a safe distance from a glob of gravy, and finds the word *courage*.

"Courage," he reads, his finger touching this word. "It's from the Romanic root *cor*, or *coraticum*, which means 'heart.'"

"Oh! So *cor* plus *age* means a heart of age. An aged heart. But wouldn't an old heart be a weak heart, rather than a strong one?"

"Maybe the heart physically weakens with time, but spiritually grows in strength."

"Ahh," she says dramatically, raising her eyebrows and smiling.

"Ahh," he says back. They grin at each other. "So this means, Judith, you're an old-hearted girl. I mean *voo-man*." He leans forward to kiss her.

"No, don't. I could make you sick."

"You could never make me sick."

"No, really."

"Really."

His lips feel soft. Then harder, more insistent. "Let's go upstairs," he says.

"No." She's feeling better than before, but still weak and feverish. "I'm tired. Maybe tonight I'll just go to sleep."

"Are you sure?"

"Yes. Let's call it a night. I'll see you tomorrow."

"Okay. I'll go home and work. I have tons to do this weekend."

She knows about the big case he is working on now for Dennis, and how stressful it is. Ever since Bobby returned from Christmas vacation, for no reason he can understand, Dennis has been piling work on him and making unusually heavy demands. All this month he's had to work nearly every evening and most of each weekend just to keep up. But no matter how hard he works, Dennis seems dissatisfied. Bobby can't do anything right. He desperately wants to be taken onto Dennis's team, but Dennis just keeps upping the bar, and it's starting to look like nothing Bobby does will ever be good enough. Even his excellent work on their latest case — which the firm won largely thanks to Bobby's outstanding background research – did not secure him the spot on Dennis's team he'd been led to expect. He is frustrated, angry, and perplexed. He can't understand what is going on.

But she can. It's because of what happened between her and Dennis at the Christmas party. She's sure of it. But now she only says, "Good idea. Tomorrow we'll be together. Thanks for bringing supper."

"No problem. Sleep well." He kisses her on her hair and leaves. She lies on the couch, figuring she'll rest for just a moment before putting away the food. Within seconds, even before Bobby's car is out of the driveway, she is fast asleep.

On Sunday night, she is still sick. Bobby comes and makes omelettes for supper, flipping them high above the pan, which makes her smile. But after one bite, she puts down her fork and lies on the couch. He sits near her in the armchair by the window.

"To go or not to go," she says. "That is the question."

"No," he says, "that's not what I'm thinking. I'm fine sitting here with you."

"I didn't mean you; I meant me." He looks at her blankly. "To school tomorrow. Tomorrow is Monday."

"School!" he cries. "You can't go to school! Just look at yourself! You can't even sit at the table for longer than five minutes."

"But I have to go. Tomorrow is the crucial day. It's the fourth week of classes, and according to Phoebe, the school administrator, I've now reached the point of no return. The first three weeks of a term are one thing, but after that it's for real. If I miss any more classes, I forfeit the whole term."

"Better than forfeiting your health," he says angrily. Then, more conciliatorily, he adds, "I'm sure you can negotiate something."

"I don't know. This email I got from Phoebe on Friday sounded so firm."

"Fuck Phoebe. Anyway, let's face it, this isn't law school; it's just social work. You could probably learn your whole term's work in a week or two in the summer."

"Stop insulting my profession," she says. "You're always putting down social work. In any case I don't plan to be here this summer. I'll be back in Israel by then."

"No, you won't," he says cheerfully but seriously. "You're staying here with me." He looks at her hoping for a positive response, but her face is tight and determined. "Either way, you obviously can't go to Dunhill tomorrow."

"Of course I can. I can do whatever I want."

"Look what happened when you went there on Thursday. It set you back another week at least. What do I have to do — come over tomorrow morning and tie you down to your bed?"

She pictures herself being forcibly restrained. Helpless. "Go away," she says. "I mean it. Go home. You have no right to talk to me that way. You're always telling me what to do. Stop trying to control me all the time."

"I'm not trying to control you."

"Yes, you are."

"No, I'm not."

"Yes. You are."

They glare at each other. Then he rises from his chair. "Fine. I'll go if that's what you want."

"Good."

"I'm going."

"Great."

But at the doorway he hesitates, turns around and looks at her half-reproachfully, half-imploringly. "Come on, Judith. I didn't mean —"

"I know exactly what you meant. Just go, okay? I want to sleep."

"Fine. I'm going."

He flicks off the light and bangs the door shut behind him. She lies alone in the darkness. *What an asshole*, she thinks. *He probably means well, but he's a control freak. Always bossing me around like a father with a child, like he's* Father Knows Best. *So obnoxious. So patronizing ...*

But she's too tired to keep this up for long. Anger takes energy and, weak as she is, she has very little of this. Two minutes later she's asleep.

— 6 —

The second she awakens the next morning, she knows she's too sick to go to Dunhill. The clock says 9:05 a.m., and today is the fourth Monday in a row she'll miss school. She imagines what's happening there now: everyone entering Corinne's class, some in cliques, others alone. Like Cindy, now that Pam's in Policy, and Aliza and she are sick. The cliques, she's sure, are whispering about her. Gossip spreads fast — by now everyone's heard what happened Thursday night at SWAC. They think she's not at school today because she's too gutless to show her face.

The phone rings. She answers it.

"I'm sorry," Bobby says immediately. "I shouldn't have said what I said."

"You're right, you shouldn't have."

"Afterwards I felt awful."

"You're always trying to control me. You have to stop trying to control me."

"It's only because I care."

"I don't care that you care. I hate when you do that."

"I know you do," he says. Then: "Do you forgive me?"

She hesitates. "Yes. Do you forgive *me*? I probably overreacted. I feel so shitty when I'm sick."

"I know. I'm worried about you. But are we done with this now? Is it over? I hate when we fight."

"Me, too."

"So let's not."

"Let's not what?"

"Fight. Ever again."

She chuckles. "Oh! Okay."

"That was easy," he says, and she hears him smiling, too. "How are you feeling today?"

"No worse than yesterday, but not well enough for school."

"I'm very glad you're staying home today. I was certain you were going to Dunhill."

"I'm not an idiot," she says. "I can be pretty stupid at times, but not *that* stupid."

He laughs, but it's a laugh that is restrained, even strained. She can feel how he is still being careful with her. "Promise," she says, "you won't tell me what to do anymore. I hate being bossed around."

"I'm not bossing you around. I'm just worried about you."

"Yes, but it's my life, Bobby, and I can do with it what I want."

There is a pause. "Look, I'll try," he says. "I'll do my level best. But you know what they say: 'It's hard to teach an old dog new tricks.'"

She laughs. "You're not old! Just keep at it, Rover. You can do it."

They talk a bit longer. This morning in a group meeting, in front of four other colleagues, Bobby got sharply denigrated by Dennis, and he isn't sure whether to bring this up when he and Dennis meet alone this afternoon. He discusses this briefly with Judith, then says he has to go. But he'll come over tonight with some supper, probably around 8:30 or 9:00 — he has to work late again.

Judith visits Bernie Braunstein for the third time this month. He tells her again what he's told her twice before: she just has to ride this out.

"You might even have been over this by now," he adds, "if you'd stayed at home last week instead of going to that mall, and then shlepping all the way to Dunhill. Try and just stay in bed. If you take good care of yourself, this shouldn't last much longer. I've seen several cases of this, and four weeks is usually the limit." He writes her a note for school, since Phoebe requested one. Handing it to Judith with a smile, he says he hopes she won't hand-deliver this until she's 100 percent well.

Arriving home, the phone is ringing. It's Cindy's Monday afternoon call. Judith says she's sure, after what happened Thursday night, that everyone at school is talking about her behind her back.

"That's not true," Cindy says. "No one said a word about you today."

"Not to you because they know you're my friend. Plus I'll bet Suzy doesn't believe I'm sick today. She probably thinks I'm faking it."

"Faking it? Why would she think *that*?" Cindy sounds affronted.

"Because last week she saw me in the mall."

"Oh, that. Well, so what? What do you care anyway what she thinks of you? Or any of these people, after that meeting?"

"You're right. I shouldn't. I just wish I didn't have to ever see them again."

"Never mind," says Cindy. "They're weird. They're" — there's a pause while she searches for the right word — "fucked."

"What did you say?!" Judith asks with a laugh. Cindy has never sworn, not once, since she's known her.

"Fucked," says Cindy. "I said 'fucked.' So there. See, Judith? You're corrupting me."

"Corrupting you? I'm liberating you!"

Cindy giggles. "It feels good to say it, actually, after hearing it all last term from you guys. But I'd better not let my mother hear that or she'll have a heart attack."

Now Cindy gives her an update on all her courses and assures her that all the teachers know she's still sick. But she suggests that Judith give each of them a call, or at least send an email, since none of them have yet heard from her directly all term. After they hang up, Judith lies in bed for a while, glowing with the pleasure of friendship. *There is goodness in the world,* she thinks. *There is darkness, but there is also light.* Then she phones both Hetty and Corinne. Not Suzy — Suzy she will have to deal with in person. But Hetty and Corinne are both lovely on the phone. Just as Bobby predicted, they tell her not to worry about their courses. She'll probably have to do an extra assignment for each course, but they both know she is a good student, and they are not worried. Hetty and Corinne both use this word, *worried*, but with different accents: one West Indian, one Eastern European. Corinne wasn't *wurrid*; Hetty wasn't *woorreed*. As long as Judith returns next Monday. Judith gets off the phone happy and relieved, and the rest of the day passes serenely. Topped off, in the evening, by Bobby's arrival with all her favourite deli foods: smoked meat, chopped liver, salami (*versht*, as her father called it), onion rolls, coleslaw, potato salad, and two huge pickles.

One week later, on Monday morning, she drives to Dunhill. It is a bright winter day and she is delighted to be well and back in the world again, even though this means that today she'll have to talk to Suzy. In addition to discussing what happened at the Christmas party and the SWAC meeting, she needs to enlist Suzy as her thesis advisor, and ask about her research grant. Judith has been counting on the RA'ship Suzy promised her, and now she urgently needs the money. She has less than $300 in her bank account: $293.03, to be precise — a prime number, she realized as soon as she saw it, which felt like an omen. Other than this $293.03, she has only a small savings account she cannot touch because it contains just enough money to cover her plane fare back to Israel and her first few months of rent there until she finds a job. Her most immediate worry is the heating bill that will arrive next week. The ancient furnace in her father's house devours oil like a Moloch devouring children. The January bill will be around $350, and she won't be able to pay it. And when she doesn't, they'll cut off her heat. She regrets that she took this chance with Suzy instead of accepting a scholarship, which would have been a sure thing. What she did back then now seems "the height of foolishness," as her father used to say. Though it made perfect sense at the time. The RA'ship would be more money than a scholarship (assuming the grant came through), and it was a generous gesture of loyalty to Suzy, an act of faith in their special relationship. But that was then. Now their relationship is strained and she is desperate for money. What if Suzy didn't get her grant? But no, that isn't very likely. Almost certainly she got her grant and all this will work out.

Judith reaches the classroom fifteen minutes before Corinne's class starts and, just as she imagined a week ago in bed, Kerry and her gang are all sitting together, gossiping, and it's the same with Lola and hers. Judith reads an article Corinne assigned until Cindy arrives and sits beside her. It's great to see her again. They hug and Cindy gives her all the materials she has saved for her. But after a few minutes of chat, Judith realizes that subliminally she is waiting for something. She is waiting for Pam and Aliza to appear, and they won't, of course. It hits her viscerally that both of them are gone. Pam's classes this term are all on Tuesdays, and Aliza — well, who knows when she'll see *her* again? And much as Cindy is wonderful, it feels strange being here at school just with her. Judith misses Aliza's brightness and lightness and Pam's tough intelligence and acerbity. *The four of us balanced each other out*, she thinks, as Cindy chatters on. *We were like four strong winds, same as in the song. North, east, south, and west meeting in the middle.*

Corinne begins her class. She is a very good teacher: smart, with a delicious dry sense of humour. This course is entitled "Sexism, Racism, and Women of Colour," and today's topic is "Women and Disability," which Judith is interested in and knows something about. So she enjoys this class and afterwards introduces herself to Corinne.

Hetty's class is also very good. She is an engaging and even charming teacher, which is a great relief to Judith, who worried that Hetty's moroseness could make for a tedious, depressing class. Judith discovers, though, that she is quite far behind in the statistics. When class is over, Cindy reassures her.

"You'll catch up," she says, patting her arm. "The first day back is always weird. I'll help you with the stats. If I can do it, you definitely can."

Then she asks Judith if Darra can join them for lunch. All this term, with Judith and Pamanaliza gone, she's been hanging out with Darra. Judith, despite a flash of jealousy, agrees. She doesn't mind Darra. She is pleasant and passionate about social work, and is taking the same two morning courses as Judith and Cindy. They eat lunch at a round pink-and-aqua table at Le Petit Café, and Judith feels a stab of sadness recalling her dinners here with Suzy. She wonders if they'll ever have another dinner together. It's only twenty-five minutes until Suzy's class, and she gets increasingly anxious as the minutes tick by. She is only half there with Cindy and Darra.

Finally they stand, bus their trays, and say goodbye, and Judith starts down the hallway alone, her hands feeling cold and clammy. When she reaches the classroom, Suzy isn't there yet. Several minutes later she enters, and after arranging her papers on the table at the front, turns to face the class. She stands there silently with a forbearing expression, waiting for them all to notice and stop talking, and meanwhile she scans the room. When she sees Judith, her eyes widen with surprise and she smiles slightly. Judith smiles back. *So it's all right then*, she thinks. *Everything is going to be okay.*

Suzy begins her class and, as Judith already suspected from the readings she has done for this course, this really is more a continuation of last term's than anything substantially new. So much so that she feels like she's barely missed anything in the first four classes. This is a comfort after feeling so lost in Hetty's class. But still Suzy's class is hard for her. With all the strain and pain in their relationship, it is hard to have to sit and look at Suzy for two hours straight. Especially since she isn't particularly looking at *her*. She is not singling her out like she used to. *Fine*, thinks Judith. *You tune me out; I'll tune you out.* So she stops listening to Suzy and summons Moshe, and he helps her get through this class.

* * *

After class, Judith waits in line outside Suzy's office. There are three people ahead of her, and whoever is inside with Suzy has been there for over ten minutes. Bored, she wanders down the hall. She has never been further than Suzy's office before, and now discovers a narrow corridor, a short alley in shadow, providing a shortcut between Suzy's office on one side and Weick's on the other. At Weick's end of the alley, there is a poster. She draws closer to see it in the poor light. Unlike the poster at Libertad, this one doesn't have an Israeli flag being burned. It has no picture at all. But it has all the same language: "apartheid state," "Zionist aggression," and so on, and like the poster at Libertad, this one is announcing a rally. *Oh shit*, she thinks, *here we go again.* This time the rally is taking place on February 17. This date rings a bell. Then she remembers: February 17 is Anti-oppression Day, just two weeks from now. This rally is part of Anti-oppression Day. It's the "rally over the lunch break" that someone mentioned at one of the SWAC meetings, meant as a follow-up to Brier's talk. An action to implement his words. Or, as Greg would say, "praxis." In Judaism, praxis would be saying the blessing over the wine and then drinking it. But this rally will not be an act of blessing, but of cursing. Cursing Israel.

The bottom half of this poster is a paragraph of text. In the dim light she squints to read it. The DSU and SLAP are calling on every good person at Dunhill, every person of conscience, to boycott all student and faculty exchanges between Canadian and Israeli universities, all joint research projects between Canadians and Israelis, and all international conferences being held in Israel. They are also calling for a boycott on Israeli exports of any kind: agricultural produce like oranges, dates, and olives, technological products like computer software, and medical inventions and devices — everything grown or developed in Israel. This poster also urges people to prohibit Israeli citizens from publishing their work in international academic journals, serving on the editorial boards of these journals, or holding honorary chairs at any university in Canada.

She feels the bottom drop out of her stomach. Then fear turns to anger. Firstly, at the malice behind this call to boycott, and secondly, at its sheer stupidity. *Are these people evil or stupid?* she wonders again. And this time answers: *Both.* Because the woman who is organizing the international social work conference in Israel next month, Dorit Benezra — someone Judith has met (she's Yonina's upstairs neighbour, and head of the Israeli social work union) — is a long-time peace activist and a founder of Peace Now. An outspoken critic of Ariel Sharon and his government, she insisted that the theme of this year's conference be "Social Workers' Responsibility as Advocates for Social Justice and Human Rights." This is the conference the poster is asking social workers around the world to boycott, so they can show their disapproval of Israelis' purported indifference to social justice and human rights. It's insane.

As for publishing — she stares at the last item on this poster — according to this boycott, Yitzchak Lichtenshtein and Sami Massarwa shouldn't be allowed to publish in any international journal their critically important cross-cultural research. Last week in *Ha'aretz* she read about this study: a significant collaboration between a Jewish Israeli and a Palestinian Israeli, both social work professors at the University of Haifa, comparing the emotional trauma experienced by Jewish and Arab children in Israel, and developing joint initiatives for addressing the mental health problems in both populations. The boycott advocated in this poster would prevent the publication of this bridge-building, peace-promoting research, since Lichtenshtein and Massarwa are both Israeli citizens. Mind-boggling. If the real purpose of this boycott is to promote more peaceful relationships and professional collaboration between Jews and Palestinians in the Israeli academe, then this project should be precisely the kind of thing they would want to support. This boycott makes no sense.

Unless ... Unless its real purpose is not to promote peace and coexistence, but to punish Israel. If that is the intent, then this boycott makes perfect sense. It's all very logical if you believe that Israel is the most evil place in the world, and therefore everything Israeli is intrinsically worthy of condemnation — even its best, most positive projects. If you view things from that angle, then this boycott is comprehensible. This also explains why there are no posters on the walls of this school calling for an academic boycott of any country other than Israel. Not Zimbabwe under Mugabe. Not China, even though China's human rights abuses are a matter of public record. Only Israel. Out of the whole world, only Israel deserves to be boycotted. This is antisemitic.

Someone should tear this poster down. It is hate literature. It encourages passersby to hate, and hurt, one specific group of people. Someone has to take it down. But who? She can't. She can't just tear down a poster.

Or maybe she can.

She peeks around the corner of the alley. There are now only two people in the hallway waiting for Suzy. Mike is holding what looks like a term paper. He is pacing back and forth, his term paper flapping at his side, obviously unhappy with his mark. He'll be in there awhile for sure, arguing with Suzy over every little point. It will be at least ten minutes till it's her turn, even if the guy ahead of Mike is quick. She ducks back into the alley and scans the poster from top to bottom. It's disgusting. It's obscene. Someone should rip it down.

But she can't. You don't go around ripping other people's stuff off walls. If you do that, you are no better than the people who put up this kind of crap. You've descended to their level.

Posters are free speech. A symbol of democracy. *If I rip down this poster*, she thinks, *I am ripping the fabric of democracy. I may not agree with what this poster says, but "I'll defend to the death its right to say it." Whoever put up this poster had a right to.*

Yes. That's true. But then, equally, I have the right to tear it down. That is democracy, too: multiple voices, each defining reality in its own terms. The person who put up this poster may perceive Israel to be the most scumbag country in the world. But I don't have to agree. I have a right to my own point of view. I also have a right, equal to anyone else's, to speak. With my lips. Or my hands.

But violence. Violence is not only wrong; it's illegal. This poster is university property, it has the university stamp on it. I could get into trouble for tearing it down.

Now she sees herself standing in front of the poster, vacillating. Like Rina vacillating about letting her kids go downtown. Rina wrote she felt as indecisive as Hamlet. *Well, so do I*, thinks Judith: *To tear or not to tear, that is the question.* Then she laughs at herself. She is being ridiculous. Look at some of the acts of courage Jews have performed throughout history, for instance in the Warsaw ghetto. Risking their lives every single day, and not to save just themselves, but also others. And here she can't even pull down a goddamn poster. Her and those namby-pamby left-wing sensibilities of hers. Keeping her from doing what she knows she should do.

She thinks of her name, Judith. Judith in ancient times lopped off Holofernes's head without even batting an eyelash. *Come on*, she tells herself. *Be strong like your name. You can doubt, dither, and deliberate all you want beforehand, if that makes you feel like a moral person. Agonize to your heart's content. But in the end, act. Sartre was right: ultimately there is nothing but action.*

She reaches out her hand. *Act. Do it. Have some impact on the world.*

She tears the poster off the wall.

— 8 —

Alone in the hallway, Judith stands outside Suzy's door, waiting for Mike to finish so she can have her turn. Her face is flushed with pride over her small act of defiance. Especially since tearing down this poster turned out to be more complicated than she expected. She was mortified by the loudness of the ripping paper and the way it resounded through the silent alley and out into the hallway. Even after the poster was off the wall, it continued to make noise — a loud crackling sound — when she tried squishing it into the nearby garbage can. The poster seemed to fight back. She felt like she was wrestling a living thing, a resisting leviathan. Eventually, panting and perspiring from the effort, she succeeded. But at that moment she sensed someone peeking into the alley. What if someone saw her? She'd destroyed school property — there must be some consequence for doing that. She is nervous, too, about being alone with Suzy again, about meeting her soon for their first real conversation since the Christmas party. She starts pacing. Finally Suzy's door opens. Mike leaves and Suzy appears in the doorway.

"Hi, come in," she says, in a friendly yet professional voice. Not warm but also not cold — somewhere in the middle. Judith enters her office and sits in the same chair as always, while Suzy closes the door behind them. She feels the seat under her, still warm from Mike's bum. She waits in silence as Suzy settles into her chair. Then Suzy speaks, in the same professionally friendly manner. "It's nice to see you back at school. Does this mean you're back now for good?"

"I hope so," Judith says.

"Good," says Suzy. But she does not sound particularly pleased, or even interested. She seems distracted and far away.

Then she returns from wherever she was, and asks, "What can I do for you?"

The abruptness of this question jolts Judith. There has been none of the chit-chat that usually precedes getting down to business; even her dentist exchanges more pleasantries than this. *Never mind*, she thinks. *We'll do this Suzy's way, getting the business over with first. Then we can have the other conversation.* So, using the language of business, she says, "I have two items."

"So do I," says Suzy. "Maybe they're the same. But you go first."

"Okay," Judith says. But she is not feeling okay. She expected some weirdness with Suzy, but she wasn't prepared for this total absence of connection. She pauses now before going on. It doesn't feel comfortable, or smart, to ask someone for a favour who is so obviously ill-disposed toward you, and in a way both of the "items" on her agenda, the RA'ship and the thesis advisor issue, are favours she is requesting of Suzy. But she has no choice now but to proceed. Suzy is glancing at the wall clock: it's 4:20, and Judith knows from last term that Suzy likes to leave school by 4:30, 4:40 at the latest, to get home in time for Natalie's schoolbus. So she plunges in.

"The first thing is, I was curious if you've heard yet about your research grant." Suzy looks at her blankly. "You know," Judith continues. "The one we talked about my RA'ing for if it came through. Exploring community-university partnerships in anti-oppression work."

Suzy frowns slightly. "Yes," she says. "I did hear back. I got the grant. I heard from them right after the Christmas vacation."

Judith stares at her, unable to absorb the good news because Suzy's nonverbals don't match what she is saying. She doesn't seem happy at all about getting her grant. But anyway, Judith is deeply relieved. She feels the anxiety that has been sitting in her bones all this time begin to seep away. She'll be able to pay that heating bill. Her house will be warm and she'll have enough money for food. Everything will be all right.

"That's great!" she cries. "I was so worried you wouldn't get funded. This is terrific."

But still Suzy is not smiling. She isn't saying anything, either — just gazing pensively at her. Judith's relief and joy turn to confusion and anxiety. Finally Suzy speaks. "I did get that grant," she says, "but I didn't know you were still interested in RA'ing for it. You and I last talked about this back in November, and I didn't hear anything from you after that. So I offered it to someone else."

Judith gawks at Suzy. "What do you mean?" she asks hoarsely. "You told me if you got this grant, I would be your RA. I was your first choice."

"Yes," says Suzy. "But that was a long time ago."

Judith doesn't understand. She has been counting on this. She passed up a scholarship for this, because Suzy asked her to. This is impossible. It can't be happening.

Suzy sits in her chair with her legs crossed, looking calm and professional. As if she hasn't done anything terrible; just some ordinary, even minor, thing, like hiring a new plumber to fix her sink instead of the guy she has used till now. Judith is still gawking at her. Suzy continues wearily, as if explaining something so obvious it shouldn't be necessary.

"You weren't here, Judith. You disappeared. You fell off the face of the earth. You didn't call, you didn't email. I had no idea what was happening with you, and I had to get started on my research. This is only a four-month grant, I was notified about a month ago, and to keep on schedule, I had to have all the preliminary interviews finished by this coming Friday, just four days from today. If I'd waited for you to resurface, I would be in very big trouble right now."

Judith can't believe what she is hearing. It's true she hasn't been in touch for the past month, but Cindy and Phoebe have been keeping her informed. "I've been sick," she says to Suzy. "You knew I was sick. Cindy told you, and Phoebe."

"I didn't know what to think." For the first time today Suzy looks at her frankly and openly. "First I hear from Cindy you're sick, almost deathly ill from the sounds of it. You have a high fever, you can barely sit up in bed, and there's no way of knowing when you'll be well enough to return to school. The next thing I know, on the same day you've missed my third class in a row, I see you gallivanting around the mall, happy as a plum. I'm sure you can understand my confusion."

Gallivanting! thinks Judith. *Happy as a plum! I was sitting on a bench trying not to vomit when you came along.* But she doesn't say this aloud. She just gapes at Suzy. Then she understands what's expected of her. She's supposed to grovel and try to convince Suzy that she is a good, honest person who really was sick. She slides her right hand into the pocket of her jeans and fingers the note from Bernie Braunstein. She has half a mind not to show it to Suzy, because Suzy should believe her without it. Suzy should have trusted her all this time, regardless of appearances, just because she knows her and the kind of person she is. *Okay*, she thinks. *I'll play your little game. Here's your proof that I'm a good person. That I wasn't lying.* She pulls the doctor's note from her pocket and thrusts it onto the desk in front of Suzy.

Suzy lifts the note, reads it, and puts it down. "You seem upset," she says empathically, looking and sounding almost like her old self. "I'm sorry if this catches you by surprise." But then her voice turns colder: "It was your responsibility, however, to be in touch with me about this RA'ship, to let me know you were still interested. I had no idea when, or even if, you were ever coming back."

These last few words, "ever coming back," sound familiar to Judith. Then she remembers Suzy saying her father had left home and never come back. *Does she think I abandoned her, too?* she wonders. *Does she think I'm like her father?* "I was sick," she says to Suzy.

But Suzy barely seems to have heard. Her face remains impassive. "I'm sorry, Judith," she says, "but none of this matters now. It's water under the bridge."

Judith peers at her. She can't really mean this — that it's all settled, and nothing can be done about it now. *I passed up a scholarship*, she thinks. *I passed it up for you. Now I'm left with nothing.*

But Suzy is unruffled. She seems perfectly relaxed in her chair, legs crossed, wearing a pink silk shirt, a black skirt, and a string of pearls.

"May I ask," says Judith, doing her best to control her emotions, "who you gave that RA'ship to instead of me?"

"I don't see what difference it makes."

But Judith sees the redness climbing up Suzy's neck. Good. At least she's ashamed. "Was it by any chance Elizabeth?" she asks.

Suzy fixes her with a sharp, probing look. "And if it were?" she asks. "Would that be a problem for you?"

Judith stares at her, then bursts out laughing. After the recent roller coaster of emotions, she can't do anything now but laugh. It's that or cry, and she certainly does not want to cry in front of Suzy. Of all people, Elizabeth. The daughter of the manager (Cindy told her) of the largest bank in Dunhill. *Blond little rich girl*, thinks Judith. *Because of her, I won't have enough money for heat or food.* Laughing, she sees herself wasting away to skin and bones in her cold, dark bedroom, feeling more and more frigid as the Canadian winter wind whistles in through the old, cracked walls of her father's house. Her laugh becomes giddy. *There is nothing left between us now. It's all over.*

You don't care, Suzy, what happens to me at all. Abruptly her laughter stops.

Suzy is regarding her appraisingly, critically. Then she asks, "What else did you have?"

Judith doesn't understand.

"You said you had two items to discuss."

She recalls, as if from far away, that she wanted to talk to Suzy about being her thesis advisor. "Never mind," she says. "It's not important." She hears the wall clock ticking loudly. *I'd better get out of here,* she thinks, *before I make a complete fool of myself. After all, Suzy is still my prof.* She rises. "I'll go now."

Suzy, still seated, looks up at her with a frown. "Actually, there were a couple of items I wanted to discuss, if you have a moment. They're quite important."

"Okay." Judith sits back down.

The first subject Suzy raises is all the work Judith has missed in her course. Suzy, comfortably in her teacher role now, launches into a description of the content she has covered so far. As she drones on, Judith only half-listens. The personal relationship with Suzy is over. So the rest of this doesn't matter. Through a haze, she answers Suzy's questions. Yes, she has gotten all the class notes. Yes, she has the handouts and the course outline. Yes, she has done the readings. But even as she talks, all that is real to her is the pain of betrayal. A deep inner bleeding. She is nothing to Suzy anymore. Yes, she replies dully, she can get last week's assignment done for next week. Yes, next week she can also hand in the topic for her final paper. Yes, all these requirements sound reasonable.

Suzy stands up to double-check on her wall calendar the due date for the final paper — yes, she had it right — and sits down again. She crosses her right leg over her left and Judith notices the shapely leg covered in silky nylon and the sharp, delicate shinbone running down its middle.

"The second thing," Suzy says, "is what happened at the last SWAC meeting."

Uh-oh. But at the same time Judith is relieved. She didn't have the guts to bring this up, yet she is glad Suzy has. Maybe she intends to explain herself.

Suzy says, "I was very disturbed by what happened there."

"So was I," says Judith, gazing at Suzy's face. So she, too, understands what a horrible thing occurred that night. How that meeting made a travesty of social justice and everything SWAC is supposed to stand for.

Suzy says kindly, "I can see things from your point of view, Judith. I can imagine why you got so upset at that meeting. But" — here her tone hardens and the kindness fades from her voice — "I felt at a certain point you lost your objectivity. Your professionalism, even."

My objectivity? My professionalism? Judith feels her bowels contract.

"And I was quite surprised," continues Suzy, "at how hard you pushed for what you wanted. After all, you were there in the role of co-chair, not just another committee member. You were supposed to help me facilitate the meeting, not advance your own agenda."

Judith stares at Suzy. *What are you talking about?* she thinks. *You're the one who fucked up at that meeting, not me. You're the one who should be apologizing.* "I didn't have an agenda," she says as evenly as she can, trying to contain her anger. "I just thought what the committee was doing was wrong. And ..." — she feels herself going out on a limb, but decides to go there anyway — "I think you felt the same."

Suzy's eyes slide to the side and then return to meet Judith's. "I have my own point of view, obviously," she says primly. "But ultimately what I thought or felt at that meeting is totally beside the point. As chair, I have to respect, and give equal time to, all sides on every issue. It's not my job to try to change people's minds and get them to vote how I want them to."

"I didn't say —"

"People have a right," says Suzy, "to vote however they wish. Last term I tried to help you. I stepped in, as you may recall, when the committee was picking Brier's topic. I tried to interfere and influence, maybe even manipulate, the committee's decision on that. I wasn't even effective, because Lola saw what I was doing and called me on it. As she was right to do."

She pauses here, as if challenging Judith to disagree or interrupt her again, but she stays silent. Suzy goes on, "A week ago Thursday I could see which way the wind was blowing, and I tried to warn you. I suggested you take a few moments and consider very carefully what you were doing before making your motion, but you wouldn't listen. More than that I couldn't do. And shouldn't do. SWAC has a right to reach its own decisions using proper democratic process."

What a cop-out, Judith thinks. *Of course the chair is not supposed to manipulate the members of a committee. But to try and influence them is something else. People try to influence each other all the time, and that is also what good leadership is. Leaders lead. You, Suzy, should have led this committee, rather than just following it.*

Aloud she says, "I'm not quite as enamoured with democracy as you. Using proper democratic process, you can still arrive at a decision that is not a good or moral one." Suzy listens attentively. "For example, what if SWAC democratically selected for its keynote speaker someone who was a racist? A member, for instance, of Aryan Truth? Or an anti-gay activist, maybe from a right-wing" — she remembers Suzy's religious beliefs and just in time omits the word *Christian* — "fundamentalist group espousing so-called family values? Would this be okay, just because this person was selected through democratic process?"

Annoyance flashes across Suzy's face. "No one like that would ever get approved by SWAC, as you well know. Those individuals would not reflect the viewpoint of our constituency."

"'Constituency'?! You sound like we're in politics."

"Don't be naive, Judith. Of course we are. Everything is political. Nothing is separate from the workings of the real world, including social work. Which is not to say that we don't have ideals. But these have to be balanced against other things."

"Like what?"

"Excuse me?"

"What exactly do our ideals have to be balanced against?"

Suzy gives her a sharp look as if she's being provocative. Which is partly true. But also she genuinely wants to know. She wants Suzy to have to say out loud, to articulate and put on the table, how she sees the world. What was so important to her that she was willing to sell her out last week. "I want to understand," says Judith. Feeling momentarily like she's again a student sitting at her teacher's feet.

"I believe you already know the answer," says Suzy. "Ideals have to be balanced against reality. Against the needs and interests of other people. This school is not just a place of learning, Judith. It is also a community. And like any community, we have to keep a balance between the different groups and their interests."

"In other words, *realpolitik*."

"No," Suzy says hotly, flushing from the neck up. "That is not what I am saying. I'm saying when you live in a democracy, you can't always get what you want."

You can't always get what you want. Hearing the Stones' song in her head, Judith is stung by Suzy's implication that she's a spoiled brat used to always getting her way. "I don't expect to always get what I want," she says. "But I also don't believe the majority is always right. At the U.N., for instance, you have one representative from Israel and one representative from each of the Arab countries, so of course everything there is skewed against Israel. Democracy has nothing to do with justice or what is morally right. Democracy is just demography."

She is feeling clever: *democracy* rhymed with *demography*. She sees Suzy's face slightly soften. Her frown is thoughtful now, rather than disapproving.

"I agree with you," Suzy says, "that democracy is far from perfect. But still it's the best we've got."

Judith nods. Her father loved quoting Winston Churchill, especially his line that democracy is the worst possible system of government — save its alternatives.

"Which is why," Suzy says, "SWAC is so committed to making all its decisions through democratic process. It is also why these decisions must be respected even if you disagree with them. That is the nature of living in a democracy."

Oh, stop it. Stop patronizing me. But aloud Judith says, trying — though not fully succeeding — to keep the bitterness out of her voice: "You win some, you lose some — is that what you mean?"

"Yes, Judith," says Suzy, leaning forward in her chair. "That's precisely what I mean. You don't flounce out of a meeting just because you didn't get your way."

"I didn't 'flounce,'" says Judith.

"Yes, you did," says Suzy. "That's exactly what you did."

"Flounce?"

"Flounce."

They look at each other, and then, unexpectedly, start to smile. Despite everything that has happened between them, their smiles broaden and their eyes laugh. But just as they are about to break through into full laughter, Suzy kills it by saying, "You have to work within democracy, Judith. There's no other choice."

Okay, thinks Judith. *Fine. Lecture me instead of laughing with me. Have it your way.* Now she knows it's really all over between her and Suzy. They will never laugh together again — not a true, open-hearted laugh, the way they used to. And this being the case, she might as well say everything she feels. Because now there is nothing to lose.

"I don't know," she says, "what choices there are or aren't. But I do know that not everything comes down to the will of the majority. There is something higher than that."

"And what is that, Judith?" asks Suzy, her voice suddenly very quiet.

"Morality," she says. "Doing what's right. Pursuing real social justice, not the ersatz kind." She pauses, probing Suzy's eyes. "You were correct when you said that SWAC would never select a keynote speaker who was anti-gay or anti-black. But that's not because all the members of SWAC are such fine, principled people. Some of them may be. But mainly it's because it would be politically incorrect, and anyone at this school who suggested a keynote speaker who hates blacks or gays would be tarred and feathered. As they should be. But meanwhile it's fine to bring here a keynote speaker who hates Israel and supports violence against Jews. Why is that, eh? I'll tell you why. It's because racism and homophobia are unacceptable at Dunhill, but antisemitism is not. Antisemitism is still acceptable here."

Suzy's eyes narrow. "What are you saying, Judith? Are you accusing everyone on SWAC, me included, of being antisemitic? Because if you are, I'd suggest you choose your words very carefully."

Judith's stomach turns over. She has spoken too freely. She still has several months at Dunhill, and Suzy is still one of her profs. "No," she says, "I'm not saying everyone on SWAC is antisemitic. God forbid. But I am saying, as we discussed last term, that there is a double standard at this school. No one here cares about human rights abuses anywhere else in the world. Only in Israel. And no other people or country gets talked about here the way people talk on a regular basis about Israel. It's fine to say anything you want about Israel. In fact, it's almost approved of: If you denigrate Israel, it shows you're a good, caring person. You care about the underdog. Things are not this way just because there's a conflict in the Middle East. This singling out of the Jewish state is a form of antisemitism."

She stops, out of breath. But she is glad she said what she had to say.

Suzy regards her pensively. Then she says, "I recall when you first shared this perspective with me. I thought it was interesting, and I still do. But I'm not sure I buy it."

Buy? I wasn't selling anything.

"To me, the reaction people have to Israel does seem very related to the political conflict there." Suzy's hair bobs prettily as she talks, reminding Judith of a photo from the 1950s she once saw of the most popular girl in a high-school class. "I'd like to believe," says Suzy, "that most of the people here at the school are good people who truly care about social justice and human rights. Who are motivated by sincere concern for the Palestinians, rather than by any" — there's a tiny pause here, like the beating of a bat's wing — "anti-Jewish sentiment."

Judith says nothing.

"Even if you don't agree with the point of view expressed at SWAC, Judith, surely you agree these people have the right to express it?"

"You mean academic freedom, free speech, and all that?"

"Yes," says Suzy. "Academic freedom, free speech, and all that."

She ignores Suzy's tone and shrugs. "I think there's a big difference between free speech and hate speech. People like Brier who advocate the use of violence against a specific group of people are using hate speech, not free speech, even if they try to justify this violence by talking about means and ends. I don't believe hate speech, against *any* group, should be tolerated. There's a book from the sixties I read called *A Critique of Pure Tolerance*, and in it Marcuse and his colleagues say that no society — not even the most open one — should tolerate everything. Because some behaviours, including certain kinds of speech, are a direct threat to a society and will undermine its existence. And one thing they say absolutely should not be tolerated is hate speech."

There is a pause while Suzy contemplates her thoughtfully. Then she says, "You're very bright, Judith. Maybe even persuasive, though I still don't know if I agree with you. But even assuming for a moment I did, what would you have me do in this situation? Anti-oppression Day is only two weeks away. It's impossible at this point to start looking for another keynote speaker."

Judith looks back at Suzy. *Nothing is impossible. As Herzl said: If you will it, it is no dream.* But she does not say this aloud. There's no point. In fact, she is starting to feel there is no point even in continuing this conversation. This game of intellectual ping-pong. Volley after volley. *Vale atque vale.* Because Suzy isn't going to do anything about Brier. She doesn't care. All she cares about now is getting her contract renewed, which means sucking up to Chris, Lola, and Weick. *She wants me to make this easy for her,* Judith thinks. *To agree with her that she has no choice. But I won't. Because she does.*

"Nothing is impossible," she says.

Suzy grimaces. "You expect a lot from people, Judith." Then, "You've changed since last term."

No. You're the one who has changed.

"Maybe it's delayed grief over your father," Suzy muses. "Or problems with Bobby." She looks at Judith almost hopefully. "I recall you saying that the two of you were having problems."

Judith flushes, embarrassed that she ever confided about this to Suzy. She's also angry. How incredibly inappropriate for Suzy to throw this in her face now — something she told her in confidence. And to try using this to explain away what is happening between them, as if this whole conflict is because of her personal problems. She glares at Suzy: *Don't you try and "social work" me. Don't even think about it.*

"In any case," Suzy says in a voice as smooth and sweet as dark honey, "I guess the question remains: Given how negative you're feeling now about SWAC, do you see yourself continuing on?"

Judith looks at her, confused. *What do you mean, "continuing on"?*

"Because if you don't believe in what we're doing," Suzy explains, her tone pleasant, "if basically you're uncomfortable with the whole direction we're moving in, then I wouldn't want you to feel obliged to stay on as co-chair. You have to do what's right for you."

Judith gapes.

"I'm not saying I want you to resign. I'm just saying if this is what you decide, I won't stand in your way."

What! thinks Judith. *Am I now being fired from SWAC? First she fires me from being her RA, and now she fires me from SWAC?!* Her cheeks feel hot.

"My preference would be for you to remain," says Suzy. "But only if you're more or less on board with everyone else. We can't have constant conflict on this committee. No committee can sustain that."

"You mean I can stay as long as I follow the majority?"

"You upset people, Judith."

"Upset people?"

"Yes. Like when you walked out of that meeting."

"I wasn't feeling well. I told you before the meeting started that I wouldn't last all the way till the end."

"Yes, you did," says Suzy. "But that's something else I've been trying to figure out. How exactly does someone know in advance that an hour and a half later they are going to be too sick to stay in a meeting? I was hoping you could explain this to me."

"I was sick."

"So you keep saying, Judith. But what a coincidence that you felt so sick you had to leave the meeting right after a vote that didn't go your way."

Judith flushes. She shouldn't have been there at all. She only came to that meeting for Suzy. "I *was* sick," she says. "But I also didn't want to sit there any longer after what they decided." Then, "After what *you* decided."

"I didn't vote. I abstained as chair."

"Yes, but you didn't do anything to stop it, did you? Other than telling everyone I'm Israeli."

"It's not my job to stop it. I did what I could to support you, and I'm sorry if you don't think it was enough. But that doesn't excuse your behaviour. And not just at SWAC. Mike was just in to see me and he was terribly upset."

Mike? What's Mike got to do with this?

Suzy looks at her intently. "He said you tore a poster off the wall. Is this true?"

She feels like shitting. So someone *did* see her. And he told Suzy. Bravely she looks right back at her. "It was calling for a boycott of Israel. Of all Israeli students and faculty —"

"I don't care what it was calling for!" cries Suzy. "You don't go around tearing posters off walls just because you don't agree with what's written on them. You have no right, Judith. This is school property."

"It's only school property because someone convinced Phoebe to stamp it with the school stamp."

"I don't know about 'convinced.' Phoebe isn't easy to convince of anything. But the bottom line is that this poster *was* stamped and therefore was school property. You are not the judge of what should and shouldn't be on the walls of this school."

"Then who is?" Judith asks defiantly, amazed at her own fearlessness. "You once said this school belongs to all of us. Well, if I, as co-chair of SWAC, can't pull down a poster that's promoting hate, then who can?"

"Being the co-chair of SWAC doesn't give you the right to pull down posters," says Suzy. "That is a misunderstanding, even an abuse, of the power of this position."

"On the contrary, I think it is a most appropriate use of the power of this position. Standing up for what is right. Opposing oppression in all its forms."

Suzy shakes her head. "No. Because when it comes to Israel, you have no sense of proportion at all. You overreact. Your judgment is flawed. If you want to stay on as co-chair of SWAC, you're going to have to be more objective and neutral."

"Objective? Neutral?!" cries Judith. "If this poster was proposing not to let Muslim faculty members sit on editorial boards or publish in any of the good journals, do you believe anyone would ask all the Muslim students and faculty to try and be objective and neutral about it? Or the Asians at this school if this poster were directed against them? Or GLBTs, or blacks? Of course not. But because it's about Israelis, you're telling me I shouldn't be upset, and I should be objective and neutral. Well, I'm not. I'm not objective and neutral, and I don't even want to be."

"That," Suzy says dryly, "is becoming clearer by the minute. You've become so emotionally involved with this issue you are quite unable to see any side but your own."

Judith laughs a small, hard laugh. "What side is that, Suzy? I'm on the side that opposes antisemitism. I should be able to see the side that supports it?"

"That's not what I meant and you know it."

"No, I don't. I don't know what you meant at all." She feels weak now, almost like crying.

Suzy says coldly, "Then I'm not sure there's any point in my trying to explain." She regards her with palpable dislike. Without the slightest hint of Unconditional Positive Regard. Or any Positive Regard at all. "But," Suzy adds, "you still have a decision to make."

"No, I don't. It's already made."

Suzy looks at her expectantly.

"I'm resigning."

Suzy isn't upset or even surprised, and Judith even sees a faint glint of satisfaction in her eyes. "As co-chair?" is all Suzy says.

She frowns. "Yes. Isn't that what I am?"

"Yes," says Suzy. "But you also have the option of resigning as co-chair yet still remaining on the committee."

She digests this for a moment. "You mean stay on as a regular member."

Suzy nods.

"No," says Judith. "There's not much point."

"No," Suzy agrees sympathetically. "Probably not."

There is that old warmth and empathy in Suzy's voice now, and a compassionate expression in her eyes. For a second, this kindles in Judith a feeling of closeness with her, and a longing for more. But then she is angry. Suzy's empathy right now is like someone kicking you in the stomach and then being solicitous that your stomach hurts. "I have to go," she says, and rises.

Suzy glances at the clock. Judith follows her eyes: 4:46 p.m. — she has already missed Natalie's bus. Judith, standing while Suzy sits, looks down at her and says, "About the Christmas party —"

"I don't want to discuss that," says Suzy.

"But I —"

"I said I'm *not interested!*"

There is a sharp finality in Suzy's voice that makes it impossible to utter another word. Judith stands perfectly still, gazing at Suzy's face. It changed the second Judith brought up the Christmas party: something deep inside Suzy's eyes snapped shut like a trap door. "Okay," Judith says slowly and turns to go. But at the door, she turns back and says, "I guess Elizabeth will co-chair with you now."

"Well, she *is* who I had in mind," says Suzy. "I checked into it, and I'm supposed to appoint your successor as soon as possible in circumstances like these."

"Circumstances like these"? What does she mean by that? wonders Judith, *or by "I checked into it"?* Then she understands. This was all pre-arranged. It was signed, sealed, and delivered before she even walked into this room. She can see Suzy, sometime after the last SWAC meeting, crossing that dark alley to Weick's office, and reviewing with him all the proper procedures for getting rid of the co-chair of a committee — in other words, her. Which Weick, disliking her as he does, would no doubt have been happy to do. So it was all settled in advance. It didn't matter, then, what she said or did in the past half-hour. She could have sat in complete silence or screamed her head off; it wouldn't have made any difference. A short laugh escapes her now: A single note — a "ha!" of epiphany.

The room is utterly silent. She stands in the doorway, gawking at Suzy. At those pretty brown eyes, which gaze back at her now with an expression of compassion and concern. *Pseudo-compassion*, she thinks, *pseudo-concern. Pseudo, pseudo, pseudo.* She turns on her heel and leaves.

— 9 —

For the next four days, Judith goes over this conversation with Suzy. Over and over again, word for word — I said, she said, I said, she said — as though it's a text that, if she studies it long enough, she'll be able to understand. Of course, at one level, she understands perfectly well what happened. She and Suzy had misunderstandings regarding her illness and the Christmas party, and different perspectives on SWAC, and these three elements affected their relationship. At another level, though, what happened with Suzy doesn't make any sense at all. Suzy sold her out. She betrayed her — with SWAC, with Weick, with the RA'ship, and with their whole relationship. In just eight weeks, Judith has gone from being Suzy's favourite student — respected, trusted, and cherished — to being someone Suzy considers untrustworthy, dishonest, and contemptible.

While she's agonizing about this, though, she is also doing her schoolwork. Despite everything, her mind is sharp and focused, and in just four days of concentrated work, she's managed to catch up on more than half the readings, and knock off one of the two short assignments she owes Suzy. At four o'clock she stops studying, goes to the kitchen, and eats a banana. She is relieved and glad to be on top of her schoolwork.

On the wall calendar she crosses off the four previous days, with four big bold red X's. Then, too superstitious to cross off today's square until it's over, she draws a little pyramid and writes in it the number of days she has left in Canada. *Only fifty-nine days*, she thinks, *until I'm back home and out of* galut. She counts all the Mondays between now and the last day of school, April 7: nine Mondays to go. Just nine more days of classes — only nine more times she has to drive to Dunhill. Anyone can get through nine days. She could survive nine days anywhere, even in prison.

Through the kitchen window she sees it's getting dark outside, so she goes upstairs and gets nicely dressed. She is going to Bobby's soon for Friday night dinner. She doesn't feel like it — she'd rather stay home and read — but they never miss a Friday night together. She bundles up and gets into the car.

Bobby looks glad to see her. He gives her a warm hug and ushers her into the kitchen where, from a pot on the stove, he ladles out for her a cup of hot apple cider. In the living room, she sits on his black leather couch, her knees pulled up against her chest, drinking her cider and holding the cup with both hands to warm them. The cider is pleasantly spicy, it warms her all the way down, and sitting here, she feels cozy. Bobby sits at the other end of the couch, smiling and watching her drink. Then he asks, "Do you know what day it is today?"

She has no idea what he means. She knows it isn't his birthday.

"It's seventeen months to the day," he says, "since we got back together."

"Wow," she says. "That's a long time."

"Time flies when you're having fun. To me it feels like nothing."

"You sound like Jacob working for Rachel. At least for me you didn't have to herd sheep from morning to night."

"I'm serious, Judith." His earnest look erases her smile. "I feel very lucky."

She looks down into her cider, embarrassed. She doesn't want things to get intense. To lighten things up, she says, "Yeah. Like I'm such a great catch."

"You are."

"No, I'm not. But anyway, can we eat now? I'm hungry."

In his dining room, she lights the Shabbat candles. They recite the blessings over the wine and *chalah*, and eat. Over soup they discuss Bobby's work: It is going slightly better than before, but still not great. Which revives in her the same old pang of guilt: *It's all my fault. It's because of that Christmas party. I shouldn't have worn that red dress …*

Over chicken-with-apricots and rice, they talk about what happened with Suzy on Monday. They have already conversed about this several times, and Bobby is disgusted with Suzy.

"What a couple, that Suzy and Dennis," he says. "I've got him and you've got her. I don't know which is worse."

For the third time in the past twenty minutes, she says, "I can't believe what Suzy did." Then she adds, "Especially how she took no responsibility for her actions and blamed it all on democracy. Like democracy is the be-all and end-all. You'd think democracy was God."

He smiles. "You know the joke about God and democracy."

"No."

"You'll love this. One night there's a meeting between Rabbi Volovich and the Ritual Committee at his *shul*. Ten men are present — a *minyan*. The committee's chairman proposes a motion, the rabbi disagrees, and all hell breaks loose. Both sides on this issue believe they're totally right, and neither side will yield. It's six against four. There's shouting, screaming, name-calling — a typical synagogue meeting dealing with sacred matters. After three hours, the chairman says, 'We're not getting anywhere. It's ten o'clock and we have to decide. I'm calling a vote.'

"They vote, and it's still six to four. The chairman is about to declare victory over the rabbi when there's a great rumbling noise. It grows increasingly loud, like thunder or an earthquake. Lightning flashes through the stained-glass windows. The sanctuary walls tremble. Everyone's terrified. Then the doors to the holy ark fly open, and out booms a deafening voice: 'Rabbi Volovich is right!' Then the ark closes, the thunder and lightning vanish, and everything returns to normal. Everyone is dumbfounded. Astonishingly, God has descended personally from heaven to express the divine viewpoint on this motion. The committee sits in stunned silence.

"Finally the chairman says: 'So what? So now, instead of four votes, the rabbi has five. I still have six, so my motion carries.'"

Judith laughs heartily. "That's great!"

"I heard it from a rabbi. Apparently the idea behind it comes from the Talmud: That God runs things in heaven, and we run things down here."

"That's depressing."

"Why?"

"Because I don't have much faith in the human race right now. If even God can't help us, we're fucked."

He looks at her tenderly. "I know you're feeling disillusioned, which is understandable. But the world is what it is. It isn't going to change, for you or anyone else, and if you keep fighting it, you're just going to keep getting hurt."

"Maybe, maybe not."

"You will. You can fight one little piece of it here or there. But this thing at Dunhill, for instance, is way too big for any one person, even you. It's just hurling yourself against a windmill."

"Stop with the windmill thing," she says irritably. "Find a new metaphor. Anyway, I don't agree. Someone has to try to change things. You can't just take everything lying down."

"There are some things I love doing lying down," he smiles. But she does not smile back. "Come on, Judith. Lighten up. It's Friday night."

She hates being told to lighten up. But she also doesn't feel like fighting. She picks despondently at her chicken-with-apricots. Her appetite is gone. She moves the chicken around on her plate, like she did as a child, to camouflage how little of it she has eaten. She hopes he doesn't notice, and he doesn't seem to. He is too busy telling her that all she has to do between now and April 7 is get her M.S.W. Show up at classes, do her homework, and graduate. He pronounces this last word in three distinct syllables: *gra-du-ate*. It sounds like "Grad Jew Ate." Like someone ate a Jew who was a grad.

"I know," she says glumly, feeling depressed. She knows he is right. He's right the same way her father was always right. Because they both reflect the voice of the world. The "real world." The world as it is, not as it should be, or as she would like it to be. She looks at Bobby across the table from her, handsome in his Ralph Lauren sweater, so solidly middle class and normal. Not like her. She has always been different. He glances up from his plate at her: his eyes are a beautiful emerald green and piercingly smart. *He'll always be okay*, she thinks. *He's a survivor.*

Now he notices her plate. "You haven't eaten a thing," he says.

"I'm not hungry," she answers guiltily. "It's very good, though — and it was sweet of you to make chicken-with-apricots. Normally I love it."

He stares at her full plate. "Okay, you're not hungry for chicken. But maybe you're hungry for something else?"

No. She is not in the mood for sex.

"Some zabaglione, perhaps?" he asks with a smile.

"Zabaglione?!" She loves zabaglione, as he knows.

"Coming right up. *Uno momento*." He disappears into the kitchen and returns a minute later bearing two tall soda fountain glasses filled with zabaglione, topped with strawberries and chocolate shavings.

"You made this?!" she asks, incredulous.

"No, it's from Fireman's. But I thought you deserved a treat."

She gazes with delight at her dessert. "I can't believe it. Bobby, you are the best." She dips her finger into the smooth, creamy foam, and with her eyes closed, slowly sucks it off. "Oh, my God," she says. "Oh, my God."

"You like it?" he asks with shining eyes.

"Better than sex, as Aliza would say."

"Really?" He sounds a little hurt.

She opens her eyes and looks at him. "Of course not, silly." She feels like she is simultaneously telling the truth and lying.

"Here." He holds out a long ice cream spoon.

She accepts it reluctantly. "Do I have to use this?"

He looks surprised. "Not if you don't want to."

"Good." She dips her finger back into the zabaglione, and again with closed eyes, slowly sucks it off. "Oh, my God," she says, and dips it in and sucks it off again. Then again. And again. But before she can do it yet another time, he comes around to her side of the table, kneels beside her, takes hold of her hand, dips her finger into the zabaglione, and inserts it into his own mouth. She moans as his tongue flicks up and down her finger, flicking-licking off the sweet foam. He leans forward and licks a tiny smudge of zabaglione from the corner of her mouth. He licks her upper lip. She smiles. He kisses her lower lip. She grins. He kisses the inside of her mouth. She flings her arms around his neck and clings to him with all her might.

On Monday morning Judith drives to Dunhill. There is snow everywhere, nothing anywhere but snow. On the radio this morning, they said this is the snowiest and coldest winter Toronto has had in twenty-five years. Even walking to her car in the driveway, the wind tore viciously through her coat as if she weren't wearing anything at all. Last night she plugged every crack around the doors and windows with rags and old socks. But *gurnisht helfn*: afterwards she still felt the cold air any time she passed a door or window — and this was with the furnace on. Yesterday she sifted through the accumulated mail, and there was the heating bill, due two days from now. There's no way she can pay it — not unless she stops buying food. She hopes they don't cut off her heat immediately; someone told her there's usually a grace period, followed by a reminder notice, maybe even two. *I must do something about this*, she thinks. *Maybe if I call them and plead ... Yes. Tomorrow. Tomorrow I'll give them a call.*

She drives past farms, fields, and houses covered with snow. Under it, she knows, lie sleeping things. Grass, earth, the worms in the earth. Hibernating animals like squirrels and groundhogs. And also her father. Her father is under the earth — inside it. And it seems to her now like he's not really dead. Just sleeping, hibernating like a bear till spring. Like her. In April she'll return to Israel, and then come back to life.

In the Dunhill parking lot she bumps into Cindy and together they walk to FRANK. They haven't spoken since last Monday, because Mikey has been sick. Cindy says he's better today, but still not entirely well; he's at home with a babysitter. Judith tells Cindy about her meeting with Suzy a week ago.

"Fuck her," says Cindy. *Fuck* seems to have become her favourite word. "I never saw what you saw in her, anyway, Judith. I always thought you overrated her."

Judith has thought all along that Cindy was jealous of her relationship with Suzy, and maybe she was. But perhaps it wasn't just jealousy. Perhaps Cindy could see Suzy's true colours all along, whereas she couldn't. Perhaps she has been not just over-rating Suzy, but underrating Cindy. Not giving her the credit she deserves.

They enter FRANK, Judith noticing with relief and gratifica-tion that the atrium is now just an atrium again, and no longer a photo exhibit. *Moshe*, she thinks, *would also be pleased about this.* Though she realizes now that lately, with everything she's had going on, she hasn't been fantasizing about him anymore.

Entering Corinne's class, Judith selects seats for her and Cindy where, as she looks straight ahead at Corinne, neither Kerry's nor Lola's gangs are in her line of vision, so she can pre-tend they're not even there. She has built for herself a little island of safety. Coincidentally, today's topic is "Women and Violence," and Corinne is lecturing about the vulnerability of women in a man's world, especially women of colour, who are doubly vulnerable, and how important it is for all women to find safe spaces for themselves. A student named Minnell says that as a black woman at this school she doesn't feel safe, and in many classes she feels marginalized and silenced. Judith thinks: *I, too, feel "unsafe, marginalized, and silenced" here, but you have to feel reasonably safe to say you feel unsafe, and I no longer do.* So she stays silent.

* * *

In her next class, Hetty begins by reviewing everything she has covered so far, and this is a big help to Judith. Then Hetty lectures on the relationship between qualitative and quantitative research. The example she offers comes from the study of rape. A quantitative researcher, she says, might investigate the characteristics of women who have been raped. For instance: Does rape in Canada happen more often to poor women than to rich ones? Women living in the country versus the city? Women of colour versus white women? And so on. On the other hand, a qualitative researcher might examine the emotional and psychological impact of being raped, and how this has affected the lives of these women and girls at the deepest levels.

"These are both important questions," says Hetty, "and contrary to what you may have been hearing from some professors, both research methodologies are completely valid. But they each have their proponents and opponents, because they come from different philosophical traditions. Putting it crudely, quantitative research deals with what might be termed 'objective reality,' and qualitative research with 'subjective reality.' But please don't approach this as if it's one versus the other. Both methodologies are valuable and they can complement each other very well. In fact, I often recommend that students use both in the same study. Are there any questions?"

There are. Mike, in his whiney yet belligerent voice, says he doesn't believe in quantitative research because, according to postmodernism, there is no such thing as 'objective reality.' Kiki pipes up in agreement. *Fuck*, thinks Judith. *Here we go again. There is no objective reality. This chair I am sitting on is not actually a chair. I can't stand this crazy world of theirs. If you don't believe the Holocaust happened, then it didn't — everything is just subjective perception.* The class discussion drags on, and to stay sane, she doodles a half-woman-half-chicken and a half-chicken-half-man. Finally Hetty, looking as irritated as Judith feels, terminates the conversation and gives the class an exercise to do. In pairs, they have to come up with a research question, define it as precisely as possible, decide which methodology they would use to explore it, and generate a list of the key questions they would ask the people in their study. Judith pairs up with Cindy — who shrugs apologetically to Darra, sitting on her other side — and they work on this exercise until the break. After the break each pair presents its work to the class, and Hetty draws on all these examples to teach them how crucial, and complex, it is to define one's research question well.

"My father always said that," Judith whispers to Cindy. "That the most important thing isn't finding the right answer; it's finding the right question."

Cindy nods vaguely, frowning and twisting her hair. She is worried about Mikey, Judith guesses, and five minutes later she is proven right. The second the bell rings, Cindy has already speed-dialled Mikey's babysitter to see how he is.

"One more thing," Hetty calls out above the chaos, and the din subsides. "Remember that next week there are no classes. But two weeks from today, please bring in the outline for your final research project. This should be on a topic of personal relevance."

Judith sighs. There is so much work due in the next couple of weeks. But at least, for some reason, they have next week off, which she hadn't realized till now. A topic of personal relevance. She begins playing with some possibilities: She could study "Women in Their Thirties Who Sacrifice Marriage with a Man They Love for a Higher Ideal." Or maybe "The Impact of a Recent Parental Death on Students Doing Graduate Studies Far from Home." She could even do "Cowardice, Hypocrisy, and Moral Bankruptcy in a Canadian School of Social Work." *Hmm. That could be fun.*

Cindy snaps her cellphone shut and says, "I'm going home. He's got a fever of 102.5." Judith wishes her luck, and she rushes off.

The room has almost totally emptied. Hetty is still at the front of the class, gathering her notes. Judith, passing her on the way out, says, "That was very interesting."

Hetty looks up from her papers. "Thanks. And how are you, Judith? Feeling well, I hope?"

"Yes, thanks. I'm fine."

"Great." Then, walking away, Judith hears "Judith," and turns around. Hetty glances all around her and says *sotto voce*, "The final decision hasn't been made yet, but ..."

Judith, following Hetty's cloak-and-dagger manner, also looks around, and sees the last of the students leaving the room. Hetty continues in the same low voice, "You've made the short-list for the B.P. Dunhill."

The B.P. Dunhill. She remembers now the essay competition she entered last term, at Hetty's invitation. Hetty submitted the paper she wrote for Weick. "Seriously?"

"Seriously," Hetty smiles. With something like a real smile for once, not her usual slightly pained grimace.

"Wow! Thank you for telling me, Hetty! And thanks for submitting my paper."

"My pleasure, Judith — it was first-rate work. Not only an incisive critique of Systems Theory, but a passionate attack on the lack of intellectual rigour and critical thinking that sometimes plagues our profession. You said everything there was to say about this in a mere ten pages, and eloquently, too. I'm looking forward to something of the same calibre for your final paper in my course."

Oy. Judith feels a thump of guilt. She hasn't even picked her topic yet. "I may do something quantitative," she says. "Unlike some people here, I think objective reality has an important place in research."

"Obviously I agree. Though perhaps this makes us both a little out of step these days, or anyway at this school. I believe I am seen here as quite old-fashioned."

"Not by me," says Judith. "I see you as a voice of sanity here. Don't pay attention to those people."

"Thank you, Judith."

"No, thank *you*. I don't think I ever thanked you properly for your support at SWAC."

"Ah," says Hetty. "SWAC. I hear you resigned from the committee."

News travels fast. Probably everybody knows. She feels slightly humiliated. She says, "Suzy suggested it."

Hetty's eyebrows rise. "Ah," she says again. "I see. I suppose I shouldn't be surprised." After a pause, she adds, "For what it's worth, Judith, I think you spoke very well at that meeting."

"Thanks, but it didn't have any effect," she says bitterly. "They're still bringing in Brier next week, and he's still going to spray his poison all over this campus."

Hetty sighs. "I know. They don't understand, Judith. I've been watching this develop here for quite some time now, and it's getting worse every year. Just between the two of us, I must say I'm not sorry about my upcoming retirement. I'm keeping a hand in, of course. I may teach a class or two each year as an emerita, but basically I'm gone from here, and not a minute too soon."

"What will you do now, Hetty?"

"I'll finally have time to write a book, and I'll work in my garden."

"Like Pangloss," says Judith, and they smile at each other. *Pang loss*, she thinks. *I feel a pang of loss that Hetty is leaving.*

"You know, Judith," Hetty says, "the main difference between people like us and people like them is that we know history, and they don't. They simply *don't know history.*" These last three words she says with intensity and emphasis, and in the silence that follows, Judith hears them echoing in her mind: *They don't know history.* She feels Hetty's steady gaze upon her. "You're right," she says.

Hetty continues gazing at her. "And if they don't know history ...?"

"They are doomed to repeat it," Judith finishes, feeling like an obedient student.

"Exactly. To my very great regret." There is a look on Hetty's face of enormous grief, of unspeakable tragedy, as if she once witnessed the whole world being destroyed, and is now watching it happen again. "Be careful, Judith," she says urgently. "Be very, very careful."

Judith looks back at her. Hetty's eyes are burning into hers as if, in this wordless way, she can somehow pour her meaning into her. Like pouring molten lava from an ancient, corroded black cauldron into a smaller, newer, shinier container. *But what exactly is she trying to tell me?* she asks herself. *What does she mean, "Be very, very careful"? Careful of what?* She's already been outvoted, kicked off SWAC, marginalized, and deprived of her RA'ship. What else could happen to her? And the way Hetty is staring at her is starting to give her the creeps. *She looks like the Oracle at Delphi or one of the prophets in the Bible, burning with divine passion and secret knowledge. But that's nonsense,* she thinks. *The days of prophecy are over.* She wonders if maybe Hetty is slightly mad.

"Thanks," she says to her. "But I'd better be going."

"Yes, of course," says Hetty, and follows her with her eyes as she leaves.

* * *

Entering her last class of the day, Judith quietly places her two assignments on Suzy's desk and sits down. Suzy begins her class with announcements. First, the Students' Union's fundraiser film night is this Friday at 7:30, and they'll be showing *Serpico*. This movie frightened Judith when she saw it and depressed her for days afterward, with its inescapable message that Evil Triumphs Over Good. Then Suzy reminds everyone that next Monday, February 17, is Anti-oppression Day. An event of such importance, she says, that all classes that day will be cancelled so everyone can attend. *That's why there are no classes.* Judith controls her face as Suzy plugs Anti-oppression Day, running through the whole schedule of events, including who all the speakers will be, and even tells them about the lunch options and free parking vouchers. Meanwhile Judith gets the distinct impression that Suzy is avoiding eye contact with her. *She's ashamed,* she thinks. *She knows as well as I do it's all a big sham. Just an excuse to dump on Israel. That's why she can't even look me in the face. Never mind. This ignoring me will stop as soon as she's finished with Anti-oppression Day.*

But it doesn't. Suzy starts her lecture, which is on nonverbal communication, yet still she won't look at her. *It's astounding,* Judith thinks, *and ironic: Here she is going on and on about the importance of nonverbal communication, and she can't manage a little eye contact. Though who knows if she even knows what she's doing. Probably not. Even if her favourite mantra is "Know thyself."*

The class continues, and Judith starts to have an eerie, invisible feeling. She has felt this way only once before: in her father's *shul* when she was a teenager. Back then it wasn't egalitarian as it is now; it was a *shul* full of old men where women were not counted in the *minyan*, and she was there that day just to keep her father company on Bubba's *yartzeit*. She recalls, even though this happened twenty years ago, how the rabbi, shortly before the service began, counted the men to make sure there were at least ten present. Counting, he pointed at her father, then skipped her, ignoring her as if she wasn't there, and pointed at the man sitting past her at the end of the row. She felt completely invisible. But still, that was different from what is happening here. That was terrible, hurtful, and sexist, but ultimately impersonal. She didn't count because she had a vagina instead of a penis. In contrast, what Suzy is doing is as personal as it gets. Highlighting this is the fact that Suzy, except for ignoring Judith, is exactly the same as usual. She doesn't appear distracted or troubled. She is the same warm, friendly teacher as always, quick to laugh at students' jokes and interested in their responses and ideas. Today she wears a mauve silk blouse, dangly earrings, and navy blue slacks, looking pretty and feminine. Everything about her is perfectly normal, except that when she does her scan of the room every minute or two — a scan that sweeps everyone in, in a big warm embrace — Judith, and only Judith, is excluded. In the sunlit circle of Suzy's class, she alone sits outside it in a cold pool of shadow.

This goes on for a half-hour. Forty-five minutes. She tries not to care. She tells herself it's no big deal. But she can't help it: the effect of this increases in intensity with time, like the gradual cumulativeness of Chinese water torture. She starts feeling like she does not actually exist. She even feels a bit panicky: If Suzy doesn't look at her soon, she will disappear. It's as if she is looking into a mirror and seeing nothing there. Dazed, longing, she gazes at Suzy: *You can't do that to someone. You can't cut someone off like this. Someone with whom you've had a bond.* She looks away from Suzy — she can't stand seeing that face anymore — picks up her pencil and fiercely begins to draw. She draws a bull devouring a deer it has just killed. The face of the bull is invisible, buried inside the deer's entrails. Like the face of a man buried inside a woman's pubic hair, as absorbed as a mute animal in inhaling the intimate powerful scent, and hungrily nuzzling, sucking, licking, tasting, and eating her. *The Lord giveth*, thinks Judith, *and the Lord taketh away.* Taketh away her mother and father, and grandparents, and aunt and uncle, and her relationship with Suzy. Soon Bobby will be taken away, too. What's the point, then? What's the point if everyone gets taken away?

Now she draws the bull again, this time after it's finished eating, its head lifted from inside the deer's entrails. Its face is covered in dripping blood. Blood that's the bright red of the freshly killed — so freshly killed it's almost still living. She hears noise: people around her are standing. "Ten-minute break," someone says, but Judith only half-understands. She is still submerged in her drawing — gaping, mesmerized, at the blood around the bull's mouth. Knowing that when it bares its lips, there will also be blood all over its teeth, staining them a dull red. She stands, still disoriented, in the almost-deserted classroom; then, with her purse and schoolbag, she leaves. She doesn't "flounce" out. She walks at a normal pace, and no one notices her stunned, absent expression — she is still seeing the bull's mouth dripping blood — or that she is walking mechanically, like a robot, with her coat wide open, out into the winter cold. Sitting in her father's freezing car, shivering, she doesn't understand how she got there, or what she should do now. For a while she just stares blankly. Then she drives back to Toronto in the falling snow.

A t home, she slips off her coat and riffles through the mail. It's almost all junk, but three-quarters of the way through there's an orange card saying *Second Reminder*, telling her she now has only forty-eight hours left to pay her heating bill. I'll call them tomorrow, she decides, throwing the card, with the other mail, onto the little table near the front door, and sits in the living room. She remembers how this room, in the final stages of her father's illness — when he was already too weak to climb stairs — became his bedroom. Then it turned into the room he died in. It became a dying-room, not a living room. But whatever room it is now, she sits awhile on its couch. She calls Bobby to tell him about today, but he can't talk. He's going into a meeting. They arrange that tonight she'll go to his place around nine and sleep over. He has a late start tomorrow, so they will be able to have breakfast together. After hanging up, she doesn't know what to do with herself. She doesn't want to study or fret anymore about Suzy. She turns on the TV and then turns it off. On her computer she googles Toronto Oil and Gas. The website reads:

> During the winter months, between November and March inclusive, failure to pay one's gas bill in a timely fashion will not result in the discontinuation of one's heating. However, it will result in the immediate withdrawal of all other services, including furnace repairs, until such time as the bill is paid.

She laughs with relief. Everything will be okay. She'll have heating throughout the winter, until it is no longer cold. As for the withdrawal of services such as repairs, this does not worry her. Her father's furnace has never, to her knowledge, broken down, so why would it do so now? She'll be fine until the end of March, and then, before leaving for Israel on April 7, she will work something out with the company.

She checks her email and browses *Ha'aretz*. Everything is all right in Israel today. And one delightful thing about Israel her friends and *Ha'aretz* remind her of: Although here in Canada everything is in the deep freeze of winter, in Israel everything is green and blooming. Tu B'shvat was almost a month ago, and as the Tu B'shvat holiday song goes, "The almond tree is in blossom." She pictures Israel now: the sap flowing in the tree trunks, the pink buds sprouting, the air softening, and the earth warm. And she feels warmed and comforted.

Bobby's meeting goes very late, so they meet at his house just in time for bed. Judith hardly sleeps all night. She wakes up frequently, upset about Suzy. How could she have done this to her? She flipped sides, like a spatula flipping an omelette — first it's on one side, then the other. How could she have betrayed her like this? At 5:45 she gives up trying to fall back asleep, and turning toward Bobby, observes his face. In sleep, it is uncharacteristically calm and at rest. Then he begins to awaken and it returns to its usual expression: vigilant, tense. He sees her, reaches out for her, they make love, and then they go downstairs. They sit at the kitchen table, he in his old blue bathrobe, and she in one of his T-shirts reaching down to her knees. Soon there are the smells of brewing coffee and toasting raisin bagels — pungent bitter mixed with sweet — and for several minutes they sit leafing through the morning papers, waiting for the coffee and toasted bagels. Then she says, "She hates me."

Bobby looks up. "Who?" She looks at him. "Come on. Suzy doesn't hate you."

"That's what it felt like when she wouldn't look at me."

"Look," he says, pushing away his paper, "you just got caught in some political crossfire, that's all this is. The good news is, eight more weeks of school and you'll never have to see her again. Only eight more weeks ..." His voice trails off.

Uh-oh. She does not want this conversation to go where it looks like it's heading.

He gazes at her with a steady, level look. "So what exactly do you see happening eight weeks from now?" he asks. "We've been avoiding talking about this, but sooner or later we're going to have to."

She looks down at the newspaper: there's a photo of a smiling woman with an arm around her dog. Judith frowns at Bobby. "I don't see why we have to," she says. "I mean, why ruin a perfectly nice breakfast, and maybe even the whole day, by discussing this? There's nothing to say we both don't already know, and I don't feel like spending our remaining two months together constantly processing this. Let's just leave it alone."

"Leave it alone?" he asks, leaning forward in his chair. "What do you mean, 'leave it alone'? You're telling me that eight weeks from now you're leaving me to return to Israel — and I'm supposed to pretend this isn't happening?"

She is silent.

Bobby continues: "Maybe I've been living in a fool's paradise. But I guess I've been hoping if we were happy together, maybe you'd change your mind about Israel and stay here with me. I don't know — it seemed to me we were doing pretty well. Like any couple we have our issues, but we're pretty happy." He looks at her questioningly. She nods. "But now you're telling me there's no chance. That I've just been deluding myself."

335

For a moment she doesn't answer. Then she says, "I've had a rough day, Bobby. I don't have it in me to get into this right now."

"Then when *do* you want to get into it?" he asks. "An hour before you get on the plane?"

"Stop it," she says weakly. He is the prosecuting lawyer again, trying to beat her down.

"I thought I could persuade you," he says more softly. "I thought if you were happy …"

Something plucks at her gut, like the pluck of a gut guitar string. A twang of guilt goes off inside her. "It's not anything you've done," she says pleadingly. "I just can't live here. It's nothing personal."

"What do you mean it's nothing personal? What could be more personal than ending our relationship?"

"I told you all along. I never lied to you. I can't live in Canada. I don't belong here."

"What does that mean, you don't belong here? You were born and raised here."

"I can't help where I was born and raised," she says. "But this will never be my home. My home is in Israel."

"Bullshit. You're not really at home there. You're an outsider linguistically and culturally. You'll always speak Hebrew with an accent. You'll never be a real Israeli."

This hurts. She says, "It doesn't matter about my accent. Israel is a country of immigrants."

But he has seen the flash of vulnerability in her eyes, the momentary flinch. Encouraged, he persists: "What's so great about Israel, anyway? Its economy is in the toilet. The crime rate is skyrocketing. The peace process is dead. Bombs are going off every Monday and Thursday —"

"So what?" she says. "Sure, Israel has its problems, but what country doesn't? I love Israel. It's my home. And whether or not I have an accent in Hebrew, that's where I plan to spend my life."

She stops. She sees that nothing she is saying is getting through to him. She is not making the slightest dent. "But how could I expect you to understand?" she adds. "You've spent your whole life in Toronto, and you think this is the centre of the world."

"No, I don't. But you're right that I don't understand when you keep saying" — here he raises his voice into a high-pitched children's taunt — "'it's my home, it's my home.'" She flushes. "I have no idea what you're talking about. You keep saying this like it's some sort of magic mantra. But when I ask you to explain it, you can't."

"Yes, I can."

"You never have yet. You just keep repeating it over and over. Like E.T. in that movie: 'E. — T. — Phone — Home.' Ju — dith — Go — Home ..."

She restrains her anger. "You're not getting it, so I'll try one more time." She looks at him hopefully: Maybe this time he will listen and understand where she's coming from. But no — his face is brick-red with anger. He's in mid-battle: a battle to keep her here in Toronto and keep her love, a battle against his rival, Israel. The last thing he's interested in now is hearing her sing Israel's praises.

With a sense of futility, she says, "I'm not saying Israel is perfect. But at least in Israel we control our own destiny. We shape our own history. Whereas here in Canada" — she looks searchingly into his eyes — "we're living in exile. A relatively comfortable exile — we're not slaves like we were in Egypt. But still we're in exile. Someone else is letting us live in their country, and 'letting' is the operative word here. It's their home, not ours. We're always just guests. Even if they are nice to us, even if they let us stay for a long time and make us feel accepted, ultimately it's not our home. The only real home for a Jew is in Israel."

"Oh, yeah? Well, *this* Jew's home" — he points to his chest — "is right here in Canada. This is where I was born and raised. This is where I belong."

"I know," she says, kindly, even sadly. "But that's exactly the problem. That's what's so sick about *galut.* After even one or two generations of living somewhere, Jews start believing that's their home. When it's not. It's just where they happen to be. It's where their parents or grandparents ended up, fleeing from somewhere worse."

"It's true my grandparents came here from Russia. But now this is my home."

"You think it's your home," she says, "but it isn't. Most Jews today, because we've been in exile for two thousand years, can't even imagine what a real home feels like. So they believe that Canada, for instance, is home. But it's not."

While she's been speaking, he has gotten up and brought the bagels and coffee to the table. Now he angrily spreads strawberry cream cheese on half a bagel. Spreading it roughly, as if he hates this bagel and wants to hurt it. He says without looking up at her, "So only in Israel can a Jew live a good or happy life. And if someone like me happens to be happy somewhere else, obviously I'm delusional, or ignorant of my people's history, or both."

Her mouth twists with impatience. "I'm not saying that. You asked me to explain what I meant by home, and I did. But if now you're raising the question of happiness, that's something else altogether. You, Bobby, can be happy wherever you want. But for me to be happy, I need to live in Israel."

He looks up at her. "I don't believe that for a moment. I believe people can be happy anywhere if they put their mind to it."

"Now you sound like my mother."

"Maybe your mother was right."

"She wasn't. She never understood about me and Israel."

"That makes two of us."

She peers at him. That's a low blow, for him to side with her mother against her.

"I mean it," he says. "I agree Israel is a special and important place. I think it's fabulous the Jewish people finally has a state of its own, and we should support it financially as best we can. But living there — why would I want to do that? Why live someplace where I could get blown up any day walking down the street? Call me selfish, call me a man with no ideals. But I'd rather not get blown up if I can avoid it. And fortunately, I can."

"I see. So your life is worth more than the life of an Israeli. It's okay for an Israeli man your age, your profession, to die defending the Jewish state, as long as you can live your life in safety and comfort."

"I'm not saying my life is worth more than his. But it's my life, and I can do with it what I want."

She stares down at the empty plate he set before her several minutes ago. Then she says, "It's true, obviously, that it's safer here than in Israel. No one can deny that. But Canada is *galut*. And it is sterile, materialistic, and capitalist."

Bobby sniggers. "'Capitalist'! Like Israel isn't?"

"Israel at least was founded on socialist principles."

He laughs. "I hate to be the one to break it to you, Judith, but whatever principles Israel was founded on, it's not a socialist country anymore."

"What do you know about Israel?"

"I know what I read in the papers and in the articles I get from the Toronto Jewish Community Board, and socialism is basically dead now in Israel. Even the kibbutzim, the symbols of socialism, are no longer dreaming the socialist dream. Even they have turned capitalist. You have this romantic vision of the sun rising and setting over artichoke fields, but there are almost no kibbutzim left that haven't moved from agriculture into industry. The Israel you're so in love with doesn't exist anymore."

She is angry. "You don't know what you're talking about. So what if the kibbutzim are privatizing? It doesn't mean the dream they represented is dead."

"Yes, it does. That's exactly what it means. The reason the kibbutzim joined the real world — in other words, capitalism — is because socialism doesn't work."

"It may not have worked well economically," she says, "but it worked in other ways."

"Like what?"

"Socially. Israeli socialists built communities. They designed a new world. A different social reality. But you wouldn't understand. Forget it. There's no point discussing this anymore." She rises.

"Fine," he says. "Walk out of the room if you want. But that doesn't make what I'm saying any less true. The Israel you love, Judith, exists only in the minds of a few idealists like you who still live in the past. Israel now is just a country like any other, except more fucked-up because it's constantly at war. And there is only so long a small country surrounded by millions of enemies can hold out. Face it: the great Zionist experiment has failed."

She stands in the doorway, trembling, poised for flight. He is attacking not just her — that alone maybe she could take — but everything she loves and believes in. He is attacking the promise she made to herself that day in the desert: the glowing throbbing orange of a vow buried in the centre of her heart, which is what keeps her alive.

"It hasn't failed," she says. "Yes, we're going through a difficult period now. We've been through difficult times before, though, and we'll come through this like we always have. But Jews like you don't make it any easier."

"Jews like me?"

"Yes. Jews with resources, education, and skills who could help build the land, but stay here in *galut*, because of the safety and comfort."

"Is that what you think?" He looks astonished. "That I don't want to live in Israel because of — what do they call it in the Bible? — 'the fleshpots'?"

She gazes at him steadily.

"What, anyway," he asks, "is a fleshpot?" The word *fleshpot* he pronounces heavily, comically, with a Russian accent.

She smiles slightly. "A pot of meat. But I'm not saying I think you're particularly materialistic, any more than anyone else. Just that life here is much easier for you than in Israel, and that's why you won't come."

"Of course it is," he says. "I won't pretend otherwise. Firstly, I don't speak the language, so over there I'd be completely lost. Also, at the material level, the fleshpot level, if you will, I won't pretend that I like poverty or deprivation. I don't. I don't see why I should leave one of the best, one of the most affluent and safest, countries in the world to go live in what is, in many senses, almost a Third World country. I also don't think that because I feel this way I'm a shallow or bad person." She still stands in the doorway, listening to him. "Sit down," he says. There is no anger in his face. Just weariness. Some sadness, too. Looking at him, she also feels sad. And scared.

"Please," he says.

She hesitates. Then she sits down.

"Look, Judith," he says, leaning toward her. "You keep saying I don't understand you, but you don't understand me, either. You act like I don't want to come with you to Israel because I don't

341

care about you enough. But that's not true. I've never loved anyone more than you. You know that."

She feels tears welling up. And again, fear.

"It isn't that I won't go to Israel, Judith. I *can't*."

"Why not? Why can't you?" she asks, bordering on a wail.
"You haven't even tried. You've never even thought about it."

"Of course I have. Other than my work, I've thought about
little else for the past seventeen months because I know how
badly you want this. But I can't do it. I don't know the language or
the culture. It's not Jewish culture over there; it's Israeli. It's something completely different from what I know. I was there once,
I told you about this, and I didn't like the food, and I couldn't
stand how people talked to each other, they shouted all the time.
To me it was an interesting country, but ultimately a foreign one.
You might as well be asking me to move to Swahililand. Not to
mention that for my first two years there at least, I wouldn't be
able to work."

"What do you mean?"

He sighs, pouring himself more coffee. "I've told you this
before, but each time you don't take me seriously. Law in Canada
is totally different from law in Israel. There it's some mixture of
British, Jewish, and Turkish law. I'd have to spend a year or two
learning Israeli law, then write Israeli bar exams, and article in
an Israeli firm. In other words, start my career all over again
from scratch." He searches her eyes. "I can't do it, Judith. I'm
thirty-three years old, I'm a junior partner in one of the best law
firms in Toronto, and I can't throw it all away to try and scrape
something together in a foreign language and foreign culture,
competing — at a huge disadvantage — with Israeli lawyers."

Her eyes are cloudy and her lips pout. "You could do it,
though. If you wanted to."

"Judith," he says, "you're not listening to me. Everyone has a line they can't cross, and this is mine. You're asking me to do something I just can't do."

She studies him: he looks totally honest and sincere. But she doesn't believe him. *If you will it …* If he loved her enough, he'd find a way to come to Israel.

"Okay," she says. "Fine."

He looks at her hopefully. "What do you mean, 'fine'? Do you mean you'll stay?"

She frowns. "No — I just meant fine. I hear you. I hear your decision." Tears fill her eyes.

"You act like I am breaking up with you," he says. "But I'm not. You're the one who's breaking up with me. You're the one who is leaving. For the second time."

She wipes her eyes and cheeks with a napkin and blows her nose. He leans forward and looks into her eyes. "What I want is to marry you," he says. "I want to spend my life with you. Have children with you."

His eyes are deep and green like an ocean, and she feels herself getting sucked down into their depths. With an effort of will she pulls herself up and out of them, like saving herself from drowning.

"I can't," she says. Looking at him, she is filled with pain.

"If it was some other guy, maybe I could compete with him," he says. "But I can't compete with a country. With a dream."

She sits there miserably. She imagines getting up and leaving, but she feels paralyzed.

He says, "This isn't only about Israel, is it?"

She looks at him uncomprehending. There is a peculiar, lit-up expression on his face, like a new idea just struck him.

"Maybe," he says, "it's true in a way this isn't personal. Your father warned me, you know. He told me last year that you could never make a commitment. That you were too afraid."

"What? He never said that!"

"Yes, he did," Bobby says, smiling smugly. "He and I had lots of time to talk last year."

"I don't believe you. But anyway, leave my father out of it. He has nothing to do with this."

"Fine. But it's true."

"It's not true. I've made lots of commitments in my life."

"Name one. One time you've ever committed yourself to anything. What job have you ever had for longer than a year before you flitted to something else?"

"'Flitted'? I don't 'flit'! I've had lots of different jobs because I'm interested in lots of different things. I'm not, like some people I know, a one-note song. I'm not someone who just went from high school to college, and then to a job that forty years later they'll probably die in."

"I'll duck that one," he says. "But name one thing. One thing you've ever stuck with."

She feels like she is on the witness stand again. "I stuck with Israel. That's one commitment I made and kept."

"Yes, but Israel is just an abstraction. An idea. An ideal."

"No, it's not. It's real. It's earth you can touch with your hands. It's as real as anything else in this world. As real as you."

"Apparently realer."

She purses her lips, but doesn't answer. He studies her awhile.

"You're like The Little Prince," he says. "Or should I say Princess. You act as if you're still twenty-three. Like time stopped when your mother died. It's like you just froze."

"That's ridiculous."

"No, it's not. I was there, remember? I know what you went through then. The guilt you felt at not coming back earlier."

She remembers.

"You're not twenty-three anymore," he says. "Sooner or later you'll have to grow up."

"Shut up. Stop lecturing me. You sound like my father."

"He and I are the two people who know you best."

"Yes, Father Knows Best," she says. "Maybe you don't know me, Bobby, as well as you think. I'm not like you, a finished pot by the age of thirty-three. I'm a work in progress. I'm still changing and becoming. I can still be all sorts of things."

"It's a bit late to become a brain surgeon, and lots of other things, too. Sometime soon you're going to have to make some hard choices, Judith. Time doesn't stand still. I love you, you know that, but even I won't wait around forever."

"I'm not asking you to."

He is silent for a moment and his mouth hardens into a straight line. "You know," he says, "your father totally nailed it."

"I said —"

"Okay, okay, I'll leave him out of this. But he was right. You're able to commit yourself to an ideal or to something abstract, but not to anything real, like another person. Or anyway, not a living person. You probably love Herzl, Rabin, and the poet Rachel better than you love anyone in the real world. Including me."

"Don't be stupid."

"No, I mean it." He looks excited, almost happy, as he always does when he gets a new idea. "You can commit yourself to a sunrise over an artichoke field. Or to a perfect political system. But to a real person, like a man? That's something different."

"That's absurd. I've been in lots of relationships with men."

"Then why have you never settled down with anybody? You're thirty-three years old. You're good-looking. Smart —"

"The same could be asked about you. Why aren't *you* married, Bobby?"

"It's different for a guy."

345

She laughs. "You're joking."

"I'm not. A guy doesn't need to be taken care of the way a woman does."

She gapes at him. "You believe that?"

"Of course I do. So did your father. In fact, he was very worried about you, and he asked me to take care of you after he died."

"Yeah, right."

"It's true. He did."

She imagines Bobby seated on the chair by her father's bed, while her father, in the old-fashioned style, talked to him man-to-man. Passing on to Bobby his only child, his daughter, his treasure (and burden) for safekeeping. Like King Lear, divesting himself of his property.

Bobby says, "He told me he hoped we'd get married, and was sorry he wouldn't live to see it. He thought I'd be good for you."

This is more than she can take. "Did he, now?" she says angrily, rising. "Well, lucky for me we're no longer in a time where fathers pick their daughters' husbands for them. Anyway, Bobby, I don't need to be taken care of. Not by you or any other man. I'm an adult, not a child, and I can take care of myself. I'm going."

"*Touché*. Whenever things get hot, whenever something gets too close to the bone, you run away. That's why you moved to Israel in the first place. You ran away."

"I did not. I didn't run away to Israel. I moved there because I wanted to, and that's why I'm returning there now. I know you're not happy about it, Bobby, but I never deceived you. I never said I'd stay here after finishing my program. Besides, I'm fed up with your criticizing me and your cross-examinations. I'm leaving."

"Fine. Do that. Go ahead — what difference does it make? You're leaving in eight weeks, anyway. You might as well leave now."

"Fine. I will."

"Fine."

She stands there glaring at him, trembling with fury. Then she runs upstairs to his bedroom, her footsteps pounding up the stairs, and presently they pound their way back down. She stands again in the kitchen doorway, now dressed in her own clothes and also wearing her coat, hat, and boots. He doesn't look at her, though. He sits at the kitchen table, staring straight ahead with a defeated expression. Now, seeing him like this, so frail and wounded, she isn't angry anymore. More than anything, she is frightened, sad, and perplexed. Just an hour ago they were in bed together, happy, making love. It is not possible that such a short time later they are ending their relationship. *This can't be happening*, she thinks. *This is me and Bobby. This is just a mistake.*

But Bobby is still staring straight ahead, refusing to look at her. She, reluctant to go, keeps standing in the doorway. She smells the warm toasted bagels. Suddenly she is very hungry. Yesterday she was too upset to eat supper, and this morning, while they argued, she ate nothing at all. The bagels smell so sweet and fragrant, her mouth waters. Outside the kitchen window, the winter wind is viciously whipping an old maple tree, and she hears the wind howl. How nice it would be if, instead of going out there, she could stay in here where it's warm and cozy and have a bagel and a cup of coffee. *I could do this*, she thinks. *I could go over to the table, sit next to Bobby, stay here with him, and have one of those wonderful bagels with sweet melted butter drizzling into its holes.*

He turns toward the door and looks at her. "If you're going," he says, "go. Don't just stand there in the doorway."

"I'm going," she says. She gazes at him wistfully. But receiving from him only a cold hard stare, she leaves.

LOVE AND HATE

The next morning, on Wednesday, Judith lies in bed. When she walked out of Bobby's house yesterday, she felt strong. She knew who she was. Someone who, as the psalm says, loves Israel "above all other joys." But now every straight line in her is turning into a question mark. Sure, when she goes back to Israel she'll have her friends again. She will have Israel itself, too. But she won't have Bobby. The man who — despite how he drives her crazy — she loves. When she returns to Israel, she'll have no one to make love to. No one to hold her when she needs to be held. No one to argue with, to sharpen herself against like a knife against flint, her flint against his making fire.

On top of this, she will be a third wheel again. She recalls how Bruria and Pinchas, or Miri and Yechiel, with a protective arm around her, would introduce her to some other new couple as "our dear friend, Judith." She doesn't want to be any couple's dear single friend ever again. She wants to be loved by someone who loves her more than anyone else in the world. Someone like Bobby. She reaches for the phone. He will already be at his desk at work. Probably alone in his part of the office, since it's only 8:05 a.m. She begins dialling his number, but then stops. They have agreed to try and not talk to each other too often for the next little while. *Anyway, even if we hadn't,* she thinks, *what would be the point in calling? We told each other the truth yesterday morning, and several more times throughout the day. There is nothing new to say at this point. There is nothing to say at all.* She bursts into tears.

Later she gets up and does some schoolwork. It's hard to concentrate at first, but that passes and she accomplishes a lot. It feels good to be distracted. Her father used to say, "Work is the great cure-all," and maybe he was right. In any case, today turns out to be much better than yesterday, which was a write-off. She even gets a load of laundry done, tidies the house, and eats two half-decent meals, finishing all the food in the house. She must go food shopping tomorrow.

Leaving the kitchen, she hears a very loud clunk, as if some metal machinery fell. She listens attentively for a moment, hears only silence, and, deciding that sound was nothing, wanders into the living room. There she notices, lying alone on the floor of the vestibule, a letter with Dunhill's blue and burgundy logo on the front. Clumsy in her anxiety, she rips it open. Inside is a letter from the Dean of the Faculty of Social Sciences, congratulating her on winning the B.P. Dunhill Award. This award, the letter says, will be presented at a ceremony in the spring presided over by the Dean, and Judith will also receive a fifty-dollar cash prize. She stands in the vestibule, gawking at this letter in her hand, and despite herself, grinning broadly. She won! Never mind SWAC. Never mind Suzy. There is still some fairness and goodness in the world, even at Dunhill.

The phone rings. It's Cindy, and she's delighted when Judith tells her the good news. Judith asks how Mikey is and Cindy says fine. Now Judith tells Cindy that she's considering switching out of Suzy's class, and Cindy cautions her that she'll need to replace it with another required course, and that it's already very late for course switching. Judith says she'll ask Phoebe.

Then Cindy brings up Anti-oppression Day and Judith's stomach jumps. She hasn't been consciously thinking about Anti-oppression Day, but still it has been with her every moment, somewhere inside her body, ever since that SWAC meeting. Now even just hearing the name, and knowing it is only five days away, is enough to fill her with dread. Cindy says everyone she has talked to is planning to attend at least the morning session,

since all the profs except Hetty expect this and have been pushing it hard. Cindy isn't sure yet if she'll go. Maybe she'll pop in
for a little of it, just to see.

Judith is silent.

Cindy says, "I'm not saying I approve of him or his message,
Judith. I just want to see for myself."

Still she does not say anything.

"Ju*dith.*"

"I'm not going," she says.

"I know. But that's why I'm calling ..."

Don't try to persuade me — don't you even try. But now Cindy
explains that the group presentation schedule for Hetty's class
was just posted, and she, Judith, and Darra will be presenting a
week from Monday, at the first class after Anti-oppression Day.

"Which means," says Cindy, "that we have to meet this coming Monday to plan it. It's the only day Darra has off work. Plus
she's going to Anti-oppression Day, so we need to meet from
noon to 1:00, over the lunch hour, and it would be best if we
could meet on campus."

"I'm not coming to Dunhill on Anti-oppression Day!"

"I know, I understand," Cindy says placatingly. "So here's
what I suggest. Dunhill's a big campus, Judith. We don't have to
meet anywhere near where Brier's speaking. We could meet in
a different building altogether, far from all the Anti-oppression
Day activities. Darra's willing to meet us anywhere on campus
you choose."

Judith is silent, but there is no objection she can think of that
doesn't sound churlish even to her own ears. "Okay," she finally
says. "Where should we meet?"

They agree on Le Petit Café. Brier will be lecturing in the
auditorium on the first floor of FRANK, just one floor above the
main cafeteria, so most likely he and his entourage — in fact,

probably everyone attending Anti-oppression Day — will converge on that cafeteria for lunch.

"They won't go to Le Petit Café," says Cindy. "It's a bit of a hike from the auditorium, and people will be in a rush."

"Okay," Judith says again. She's full of misgivings, but they are as nebulous as fog. She says goodbye and hangs up.

She returns to work on her paper for Hetty, but frequently glances at her watch. It is seven o'clock, then 7:30, then eight o'clock, and still not a word from Bobby. They agreed he would phone her sometime today in between his clients. But so far not a peep. She thinks of calling him but doesn't dare. Because yesterday he said, "We can't keep doing this, Judith. If we're breaking up, we have to start acting like we are: we have to put some space between us. We can't talk on the phone five times a day. Even if we feel like it."

"Of course," she said. "You're right." But now it has been more than twenty-four hours since she heard his voice, and she wants to talk to him. She wants to tell him about winning the B.P. Dunhill Award and about having to go into Dunhill on Anti-oppression Day. Yet she knows she shouldn't call. So she tries to keep working, meanwhile missing him. Even missing some of the things about him she never could stand, like his paternalism. *No*, she thinks, *that's wrong. It's not his paternalism I miss — his patronizing attempts to control me — it's his paternalness. His pater-ness. It's the best part of fatherliness I am missing: his caring and protectiveness.* She puts down her work and lies on the couch, aching for him. She hopes right now he is aching for her, too. Though probably not. She knows him better than that. When he works, he works, and he doesn't let anything get in his way. His office building could burn down around him and he wouldn't even notice. He is probably immersed in his work now and not thinking of her at all.

She lies there waiting for the phone to ring. This is all much harder than she expected. She wishes she had more of a life here — that would make this breakup so much easier. She has no one here now except Cindy. She no longer has Pam, Aliza, or Suzy. It wasn't supposed to be this way. At dinner with Suzy back in the fall, after confiding in her about her troubles with Bobby, Suzy leaned forward and put a hand on her arm.

"Just remember, Judith," she said, looking at her affectionately, "whatever happens between you and Bobby, you still have me and all your friends here at this school. You are not alone here in Canada. You have friends who care about you."

Liar. You're a liar and a phony. You're not here for me right now. You couldn't care less what happens to me.

The phone rings, startling her. It's Bobby, explaining he has had a terribly busy day so he couldn't call. Even now he can't talk for very long because he has an important meeting starting in just a few minutes.

A meeting? That's weird. He often works late in the evenings, especially since they returned from Vancouver, but always alone. What sort of meeting could he be having at 8:30 at night? She imagines him with a tall, statuesque blonde on his arm, bar-hopping, out on the town, laughing together. She doesn't exactly believe this image, but she sees it so clearly it feels real.

"Who is your meeting with?" she asks.

"What do you mean?"

"Is it a woman?"

"Yes, as it happens." There is a pause. "Come on, Judith. You don't mean —"

"I'm just asking. Anything is possible."

"This isn't. I'm meeting with Bernice McIvor. You met her at the office party last spring. Do you remember her?"

"No."

"We're working on that big case together. We're going to court first thing tomorrow morning and there are still some details to work out."

"How old is she?"

"What?"

"How old is she?"

"I don't know. Fifty, maybe."

"What does she look like? Some women are still very attractive at that age."

"Short grey hair and about 250 pounds."

"Seriously?"

"Yes."

She feels her breath release. "Okay, then."

"I suppose I should be flattered you're jealous," he says. "But you have no cause to be. You don't remember her from that party?"

"No. There were 160 people there."

"She's on Dennis's team. She's senior counsel on this case."

"Okay."

"Is it?"

"Yes. I just thought ..."

"Don't worry. I'm nowhere near anything like that yet. It's going to take me a very long time ..."

She wants to weep with relief. But she also wants to weep because she knows that even though she still loves him, and he still loves her, sooner or later they aren't going to love each other anymore. They will love each other, of course, in that vestigial place somewhere in the bone where until you die you love anyone you have ever loved. But in the normal sense of loving, they won't love each other anymore. She knows, too, that this could happen even in a surprisingly short amount of time. She sees with cold clarity how at some point in the future they will both find other people to love and probably marry. And that will be that. And this moment will one day be nothing but a memory. One small part of a huge pile of memories, like a huge pile of shoes.

"Are you there?" he asks.

"Yes," she says. Then she asks him how his big case is going. Not bad, he says, and they talk a bit about his work, and now it feels perfectly normal to be having this conversation. Then she tells him about winning the B.P. Dunhill Award, and he is so happy for her, and so proud, that it's almost like things between them are the same as always. Yet simultaneously she feels how things are not the same at all. There is a strangeness between them now: there are silences, and a certain forced quality in the conversation. After one such silence, Bobby asks, "What do you want to do about Friday night?"

She does not understand the question. It is her turn this week to cook the Shabbat meal, and they both know this. "What do you mean?"

"Well," he says carefully, "should we eat together as usual?"

She feels a blow to her stomach like that time in grade five when, playing dodgeball, a ball went right into her stomach. She didn't see it coming. This from Bobby she didn't see coming, either. But now that it's here, she recognizes this as one of those questions whose answer is contained within it. Like that riddle, also from grade five: *What colour was George Washington's white horse?*

She replies cautiously. "What do *you* think?"

A lawyer who never enters court unprepared, he answers without a moment's hesitation. "Maybe we should take a week off and see how we feel."

See how we feel? What do you mean, see how we feel?

"If you really want to," he says, "we can still —"

"No," she says. "It's okay." Then, "I just thought —"

"What?"

"I don't know. We're not completely broken up yet, are we? I mean, we're in a process, but we don't have to stop everything cold turkey, do we?"

"No," he says. "But if that's where we're heading, then maybe the best thing is to just tear the band-aid off all at once. Rather than inch by inch."

She is silent.

"I thought," he says, "of going to my brother's tomorrow night. They're always inviting me, and I never go."

Because of me, she thinks guiltily. *You never go because you know I can't stand them. It's my fault. I've come between you and your brother.*

"What about you?" he asks.

Again she doesn't understand the question.

"Where will you go?" he asks.

Oh. Now she understands. Where will she go for Friday night dinner? She has no idea. She can't picture a single place in Toronto. "I'll manage," she says.

"Are you sure?"

"Yeah."

There's a pause.

"I'll call you tomorrow," he says. "I have to go. Bernice is waiting — she's signalling me."

She doesn't answer.

"Are you okay?" he asks.

"No. I miss you."

"I miss you, too."

"I can't believe this is happening," she says.

He doesn't answer.

"I'm so mixed up."

"Don't ask me to comfort you, Judith. This is your doing, not mine. You can change it back anytime you want."

"This is so hard."

There's another pause.

"Bobby, do you love me?"

"Yes."

"I love you, too."

"I have to go," he says.

"Okay."

"Bye."

She lies on the couch with her arm over her eyes. *Am I making a terrible mistake?* she wonders. *Am I making the worst mistake of my life? I love this man and he loves me. Something like this may never come my way again.*

But Israel. She can't imagine her life without Israel. Now she thinks of her friends there and tries picturing what they are doing. Then, as if her legs have a will of their own, they have walked her to the dining room, where she checks her email for letters from home.

— 2 —

The next day, Thursday, is much like the one before. But on Friday morning she awakens exhausted from a terrible night. She woke up three times, each time after a horrible dream. In the first one, she saw two yeshiva boys, lynched, swinging from a tree. She recognized them: the two sons who get lynched in the novel *The Sacrifice*. In her dream, their bodies were swinging in the wind. She awakened sweating and nauseated, and then lay there listening to the wind wailing outside her window. She noticed yesterday on the kitchen calendar that something called Purim Katan is in just three days, and after she woke from this dream, she thought about Purim, Haman, and his ten sons swinging back and forth on their gallows trees.

Then she slept again, and dreamed she was at Anna Ticho's House, one of her favourite places in Jerusalem. She was sitting on a bench in the charming restaurant-garden of this artist's house, sipping lemonade, when a man came and stuck his hand down her pants. In her dream, before entering the garden she had toured this house, enraptured by Anna's powerful, evocative sketches of the Judean hills. After awakening from this dream, her first thought was: *How could that man do this to me in the midst of all that beauty?*

She dozed a third time and dreamed she was strolling in an orange grove somewhere near Netanya. She was happy and slightly dazed, intoxicated by the fragrance of the oranges. The trees around her swished gently in the breeze and the oranges above her head were plump and glowing. She reached up, plucked one, and gazed at it in her palm. But as she did so, the orange began to change before her eyes. Almost imperceptibly at first, because the change was so gradual, like a slow-motion film of a rose opening its petals. It was only when the transformation was complete that she recognized what it had become. An orange grenade. And at the exact moment that she understood this, it exploded suddenly in her hand, its sticky mess all over her like some deadly spore or sperm.

She snuggles under the covers. She feels wretched after all these dreams and is in no mood to get up. Plus the house is freezing, and she wants to stay here in bed where it's warm for as long as possible. But after a while, bored and hungry, she gets out of bed. She is shocked by the wave of coldness that hits her: a physical force like a wall of icy air slapping against her. She hurries downstairs, and from the hall closet takes out her father's long, heavy army coat. It smells vaguely of him, a manly smell, and she wraps herself in it as if wrapping herself in her father, in his large, safe warmth. The closet is still full of his things. She has not yet gone through all the closets and drawers; she must do this sometime, and decide what to give away. But now she gazes transfixed at a sweater. Every time she sees this sweater, fishbones comes to mind, and how if you are not careful, and swallow one, it can stick in your throat and kill you. Flora, who many years ago was their next-door neighbour, once came for supper, and halfway through the meal she swallowed a fishbone. Daddy was worried about her, but Flora laughingly brushed off his concern.

"Never mind, Izzy, I'm fine," she said to him when he suggested driving her to the hospital. Several minutes later, though, he prevailed, as he often did in his gentle but persistent way, with Flora coyly succumbing to his caring — flattered by it, in fact, the lonely single woman. Judith can still see her protesting as her father helped her on with her coat: "This is so unnecessary, Izzy. I'm 100 percent fine."

But the second Daddy and Flora walked into the emergency room, Flora began to cough, and then choke, and the doctor afterwards said that if she hadn't been in the emergency room at that exact moment, she would be dead by now for sure. It was soon after this that Flora started knitting for Daddy. Every year on his birthday she would present him with another sweater, to Mummy's thinly disguised annoyance. Flora's sweaters were always 100 percent wool, sufficiently thick and warm for Canadian winters. They were also all simple in design: solid colours, or at most with a single stripe. Judith removes her father's coat and puts on the first sweater Flora ever made for him. A plain, solid grey, rather lumpy in places. Then on top of this she rebuttons her father's coat. Now she sees another of Flora's sweaters hanging in the closet: bright blue with a yellow horizontal stripe, same as the cover of Suzy's book. She closes the closet door.

She sneezes. Shivering, she checks the thermostat at the entrance to the kitchen. It says sixty degrees instead of the usual sixty-eight. Why has it gone down to sixty? Could Toronto Oil and Gas have already cut off the heat? That's doubtful. Their policy was quite clear about not cutting off people's heat in the winter. No, they would not do something as drastic as that. As her father liked to say, this isn't Communist Russia.

But what about that metallic clunk she heard yesterday? Could that have been the furnace breaking down? She hurries to the basement to check. It is absolutely quiet down there. The furnace is not making any of its usual hissing, clanking, groaning sounds. And it is perfectly still — not vibrating or trembling as it always is. It looks like an enormous dead thing. A dead mammoth.

She runs upstairs, alarmed. In front of the thermostat, she stares anxiously at the number. *Oh my God. It's just going to keep getting colder and colder. Now it's at sixty, soon it will be fifty-nine. Then fifty-eight. Then fifty-seven.* And she can't call Toronto Oil and Gas to come fix it, because there is "immediate withdrawal of all other services" if you haven't paid your bill. For a second she thinks of calling Bobby and asking him to lend her the $362 for the heating bill. He would agree, of course. But she can't do this. They are in the middle of breaking up. *I'll manage somehow for the next eight weeks. All I really need during this time is food and gas for the car.*

Food. She came downstairs automatically for breakfast, forgetting there isn't any food in the house. Literally nothing except a dozen crackers. Yesterday she felt lazy, and instead of going shopping she just ordered in pizza. She really must buy food today. But looking out the living room window, she sees it snowed again last night. Everything is buried under snow: her front lawn, the front lawn of the neighbour facing her, and the street in between (which, not having been driven on yet this morning, is nothing but a slight dip in the snow between the two lawns). Her car in the driveway is a white snow-covered hump. It will take her twenty minutes at least to dig it out from under all that snow, and anyway, what's the point? The street is impassable. She'll have to postpone going food shopping until they've cleared it. Not that she minds. She is so cold now that she is sneezing again, and all she wants is to be warm in bed. She grabs the crackers and some articles she has to read for school, and runs upstairs. Quickly she pulls on some extra clothing — *gatkes*, ski pants, hockey socks — adds two more blankets to the bed, and dives under the covers. Then she reads an article for Hetty's course, the first chapter of a "stats-for-dummies" book, getting caught up instantly in the joy of numbers and the games you can play with them. She reads it with interest and pleasure. Then she reads another article. And another. Then she dozes off.

At 4:15 she awakens very hungry. Except for the twelve crackers, she has eaten nothing all day. She looks out the window: the street has been cleared, so she could go shopping now. But she is tired and doesn't have the energy to shovel off her car. I'll order something in, she decides. Something fancier than just plain pizza for my Friday night dinner. But first, before Shabbat begins, I'll check my email.

Downstairs, she sits shivering at the dining room table with a blanket over her shoulders and turns on the computer. She has a letter from Bruria — the first in two weeks — so she clicks on it right away. Reading it, she sharply sucks in her breath. In Netanya today, exactly when she was dreaming about that orange grove near Netanya, there was a suicide bombing in the main shopping mall, and Bruria's neighbour's sister, Chana, was seriously hurt. *In Hebrew*, thinks Judith, *"Netanya" means "given by God," but it keeps having suicide bombings. The Lord giveth, the Lord taketh away.* It seems Chana had already finished her food shopping for Shabbat, but realized she had forgotten lettuce for the salad, so went back into the mall to buy some. Now she is internally hemorrhaging and may die.

Bruria has other bad news, too. Rina's son Gidi is doing his army service in Ramallah. *Ramallah*. In Arabic *Ram* plus *Allah* means "the height of God." There, in the Height of God three days ago, according to Bruria, Gidi got injured.

> *Don't worry. It's not life-threatening. Just shrapnel in his right leg, and they've already managed to get out most of it. They couldn't get all of it out because some of it was too close to the bone. But the doctors say his leg should be okay in time. Though he may end up walking with a bit of a limp.*

A bit of a limp?! Judith envisions clearly the red-haired freckled boy — *no*, she tells herself; *man* — who recently led his younger brother and sister in rebellion against their parents, and got them to agree to let them go to a club in downtown Jerusalem. Now that spirited young man will be one of Israel's war veterans, limping down the stairs into the same downtown club. She shudders, feeling the circle of violence and death winding its way closer to her. Like a lasso that formed itself around her and Israel at a distance of six thousand miles, and then, tightening, at six hundred miles, then sixty, then one mile — until now it encloses her within it, and she can feel its noose around her neck.

I'm sorry to be the bearer of bad news, Bruria writes. *But I know you would rather know than not know.*

This is true, thinks Judith.

Then Bruria writes, responding to Judith's last letter: *As for this Suzy chick, I can't believe she kicked you off that committee. That is so sick and fucked-up. But anyway, soon you'll be back here, and I'll have you on more committees than you'll know what to do with. Seriously — I have some ideas.*

Judith smiles. *That is so Bruria.* Next Bruria expresses concern about Judith's health. She feels Judith's illness has dragged on way too long. *Don't they have any decent doctors in Canada? What's happening to you there?*

What is happening to me here, Judith thinks, *is a sickness called* galut. *Which unfortunately there is no pill for. But don't worry, Bruria — I'll be home again soon, and then I'll be fine.*

Bruria signs *With love*, and adds a P.S.: *Do you know that in your last few emails, you've been typing* aslo *instead of* also? *Maybe you long for Oslo — for peace. What can I say? Don't we all.*

The blanket has fallen off her shoulders. She stands, wraps it tighter around her, and as she sits back down, the computer screen goes blank and the dining room lights go off. She feels her way downstairs to the electricity box in the basement and flicks all the usual switches, but nothing happens. Back upstairs, she looks out the living room window: the whole street is a deep indigo. There are no lights on anywhere, not in the houses, not even the street lamps. She sees trees thrashing around violently in the wind and a hydro pole lying across the road. If the electrical wires are down, all the roads will be closed. This is a major storm. The last time there was a storm like this, the power was out for two days. The phones were cut off, too. She checks the phone. Nothing. Nada. She is filled with dread. It is dark outside, she is all alone in a freezing house with no food, and she is cut off from the rest of the world. In theory, she could knock on a neighbour's door. But that would be very awkward. They are her father's neighbours, not hers, and she doesn't know any of them. There is no one left on this street from when she lived here.

She sits on the couch, gazing out the window. The sun is setting and she watches the light fade until the once-indigo sky is black. This will be her first Shabbat alone in … she tries but can't recall when she last spent a Shabbat all by herself. In Israel Friday nights were always spent with friends, sharing an elaborate meal with laughter, singing, talk, and the joy of human company. In Canada too, for the past eighteen months, Friday night was a time spent always with people she loved. At first with her father, and then with Bobby. She visualizes Bobby now at his brother's, sitting around the Shabbat table — white tablecloth, fresh flowers, crystal decanter of wine, the whole deal — with Richard, Annette, and their two kids, a boy and a girl, the picture-perfect family. No doubt they are eating chicken paprikash, the only recipe Annette seems to know how to make, since she has served it every time Judith has eaten there. No doubt also Richard and Annette are glancing surreptitiously at Bobby and then exchanging looks with each other, looks of subtle — or even not so subtle — gloating that finally Bobby has broken up with her. That is what they'll assume, of course: that Bobby broke up with *her*. It is inconceivable to them that anyone would ever break up with someone from their family. She imagines the conversation around the table. Probably talking about the suicide bombing in Netanya, with Richard making his usual Arab-hating remarks. She can hear his deep, not-quite-bass, voice saying, "The only good Arab is a dead Arab." The comment that prompted her first fight with him. In response to whatever Richard says, Annette, as usual, will nod like a moron. Then their kids will pipe up too with their opinions, parroting these same disgusting views. Picturing this scene, she is very glad not to have to be there tonight, struggling to keep her mouth shut and stomach these smug, stupid people.

Then again, she thinks, *here I am all alone on a Friday night. No food, no heat, no lights, no friends, nothing.* She is angry at Bobby for insisting on this night apart. He called her this morning, probably out of guilt, and they talked for only a minute or two. Which afterwards she thought was just as well, since they didn't have much to say to each other. It was just chit-chat, uncomfortable and surreal. Then he commented that she sounded hoarse, and he hoped she wasn't sick again. She did not want to tell him she hadn't used her voice — had not talked to another human being — since speaking to him the day before. Or that she was lying in bed, and had been all day, because there was no other way to keep warm in this house. So she said she hadn't slept well.

"Why not?" he asked, sounding wary, like he wasn't sure he wanted to know.

She cast around for something to say. Her nightmares were another topic she didn't want to tell him about. Inspired, she answered, "Because Dunhill hath murdered sleep."

There was a pause, and then he chuckled. "Remember that?" he asked.

"Yes." She smiled.

In grade nine when their class put on *Macbeth*, she was Lady Macbeth and Bobby was Duncan. From then until the end of high school, whenever anyone complained they hadn't slept well, Judith or Bobby, or someone else who had been in the play, would say ominously, "Glamis hath murdered sleep." Or "The geometry test hath murdered sleep." Or "Last night's party hath murdered sleep." Or drinking. Or sex. "Sex hath murdered sleep" was what Bobby often said to his best friend, Roy, who had his first girlfriend in grade eleven and all that year was chronically tired.

She and Bobby hung up soon afterward, after he suggested they speak on Sunday and maybe meet on Monday night. She agreed and they said, "*Shabbat shalom.*"

Now she feels weak and dizzy from not eating anything all day. Again she tries the phone — an old phone her father had forever, and that lacks battery backup. It still isn't working so she can't call out for food. She wishes she had a cellphone. Bobby kept urging her to get one, but she never did. She checks the thermostat again. It says fifty degrees. As she peers worriedly at this number, it drops to forty-nine. Now she is afraid. After forty-nine it will be forty-eight, forty-seven, forty-six … She doesn't know how to stop this. She has no idea what to do. But since it is now time to light the Shabbat candles, she goes to the dining room table, inserts two candles into her great-grandmother's candlesticks, and strikes a match. Then she waves her hands gently in circles above the lit candles. She performs this traditional gesture to spread the peacefulness of Shabbat throughout her home, and maybe the whole world. But now, because her hands are so cold, she holds them a while longer above the flames.

Then she goes into the kitchen, searching for food. She opens and closes cupboards. There is nothing in any of them. *Empty, empty, empty*, as she slams them shut one after another. Not a single crouton. The same thing in the fridge and freezer, too. Not a single stalk of limp celery, or a freezer-burned but still suckable popsicle. Nothing. In desperation she looks in the cupboard under the kitchen sink, where the cleaning supplies are kept. There, buried at the very back, behind two big plastic bottles, spray cans, sponges, steel wool, and silver polish, she sees a small unfamiliar-looking can resting against the wall. It's SPAM. *SPAM! What is* this *doing here?* SPAM is made of pork which, although she is not strictly kosher, she has not eaten for the past twelve years. Even her father, who did not keep kosher, would never have eaten SPAM. How did it get here? Maybe it was brought into the house by one of her father's caregivers. She looks at the can of SPAM with disgust. Canned meat. Canned pork meat. Ground-up pig. Yuck. She closes the cupboard door.

But then she opens it again. Because she knows this is all there is to eat in this house. And she's starving. She is so weak she feels faint. Survival above all. She removes the square-shaped can, hooks her finger through the metal loop, rips off the top, and stares at the pink, spongy mass inside. It doesn't bear the slightest resemblance to meat. She sniffs it. It smells awful. She sets the can on the counter and turns away. But then she sniffs it again. Now it doesn't smell quite so bad. *It's not that terrible*, she thinks. *When Daddy was in the army, he ate worse stuff every day. He'd probably have been grateful for some meat, even this kind.* She smiles. One of his favourite jokes was about a yeshiva student who has been drafted into the Czar's army, and asks his rabbi what to do if they serve him pork and there's nothing else.

"Eat the pork," says the rabbi. "But don't suck the bones."

So, holding her breath, fighting the impulse to gag, and telling herself, *It's just meat — it'll give you strength,* she eats every last bit in the small tin. It's not that bad, she decides, once you get used to it. Not that she plans to. And she didn't "suck the bones."

She sneezes. Then twice more. This house is freezing. She'd better go back to bed. Leaving the kitchen, she passes the thermostat but deliberately avoids looking at it, like snubbing a former friend. She carries the candlesticks upstairs, feeling, as they light her way to bed, like someone in a nineteenth-century novel. She places the candlesticks on her night table, blows them out, and gets under the covers. She is almost contented. But then she feels nauseated and wonders what, in fact, she just put into her body. *Spam* in computer language means garbage. Is this what she just filled her body with? With virtual garbage? She pictures the inside of her body — the inside of limbs and organs — filling up with flashing smiley faces selling pornography, get-rich-quick schemes, hate propaganda, and endless other mental garbage. Are these her insides now? Or maybe, from eating SPAM, she has become half-human-half-pig? What a horrible Friday night. Among the worst of her life. Feeling miserable, she falls asleep.

— 3 —

It is very dark when she awakens panting and sweaty. Wild animals were chasing her down a forest path. They were gaining on her, and she woke up just an instant before they pounced and tore her to pieces. Although she is awake now, she keeps panting: it is hard to catch her breath, as if she has really been running, really been chased. She does not want to go back to sleep now: she is afraid of dreaming again. *To sleep perchance to dream.* She leans over and switches on the lamp near her bed to see if the electricity is back, but nothing happens. She lifts the phone. Dead.

"Shit," she says. Her stomach aches with hunger. *Never mind,* she comforts herself. *Everything will be back to normal in the morning. This is just one of those strange, abnormal nights. Like "A Night," the Yiddish poem by Moyshe-Leyb Halpern. A night you just have to get through. Survive. Same as the long, hellish night Israel is experiencing now.* Lying in bed, she muses not just on suicide bombings and the threats to Israel's physical survival, but also about what is happening to Israel's soul. Last week in *Ha'aretz* she read that the Israeli government recently "appropriated" — in other words, stole — some land belonging to Abu

Ghosh, an Arab village just outside Jerusalem that for years has lived in peaceful and friendly harmony with Israel, even sometimes demonstrating impressive loyalty. Now the Israeli government reciprocates this loyalty by stealing some of their land. It's disgusting. It's outrageous. As is that euphemistic verb, "to appropriate," when it is utterly *in*-appropriate to steal.

Yesterday she read about another Arab village where a grove of olive trees was uprooted by religious settlers. In response, several dozen Israeli peaceniks, including some prominent writers, went to this village and fought with the settlers, preventing further uprooting; but already considerable damage had been done. *Don't uproot what's been planted*, goes a line in "The Honey and the Bee Sting," and there is also in Jewish law a prohibition against uprooting fruit trees, even in times of war. Talk about those settlers being selective when it comes to their religious observance.

Reflecting on these recent Israeli actions against Palestinians, she is ashamed. Ashamed and grieved. What was it Maimonides said about grief? "If a man" — *of course a man!* thinks Judith — "wanted to wax wroth about the ignorance of man, he would never stop being angry, and would have to lead a life of grief and affliction." That is how she feels now: grieved and afflicted. She feels it burning inside her like a cancerous ulcer eating away at her stomach. A cancerous ulcer like the occupation. *A moral decay at the core of our country, eating away at us — devouring us — from within.*

Not that the Palestinians are exactly moral paragons, either. There are Palestinians like Jaber who believe Jews are "the sons of dogs and monkeys" and should be wiped off the face of the earth.

Where is there hope? What can one cling to?

Then she smiles. Samah. Samah was her partner when she worked on that dialogue project in Israel for Jewish and

Palestinian teens. The leaders of the dialogue groups always worked in pairs, one Jew and one Palestinian, and she and Samah were matched together. Samah was, like her, a feminist, and a few years older. They had different points of view, obviously, on certain issues, but they had real respect for each other, and genuine affection, too. That was building, instead of destroying. That was increasing the peace in the world, rather than the hate. That is the only hope.

She feels drowsy. *No*, she tells herself. *Don't fall asleep. If you fall asleep, you'll have another nightmare.* But how can she keep awake without caffeine, without electricity, and without having to leave this bed, which, though no longer warm, is still the warmest place in this house? Then she knows. She'll play with words. Whenever she was ill and bedbound as a child or teen, this is what she did. She picked a word and played with it. What word should she pick first?

"Exile," she says aloud. As she says it, it sounds like *Eggs Isle*. Eggs on a desert isle. An island full of eggs. Eggs in Hebrew are *baitzim*. *Baitzim* means eggs, but also testicles. So broken eggs are broken testicles. No babies can come from broken testicles. So there can be no future. No future for the Jewish people. In Eggs Isle. In Exile.

She laughs. This is fun. What word should be next? Dunhill. She snickers. Dunhill is a brand of cigarette. Something cancer-causing, potentially fatal. And if you add a *g* to Dunhill, Dunhill becomes Dunghill. Like the dunghill outside Dung Gate — one of the gates to Jerusalem's Old City — where camels in previous centuries dumped their dung. Which formed a hill. A dunghill. *Dunghill University,* she sneers. *The real name of the shitty school I attend.*

She is happier now, but colder. Especially her hands and feet. Her teeth chatter. She burrows deeper under the covers, pulling them tighter around her, but it does not help. It must be forty-seven degrees in here, maybe less. Fuck Suzy. If she hadn't given that three-thousand-dollar RA'ship to Elizabeth, if she had kept her promise, then this house wouldn't be freezing cold. And she wouldn't be freezing and starving, while Suzy does just fine in her warm, plush, carpeted house, with its fridge crammed full of food.

There is a loud growling sound: it's her stomach. She doesn't feel at all hungry, though; just weak and light-headed, like she could laugh and laugh and never stop. Her stomach continues making noises. Like the wild animals in the forest who were chasing her. As if they were all inside her stomach now. Along with the pig she ate for supper tonight.

I need help, she thinks. But she doesn't know how to get it. She can't call Bobby or Cindy, or even her friends in Israel, because the phone is dead. *I'm alone — 'mAlone.* She laughs, more and more shrilly, and can't stop. Her face feels wet. She touches it — it's tears, her face is soaked in tears. *I'm falling apart,* she thinks. *Maybe I'm going mad.* She doesn't think so. But then again, almost by definition, mad people never think they're mad; they always think that they're okay and everyone else is crazy. *So how would I know? How would I really know if I were mad? Around the bend? Insane?*

No, she decides, *I'm not mad. Just lonely. And a person can't go mad from loneliness, can they? From not having one person to talk to closer than six thousand miles away who understands what I am doing with my life? Or from losing the people I love, one after another after another? A person can't go mad from that, can they? Or from living far from home in galut? Of course, one can go mad in galut. Which sounds like the title of a movie:* Sleepless in Seattle. Going Gaga in Galut. *But can one actually go mad from galut? From living for a protracted period in a spiritually unnatural condition like exile? Maybe. After all, there is the*

Jerusalem Syndrome, where people who come to Jerusalem for the first time become clinically insane, believing themselves to be Moses, Jesus, or Mohammed (and sometimes all three). Perhaps I have the opposite of this. Perhaps there is a psychiatric disorder called the Galut Syndrome, a mental illness caused by living in exile, a place intrinsically antithetical to one's emotional and psychological health. A syndrome that would likely be exacerbated on Friday nights spent alone, the way werewolves go especially crazy whenever there's a full moon.

This is probably all that's wrong with me. I'm feeling crazy now, but I'll be okay once I'm back home in Jerusalem. In just seven and a half weeks. Only fifty-two days.

A half-hour later, Judith is sitting up in bed. On the night table the Shabbat candles are lit, and she feels peaceful and content. With a pencil and paper she is doing *gematriya*, the Jewish system for relating numbers and words. It all started because of *only fifty-two days.* She began playing with the number fifty-two. Fifty-two weeks in the year. Fifty-two is composed of a five and a two. Five plus two equals seven. Seven is the number of days in the week. The seventh day of the week is Shabbat, which is today. Which feels, as they said in high school, "cosmic."

Numbers, she thinks, *tell the truth.* They never change or die like words and people do. They're perfect, unchanging, and eternal. Something like the language of God. She learned *gematriya* three years ago in a half-day workshop at Beit Ha'am in Jerusalem, and hasn't done it since, but when she started doing it tonight, it came back quickly. First she wrote the Hebrew alphabet vertically, one letter under the other. Then next to each letter she wrote its assigned numerical value. The first ten letters, from *aleph* to *yud*, have values from one to ten. *Aleph* equals one, *bet* (the *b* sound) equals two, and so forth. The letters following *yud* have values in increments of ten. So the eleventh letter of the alphabet, *kaf*, is worth twenty. The twelfth letter, *lamed*, thirty. And so on up to *kuf*, which is one hundred. After that come the last three letters of the alphabet: *resh, shin,* and *taf*, with values respectively of two hundred, three hundred, and four hundred. If you need to go higher than four hundred, you just combine letters to add up to the number you want.

The Hebrew words she plans to do *gematriya* on are important. They're the Hebrew words for Friend, Peace, War, God, Love, Hate, Life, Death, Goodness, Evil, Trust, Betrayal, Exile, and Redemption. She picked these words because, to make it through this night, and also through her fifty-two remaining days in *galut*, she needs to know what things are worth. *Gematriya* will tell her the true value of things. She carefully calculates each of these words and then studies the result. It's interesting. For example, Love, *ahava*, has a numerical value of thirteen. Which is also the age at which, according to Jewish law, one is considered an adult and therefore morally responsible for one's actions. Is this implying a connection in life between love and responsibility? Also interesting is the word Friend. The male form of Friend, *chaver*, is 210, but the female form, *chavera,* is 215. Does this mean that to a woman a female friend is more valuable than a boyfriend? Possibly. Feminists have been saying that for years.

Now she writes the letters of the English alphabet vertically, and next to each letter a number: A equals one, B equals two. To parallel Hebrew *gematriya*, at the eleventh letter of the English alphabet, K, she starts going up ten at a time. K equals twenty, L equals thirty. Up to one hundred, which is S. So T equals two hundred, U equals three hundred, and so on until Z, eight hundred. *Eight hundred Z's*, she thinks. In Hebrew, eight hundred letters of the *z* sound is eight hundred *zayins*. But a *zayin* is also a penis. So picturing this, eight hundred penises, she laughs. She laughs and laughs, she can't stop laughing, and the next thing she knows she is sobbing, then screaming, "What's the point? What is the point?!" She sits awhile, calming down. When she's calm, she calculates the numerical value of God, and all the other words she just did in Hebrew, but this time in English. She also calculates Bobby's name in both English and Hebrew, and her own.

When she's finished, she takes a deep breath. This is the moment of truth. Now she'll compare the Hebrew and English. Now she'll find out if things are worth more in Israel than in Canada: for instance, is love worth more in Hebrew than in English? Is an Israeli man worth more than a Canadian one? A Moshe, for example, compared to a Bobby? She starts laughing again — something about this question strikes her as very funny — and it takes several minutes till her laughter subsides. Again, when she touches her face, it's wet with tears.

She goes down her list word by word, comparing the numerical values in English and Hebrew, drawing a square around each word that achieves a higher score in English. Love, for example, is 495 in English and only 13 in Hebrew, so when it comes to love, English wins. Around all the words where the Hebrew word trumps the English, she draws a circle. Then she surveys the results.

English wins on Judith, Bobby, Love, Trust, Goodness, Evil, God, War, Truth, Betrayal, Exile, and Redemption. She contemplates Judith, Bobby, and Love. Does this mean she should stay here with Bobby in English-land, rather than look for someone in Hebrew? Also, she can't understand how War won in English. It's counterintuitive: almost everything she knows about war she's learned in Israel. But English winning on Betrayal feels correct. In Israel she was never betrayed like she was here. As for Exile, this one's obvious. Of course Exile wins in the language spoken in exile rather than in the language spoken at home.

She looks to see where Hebrew wins. Hebrew wins on Death (because of all the wars?), but it also wins on Hope. This makes sense: Hope, *Hatikva* in Hebrew, is the name of Israel's national anthem.

Last but not least, Hebrew wins on Life. And, as if this were the overall score of the entire exercise, like one's final mark in a course, this feels very true to her. Life *is* better there than here.

She is dizzy and lies down, pulling the covers up to her neck. She also feels drowsy, and now she isn't afraid of falling asleep. But first she wants to sing something, like singing herself a lullaby. It's the *kaddish*, the mourner's prayer one recites after the death of a parent, thrice daily for eleven months. "*Yitgadal v'yitkadash …*" she begins: "May God's great name be magnified and sanctified." But as she continues singing this prayer, entering into it through its secret gate, she has the odd sensation that she is not reciting it for her father. Coming to the end of the *kaddish* — "May the Lord who makes peace in heaven make peace as well for us" — she knows she has been singing it also for herself. As if a part of her has recently died.

— 4 —

Monday morning, she drives to Dunhill. The sun is shining, and it is a glorious winter day with a crisp, clean feeling in the air. She is going to meet Cindy and Darra, to plan their presentation for Hetty's class next week. She reassures herself that she won't be anywhere near any of the Anti-oppression Day events. She must protect herself. She doesn't know exactly where the line between madness and sanity is, but she knows that on Friday night, if she did not actually cross that line, she was dancing right on top of it. Luckily, when she awakened on Saturday morning, the sun was shining, the storm was over, the electricity was back, the phones were working, and her street had been cleared of the fallen electrical pole. Without even showering or properly shovelling off her car, she drove to the nearest open restaurant, a diner, and ordered an enormous breakfast: pancakes with syrup, scrambled eggs with hash browns and onions, toast with butter and strawberry jam, a large cinnamon bun, a yogurt, fresh fruit salad, orange juice, and coffee. She ate as much of it as she could — which was not much since her stomach had shrunk — and brought the rest home.

She hated being at home, though. After the warmth of the diner, her house was terribly cold. So she packed some schoolwork and a pannier of food and spent the day at the University of Toronto library, studying there in snug comfort until it closed at midnight. By the time she got home the house was thirty-eight degrees, and after two hours of tossing and turning in her almost freezing bed, she went downstairs to the kitchen. To heat some leftover pancakes, she turned on the electric oven. (Her father had refused to buy a microwave: he was convinced they emitted carcinogenic rays.) While waiting for the oven to warm, she got an idea. She carried into the kitchen from the living room the two bottom cushions of the couch, a throw pillow, and a ratty old blanket, and built herself a little nest in front of the stove. When the oven hit 350 degrees — a good temperature for defrosting foods and bodies — she opened the oven door, lay down, pulled the blanket over her, and curled up like a cozy contented dog in front of a fireplace.

She slept deeply and well. On Sunday she spent all day at the library, and at midnight returned to her pallet in front of the stove. On Monday morning she turned off the oven, ate breakfast, and got on the road.

Now she is a third of the way along the highway, and since it's eleven o'clock — well past rush hour — the road is almost empty. By now Brier has finished his keynote and the panellists are speaking. *This whole nauseating event,* she thinks, *is the product of Dunhill's — Dunghill's — version of democracy. Yay democracy. Which rhymes with hypocrisy.* She flies down the highway, singing a Purim song, because today in Jerusalem it's Shushan Purim Katan, the second day of Purim Katan, or Little Purim. She hadn't known until four days ago that there was a little Purim as opposed to the regular (big?) one. As a girl, on Purim, she loved dressing up as Queen Esther, the hero of the Purim story. She loved Queen Esther because Queen Esther was brave. She risked her life to save her people and, thanks to her, the Jews of Persia were spared death. The Purim song Judith is singing now is the first one she ever learned, "Today Is Purim," which her father sang with her in Yiddish. Then she starts "My Hat Has Three Corners," a Purim song in Hebrew. Partway into it she notices she is low on gas. She pulls into a gas station and, still happily singing in Hebrew, inserts the hose from the pump into her gas tank. But sensing something, she turns: the man at the neighbouring pump, filling his car, is glaring at her. Immediately she stops singing. Then she wonders, *Why did I do that? There's no reason I can't sing a Hebrew song in public. A song in Israel's tongue is no worse than a song in Canada's.* Defiantly she starts singing again. But now the joy has gone out of it, so she stops. *Life in* galut …

Soon she reaches Dunhill. In her usual parking lot, the one closest to FRANK, she sees a very good spot and grabs it without thinking. Then she realizes she could have kept going and parked in the second lot, nearer to Le Petit Café. But she decides not to bother switching spots now. It isn't a long walk and it's a beautiful day. As she ambles down the path toward Le Petit Café, the magnificent weather makes her feel invigorated and alive. She recognizes a tree with gnarled, powerful branches reaching skyward. Soon it will sprout pink buds. Soon it will be spring.

But then her stomach clenches. She is approaching FRANK, where Anti-oppression Day is being held. In a minute the path she is on will diverge and she'll veer off to the left, away from FRANK and toward Le Petit Café. But now the path is taking her straight toward FRANK, and all she feels is fear.

Then shame. To be afraid right after singing these songs about Purim. When Esther was so brave. And when she knows there is nothing really to fear. Today she won't set even a toe inside FRANK. She won't have to see any of those horrible people. *So relax*, she tells herself. *Just have a nice meeting with Cindy and Darra.* Feeling slightly calmer, she continues on her way.

At Le Petit Café, Cindy sits alone at a round pink-and-turquoise table, like the one Judith sat at with Suzy for their suppers last term. Cindy gives her a hug. They sit and chat, waiting for Darra who is in the bathroom. Cindy asks Judith about her weekend, and she answers selectively. She tells Cindy about the fallen electrical pole and being stuck in a cold house without any food. But she tells it humorously, giving no hint of what Friday night was truly like for her. She also does not mention that her house is still without heat, so she is sleeping on the floor like a dog in front of the stove. Still, Cindy looks concerned.

"That's terrible, Judith," she says. "I wish I'd known. You could have stayed at our place."

She looks at Cindy, astonished. Such a thought never crossed her mind. "Thanks," she says, touched.

"Seriously. If this happens again, come stay with us. And get a cellphone."

Judith nods vaguely. She can't afford a cellphone. To change the topic, she asks Cindy how it went this morning with Brier.

Cindy makes a face. "He's a weird guy. At first, he seemed okay. He's smart and good-looking, and he has charisma, so you're listening and you kind of want to agree with what he's saying. But after a while I started to feel — I hate to say it, Judith, but he totally hates Israel. I think he hates Israel more than he even cares about the Palestinians."

She stares at Cindy. "That's amazing you said that. Golda Meir once said something similar. She said Israel will only have peace with the Arabs when they love their own children more than they hate us. Were there a lot of people there?"

"You wouldn't believe it, the place was packed. The whole auditorium was filled — all 350 seats — and there were tons of extra people crammed in, standing against the back wall. Also sitting on all the steps inside the auditorium, from the top to the bottom, even though it's not allowed."

Judith's stomach turns over as she pictures all those students eagerly squeezing into the auditorium to hear this hate-monger peddling his hatred of Israel and Jews. She can almost smell the hot, overcrowded room and see the gullible students opening their mouths like baby birds to receive Brier's poisoned worms. "How did Darra react?" she asks Cindy. "Did she feel like you?"

Looking pained, Cindy shrugs. Judith realizes she has made Cindy uncomfortable and also put her in an awkward position, and she is sorry. But she needs to know where Darra stands on all this before spending the next hour with her. Also, she feels jealous, and wants to check if Cindy's loyalty lies with Darra or her.

"She liked Brier." Cindy frowns. "Don't get me wrong, Darra's a good person. But she always has to side with the victim. Or anyway with whoever she sees as the victim."

Judith smiles, gratified that Cindy has sided with her.

"But I see the situation in the Middle East," Cindy continues, "differently than most people, because of knowing you. Maybe if I hadn't heard from you all last term about Israel, I wouldn't have seen through Brier, either."

"You would have. You're discerning."

"I don't know. He's an extremely good speaker, very persuasive. You should have seen those people, Judith — they ate it all up. He got that whole auditorium frothed up against Israel."

Frothed up. Judith pictures a mad dog frothing at the mouth. Then a whole auditorium full of mad dogs with frothing mouths.

"Darra's just like everyone else who was there," says Cindy. "She thought Brier was sincere. That he was fighting for the Palestinians, a champion for the underdog and all that. Shh. Here she comes."

Lo, here she comes, thinks Judith, following the direction of Cindy's eyes. Darra, briskly walking toward them, is rubbing her hands together repeatedly, reminding Judith of Lady Macbeth in the mad scene trying to wash the blood off her hands. Reaching their table, Darra says laughingly, "That bathroom always runs out of paper towels," and finishes drying her hands on her pants. They eat the Anti-oppression Day pizza special while working on their presentation. It quickly becomes obvious to Judith that Cindy and Darra have done much more reading than her, both for Hetty's course generally, and specifically for this assignment. But it also seems like neither of them minds, and they both assume they will take the lead in presenting next Monday. By the end of the hour, they have mapped everything out in detail, and all she will have to do is read, and report on, one small section. Gratefully, she thanks them.

"It's nothing. You've been sick," says Darra, then rushes off to the afternoon session of Anti-oppression Day. Judith restrains herself from saying anything about her to Cindy, and watches silently as Cindy wipes some crumbs off the table. Judith says, "Where are you parked? I'll walk out with you."

"Actually, I'm staying. My cellphone is broken, so I'm going to use the pay phone here. I have to call Mikey's doctor."

"Mikey's doctor! I thought you said he was okay."

"He is. Don't worry. But his doctor's latest theory is that he has allergies, so we're checking into that. I have to phone him before one o'clock when he starts seeing his afternoon patients."

"I see. I'm glad Mikey isn't sick again. He's been sick so much."

"I know."

"Are you sure you don't want me to wait for you?"

"No. Go ahead."

"Thanks again, Cindy, for organizing this."

"Don't be silly."

Walking to her car, she feels very lucky to have a friend like Cindy. This whole year, this term especially, would have been so much worse without her. She strolls along in reverie, barely noticing the brilliant spring-like sun or anything else around her. She is cogitating about what she has to prepare for their presentation next week, and all the other work she still has to do in the remaining seven weeks of school: a research project, two major term papers, and two medium-size assignments. It is daunting but doable, she decides. Liking the sound of that, she repeats this in her mind a few times: *Daunting but doable. Daunting but doable. Daunting but doable ...*

Meanwhile, she has been walking automatically toward her car, oblivious to her surroundings. So only now does she notice there is a sizable crowd up ahead that will soon block her way. She frowns and slows down. What is this? It can't be anything to do with Anti-oppression Day; that's all happening inside FRANK. But glancing in that direction, she sees a huge crowd filling the area between FRANK and where she is now. There must be five or six hundred people. There is noise and excitement and placards waving in the air.

Now she understands: this is the "rally over the lunch break" — the anti-Israel demonstration she read about last week in the alley near Suzy's office. She can't believe she forgot. If she had remembered, she never would have parked her car where she did. She'd have parked in the second lot, next to Le Petit Café. Now she will have to walk through this rally. Right into the heart of it. Like into "the heart of darkness." Before her there is a wall of people, mostly students but also several faculty members, and some outsiders, demonstrators from the community with no university affiliation. Everyone is looking toward the quad, so she does, too, and recognizes Michael Brier standing on the front steps of FRANK. He is, as Cindy said, good-looking. He speaks into a microphone, but she can't hear anything. The mike is not working. Near him a guy of about forty with greasy hair fiddles with the equipment. Surveying the people around her, she sees Darra in the crowd. She is about to call out and wave to her, but something restrains her. Darra seems too happy somehow, too relaxed and at home here. She is smiling and laughing with the guy beside her. Judith, turning away, sees a horizontal yellow stripe along the outside of the crowd. It's a line of campus policemen in their yellow uniforms, with something (clubs?) dangling from their hips.

Reluctant to advance, she looks in the one direction she has not yet: upward. In the highest windows of FRANK there are faces peering down at the rally below. *What are they seeing?* she wonders. How much do they understand about what they are viewing? She spots an orange curtain in one of the top windows and recognizes it as the very window from which, on Orientation Day, she first looked down and saw this quad. She contemplates the crowd ahead of her. If she wants to reach her car, she will have to start advancing. But she can't; it's as if her feet are nailed to the ground. Some distance away from her, but close enough to read, are two signs:

ISRAEL = APARTHEID

and

END ZIONIST OPPRESSION

Par for the course, she thinks, observing with satisfaction that she is not that upset by these signs anymore, in contrast to her reaction two weeks ago to the poster near Suzy's office. Maybe she is becoming inured to all this. Maybe she is learning to grow a tougher skin. She scans the crowd and the area beyond it, searching for an alternate route, but there isn't one. The only path to the parking lot where her car is parked is on the other side of this demonstration. It's like that song:

> *So high you can't get over it,*
> *So low you can't get under it,*
> *So wide you can't get around it …*

You've just got to go right through it. So she starts weaving politely through the crowd: "Excuse me, excuse me. Excuse me, excuse me." After what feels like a great deal of work, she peeks behind her and discovers she has come only about the length of her bedroom. She is making progress, but at the rate of an inchworm. Furthermore, she is feeling breathless — it is claustrophobic in this dense herd — but she tries to stay calm. She tries also not to think about the fact that she is surrounded by hundreds of people, many of whom hate Israel, and who would probably hate her too, if they knew she was Israeli. Not that there is any way they could know, she reassures herself: there is nothing about her that could give her away, like a *kipa*, or a Jewish star around her neck. She continues through this throng, feeling anxious and wishing she weren't here alone. She regrets she didn't wait for Cindy; if she had, they would be walking through this together, which would feel completely different. Suddenly a thunderous voice booms overhead.

"We must — stand — together," this voice roars. She glances at the steps in front of FRANK: Brier, alone there, is speaking. Evidently the greasy-haired guy fixed the sound system.

Brier shouts: "We must stand together against Zionist aggression! We must stand together against Zionist oppression!"

She pushes and jostles her way more forcefully through the crowd. *I have to get out of here*, she thinks. *I can't listen to this.* Some people, irritated, push or jostle her back. But she keeps advancing, one person at a time. "Excuse me, excuse me. Excuse me, excuse me." Meanwhile she tries to block out Brier's words, which continue to blare over the loudspeaker, and to concentrate only on her slow but steady progress through this mass of people. But this is not possible. Brier has taken over the airspace. His booming voice dominates every cubic inch of the air, penetrating not just her ears, but even her nostrils, forcing her to inhale his voice. To take it into her body and mind.

"Repeat after me: Zionism is apartheid!"

"Zionism is apartheid!" the crowd shouts back.

"Louder!"

"Zionism is apartheid!" the crowd shouts louder.

"Good! Now repeat after me: Get the Zionists out of Palestine!"

"Get the Zionists out of Palestine!"

"Get the Zionists out of Palestine!" Brier cries again.

"Get the Zionists out of Palestine!!"

She keeps walking. *I have to get out of here.* These repeat-after-me's scare her. The content of them, but even more than that, their anger and hatred, and their mindlessness, like a mountain echoing a yodeller. *A mountain has no mind*, she thinks, *and neither does a mob.*

"Palestine for the Palestinians!" shouts Brier.

"Palestine for the Palestinians!" the mob shouts back.

"All of Palestine for the Palestinians!" screams Brier.

"All of Palestine for the Palestinians!" the mob screams back.

"From Haifa to Eilat!"

"From Haifa to Eilat!"

"With Jerusalem the capital of Palestine!"

"With Jerusalem the capital of Palestine!"

"Jerusalem the capital of Palestine!" shrieks Brier, shaking his fist.

"Jerusalem the capital of Palestine!"

She stops walking. She stands, frozen. *Jerusalem*, she thinks. *Jerusalem is my home. You can't have my home.* She is having trouble breathing, she's panting slightly and holding her chest. *It's nothing*, she tells herself. *It's just stress. Brier's words can't hurt me — they're only words. Sticks and stones can break my bones …* She looks around to get her bearings. She has come almost halfway through the crowd, and here the view is different. She is smack in the middle of the demonstration, about fifteen rows from the front, and Brier is almost straight ahead of her. A real demagogue. He reminds her of a newsreel she once saw of Hitler at a rally. He shouted and shook his fist in exactly the same way.

"No Israeli products at Dunhill!" Brier is hollering.

"No Israeli products at Dunhill!" hollers back the mob.

"No academic exchanges with Israel!" Brier shouts.

"No academic exchanges with Israel!" the mob shouts back.

What this mob is really calling for, same as that poster, is a Dunhill that is Judenrein. *Or anyway "Israel-rein." Next they'll be shouting, "No Israeli students at Dunhill!"* Which means her. Feeling panic and horror, she starts pushing her way through the crowd again, but harder, more urgently, than before. Desperately.

"Hey, watch out," says a guy she just squeezed past. She turns around. "Sorry." Then she recognizes the guy with the long greasy hair who fixed the mike. He holds a sign. She glances at it — it's not like the other two she saw. This sign has words but also a picture. She studies it, frowning, feeling watched by the greasy-haired guy. The picture is of a can — a regular can, a soup can — and on the front of it there is a picture of a boy, seven or eight years old, and below that some words. She squints to read them:

ONE PALESTINIAN CHILD
Ground up with his Bones and Blood
Still Fresh — Good Until April 25, 2003
Murdered by the Israelis Only One Week Ago
(Feb. 10, 2003)
Certified Kosher by the Chief Rabbi of Israel
For Use in Making Passover Matzos

She turns away, holding her stomach so she won't vomit. A child ground up with his bones and blood. Her stomach heaves and she struggles to control it. Then with shock she understands what this poster is. It is the medieval blood libel, translated into the contemporary Palestinian narrative. She can hardly believe it. She takes some deep, slow breaths to calm herself. She does not dare glance again at the sign or at the guy holding it. Because if she does, she'll go crazy: she'll lunge at him and start pummeling him and screaming. But what's the point? Nothing she says or does will make any difference. She can't change the mind of anyone here about Israel. She pictures Bobby and knows what he would advise: Just keep walking, get into your car, and drive home. That's all. She begins to walk away.

"Hey, where you goin'?" asks the greasy-haired guy. "Don't you like my sign?"

She tries to ignore him and keep walking, but the way in front of her is blocked by a little knot of people having an intense conversation.

"You," she hears from behind her. "*You*. I'm talkin' to *you*."

She turns around and faces the greasy-haired guy. He has pockmarks on his face and an arrogant smile.

"No," she says, "I don't like your sign. It's a lie."

"Oh, yeah?" says the guy. "Well, maybe you don't know all the facts."

"I know all the facts."

"You do? Do you know how many Palestinian children have been killed by the Israeli army in the past three years? Do you?"

She frowns. "Not exactly, but —"

"I'll tell you. And I do know exactly, because I work with Brier. Me and my friend here." He nods toward a fat guy, also about forty, in a grey knitted hat. "Hundreds. Hundreds of kids have been killed by the Israelis. Maybe even thousands. And you know why? Because the Israelis target the children."

"That's ridiculous," she says. "That is total bullshit."

"It's what?"

"Bullshit. Firstly, your numbers are way off. Secondly, yes, there are some Palestinian children who have gotten caught in the crossfire, and that's tragic. But it doesn't mean Israel deliberately targeted them."

"Yes, it does."

"No, it doesn't."

"What are you saying?" he asks menacingly. "You don't believe me?"

"Of course I don't. What you're saying isn't true."

"Yes, it is."

"No, it isn't. It's a lie. A disgusting lie. And so is that sign you're holding."

He brings his pockmarked face closer to hers, his grey eyes glinting dangerously. "Are you calling me a liar?"

She draws back. She wants nothing more than to get away from this man. But she knows that to do this, she will first have to appease him. Crazy people have to be dealt with carefully. She flashes momentarily onto Suzy interviewing that pedophile.

"No," she says evenly, forcing herself to look at him and not lower her eyes. "I'm not saying that. I'm just saying I don't agree."

"In other words, I'm wrong." Now he turns and calls to the people around them, appealing to them. "Hey, everybody. Here's someone who says Israel doesn't kill Palestinians. She thinks what Israel's doing to the Palestinians is just fine."

"I didn't say that," she starts to say, but her voice falters. Several people have now turned to listen to the greasy-haired guy. Some of them also look at her, and others read his sign. She watches their faces as they read it. She is filled with rage.

"Give me that," she says, and tries grabbing the sign away. But he takes a step backwards and the sign spins around in his hand, showing its naked back: two sticks of wood nailed together into a cross. "Give me that!" she says again, and once more lunges at the sign.

But this time he steps forward and pushes her. Shoves her in the shoulder. Hard. "Get out of here," he says. "Get out of here while you still have the chance."

"No. Not till you give me that sign." For the third time she flings herself at it. This sign now feels like the most important thing in existence. If only she can destroy it, it will be like she has destroyed all the lies in the world against Israel. But for some reason she can't reach that sign — she can't move forward at all. Something is restraining her. Annoyed, she glances behind her: the fat man with the grey knitted hat is holding her by the back of her coat.

"Let me go!" She tries to yank herself loose.

"No," says the guy in the hat. "Not unless you promise to leave that sign alone."

"I'm not leaving that sign alone. It's a lie. A vicious, disgusting lie." Meanwhile she is twisting and turning to get herself free.

"No, it's not," says the greasy-haired guy, standing too far away for her to reach. "You're the one who's lying. Everyone else knows the truth about Israel: it's an apartheid state that oppresses and murders Palestinians, especially children."

"You're insane," she says. "You're out of your mind. It's Michael Brier, not us, who believes in murdering children. Listen to him." His voice is still blaring rhythmically over the loudspeaker. "He's a nutcase. A hate-monger. Spreading lies …" To free herself, she jerks sharply on her coat, twice, but is unsuccessful, so she turns around quickly and hits the arm that is holding her back. The guy in the grey knitted hat is stronger than her, though, and just laughs. Now the guy with the sign, stepping forward, grabs her right wrist. Tightly, with pincer fingers, hurting her.

"Brier is a great man," he says, tightening his grip on her. "He's a fighter for the oppressed, a visionary —"

"Let go of me!" she cries, pulling away as hard as she can. But the harder she pulls, the more it hurts. Pleadingly, she looks at the people standing around, but they all just look back at her blankly. She, having just her left arm, flails around with it, trying to free her right arm and also her coat. She struggles furiously, valiantly, with tears in her eyes.

Then she does not have her left arm anymore either. Someone has grabbed it from behind. She glances backward and sees a woman in a red coat. Now without either of her arms, she feels helpless and terrified, like a small animal caught in a trap. She has no way of defending herself. Adding to her terror, the greasy-haired guy, who is still hurting her wrist, is standing calmly in front of her, grinning a triumphant and cruel grin. A grin of "I've-got-you-where-I-want-you." Seeing this, she knows he wants to hurt her and has the power to.

She struggles even harder against the two people restraining her. She twists and turns more frantically, and then realizes that — though armless — she still has her legs. She kicks at the guy in front of her, kicking furiously and wildly, and gets him hard in the shin. With satisfaction, she sees his hideous grin transform into a scowl of pain.

Her right knee buckles under her. The fat man has tripped her, and she falls onto her knee. Then onto both knees. She starts to get up, but someone trips her again. She tries a second time to stand, and again someone trips her. Somehow she is lying on her side on the snow-covered ground and the two men are standing above her. They look very tall, like trees. At eye level all she can see is their boots: tall boots made of black and brown leather. Cossack boots. These boots advance toward her and kick her four or five times each. They kick her quickly and hard, in her stomach, legs, back, shoulders, chest, and head, and in less than half a minute her body is a ball of pain. She is on the ground curled up, moaning, bleeding. At one point there is a very loud crack followed by a crunching sound — the sound maybe of metal crushing bone — and her leg is on fire. Something warm and sticky is dribbling down her face. She is lying on the cold snowy ground and there is shouting all around her. Between the boots she glimpses something yellow: the campus police off in the distance. She touches her face, it's wet, and now the wetness is on her hands and it's red. It's blood, but whose blood? The snow is also red. But it can't be; snow isn't red. Snow is white.

One of the last things she hears before passing out is a galloping sound. Cossacks' horses. It's a pogrom. Then she hears a voice. One single voice cutting through all the other noises around her. Cindy's voice. She's screaming, "No! *No!*"

Then from closer, she hears her name being shouted: "Judith! Judith! Answer me!"

But she can't. She can't answer Cindy, even though she wants to. She is too far down below. She can't see or do anything now. She doesn't know Cindy has knelt beside her and taken her bleeding head into her lap. She is sinking too fast. Sinking into a strange, cold, incandescent light that has just appeared in front of her. Sinking into that shimmering, beckoning, heatless, heartless light.

— 5 —

Cindy, holding her hand, rides with her in an ambulance to the nearest hospital, where she spends the next month. At the rally her leg was smashed in two places by what her doctor guessed were steel-toed boots, and her spine was damaged, too. For the first two weeks she cannot move her leg at all without pain screaming up her back. Adding to her misery, anytime the pain has finally been dulled by enough painkillers and she is managing to doze off, someone comes and sticks something into her — a needle in her arm or tubes down her throat — all supposedly for her own good, but she never gets any sleep and everything hurts and makes her cry. After one month, though, she is moved to a rehab centre where she spends eight weeks recuperating and gradually learning to walk again. This rehab centre, compared to the hospital, isn't bad at all. As she writes Bruria several days after arriving, *this place is quiet and peaceful*, and they leave her alone a lot of the time to just read or rest. No one pushes or pulls at her all day long like at the hospital, except the physio, but that's just once a day, and she's very nice. Plus every day at lunch they serve a butterscotch pudding she likes, and across the hall there's a grey-haired Jewish philosophy professor who fell off a ladder, with whom she has a running argument about Spinoza's relationship to God. He thinks Spinoza ceased to believe; she thinks Spinoza still believed but simply with a different conception of God. "Same thing," says the philosophy professor. "Not at all," she says. And so on.

She also writes Bruria that Bobby has been fabulous during all this. He visited her at the hospital every day, and on weekends he was there almost all the time, a familiar sight to the nurses, working quietly on his laptop on a chair near her bed while she watched TV or slept. He was there so often, and was so obviously devoted to her, that the nurses thought he was her husband. Once a nurse even called him *Mister Gallanter,* but Judith quickly set her straight on that.

At the rehab centre she makes progress, and after two months she leaves and moves in with Bobby. It seems like the logical thing to do. Her own house is still unheated and probably filthy after her three-month absence, and she still can't manage entirely on her own. And Bobby begged her to come stay with him. He was like a kid, so excited about the prospect of them living together. So she moves from the rehab centre into his house, which, compared to hers, is delightful. It is deliciously warm no matter what the weather outside, the fridge is always crammed with her favourite foods, and Bobby comes home every day as early as possible to be with her.

For the hours he is at work, he has hired the cousin of his once-a-week housekeeper to help Judith. Faith is a kind, maternal woman who comes in the mornings, gives Judith breakfast, helps her to the bathroom to do her "morning ablutions," and then assists her with dressing. For the rest of the morning, Judith reads, watches TV, or does email or schoolwork on her computer while Faith cooks lunch and does housework. At noon she gives Judith lunch, and for the rest of the day does this and that, but mainly just hovers around at a polite distance in case Judith needs anything.

And it is astounding to Judith how many things she needs. Initially she thought having Faith around would be a waste of money and a nuisance, but after just a few days she can't imagine how she'd have managed without her. She feels the same way for the next six months. Because instead of gradually recovering as she expected, she develops complications. The fractures in her leg do not set well, and five weeks after her move to Bobby's, the doctor at the hospital recommends two follow-up operations. These turn out to be very painful and only partially successful, leaving her with a limp. And quite a marked one at that — marked enough that strangers cast their eyes aside when they pass her in the street. She tries putting a brave face on it, writing to Bruria ten days after the second operation:

> *I still have that limp and there is still quite a lot of pain. My surgeon says that both of these might improve over the next month or two, and I hope he's right. But at this stage anyway, my leg is a write-off. Oh, well. Better my right leg "loses its cunning" than my right hand. According to the psalm, that would mean I had forgotten Jerusalem, which I haven't.*

Her bravado starts wearing thin, though, after another ten days, when the pain continues unabated and her surgeon refuses to prescribe any more painkillers, because, he tells her, they are potentially addictive and this pain could go on indefinitely. She gets depressed. It finally hits home that this is real. For the rest of her life she will be in pain and walk with this limp, and be perceived, by everyone who sees her, as a disabled person. As "handicapped." "Crippled." She knows, even thinking this, that these words are politically incorrect. But she feels that what has happened to her is cruel, and her body is now ugly, so she wants to use cruel, ugly words to describe herself. *I am crippled*, she tells herself over and over again. *I am deformed. I am flawed.* Soon this mantra enters her bloodstream like an injection of self-rejection, and she can't imagine anymore how Bobby could possibly be attracted to her. He seems to still desire her, but she can't believe this. Maybe he is pretending out of pity. One day when he comes and puts his arms around her, she pushes him away.

"Come on," she says. "You don't really want to."

"What do you mean? Yes, I do."

"How can you? Look at me."

"I am looking at you."

"You know what I mean," she says impatiently.

"You mean because of your leg."

"Yes. I'm lopsided now. I'm not … normal."

"You've never been normal." He smiles. "You've always been different from everyone else."

"I'm serious."

"So am I. It doesn't bother me. I guess I'm lucky — we're both lucky — that I've never been a leg man. I've always been a boob man, as you know. And your boobs are still as beautiful as ever."

Feeling the beginning of tears of relief and gratitude, she asks, "Are you sure? If you don't want me anymore, you have to tell me."

"Do I look like I don't want you?" he asks. He lifts her shirt and starts kissing her left breast.

"No. But —"

"But what?" He lifts his face from her breast. "Do you mind if we stop talking for a moment?"

They stop talking and make love. And that was the end of that.

NEXT YEAR

Well, not quite.

Now, eighteen months later, Judith sits in an easy chair with her leg up on a footstool, resting it and reminiscing. *No, she thinks, that was not the end of that.* Because that night eighteen months ago, she got pregnant. When she first found out, her reaction was that there had been a mistake. There was no way she could be pregnant just because one time they hadn't used a condom. There was also no way she could be pregnant because a defective, shattered body like hers could not possibly create anything of value. A cracked clay vessel can't contain even a teaspoon of water; how could her body be containing a baby? At this point she could not walk even a city block without aid. It was inconceivable that she could be the source of life for another human being.

But apparently she was. And Bobby was so overjoyed at her pregnancy that soon she began believing it was true. Even then, though, she did not believe the baby would be okay. She was convinced that her ruined right leg would somehow be transmitted to the baby, and it would be born crippled like her.

But it wasn't. It was perfect. They named him Israel Chaim. Chaim after Bobby's father and Israel after hers. And Israel also after Israel. She nicknamed the baby Issy — not Izzy, her father's nickname — so she could keep them separate in her mind. Issy was a happy baby from day one, cherubic-looking with big blue eyes like Judith's mother. Now eight months old, he is quick to smile and laugh, enthusiastically waving his arms and legs. She gazes at him sleeping contentedly on the floor next to her in his flannel-lined baby seat, and she feels contented, too. Her life is good.

Except, of course, for her leg. Her leg hurts. It always hurts when she does even a moderate amount of standing or walking, and she has been doing a lot of both this past week, preparing for Pesach. Tuesday she scoured the kitchen and then taped waxed paper onto all the counters and the shelves of the cupboards and fridge. On Wednesday, although it transgressed doctor's orders, she stood on a rickety stepladder and replaced all their regular dishes with the Pesach ones. Afterwards she went food shopping. On Thursday and Friday, in her shiny, now kosher-for-Pesach kitchen, she cooked. She made chicken soup with *matzo* balls, chicken, *kugel, tzimmes*, salad, and a kosher-for-Pesach chocolate cake, and she roasted the egg and shank bone for the Seder plate.

Now it is Saturday afternoon, she has had a restful, peaceful Shabbat, and tonight is the Seder. On Shabbat she never works, which includes not doing any major cooking. But twenty minutes ago she skimmed the chicken soup, leaving her with just one more minor food task to do. This one is fun. It's making *charoset*, her favourite Pesach food. Before starting that, though, she is taking a rest. She has learned the hard way that if she doesn't listen to her body and put her leg up as soon as the pain starts, it just gets worse and worse until she does. And if it gets very bad, she has to take painkillers, which dull her mind and make her weepy, and she hates this.

So now she rests. Rests and smiles. Because five days ago she mailed her last term paper to Dunhill. The last paper required for her M.S.W. She can hear Martin Luther King's voice saying, "Thank God Almighty, free at last!" She is, thank God, free at last of Dunhill. *Of Dunghill.* She leans her head back and closes her eyes. It's wonderful to be able to just sit here like this for a while with nothing to do, with the sun streaming in through the living room window, warming her face, chest, and arms on this splendid spring day. For once to have no schoolwork hanging over her head. Nothing left to do for Pesach, either. Nothing at all, except make *charoset*, until it's time to shower and dress for the Seder. How apt to feel this way — so free — just before the beginning of the Festival of Freedom. She will receive the official letter soon in the mail, Phoebe told her yesterday on the phone, but that is just a formality. She is done. She has earned her M.S.W. Daddy would be proud. She is proud, too: she has kept her promise to him. She did what she said she would. Though it has taken her almost three years to get this degree, instead of just one year, as expected. Plus her journey getting here, she is sure, is nothing like what her father imagined. *Yes, I've gotten an education*, she thinks darkly. *I've acquired knowledge and learned a lot of lessons. But not necessarily the ones Daddy had in mind.*

Morosely she rubs her leg. She is different now than when she started her M.S.W. That rally broke not only her leg, but something else in her, too. She is tougher now. Maybe even hard. And all sorts of things she used to care about don't matter much anymore. Gazing at the sunlight, she ruminates, as she does several times every day, about that rally. She remembers how they kicked her. She will never forget the physical pain, the terror she felt, or her despair in the weeks and months that followed — despair so deep it sometimes seemed there was no point in living. Nothing could ever compensate her for what she has been through. Not even a million dollars.

But still she is suing Dunhill. She is suing them for every penny she can get. At her lawyer's request, she has been documenting everything that happened to her, including the visit of the rector of the university on her third day in hospital. He stood at the end of her bed and said that what had occurred at that rally was very unfortunate. He stared at her swollen, gashed, disfigured face, her head and neck that could not be moved, her torso in its cast from neck to hip, and her right leg in a second cast, and added, "Very, *very* unfortunate." However, he said, according to the university's legal counsel, this event could not be attributed in any way to the negligence of the university, which had not been, in terms of even the strictest definition, derelict in its duty. Furthermore, he explicated, the university's lawyer, in consultation with the university's equity officer, had also ruled that this incident could not be classified as a hate crime. What had occurred, unfortunate though it was, was ultimately just an interpersonal conflict. Academic freedom, differences of viewpoint, must be allowed to flower on campus. Therefore the university would not be laying charges against anyone involved. Not Michael Brier, his staff, or the Dunhill Students' Union or the Social Work Anti-oppression Committee, the co-organizers of the rally. According to the university, no one was responsible. It was an unfortunate incident — "very, *very* unfortunate." But no one was to blame.

She nearly spat at him from her hospital bed. But a week later the university did make a minor gesture. Phoebe called to say that Dunhill would give her as long as she needed to finish her degree, and would charge no additional tuition fees until then. All she had to do to graduate was submit her written assignments; they were waiving the usual requirement for class attendance. This last point pleased Judith to no end. *Great!* she thought. *I won't have to set foot on that campus, or see any of those horrible people, ever again!* Phoebe also said that Judith could, instead of a thesis, just hand in one extra paper, something slightly longer than the typical twenty pages. (Which Judith subsequently did for Hetty, a paper titled "Defining the Difference Between Free Speech and Hate Speech On Campus.") All these special conditions, Phoebe explained, were just an informal arrangement between the rector and Judith, with the school's participation. Nothing would be put in writing. *Of course not,*

Judith thinks now. Nothing was ever written down so that this arrangement could not be construed as an admission of guilt, or even responsibility, on the university's part. *Assholes. Especially that rector. Rector, rectum — perhaps the two words are related? Of course they are. At least when a rector, like this guy, is a rectum.*

She goes to the kitchen and collects the ingredients for making *charoset*: a half-dozen apples, two bags of walnuts, a bottle of sweet red wine, and cinnamon. She finds the cutting board, paring knife, grater, hammer, spoon, and mixing bowl, and places everything on the dining room table. Meanwhile she is thinking, *A person, if they let themselves, could get as bitter as horseradish. Here I am with a ruined leg that hurts twenty times a day, and almost every night I have nightmares, but the people who did this to me, they get off scot-free. They're doing just fine. For them this was an almost insignificant incident. It probably never even crosses their minds.*

She sits at the table, places an unopened bag of walnuts on the cutting board, lifts the hammer, and starts smashing the walnuts inside the bag. The hammer in her hand reminds her of a Pete Seeger song, and she sings, "It's the hammer of justice ..." And she thinks about bells of freedom, and love between brothers and sisters, as she sings and pounds away.

When she's done, she examines the bag of nuts. No big chunks are left, just a few little bumps of walnut, and the rest has been ground into powder. Walnut powder. Walnut dust. Ashes to ashes, dust to dust. She tears open the cellophane bag, empties its powdery contents into the plastic bowl, and peels the apples. Then she begins grating them, musing about *charoset*. It's supposed to symbolize the mortar for the bricks we made when we were slaves in Egypt — it's a symbol of our suffering and affliction — yet it tastes delicious. Is pain supposed to be tasty?

No. But justice is. Yesterday Cindy told her that Weick was arrested last weekend for drunk driving. He nearly killed a ten-year-old girl and then drove off. It's all over the Dunhill papers: Director of Social Work School Arrested in Hit-and-Run. Judith grates an apple. Weick's dissoluteness and cowardice are now in view for all to see. Maybe, after all, there is some justice. And its taste at this moment is sweet. Like the sweet juice dripping now from the apples.

She pours the grated apples, already starting to turn brown, into the bowl with the smashed walnuts, and stirs. The proportions aren't quite right. It needs more apple. So she peels and grates one more apple, a perfect shiny red one that reminds her of the very first apple, the one stolen from the Tree of Knowledge. *What is knowledge?* she recalls, was the theme question of her time at Dunhill. Now she answers: *True knowledge, or wisdom, is the understanding that there is evil in the world — but also goodness.* Goodness like Cindy. Goodness also like some of the other students in her class — Genya, Samantha, Darra, and Mary Martha — who sent her a get-well card when she was in hospital, with a picture of a wicker basket full of wistful-looking kittens. The card on the inside said all the usual things, but also that they had put together a binder of readings about Israel, Judaism, antisemitism, and anti-Israelism, and it was already on the Anti-oppression shelf in the Social Work Library, with a note on the cover saying it was in honour of Judith Gallanter. She was still in enormous physical pain then, and too cynical to believe that anyone at Dunhill would ever open that binder. But still she was very touched by this gesture. As she is again now.

She stirs the mixture and, satisfied this time with its consistency, adds a slosh of the sweet red wine and a shake of the cinnamon. The smell of the mixture is spicy but also sweet and pungent, and it makes her mouth water. It's the smell of life itself.

When she was a little girl making *charoset* with Bubba — or as Bubba pronounced it in Yiddish, *charoises* — they chopped the walnuts with a hand chopper, a semi-circular blade with a wooden handle that Bubba also used for chopping liver. Making *charoises*, she and Bubba sang Pesach songs in Yiddish, along with the songs from the Haggada, which are in Hebrew and Aramaic, refreshing their memories so that they would know them for the Seder that night. Bubba had a sweet, lyrical voice, and together they sang "It Would Suffice," "One Kid," "Mighty Is God," "It Is Proper to Praise Him," and "Who Knows One?" Also, of course, they practised the Four Questions, which — although she wasn't the youngest child at the Seder — she had to recite until her cousin Paul learned how to say them.

"Why are there only four questions?" she once asked Bubba. "I have more than four."

"That's good," said Bubba. "It's good to have questions."

Now humming "Who Knows One?" Judith gives a final stir to the *charoset*, and puts a spoonful of it into her mouth. It is delicious. Perfect. *Perfecto,* as Daddy always said. She transfers the *charoset* from the mixing bowl into a pretty, round aqua dish, and, using the second bag of walnuts, decorates the *charoset* with a circle of nuts all around the perimeter, plus one perfect nut in the middle. She covers the whole thing with plastic wrap and puts it in the fridge. *Mortar,* she thinks, *for remembering.*

— 2 —

Judith returns to the couch and puts her leg up on the footstool. It's aching again. But despite this, she feels cheerful: she is pleased with her *charoset*. She watches Issy awhile and then starts singing to him in Hebrew. Softly, so as not to wake him. She sings "Who Knows One?" and realizes this is a numbers song. A song built on numbers. Ever since that terrible Friday night twenty-six months ago, the one before the rally, she has felt toward numbers a special affection. She sings to Issy:

> "Who knows One?
> I know One.
> One is our God.
> Our God, our God, our God, our God,
> Who is in heaven
> And the earth."

She smiles at the sleeping baby. *Who knows One?* she asks herself. *If I were counting my blessings, you would be Blessing Number One.*
> *Number one*
> *Is my son.*

Now she softly sings the second verse of the song:

> "Who knows Two?
> I know Two.
> Two is the tablets
> Of the Ten Commandments."

Two, though, is also a man and a woman. And Blessing Number Two in her life is Bobby. Which feels almost as miraculous as having had a baby. It astounds her that she and Bobby have ended up together. Even in those first weeks after the rally when she couldn't move a bone in her body without pain, and he was incredibly solicitous and kind to her — even then she was sure they wouldn't end up together. She was grateful for his love, caring, and constancy, but she also felt guilty, like she was just using him. She knew there was no way she was staying here in Toronto and settling down with him. As soon as she was back on her feet — standing on her own two feet, both literally and figuratively — she would be on the first plane back to Israel. And she would be on that plane alone, without Bobby in the seat next to her.

But then she got pregnant. And discovered to her astonishment how much she wanted this baby. Then, shortly after, how much she wanted Bobby, too. To be the three of them together. A family. So they got married in a small ceremony in his living room, with just his brother and sister and their spouses, Cindy and Tom, and the rabbi. But before agreeing to marry him, she insisted they come to an understanding about Israel. This was her only condition for marriage: that within five years at the most — and hopefully sooner — they would move to Israel to live. Bobby, half-joking that anything — even Israel! — was better than losing her, agreed. Though he added almost parenthetically that living in Israel would be very difficult financially, much harder than in Canada, so they had to make some money before they went. With a little luck, he said, they could save enough in four to five years. Judith, who had been poor both in Canada and Israel — so poor in Israel that, in exchange for groceries she couldn't pay for, she sometimes put up with being groped by the grocer — told Bobby he was probably right. They should go with a nest egg. But they never defined exactly how much would be enough. They never nailed down a magic number. He said they needed to go with at least half a million dollars, and a million would be even better. She thought that sounded like a lot. But by this time Bobby had left BBB and moved to another firm, BRJ, where he felt very optimistic about his prospects, and was so confident about his future earning capacity that she deferred to his judgment. Even though she would have been willing to go to Israel with much less than half a million dollars. She would have been willing to go with nothing.

But none of that matters now. The main thing is, they have an agreement in principle that they're moving to Israel. Everything else is mere detail. As it says in the Talmud, "The rest is commentary."

She stands and stretches, looking out the window, feeling satisfied with life. She may be temporarily in *galut*, but still she is a lucky woman. She has a husband, a child, and even ("Who knows Three?") a dear woman friend. A true friend — after all, who could be truer than someone who has saved your life? With shame she recalls how, during her first months at Dunhill, she sometimes took Cindy for granted, or undervalued her, because she wasn't as intellectual as the rest of their group. Also because she seemed so sunny, uncomplicated, and innocent. *Yet she's the one who saved me*, thinks Judith. *Maybe with the power of her innocence. Like Scout in* To Kill a Mockingbird, *when she stopped a mob from lynching a black man. I love Cindy. And always will.*

She bends down and touches Issy's cheek. "Mama loves you," she whispers, and goes to check on the chicken soup. It is gently bubbling and has come out well. It smells rich and fragrant and has a few of those floating fat globules on the top, broken up by protruding celery, carrot, and chicken bone. She stirs it and, careful not to burn her mouth, slurps a little off the spoon. It is, as Annette would say, "marvellous." Judith turns off the flame and moves the soup to the back burner to cool. She'll bring this tonight as their contribution to the Seder meal. They are going to Richard and Annette's. Over the past year she has made her peace with them. In a limited way, of course, which is all that's possible with people like that. But last year she and Bobby went there for the Seder, and this year it was just assumed they'd return. Which was fine with her. Annette, who always plans far ahead, called her five weeks ago, asking if this year she would again make her marvellous chicken soup. She agreed, and offered to also make the *charoset* and roast the shank bone and egg, an offer gratefully accepted. She also bought flowers for Richard and Annette. The red tulips and yellow daffodils mixed together look bright and cheerful on the kitchen counter, and nearby, in shiny purple-and-silver gift wrapping, are presents for the children in exchange for the *afikoman*. Surveying all these preparations for tonight reminds her that she promised Annette she would bring some Haggadas, too. Last year they didn't have enough and people had to share.

She crouches gingerly — her back is still fragile: such movements need to be undertaken gradually — and from the bottom cupboard pulls out a pile of Haggadas. She carries them into the living room and sets them next to her on the black leather couch. This couch that used to be just Bobby's, but now — she feels with proprietary pleasure — also belongs to her. She sifts through the Haggadas, creating a separate pile for all those of artistic value or with interesting commentaries. To this pile she adds the Szyk Haggada Bobby got for his bar mitzvah, and which he wants to use tonight. For herself she selects the first feminist Haggada ever published, Aviva Cantor's.

She senses Issy stirring in his seat. She strokes his cheek, murmurs, "Yes, yes, okay," and he falls back asleep. She returns to browsing through the Haggadas, putting into the good pile the ones by Lehmann, Zion/Dishon, and Moss. Then she discovers a stack of little two-dollar Haggadas, obviously much-used, stained by wine and food. There are ten, all identical. *These are good*, she thinks. *This way Richard can call out a page number and we'll all be on the same page.* She opens one and smiles at the lively, cartoon-like illustrations in purple and lime-green. Issy will like this. So will the other kids. She adds these ten Haggadas to the pile.

Feeling tired, she glances at her watch. Almost five o'clock. Just three hours until the sun sets and Pesach begins. Annette wants them there for 7:30, so she and Bobby agreed they'd leave the house at 7:15. Bobby is still at the office. There was an emergency to deal with today; he doesn't usually work on Saturdays. But he promised he'd be home no later than seven o'clock. That's not for another two hours — she's still got lots of time till she has to shower and dress. She is looking forward to dressing up. It's an Israeli custom to wear new clothes on Pesach, and she has bought a new outfit for tonight. Something pretty: white with small red flowers. And shiny red shoes to match. She laughs. For no special reason. Just out of sheer joy. Because life is good. She glances down at her sleeping baby and is flooded with love. Leaning her head back, she closes her eyes and feels on her face the warmth of the late afternoon sun beaming in through the window. She hears the peaceful silence of the house. There is no sound at all except the quiet ticking of a clock. Half-smiling, she dozes off.

— 3 —

She jolts awake, feeling panicky. She has had another bad dream, and the room around her is cold and full of shadows. She glances at the baby — he's fine, still sleeping — and checks her watch: 6:15. She'll have to start getting ready soon. Her leg hurts again, which is depressing — *Am I going to spend my whole life in pain?* — and this dream she just woke from was scary and disturbing. It wasn't her usual nightmare: boots kicking her, crowds jeering, Cossacks on horses. In this one, there's something she can't put her finger on that is wrong. Very wrong. She tries retrieving this dream, but can't — it feels like it's lost to her forever. Now, though, she remembers something else. It's as if this dream shook loose from its moorings, like poorly nailed-down flooring, an incident she has suppressed since it happened. It was a small but troubling event. Three days ago, Richard and Annette phoned with some last-minute details about tonight's Seder. Then they mentioned — laughing at themselves for planning so far in advance — that on that exact date four years from now, their son, Ryan, would be celebrating his bar mitzvah. After hanging up, Bobby said that, knowing how compulsive a planner Annette is, she'll probably ask them tomorrow if, during the bar mitzvah weekend, they can put up her parents and sister from Calgary. He assumed, he said jokingly, that this would be okay with Judith — that she didn't have any plans yet for that weekend four years away.

Diapering Issy, she had her back to him, and didn't answer.

"You wouldn't mind, would you?" he asked, sounding surprised.

She spun around to face him and cried, "What are you talking about? Are you out of your mind?"

He stared at her, dumbfounded. As he continued staring at her blankly, obviously not understanding, she said, "We're not going to *be* here four years from now, remember? We're going to be living in Israel."

"Oh, yeah," he said glumly. Then, on some pretext, he left the room.

This brief interchange shocked and frightened her. It was clear that Bobby, for those moments at least, had totally forgotten about their plan to move to Israel within five years of their wedding. *How do you forget something like that?* she asked herself. *How do you forget your plan for the rest of your life? How do you forget a dream?*

But she didn't make a big deal of it. After her little outburst she went on diapering Issy, and she didn't raise this incident again. *Don't make a mountain out of a molehill,* she told herself. She pushed it away. She'd learned at that rally two years before, learned "on her own flesh," as the Hebrew expression goes, what happens when you fight back. So she is no longer a fighter like she was. She tries as much as possible to avoid conflict, with Bobby and everyone else.

But now she wonders if this really was just a molehill. In several months she will have been in Toronto for four full years, and she needs to know that sooner or later she'll return to Israel. It doesn't have to happen next year, or the year after that. But it does have to happen. This episode on Sunday was not the first. Bobby just doesn't seem to be onside when it comes to moving to Israel. It feels like it's only her plan, and not his.

A terrible thought strikes her. It is so terrible that she immediately dismisses it as impossible. It can't be. She doesn't believe it. But now that it's in her mind, she can't get it out. What if Bobby has just been stringing her along all this time? What if he never truly intended to live in Israel, and just pretended he would so she'd marry him? What if he keeps postponing going — constantly upping the ante (they need another quarter of a million, and then another, and then another) — until they never end up going at all? She feels short of breath. No, it isn't possible. Bobby wouldn't do that. He wouldn't outright lie. He might avoid doing things he doesn't want to but must, like visiting the dentist. But to actually promise he'll move to Israel when he never had any intention of it? No. That's not Bobby. Not the Bobby she knows.

Anyway, it can't be true, because if it were, then their entire marriage would be a lie and a sham, and there would be nothing between them that was real. This can't be.

Also, it can't be true because it would be too ironic, and too cruel, if ultimately she got stuck permanently in *galut* as a result – indirect but indubitable – of her standing up for Israel at that rally: *I fought for Israel so I lost Israel.*

No. It's inconceivable. In the darkness falling around her, she tells herself that everything is fine. Everything is okay. Sure, Bobby is a bit funny about Israel. But it will all work out in the end. They had a good trip to Jerusalem four months ago during Chanukah, and Bobby got along well with her friends. Sooner or later they'll end up in Israel. Meanwhile, in the years they spend here — whether that will be five years or six — they'll enjoy what there is to be enjoyed in Canada. And there are things to enjoy. Their life here, though temporary, is very pleasant. They have some good friends, Bobby likes his work at BRJ, and she is finding a niche for herself. Last year, prodded by Mendl, she agreed to chair fundraising for Friends-of-Peace, and discovered to her amazement that she has a knack for raising money. In six months she alone raised what everyone at Friends-of-Peace had raised in the previous twelve. Friends-of-Peace is currently seeking a part-time fundraiser and she might apply for this position, or else hunt for a "real" job — a social work job — now that she has her M.S.W.

And yet … She sighs. All this pleasantness, all this enjoyment of *galut*, is based on the assumption that their life here is temporary. The same way you enjoy a one-week sun holiday on the assumption that one week later you'll be home. Making a permanent life at a sun resort would be not only deeply unsatisfying, but miserable. She tries to picture, even for a moment, staying in Canada for good, and the idea of ending up like Micky, Efraim, Lily, and the other old-timers from Friends-of-Peace makes her shudder. It repulses her to envisage turning into one of them: still here in Toronto in eighteen years — being in her fifties, and grey-haired, like they are now — and having become one of those people who are emptied of their dreams. People living pointless, disappointed lives. *Yordim.*

No, she thinks. *I won't let this happen to me. I won't. We have a plan. We're going to live in Israel. He promised.*

She imagines Issy growing up in Jerusalem, walking to *shul* on Shabbat in those Biblical sandals they have there, and wearing shorts and a white shirt with a collar like her friends' kids always wore. And of course he'll be speaking Hebrew. Perfect Hebrew. Hebrew with the right accent, not like hers. He'll be a real Israeli.

She hears a gurgling sound and looks down at Issy. He is awake now and his beatific face is smiling at her. His blue eyes are expectant and hopeful, and he is waving around his arms and legs, wanting to be picked up. She takes him in her arms. He smells sweet — that unique sweet smell of babies and baby powder. She nuzzles his neck, and when he laughs she laughs too, and hugs him.

"Come, I'll read to you," she says, and seats him on her lap. He is used to her reading to him. Mainly alphabet books and some with very simple stories, just a few words here and there, illustrated with fields of flowers or kind-looking animals, people, or birds. There is even a book called *Pat the Bunny*, where Issy pats some soft, fluffy cotton batting in the shape of a rabbit. So he snuggles in happily as she reaches for the nearest book. But all she can put her hand on is the two-dollar Haggada on top of the pile she is bringing tonight. She thinks of getting up and looking for a baby book instead, but her leg hurts, and anyway, why not read him the Haggada? In a couple of hours it will be Pesach, and on this holiday you are supposed to Tell Your Children this story of deliverance. Her left arm is around Issy, and in her right hand she holds the Haggada, showing him the lively, cartoon-like illustrations in purple and lime-green. He looks at them eagerly. The Haggada has opened by chance to the end of the Seder.

"Look," she says, pointing to a picture of Jerusalem with its spires, domes, and arched doorways. *Doorways I entered through*, she thinks. *Doorways I left through. The only city I have ever loved.* "Jerusalem," she says to him. "*Yerushalayim.*"

"Umma," he says, and points to the picture.

"Yes," she says, "Jerusalem."

"Baba," he says, and reaches out and touches the page. Touches the walls of the old city. Like baby Moses touching the hot coal.

"Yes," she says. Now she points to the concluding words of the Seder in both Hebrew and English. She wants him to hear the Hebrew, even though she knows he won't understand it. She wants him to hear the cadence of the language, the music of the holy tongue. So she reads him the Hebrew words. Then she sings them to him, using the traditional tune for this part of the Seder. He listens intently and, as if beating time, hits the Haggada a few times with glee. She finishes singing and scans the English text. It is a very loose translation, even an adaptation, from the Hebrew. Someone has obviously written this with children in mind, using very simple language. She reads to Issy:

> "Our Seder is now almost over.
> We have done the best we could.
> We hope God is pleased with our offering."

Issy wriggles slightly. She feels the warmth and aliveness of his body on her lap, and hugs him tightly. Then she continues:

"We hope God, who led us out of Egypt long ago,
Will lead us out of exile now,
And bring us home to the Promised Land."

She pauses. She can't go on. A yearning so sharp that it is pain has risen inside her. She is silent, struggling against the tears starting up. Then, when she thinks she has control of herself, she reads to her baby the final words of the Seder: "Next year in Jerusalem," her voice breaking before the end.

GLOSSARY

Here are brief definitions of all the non-English terms in this novel that are not explained in the text, as well as a few relevant English-language ones. Please keep in mind that a number of the terms below have several different meanings, and our explanations relate only to the way each term is used in this novel.

Afikoman (Hebrew)	A piece of matzo hidden at the start of the Passover Seder to be found later by the children present and exchanged for small gifts or money so the Seder can be concluded.
Aliya (make *aliya* or go on *aliya*) (Hebrew)	Move permanently to Israel.
Avanti Popolo (Italian)	Literally: Forward, people. The nickname of a song officially titled "Bandiera Rossa" (Italian for *red flag*), famous from the Italian labour movement, that glorifies the symbol of the socialist, and later communist, movement.
Binding of Isaac	The Biblical story where God tests Abraham by telling him to sacrifice his son Isaac (Genesis 22).
Blood libel	The false allegation that Jews use the blood of non-Jews in the making of Passover matzos. Cases of blood libel are reported even nowadays.

Es gezunterheyt (Yiddish)	Eat in good health. *Bon appétit.*
Ethics of the Fathers	A tractate of the Mishnah (which is the earliest code of Jewish oral law), composed of ethical maxims of the rabbis.
Four Questions (The)	Four questions traditionally asked (sung) at the Passover Seder by the youngest child present. These questions pertain to four elements that make the night of the Passover Seder special.
Galut (Hebrew)	Exile.
Gatkes (Yiddish)	Long underwear.
Gurnisht helfn (Yiddish)	It's no help.
Haggada (Hebrew)	The text read during the Passover Seder recounting the story of the Exodus.
Kipa (Hebrew)	A skullcap worn by a Jew.
Kugel (Yiddish)	A noodle pudding traditionally served on Shabbat or on holidays.
Moshav (Hebrew)	Co-operative agricultural village in Israel whose inhabitants possess individual homes and holdings, in contrast to the system of communal ownership on a kibbutz.
Pesach (Hebrew)	Passover.
Purim (Hebrew)	A holiday commemorating the deliverance of the Jews of

Persia about 2,500 years ago. During Jewish leap years only, an additional Purim holiday occurs, called Purim Katan (literally "little Purim"), which precedes the regular Purim by about one month. Shushan Purim and Shushan Purim Katan refer to a second day of celebration, nowadays celebrated only in Jerusalem.

Rugelach (Yiddish)	A crescent-shaped Jewish pastry originating in Eastern Europe.
Shabbat (Hebrew)	The Jewish Sabbath, beginning around sundown on Friday night and ending approximately one hour after sundown on Saturday night.
Shaheed/a (Arabic)	Holy martyrs, a term used by Palestinians to refer to suicide bombers.
Shiva (Hebrew, Yiddish) / *Shiva* house	The week-long mourning period in Judaism for first-degree relatives. The ritual is referred to in English as "sitting *shiva*." A "*shiva* house" is a house where people are sitting *shiva*.
Shofar (Hebrew)	A ram's horn blown primarily on Rosh Hashana and Yom Kippur.
Shtetl (Yiddish)	A small village in Eastern Europe where Jews lived prior to World War II.

Shul (Yiddish)	Synagogue.
Shvartzes (Yiddish)	Blacks.
Talmud (Hebrew)	A collection of discussions on the Mishnah (which is the earliest code of Jewish oral law) by generations of scholars in Babylonia and Palestine, redacted about 500 CE.
The Protocols	Short for *The Protocols of the Elders of Zion*, a piece of antisemitic propaganda claiming Jews are plotting world dominion. It was translated into many languages over the past century, encouraging and widely spreading antisemitism. Long repudiated as an absurd, hateful lie, it continues to be reprinted and circulated today.
Tu B'shvat (Hebrew)	A Jewish holiday also known as "The New Year of the Trees."
Tzimmes (Yiddish)	A traditional Jewish casserole usually made with carrots, served at festive meals.
Vale atque vale (Latin)	Farewell and farewell. A play on *"Ave atque Vale"* ("Hail and Farewell"), a poem by Catullus.
Vesti la giubba (Italian)	Put on the costume. Put on your mask. An aria in the opera *Pagliacci*.
Yartzeit (Yiddish)	The annual anniversary of a death.
Yediot (Hebrew)	Short for *Yediot Achronot*, a popular newspaper in Israel.

Acknowledgements

It is a pleasure to thank here the people who have played a central role in the development and realization of this book. I extend my grateful thanks to:

All the courageous individuals and groups, within academe and in the community at large, who — over the past two decades — have stood up against the antisemitism prevalent on campuses worldwide. In particular, I wish to thank the students who have bravely fought anti-Israelism at their universities, sometimes at great personal cost. Their efforts have often intersected my own activism in this area, and were one of the sources of inspiration for this novel.

My esteemed academic colleagues whose thoughtful and original scholarship on "the new antisemitism" has provided the theoretical groundwork both for my own research in this field, and for this book.

The distinguished and talented authors and the extraordinary, devoted volunteers associated with *Jewish Fiction .net*, the online literary journal that publishes first-rate fiction from around the world. Since founding *Jewish Fiction .net* in 2010, I have become part of an international literary community that nourishes me with a sense of belonging and support. This is a great gift to any writer.

Dundurn Press, an excellent publishing house with which I am proud to be affiliated, and its dedicated and very capable staff. A special thank you to Sylvia McConnell for her enthusiastic support for this book from the outset.

Diane Schoemperlen for her helpful comments on an early draft of this manuscript.

My son, Joseph Weissgold, for assisting with the design of the cover of this book, and whose *joie de vivre*, creativity, and constantly evolving plans for bettering the world are a never-ending source of delight and pride.

Last but not least, my husband, Dr. David Weiss, for his unwavering confidence in this novel and in me, his passionate loyalty, his good humour, and suggestions throughout the writing of this book, and most of all, his love.